The FLIP SIDE

CREATED BY

PENDLETON WARD

ROSS RICHIE CEO & Founder • **MARK SMYLIE** Founder of Archaia • **MATT GAGNON** Editor-in-Chief • **FILIP SABLIK** President of Publishing & Marketing • **STEPHEN CHRISTY** President of Development
LANCE KREITER VP of Licensing & Merchandising • **PHIL BARBARO** VP of Finance • **BRYCE CARLSON** Managing Editor • **MEL CAYLO** Marketing Manager • **SCOTT NEWMAN** Production Design Manager
IRENE BRADISH Operations Manager • **CHRISTINE DINH** Brand Communications Manager • **DAFNA PLEBAN** Editor • **SHANNON WATTERS** Editor • **ERIC HARBURN** Editor • **REBECCA TAYLOR** Editor
IAN BRILL Editor • **CHRIS ROSA** Assistant Editor • **ALEX GALER** Assistant Editor • **WHITNEY LEOPARD** Assistant Editor • **JASMINE AMIRI** Assistant Editor • **CAMERON CHITTOCK** Assistant Editor
KELSEY DIETERICH Production Designer • **JILLIAN CRAB** Production Designer • **DEVIN FUNCHES** E-Commerce & Inventory Coordinator • **ANDY LIEGL** Event Coordinator • **BRIANNA HART** Administrative Coordinator
AARON FERRARA Operations Assistant • **JOSÉ MEZA** Sales Assistant • **MICHELLE ANKLEY** Sales Assistant • **ELIZABETH LOUGHRIDGE** Accounting Assistant • **STEPHANIE HOCUTT** PR Assistant

ADVENTURE TIME: THE FLIP SIDE, December 2014. Published by KaBOOM!, a division of Boom Entertainment, Inc. ADVENTURE TIME, CARTOON NETWORK, the logos, and all related characters and elements are trademarks of and © Cartoon Network. (S14) Originally published in single magazine form as ADVENTURE TIME: THE FLIP SIDE No. 1-6. © Cartoon Network. (S14) All rights reserved. KaBOOM!™ and the KaBOOM! logo are trademarks of Boom Entertainment, Inc., registered in various countries and categories. All characters, events, and institutions depicted herein are fictional. Any similarity between any of the names, characters, persons, events, and/or institutions in this publication to actual names, characters, and persons, whether living or dead, events, and/or institutions is unintended and purely coincidental. KaBOOM! does not read or accept unsolicited submissions of ideas, stories, or artwork.

A catalog record of this book is available from OCLC and from the KaBOOM! website, www.kaboom-studios.com, on the Librarians Page.

BOOM! Studios, 5670 Wilshire Boulevard, Suite 450, Los Angeles, CA 90036-5679. Printed in China. First Printing.
ISBN: 978-1-60886-456-0, eISBN: 978-1-61398-310-2

WRITTEN BY
PAUL TOBIN & COLLEEN COOVER

ILLUSTRATED BY
WOOK JIN CLARK

COLORED BY
WHITNEY COGAR

LETTERED BY
AUBREY AIESE

COVER BY
WOOK JIN CLARK

DESIGNER
JILLIAN CRAB

ASSISTANT EDITOR
WHITNEY LEOPARD

EDITOR
SHANNON WATTERS

With Special Thanks to Marisa Marionakis, Rick Blanco, Jeff Parker, Laurie Halal-Ono, Nicole Rivera, Conrad Montgomery, Meghan Bradley, Curtis Lelash and the wonderful folks at Cartoon Network.

CHAPTER ONE

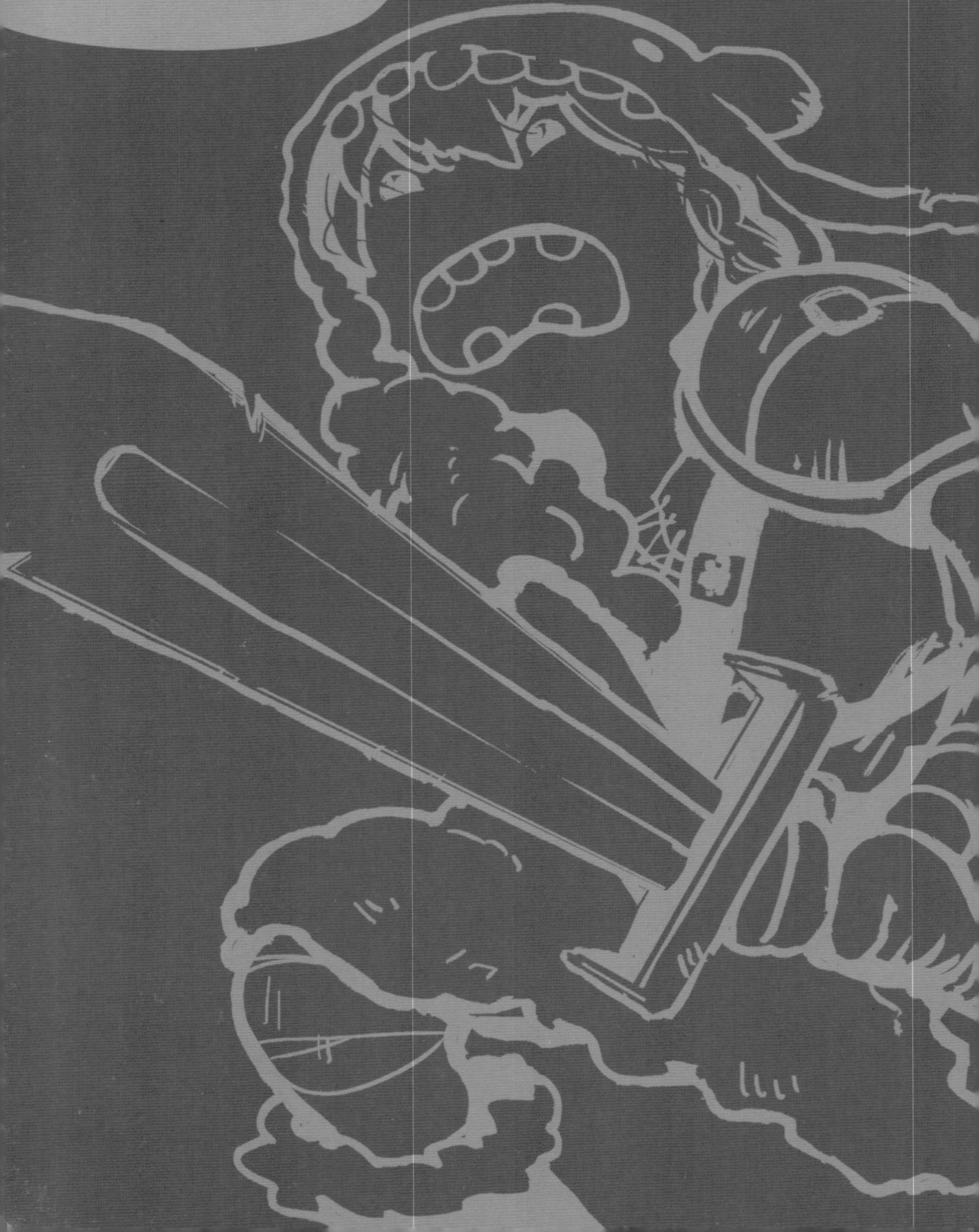

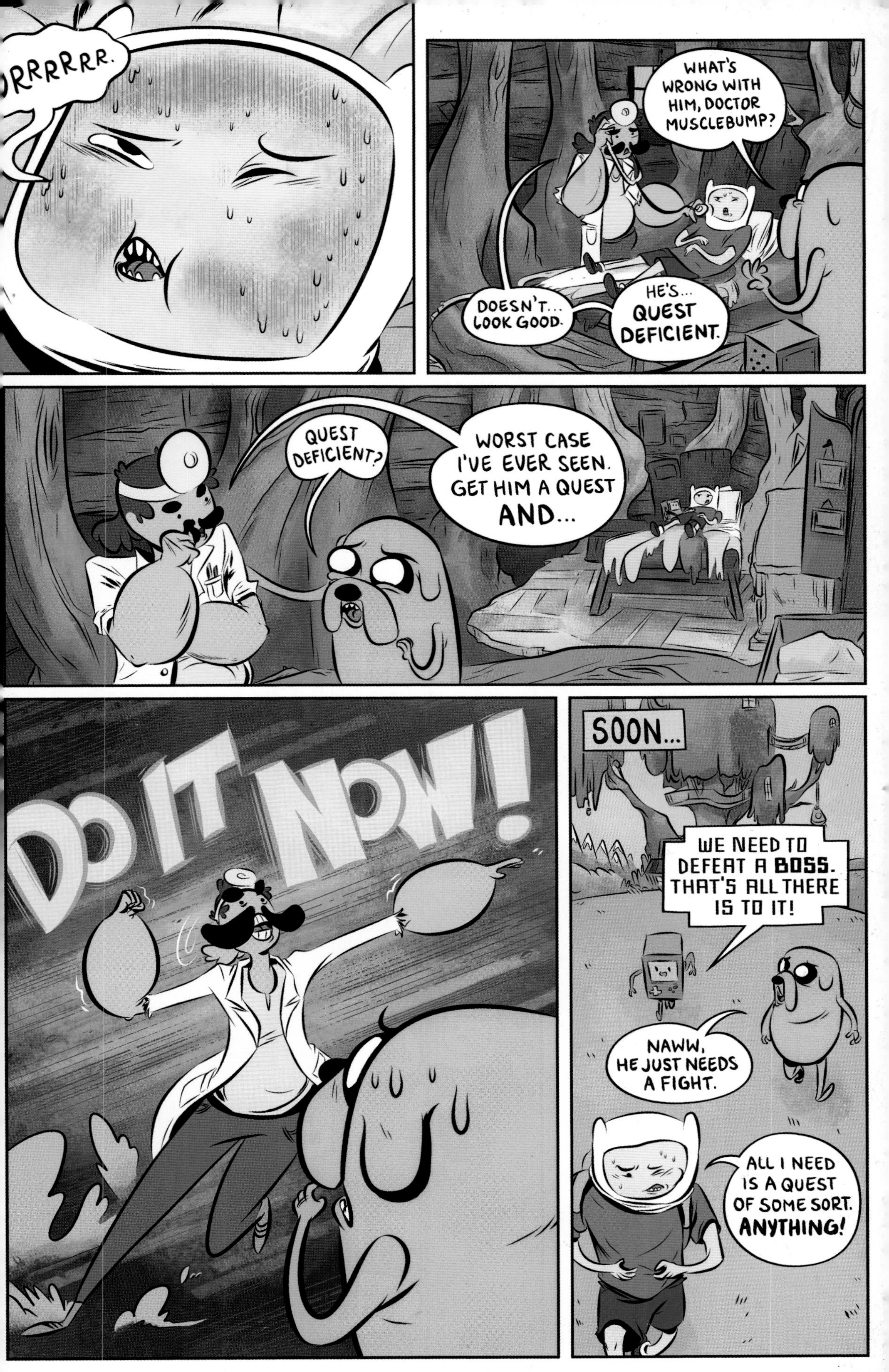
RRRRRRR.
WHAT'S WRONG WITH HIM, DOCTOR MUSCLEBUMP?
DOESN'T... LOOK GOOD.
HE'S... QUEST DEFICIENT.
QUEST DEFICIENT?
WORST CASE I'VE EVER SEEN. GET HIM A QUEST AND...
DO IT NOW!
SOON...
WE NEED TO DEFEAT A BOSS. THAT'S ALL THERE IS TO IT!
NAWW, HE JUST NEEDS A FIGHT.
ALL I NEED IS A QUEST OF SOME SORT. ANYTHING!

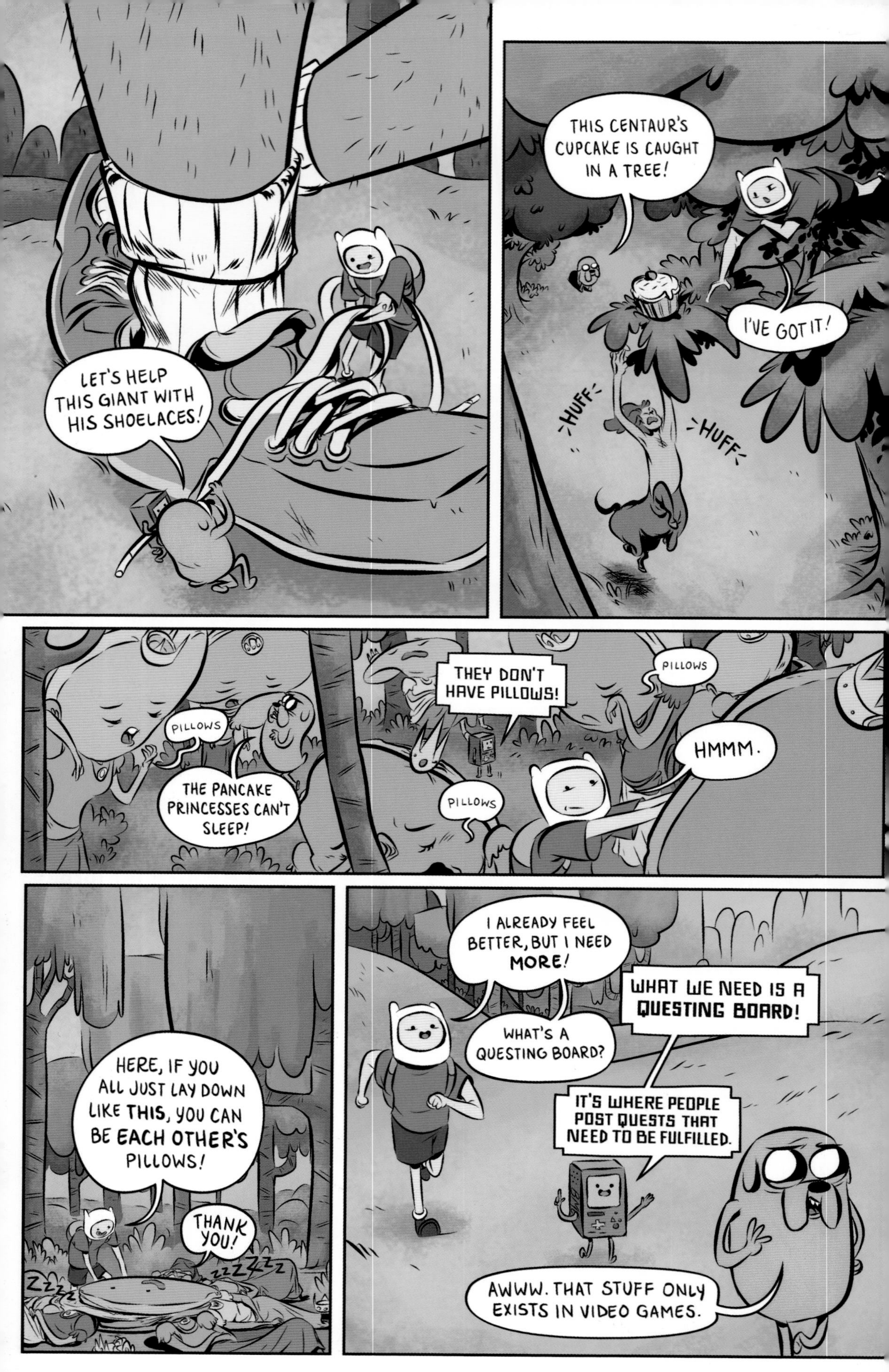
LET'S HELP THIS GIANT WITH HIS SHOELACES!
THIS CENTAUR'S CUPCAKE IS CAUGHT IN A TREE!
I'VE GOT IT!
HUFF
HUFF
THE PANCAKE PRINCESSES CAN'T SLEEP!
PILLOWS
THEY DON'T HAVE PILLOWS!
PILLOWS
PILLOWS
HMMM.
HERE, IF YOU ALL JUST LAY DOWN LIKE THIS, YOU CAN BE EACH OTHER'S PILLOWS!
THANK YOU!
ZZZZ
ZZZZZZ
I ALREADY FEEL BETTER, BUT I NEED MORE!
WHAT WE NEED IS A QUESTING BOARD!
WHAT'S A QUESTING BOARD?
IT'S WHERE PEOPLE POST QUESTS THAT NEED TO BE FULFILLED.
AWWW. THAT STUFF ONLY EXISTS IN VIDEO GAMES.

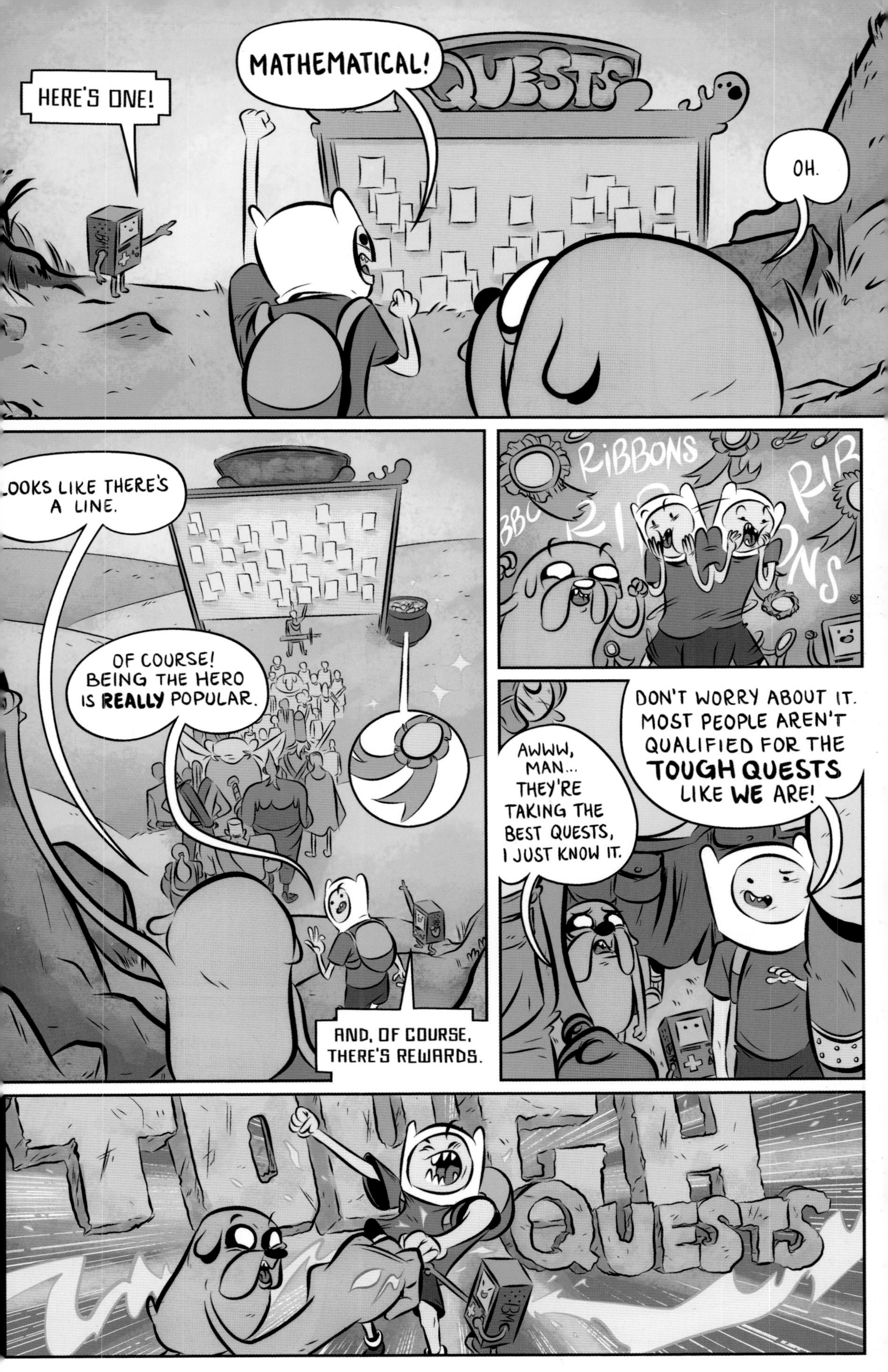
HERE'S ONE!
MATHEMATICAL!
QUESTS
OH.
LOOKS LIKE THERE'S A LINE.
OF COURSE! BEING THE HERO IS **REALLY** POPULAR.
AND, OF COURSE, THERE'S REWARDS.
RIBBONS
DON'T WORRY ABOUT IT. MOST PEOPLE AREN'T QUALIFIED FOR THE **TOUGH QUESTS** LIKE **WE** ARE!
AWWW, MAN... THEY'RE TAKING THE BEST QUESTS, I JUST KNOW IT.
QUESTS

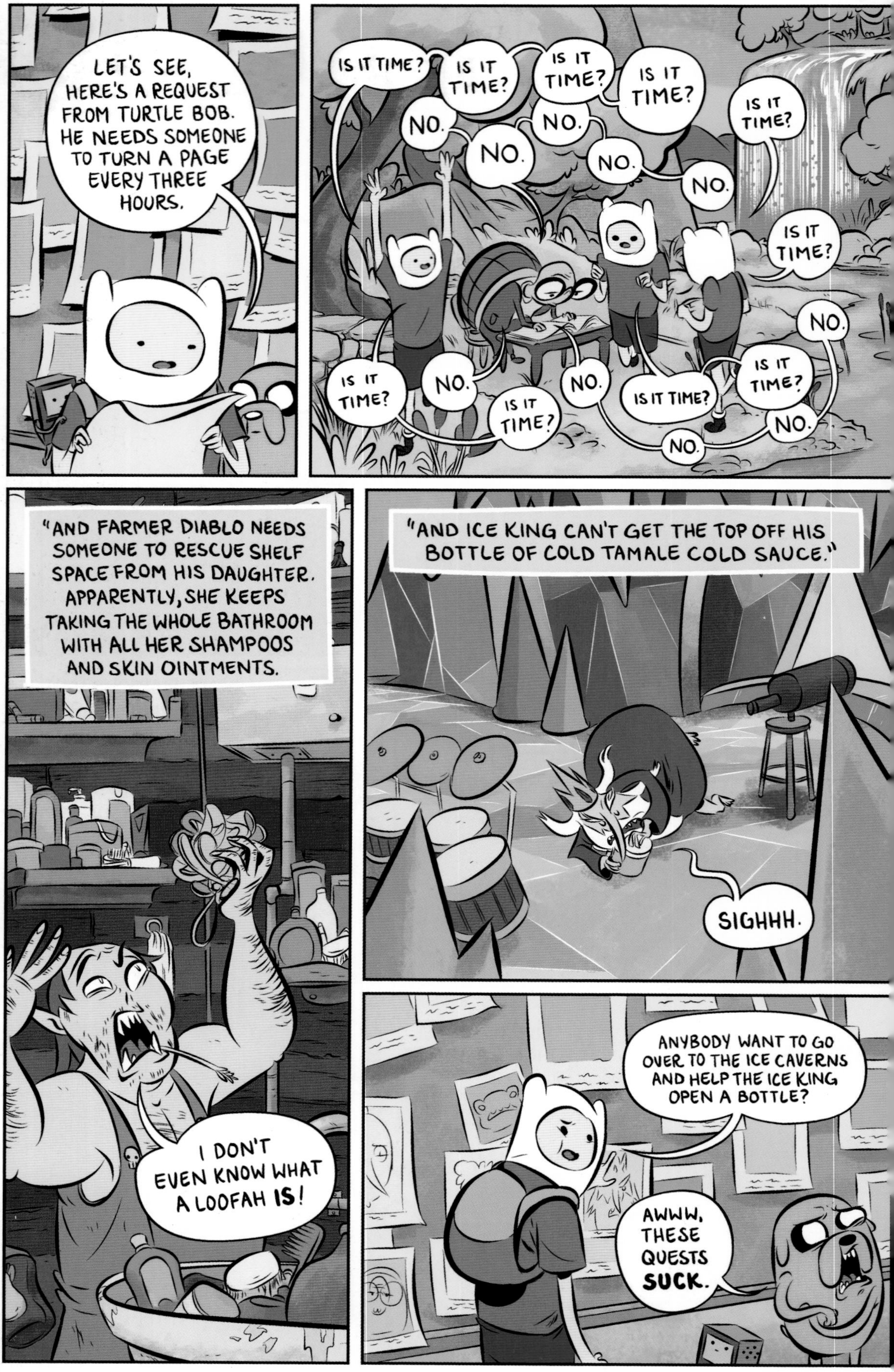
LET'S SEE, HERE'S A REQUEST FROM TURTLE BOB. HE NEEDS SOMEONE TO TURN A PAGE EVERY THREE HOURS.
IS IT TIME?
IS IT TIME?
IS IT TIME?
IS IT TIME?
NO.
NO.
NO.
NO.
IS IT TIME?
NO.
IS IT TIME?
NO.
IS IT TIME?
NO.
IS IT TIME?
NO.
IS IT TIME?
IS IT TIME?
NO.
NO.
"AND FARMER DIABLO NEEDS SOMEONE TO RESCUE SHELF SPACE FROM HIS DAUGHTER. APPARENTLY, SHE KEEPS TAKING THE WHOLE BATHROOM WITH ALL HER SHAMPOOS AND SKIN OINTMENTS.
I DON'T EVEN KNOW WHAT A LOOFAH **IS**!
"AND ICE KING CAN'T GET THE TOP OFF HIS BOTTLE OF COLD TAMALE COLD SAUCE."
SIGHHH.
ANYBODY WANT TO GO OVER TO THE ICE CAVERNS AND HELP THE ICE KING OPEN A BOTTLE?
AWWW, THESE QUESTS **SUCK**.

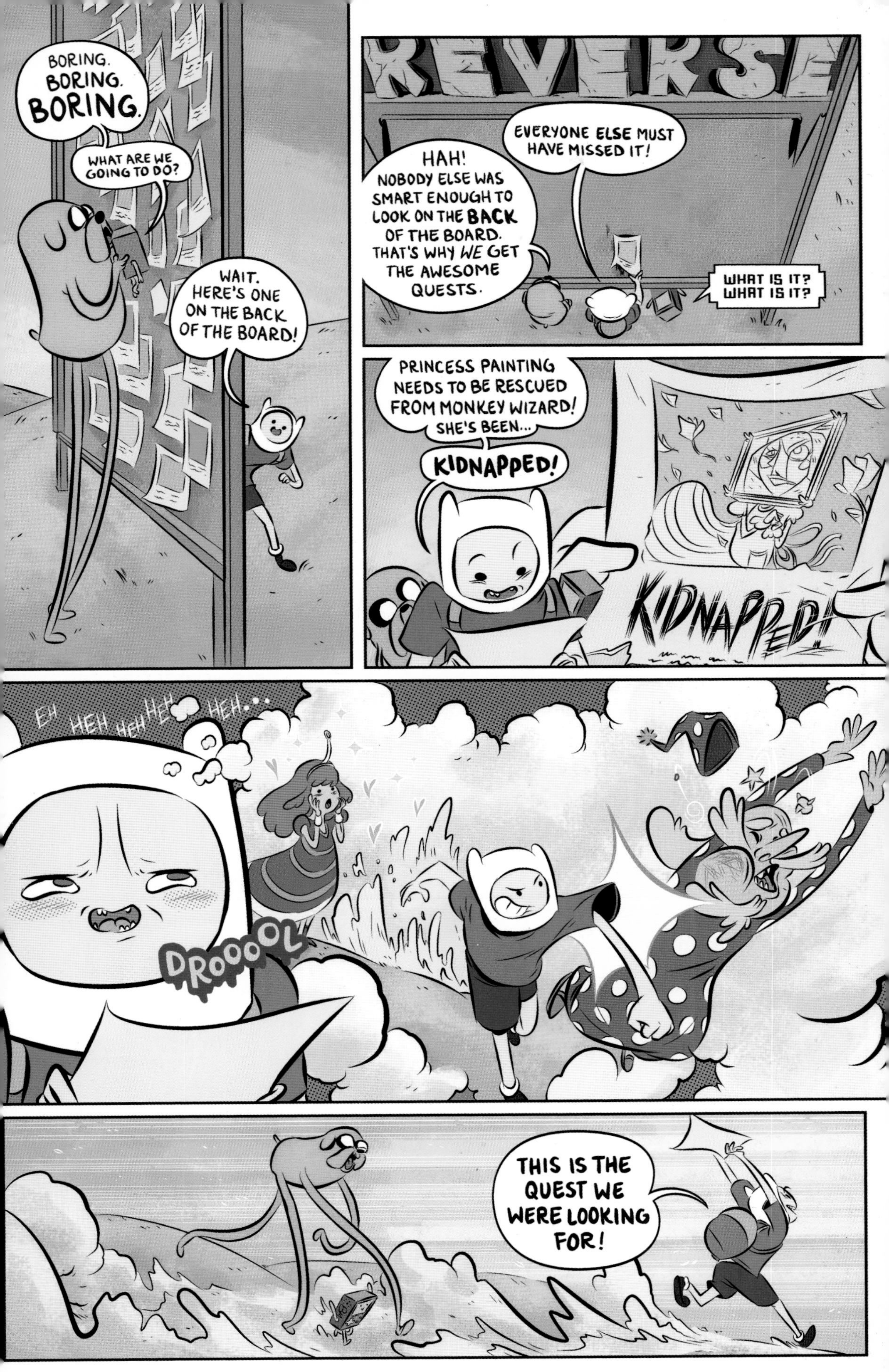
BORING.
BORING.
BORING.
WHAT ARE WE GOING TO DO?
WAIT. HERE'S ONE ON THE BACK OF THE BOARD!
REVERSE
EVERYONE ELSE MUST HAVE MISSED IT!
HAH! NOBODY ELSE WAS SMART ENOUGH TO LOOK ON THE BACK OF THE BOARD. THAT'S WHY WE GET THE AWESOME QUESTS.
WHAT IS IT? WHAT IS IT?
PRINCESS PAINTING NEEDS TO BE RESCUED FROM MONKEY WIZARD! SHE'S BEEN...
KIDNAPPED!
KIDNAPPED!
EH HEH HEH HEH HEH...
DROOOOL
THIS IS THE QUEST WE WERE LOOKING FOR!

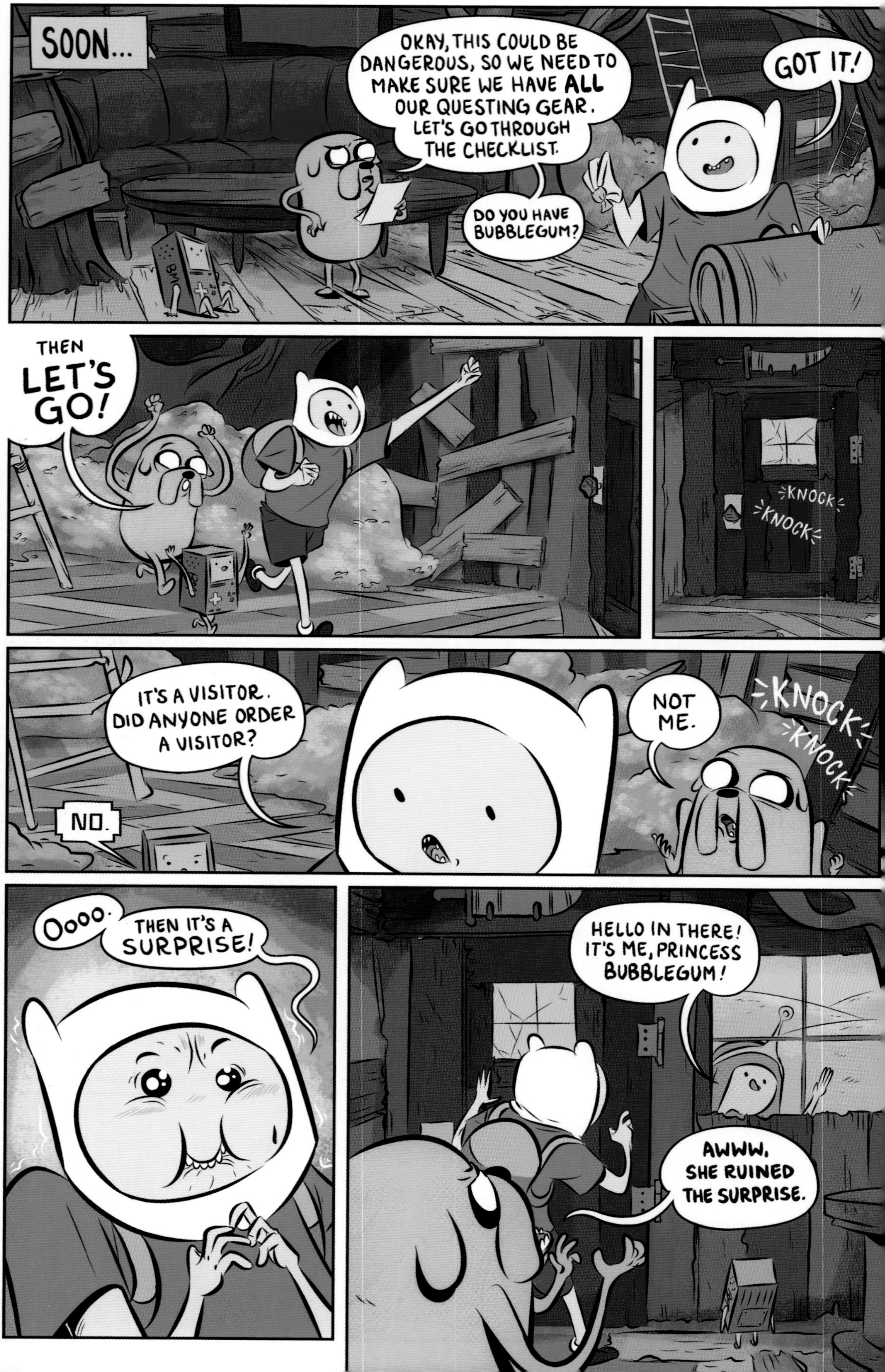
SOON...
OKAY, THIS COULD BE DANGEROUS, SO WE NEED TO MAKE SURE WE HAVE ALL OUR QUESTING GEAR. LET'S GO THROUGH THE CHECKLIST.
DO YOU HAVE BUBBLEGUM?
GOT IT!
THEN LET'S GO!
KNOCK
KNOCK
IT'S A VISITOR. DID ANYONE ORDER A VISITOR?
NO.
NOT ME.
KNOCK
KNOCK
Oooo.
THEN IT'S A SURPRISE!
HELLO IN THERE! IT'S ME, PRINCESS BUBBLEGUM!
AWWW, SHE RUINED THE SURPRISE.

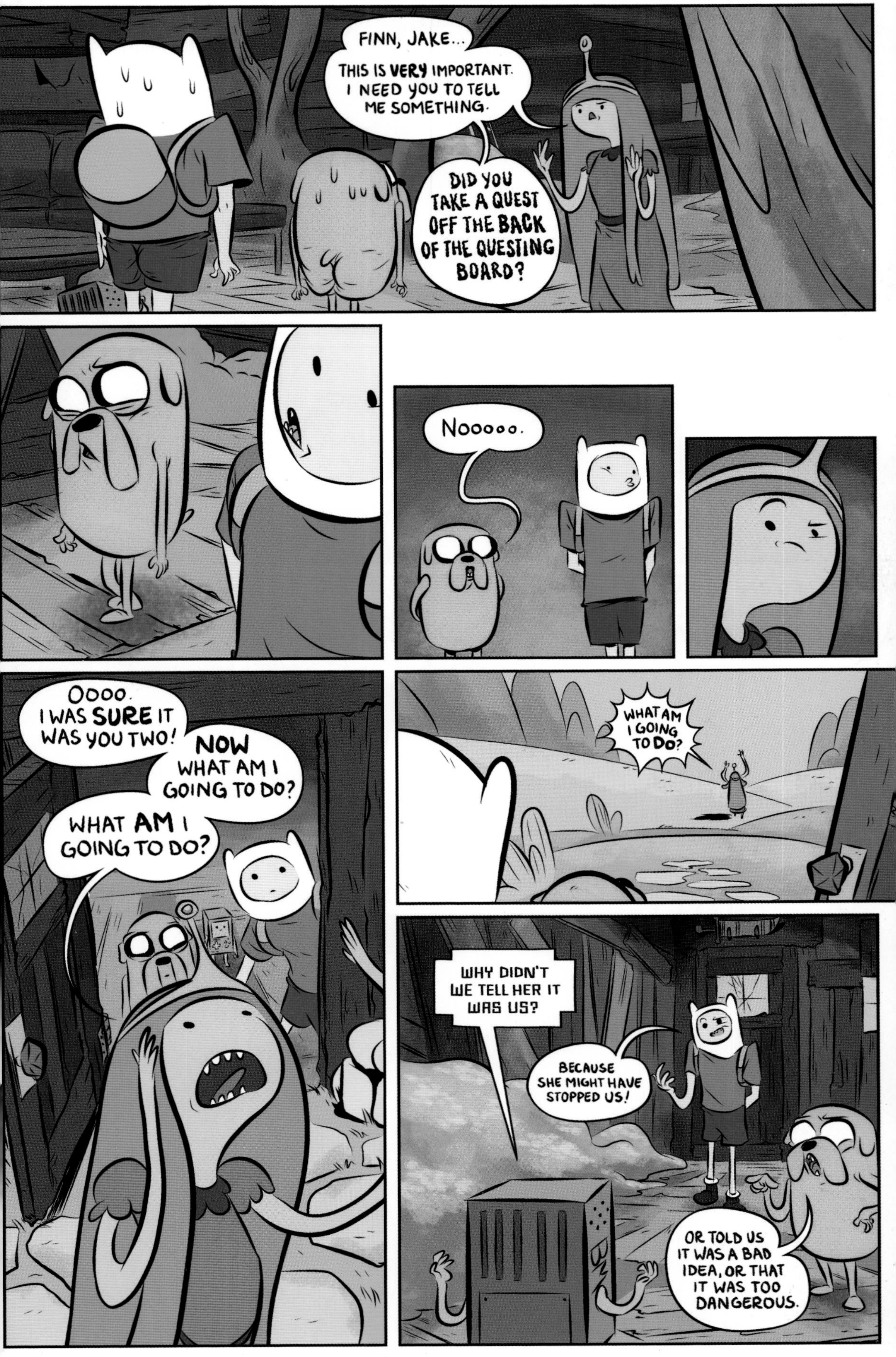
FINN, JAKE...
THIS IS VERY IMPORTANT. I NEED YOU TO TELL ME SOMETHING.
DID YOU TAKE A QUEST OFF THE BACK OF THE QUESTING BOARD?
Nooooo.
OOOO. I WAS SURE IT WAS YOU TWO!
NOW WHAT AM I GOING TO DO?
WHAT AM I GOING TO DO?
WHAT AM I GOING TO DO?
WHY DIDN'T WE TELL HER IT WAS US?
BECAUSE SHE MIGHT HAVE STOPPED US!
OR TOLD US IT WAS A BAD IDEA, OR THAT IT WAS TOO DANGEROUS.

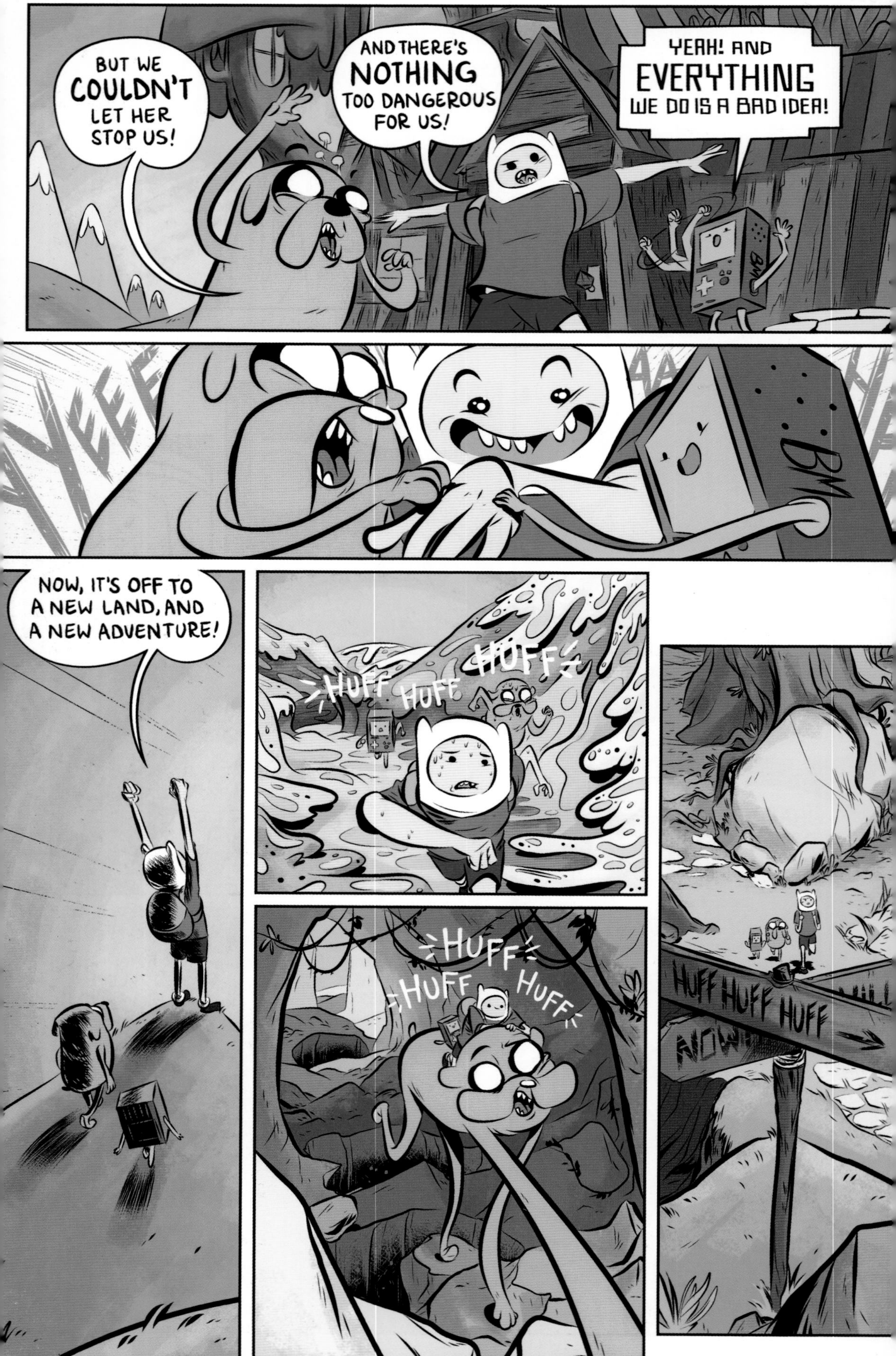
BUT WE COULDN'T LET HER STOP US!
AND THERE'S NOTHING TOO DANGEROUS FOR US!
YEAH! AND EVERYTHING WE DO IS A BAD IDEA!
NOW, IT'S OFF TO A NEW LAND, AND A NEW ADVENTURE!
HUFF HUFF HUFF
HUFF HUFF HUFF
HUFF HUFF HUFF

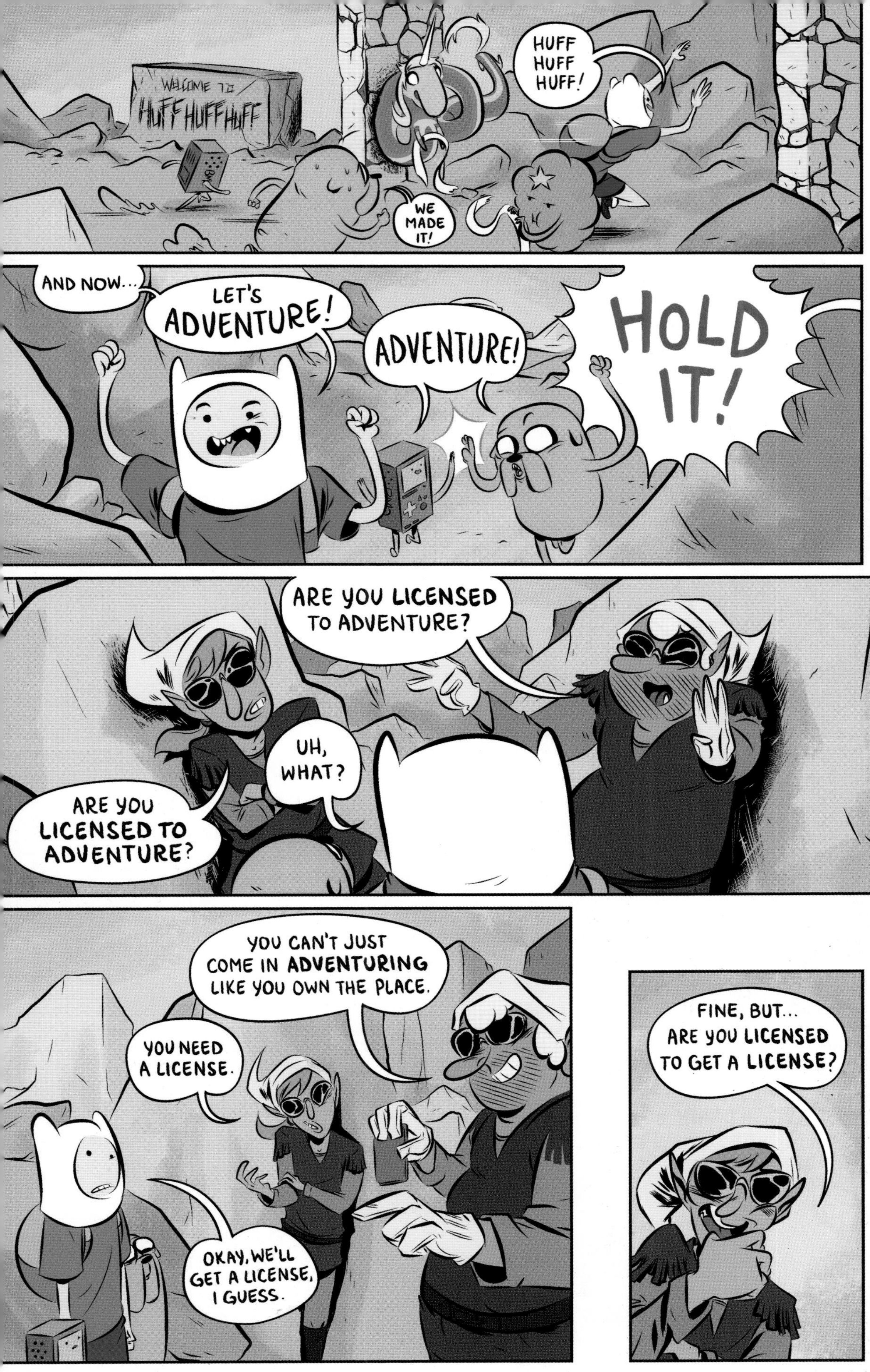
WELCOME TO
HUFF HUFF HUFF
HUFF HUFF HUFF!
WE MADE IT!
AND NOW...
LET'S ADVENTURE!
ADVENTURE!
HOLD IT!
ARE YOU LICENSED TO ADVENTURE?
UH, WHAT?
ARE YOU LICENSED TO ADVENTURE?
YOU CAN'T JUST COME IN ADVENTURING LIKE YOU OWN THE PLACE.
YOU NEED A LICENSE.
OKAY, WE'LL GET A LICENSE, I GUESS.
FINE, BUT... ARE YOU LICENSED TO GET A LICENSE?

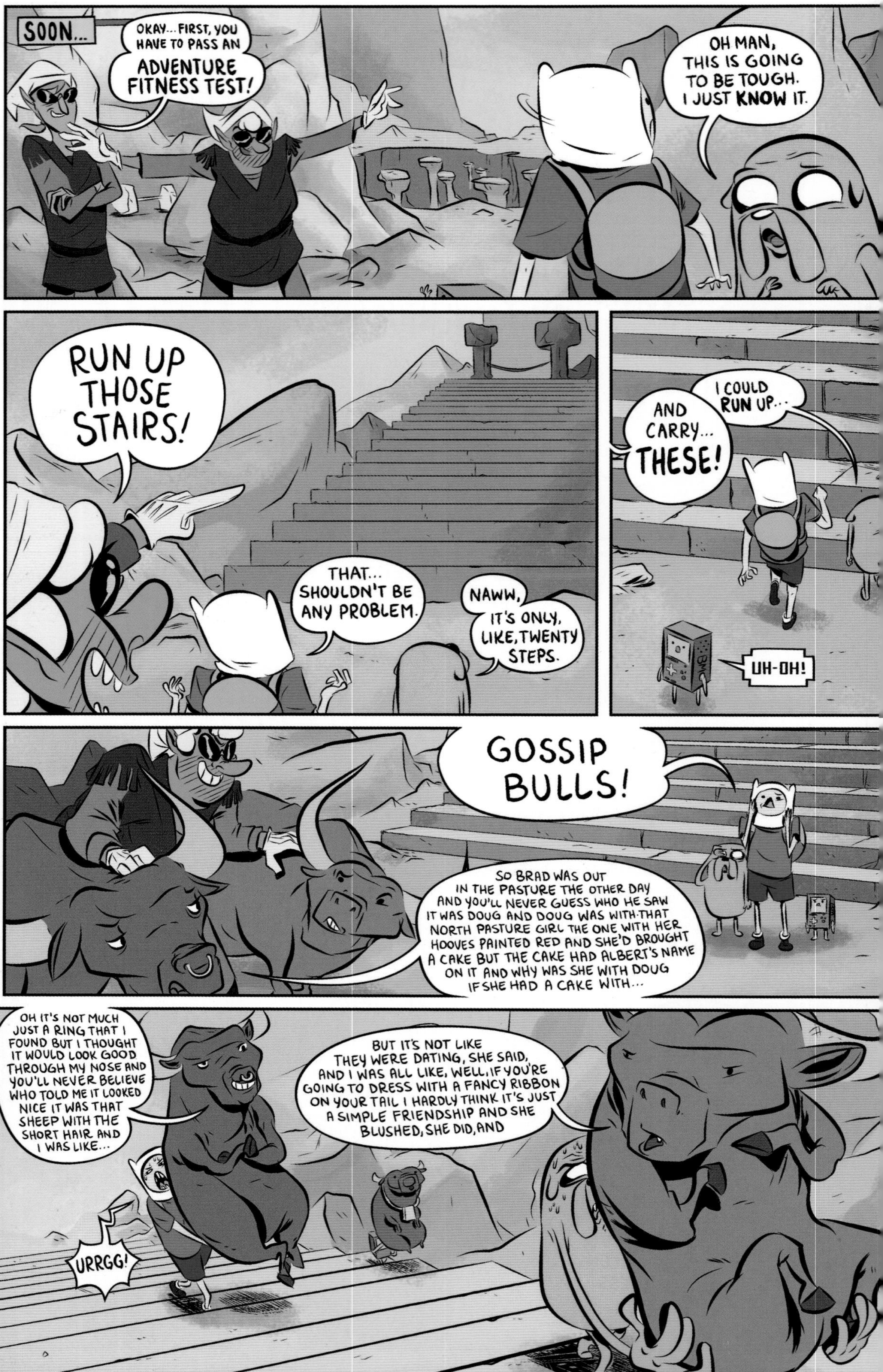

SOON...
OKAY... FIRST, YOU HAVE TO PASS AN ADVENTURE FITNESS TEST!
OH MAN, THIS IS GOING TO BE TOUGH. I JUST KNOW IT.
RUN UP THOSE STAIRS!
THAT... SHOULDN'T BE ANY PROBLEM.
NAWW, IT'S ONLY, LIKE, TWENTY STEPS.
I COULD RUN UP...
AND CARRY... THESE!
UH-OH!
GOSSIP BULLS!
SO BRAD WAS OUT IN THE PASTURE THE OTHER DAY AND YOU'LL NEVER GUESS WHO HE SAW IT WAS DOUG AND DOUG WAS WITH THAT NORTH PASTURE GIRL THE ONE WITH HER HOOVES PAINTED RED AND SHE'D BROUGHT A CAKE BUT THE CAKE HAD ALBERT'S NAME ON IT AND WHY WAS SHE WITH DOUG IF SHE HAD A CAKE WITH...
OH IT'S NOT MUCH JUST A RING THAT I FOUND BUT I THOUGHT IT WOULD LOOK GOOD THROUGH MY NOSE AND YOU'LL NEVER BELIEVE WHO TOLD ME IT LOOKED NICE IT WAS THAT SHEEP WITH THE SHORT HAIR AND I WAS LIKE...
BUT IT'S NOT LIKE THEY WERE DATING, SHE SAID, AND I WAS ALL LIKE, WELL, IF YOU'RE GOING TO DRESS WITH A FANCY RIBBON ON YOUR TAIL I HARDLY THINK IT'S JUST A SIMPLE FRIENDSHIP AND SHE BLUSHED, SHE DID, AND
URRGG!

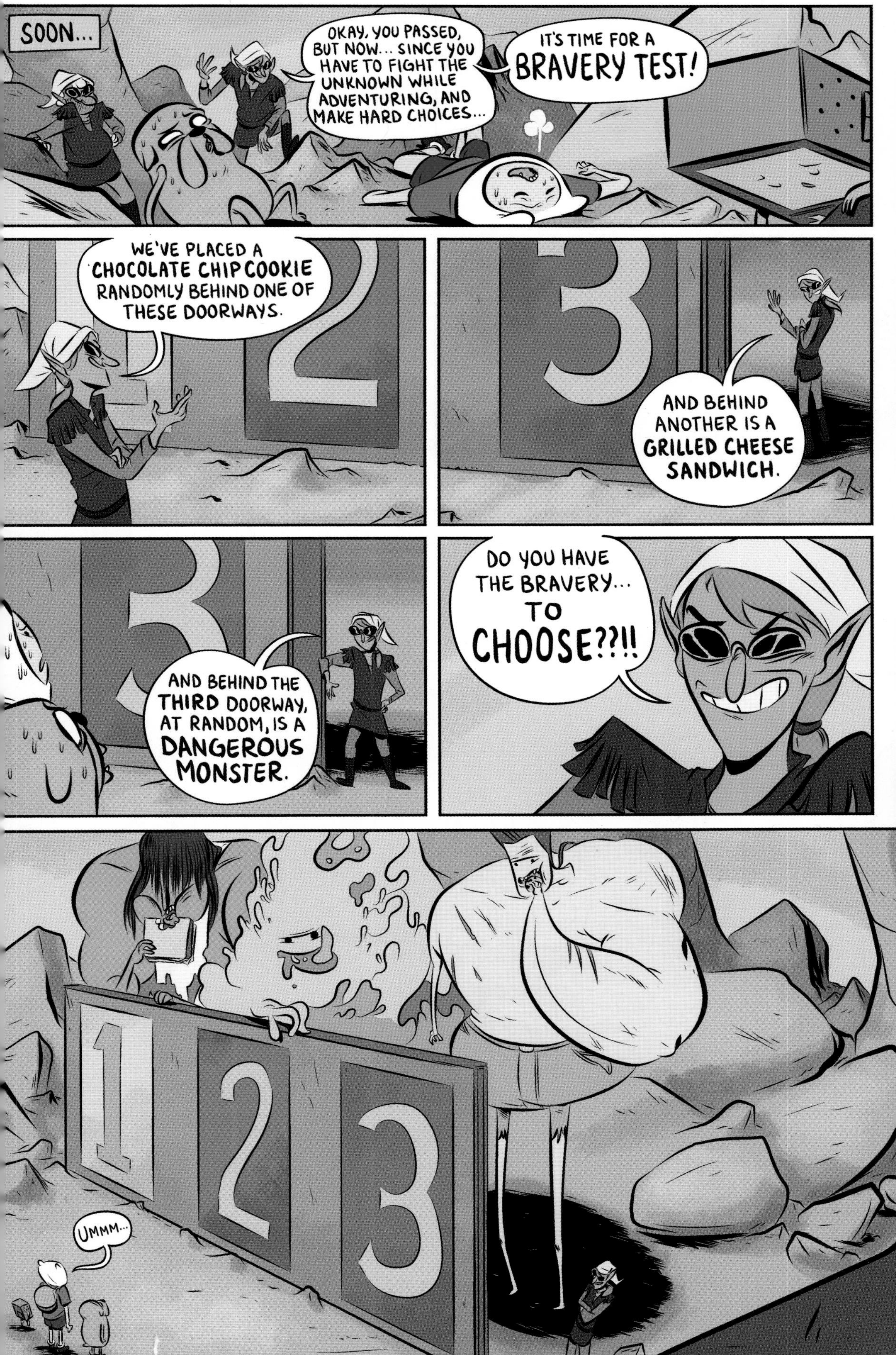
SOON...
OKAY, YOU PASSED, BUT NOW... SINCE YOU HAVE TO FIGHT THE UNKNOWN WHILE ADVENTURING, AND MAKE HARD CHOICES...
IT'S TIME FOR A BRAVERY TEST!
WE'VE PLACED A CHOCOLATE CHIP COOKIE RANDOMLY BEHIND ONE OF THESE DOORWAYS.
AND BEHIND ANOTHER IS A GRILLED CHEESE SANDWICH.
AND BEHIND THE THIRD DOORWAY, AT RANDOM, IS A DANGEROUS MONSTER.
DO YOU HAVE THE BRAVERY... TO CHOOSE??!!
1
2
3
UMMM...

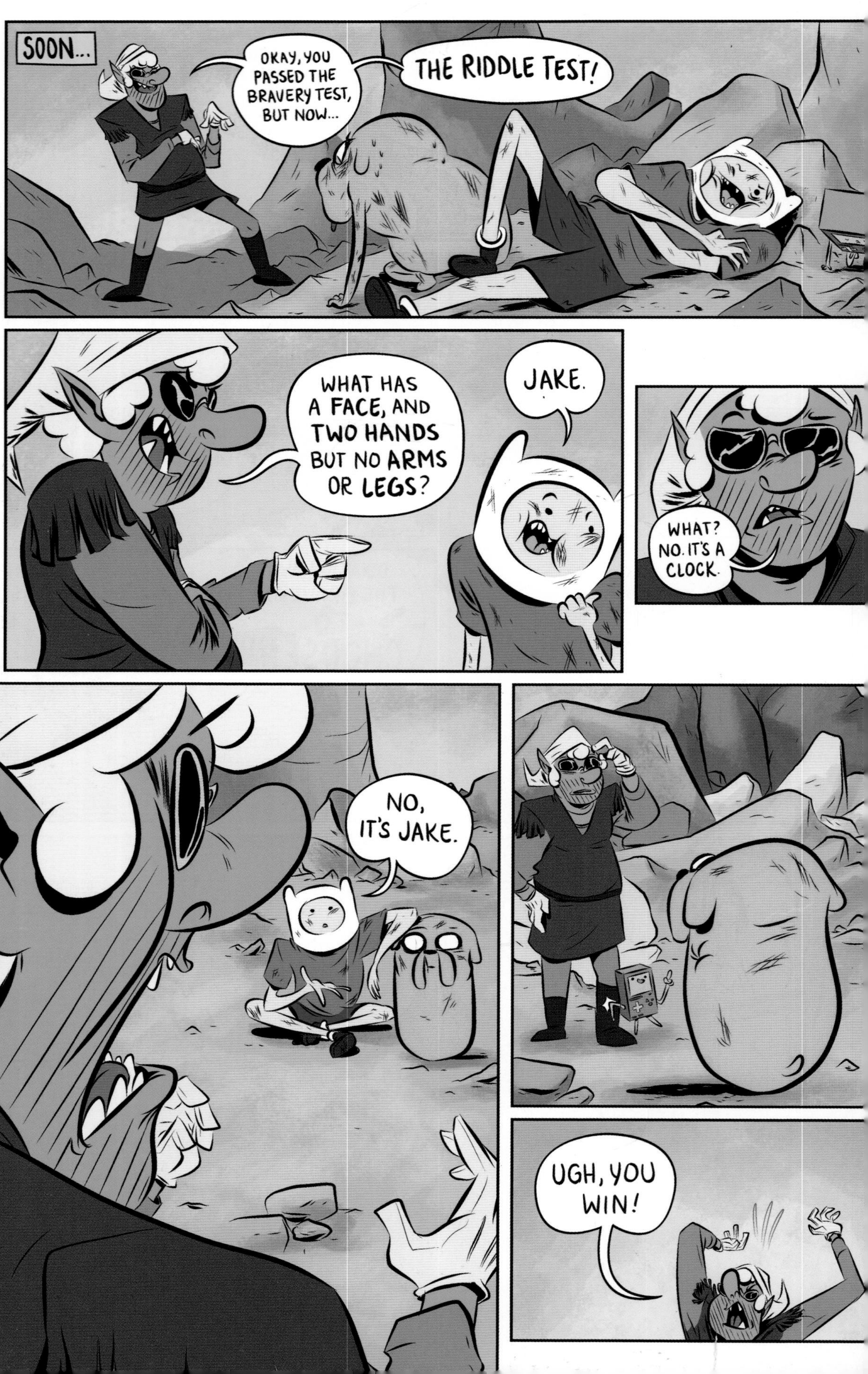
SOON...
OKAY, YOU PASSED THE BRAVERY TEST, BUT NOW...
THE RIDDLE TEST!
WHAT HAS A FACE, AND TWO HANDS BUT NO ARMS OR LEGS?
JAKE.
WHAT? NO. IT'S A CLOCK.
NO, IT'S JAKE.
UGH, YOU WIN!

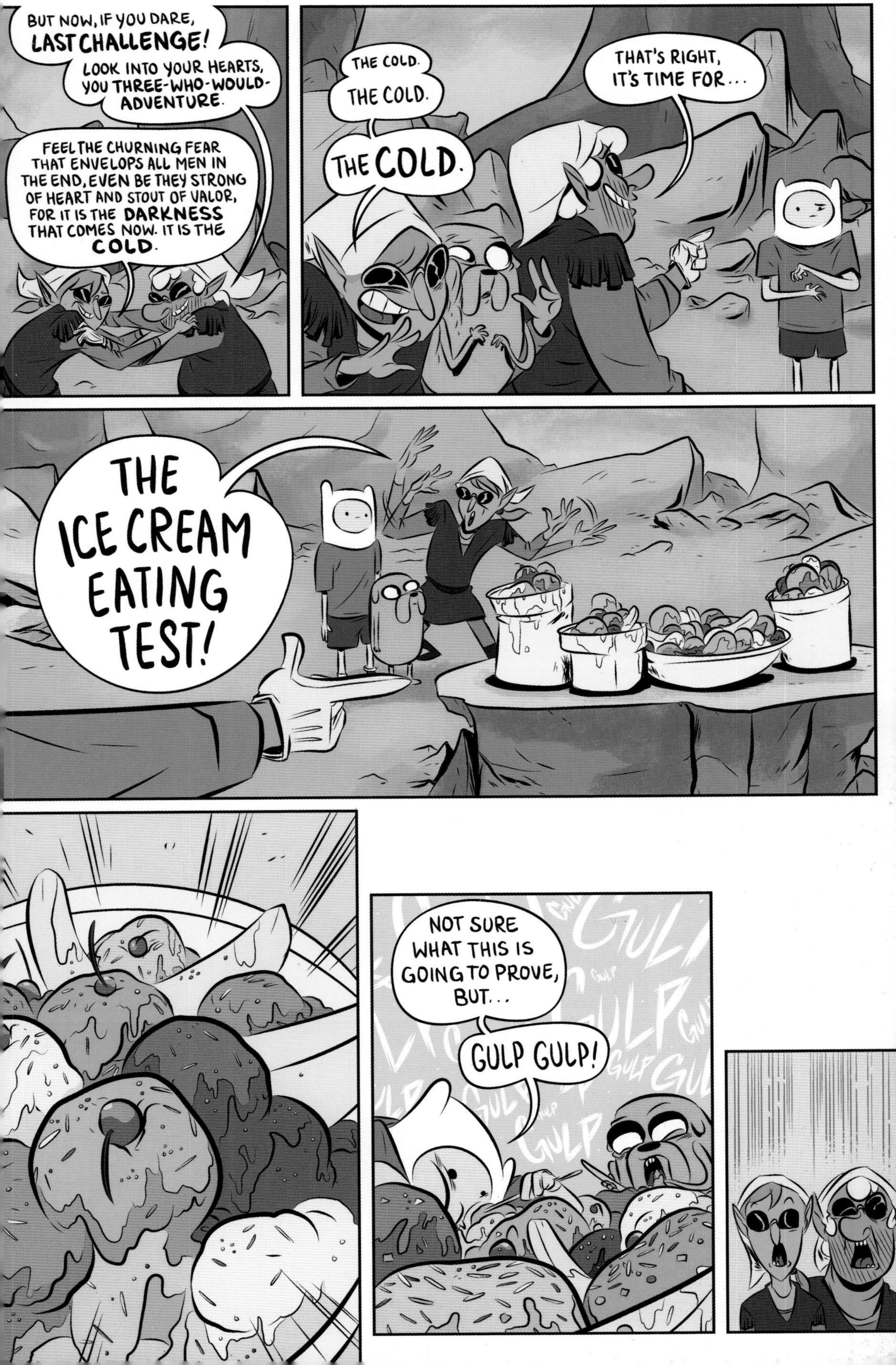
BUT NOW, IF YOU DARE, LAST CHALLENGE!
LOOK INTO YOUR HEARTS, YOU THREE-WHO-WOULD-ADVENTURE.
FEEL THE CHURNING FEAR THAT ENVELOPS ALL MEN IN THE END, EVEN BE THEY STRONG OF HEART AND STOUT OF VALOR, FOR IT IS THE DARKNESS THAT COMES NOW. IT IS THE COLD.
THE COLD.
THE COLD.
THE COLD.
THAT'S RIGHT, IT'S TIME FOR...
THE ICE CREAM EATING TEST!
NOT SURE WHAT THIS IS GOING TO PROVE, BUT...
GULP GULP!
GULP
GULP
GULP

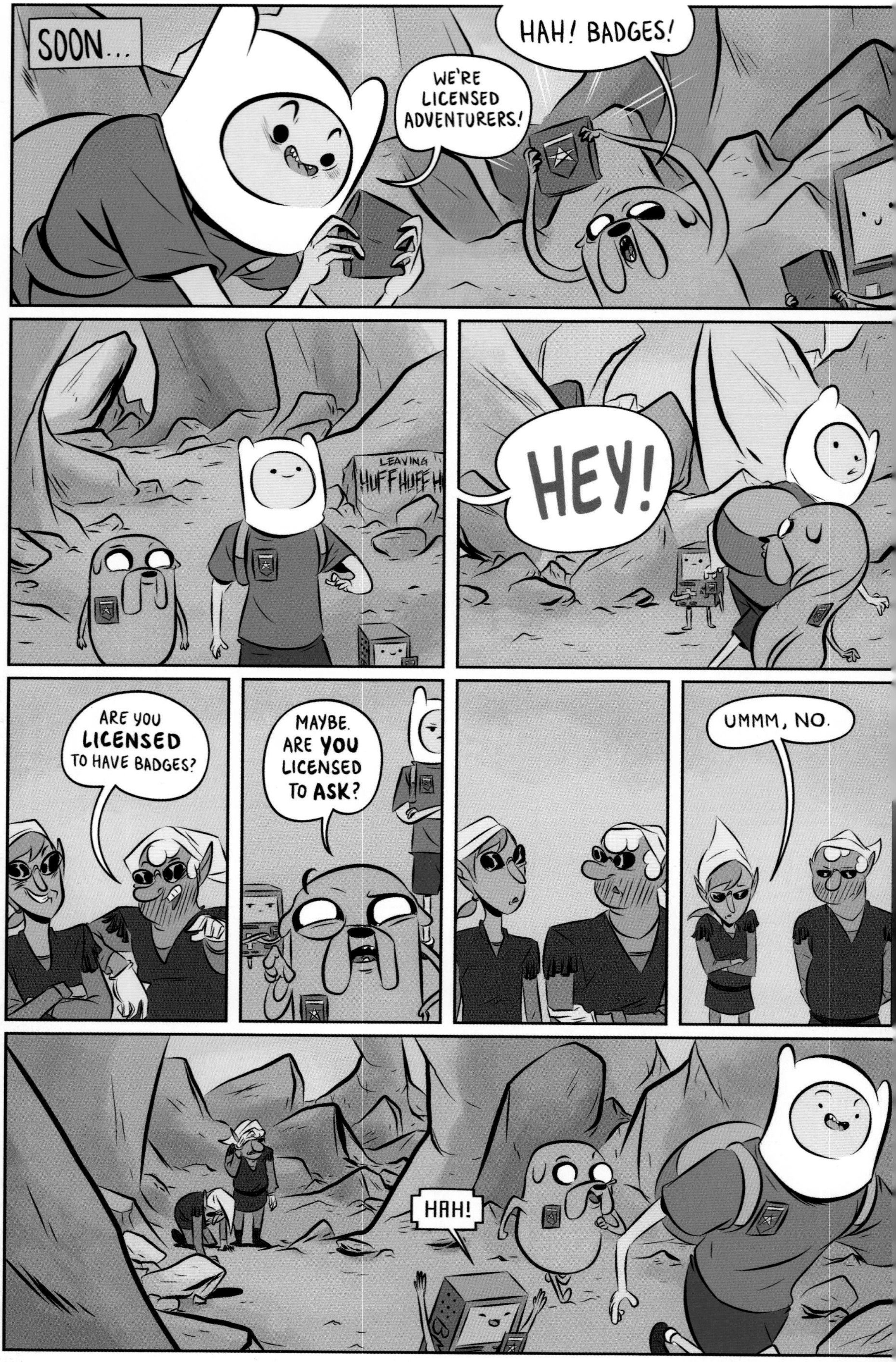
SOON...
WE'RE LICENSED ADVENTURERS!
HAH! BADGES!
LEAVING HUFFHUFF H
HEY!
ARE YOU **LICENSED** TO HAVE BADGES?
MAYBE. ARE **YOU** LICENSED TO **ASK**?
UMMM, NO.
HAH!

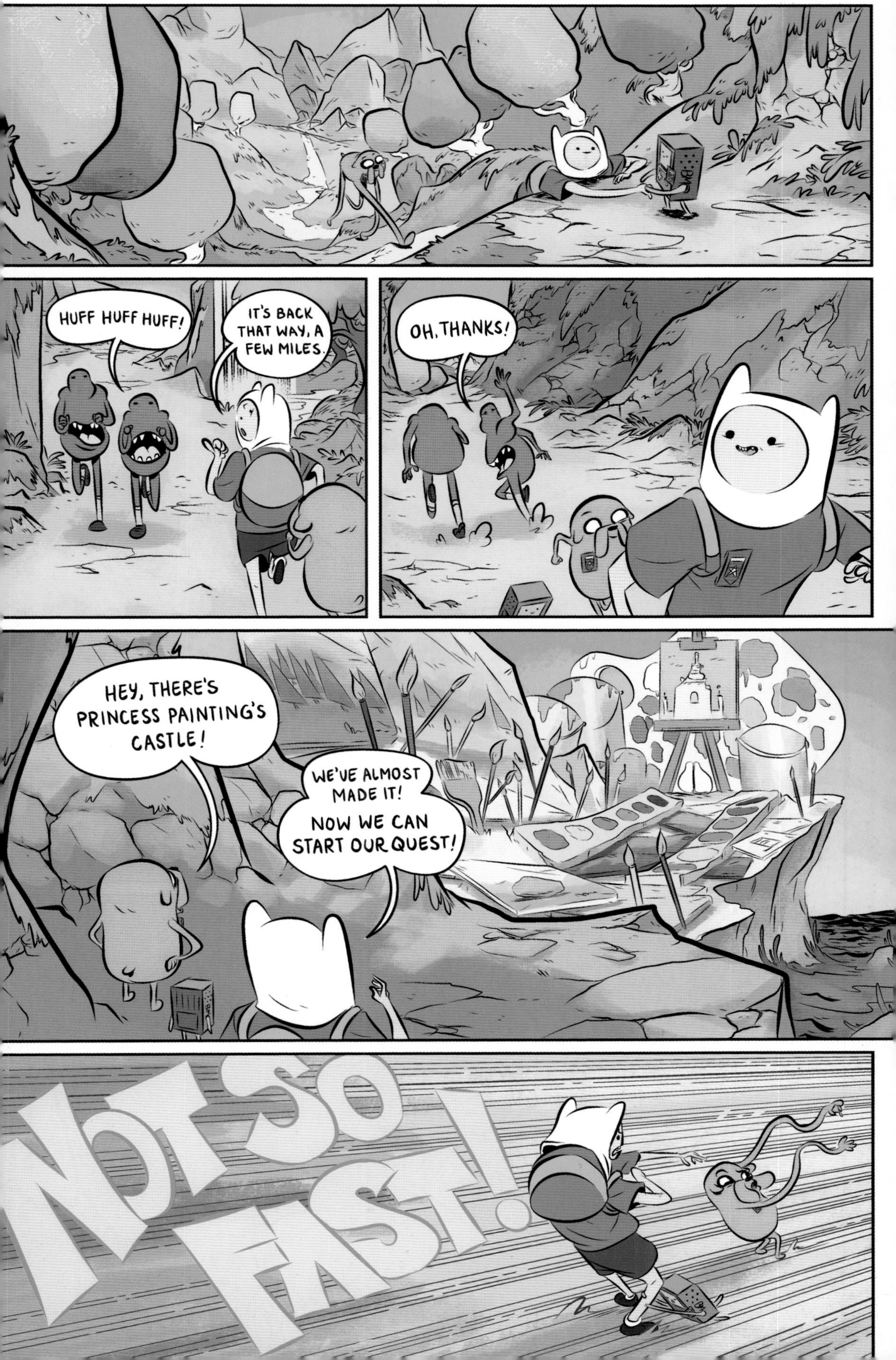
HUFF HUFF HUFF!
IT'S BACK THAT WAY, A FEW MILES.
OH, THANKS!
HEY, THERE'S PRINCESS PAINTING'S CASTLE!
WE'VE ALMOST MADE IT!
NOW WE CAN START OUR QUEST!
NOT SO FAST!

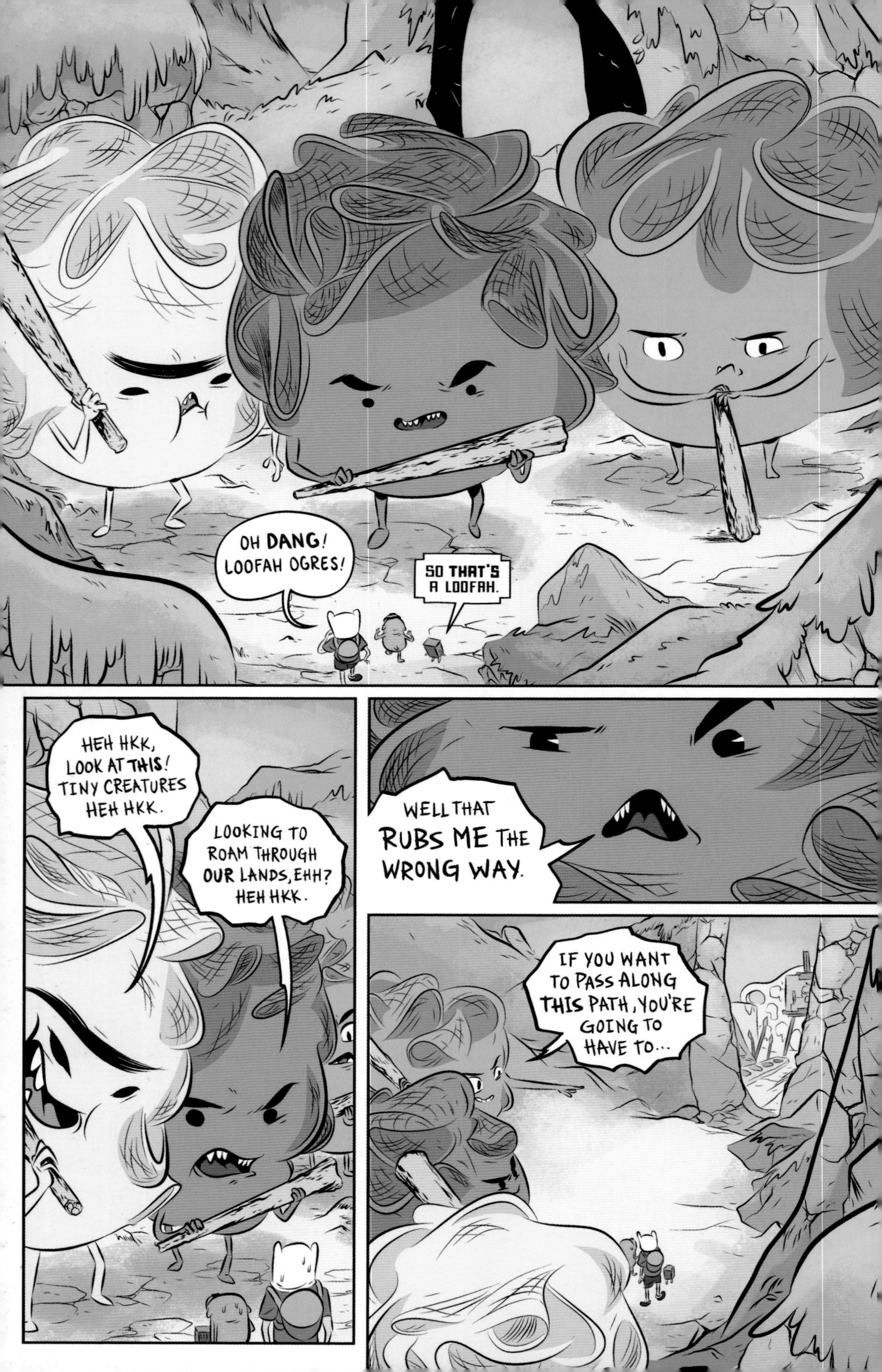
OH DANG! LOOFAH OGRES!
SO THAT'S A LOOFAH.
HEH HKK, LOOK AT THIS! TINY CREATURES HEH HKK.
LOOKING TO ROAM THROUGH OUR LANDS, EHH? HEH HKK.
WELL THAT RUBS ME THE WRONG WAY.
IF YOU WANT TO PASS ALONG THIS PATH, YOU'RE GOING TO HAVE TO...

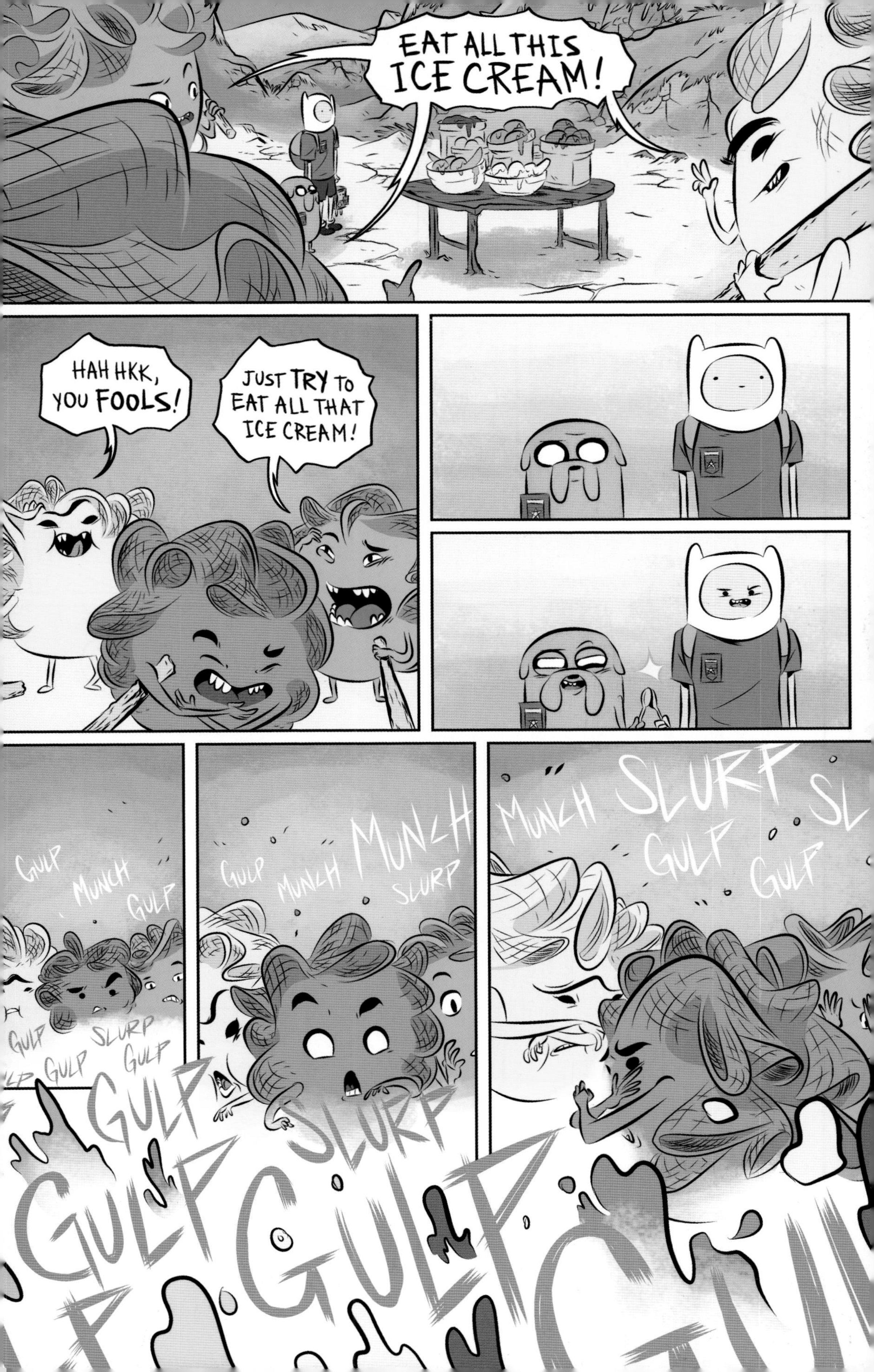
EAT ALL THIS ICE CREAM!
HAH HKK, YOU FOOLS!
JUST TRY TO EAT ALL THAT ICE CREAM!
GULP
MUNCH
GULP
GULP
SLURP
GULP
GULP
GULP
MUNCH
MUNCH
SLURP
MUNCH
SLURP
SL
GULP
GULP
GULP
SLURP
GULP

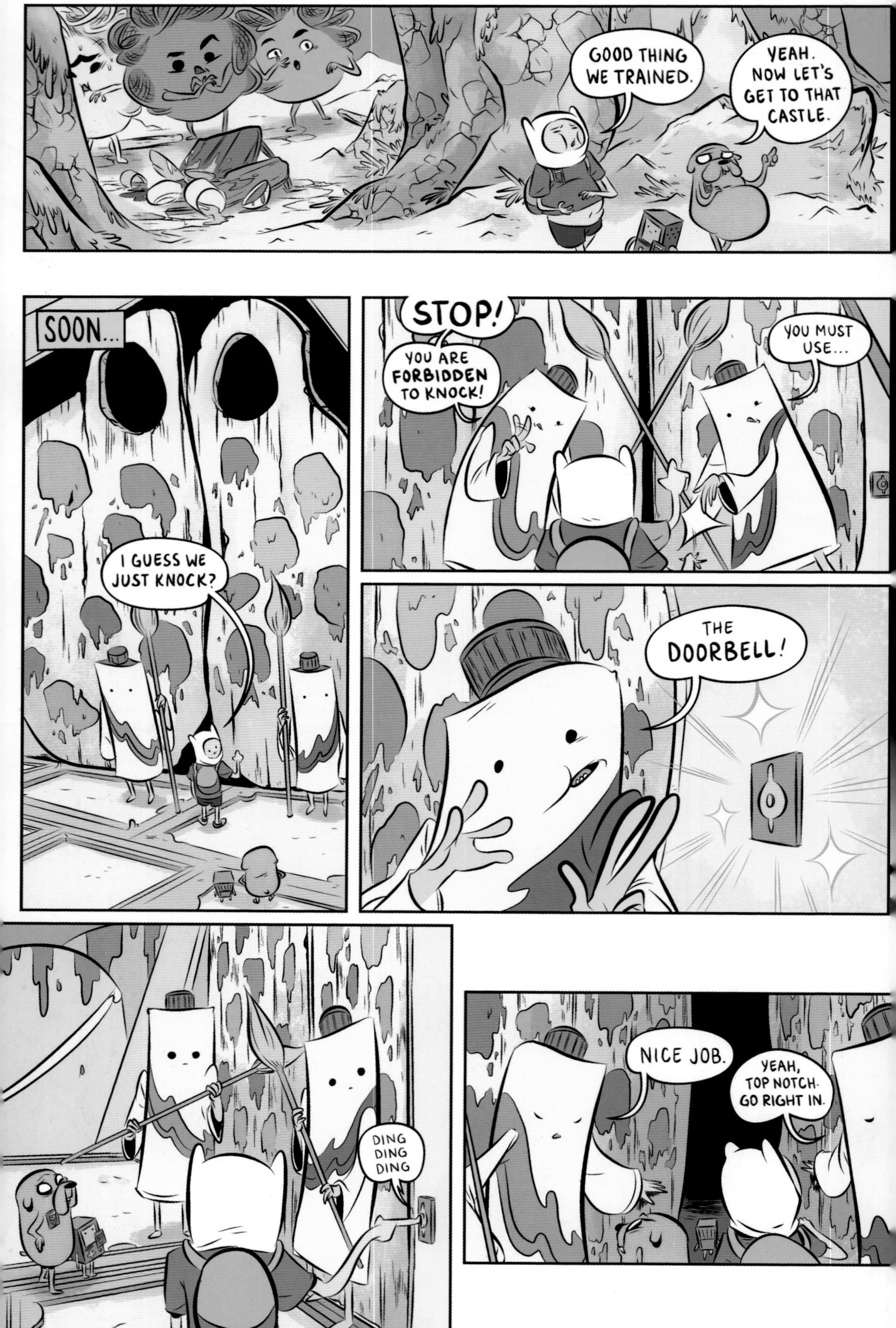
GOOD THING WE TRAINED.
YEAH. NOW LET'S GET TO THAT CASTLE.
SOON...
I GUESS WE JUST KNOCK?
STOP!
YOU ARE FORBIDDEN TO KNOCK!
YOU MUST USE...
THE DOORBELL!
DING DING DING
NICE JOB.
YEAH, TOP NOTCH. GO RIGHT IN.

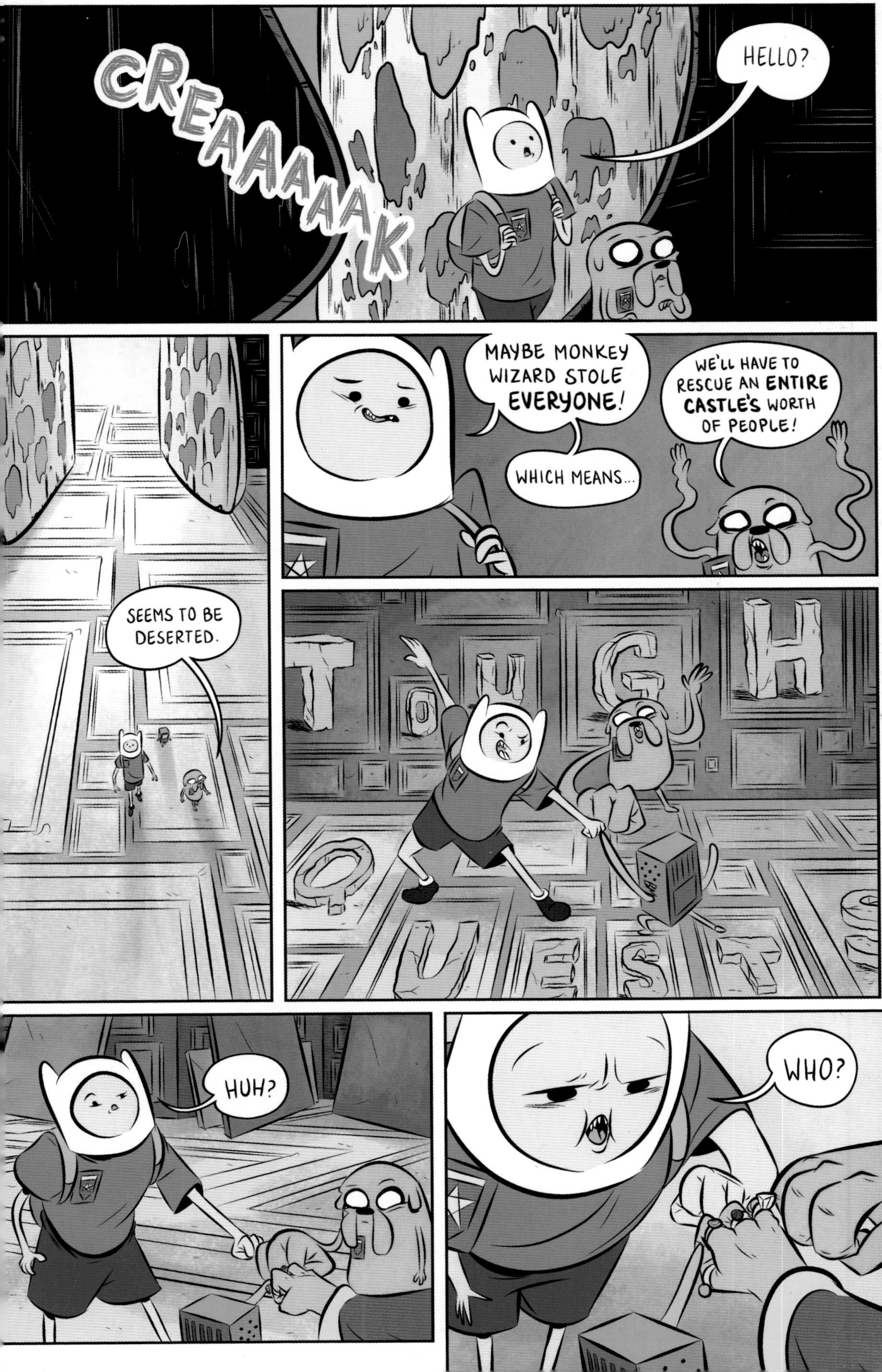
CREAAAAAK
HELLO?
SEEMS TO BE DESERTED.
MAYBE MONKEY WIZARD STOLE EVERYONE!
WHICH MEANS...
WE'LL HAVE TO RESCUE AN ENTIRE CASTLE'S WORTH OF PEOPLE!
HUH?
WHO?

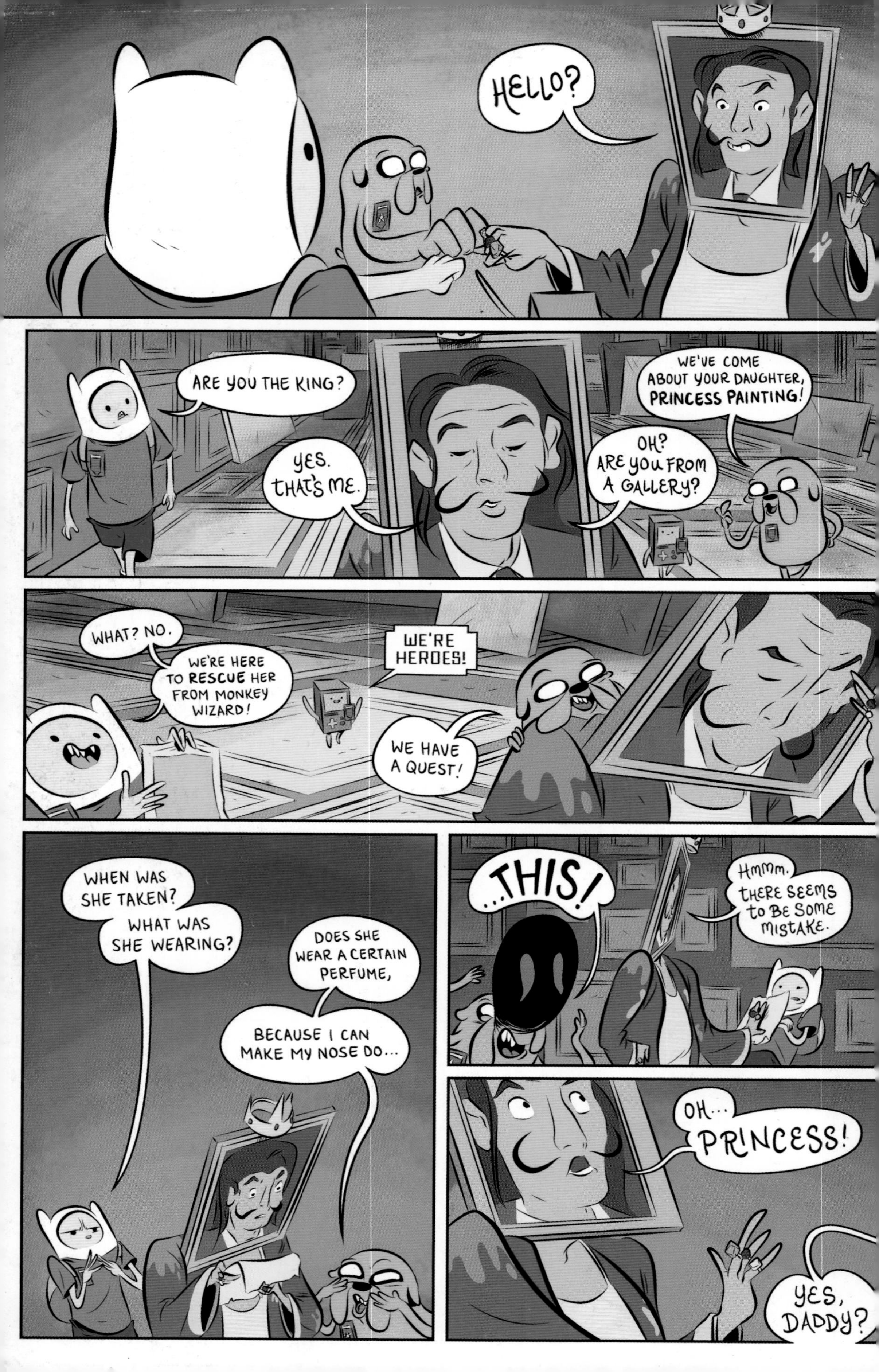
HELLO?
ARE YOU THE KING?
YES. THAT'S ME.
WE'VE COME ABOUT YOUR DAUGHTER, PRINCESS PAINTING!
OH? ARE YOU FROM A GALLERY?
WHAT? NO.
WE'RE HERE TO RESCUE HER FROM MONKEY WIZARD!
WE'RE HEROES!
WE HAVE A QUEST!
WHEN WAS SHE TAKEN?
WHAT WAS SHE WEARING?
DOES SHE WEAR A CERTAIN PERFUME,
BECAUSE I CAN MAKE MY NOSE DO...
...THIS!
Hmmm. THERE SEEMS TO BE SOME MISTAKE.
OH... PRINCESS!
YES, DADDY?

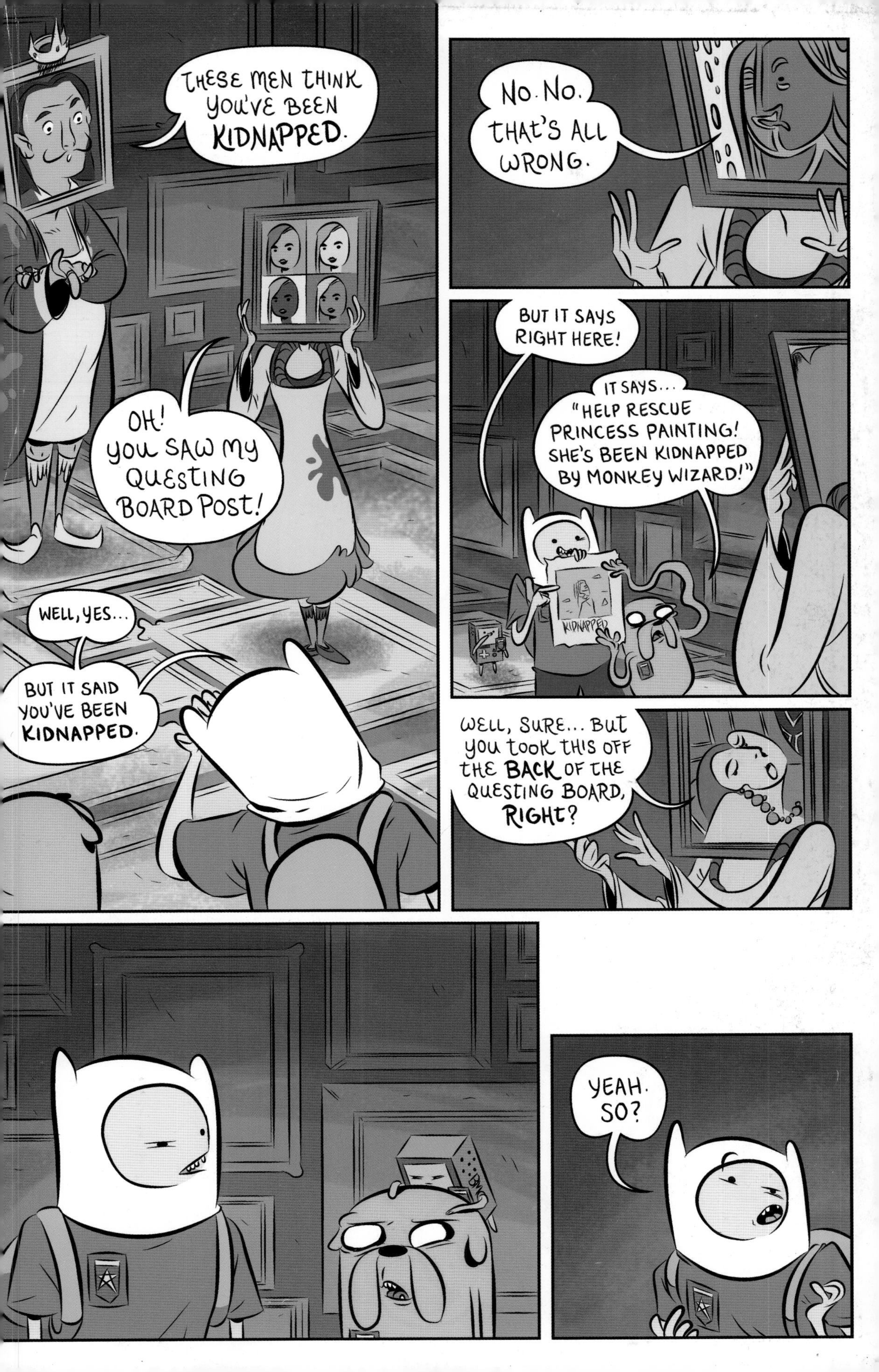
THESE MEN THINK YOU'VE BEEN KIDNAPPED.
OH! YOU SAW MY QUESTING BOARD POST!
WELL, YES...
BUT IT SAID YOU'VE BEEN KIDNAPPED.
NO. NO. THAT'S ALL WRONG.
BUT IT SAYS RIGHT HERE!
IT SAYS... "HELP RESCUE PRINCESS PAINTING! SHE'S BEEN KIDNAPPED BY MONKEY WIZARD!"
KIDNAPPED
WELL, SURE... BUT YOU TOOK THIS OFF THE BACK OF THE QUESTING BOARD, RIGHT?
YEAH. SO?

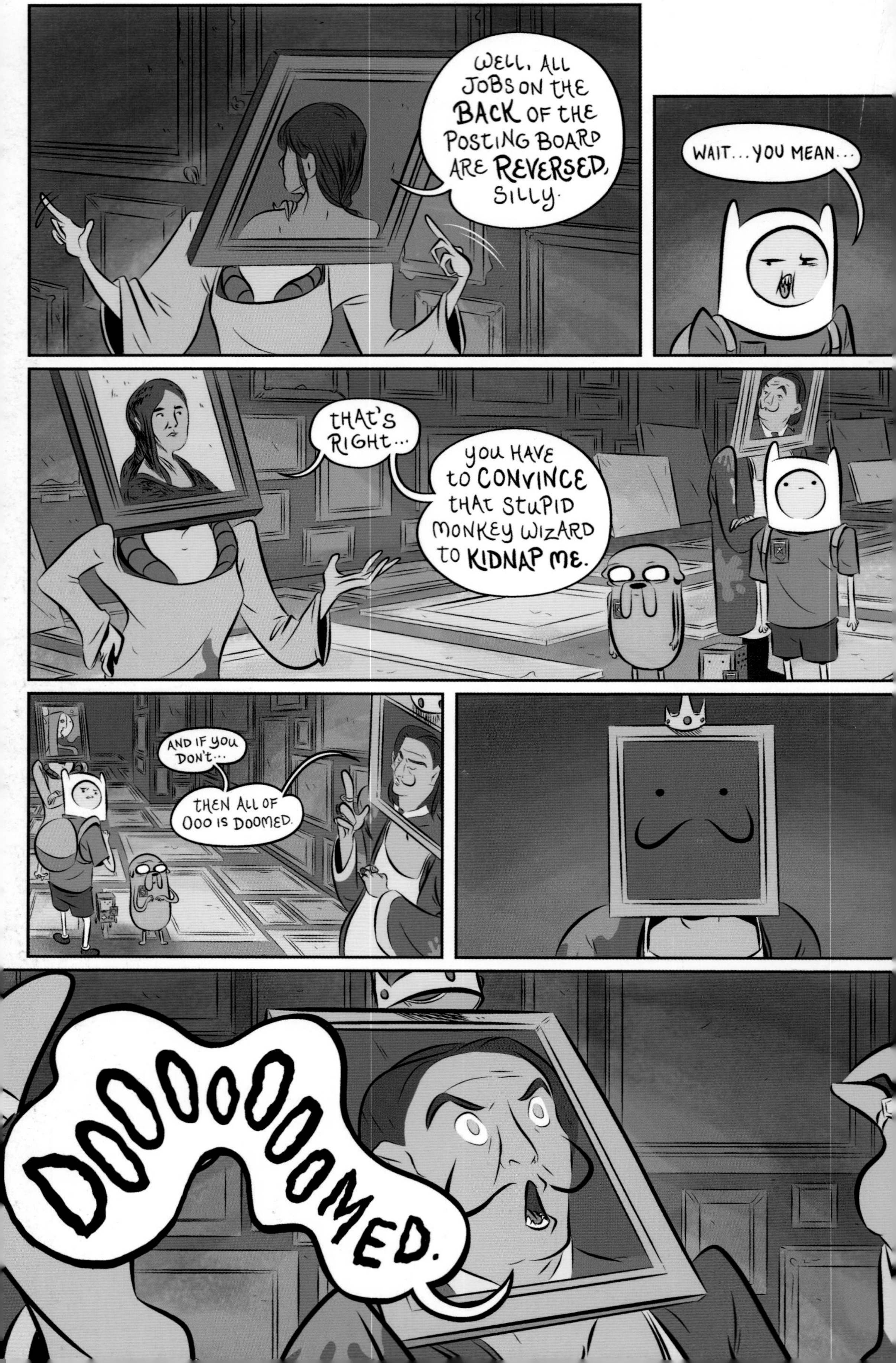
WELL, ALL JOBS ON THE BACK OF THE POSTING BOARD ARE REVERSED, SILLY.
WAIT... YOU MEAN...
THAT'S RIGHT...
YOU HAVE TO CONVINCE THAT STUPID MONKEY WIZARD TO KIDNAP ME.
AND IF YOU DON'T...
THEN ALL OF OOO IS DOOMED.
DOOOOOOOOMED.

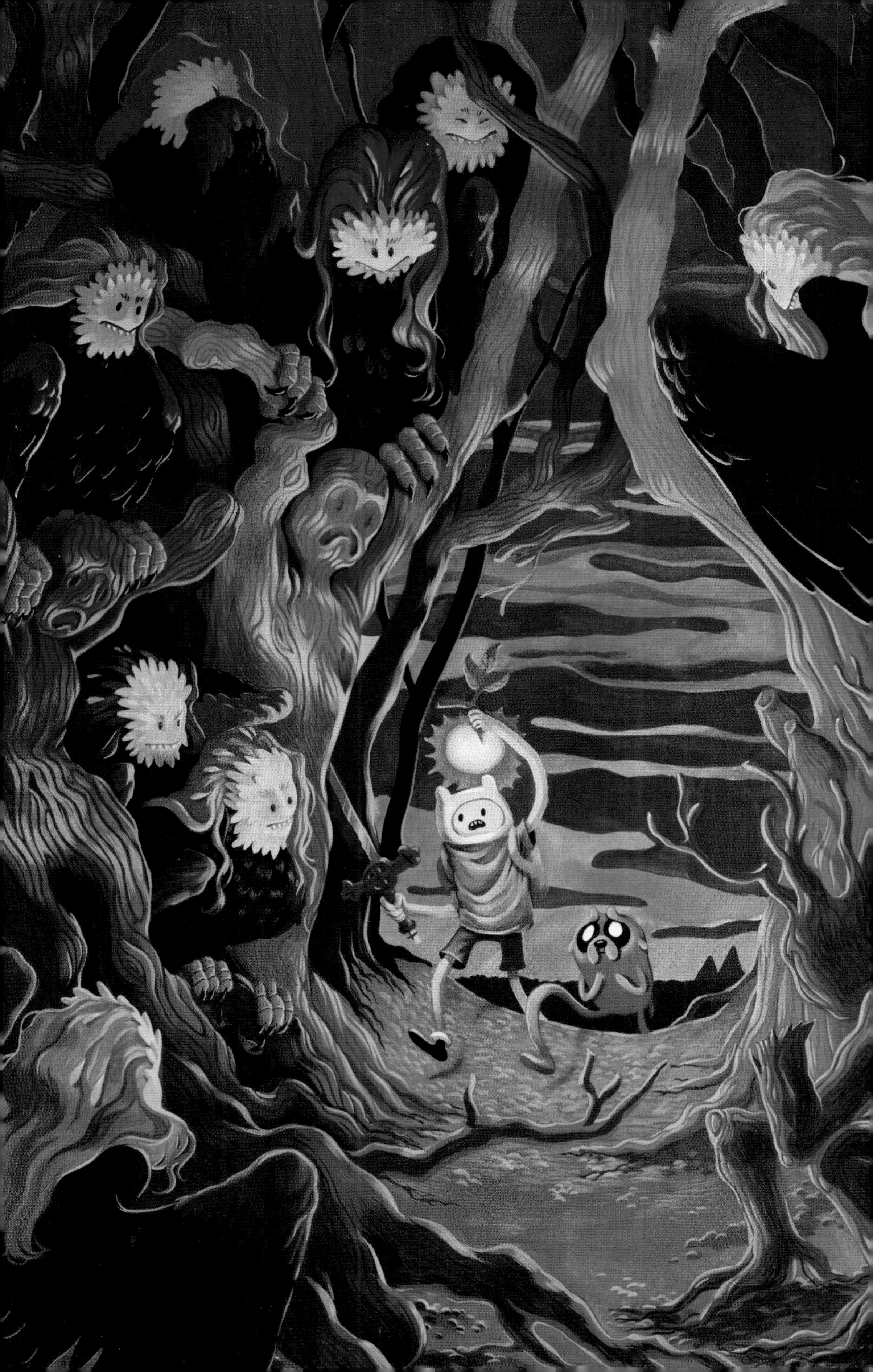

CHAPTER TWO

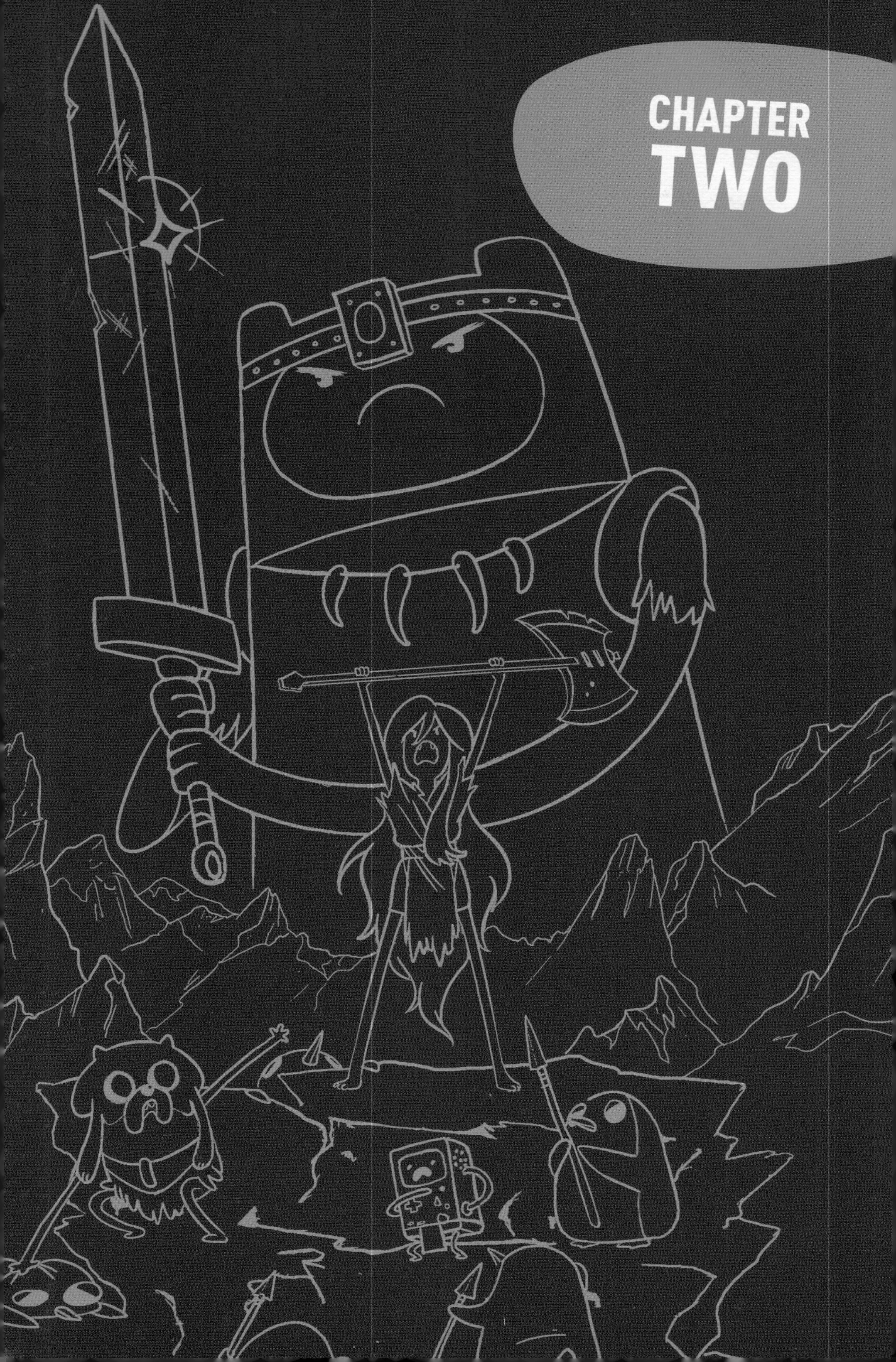

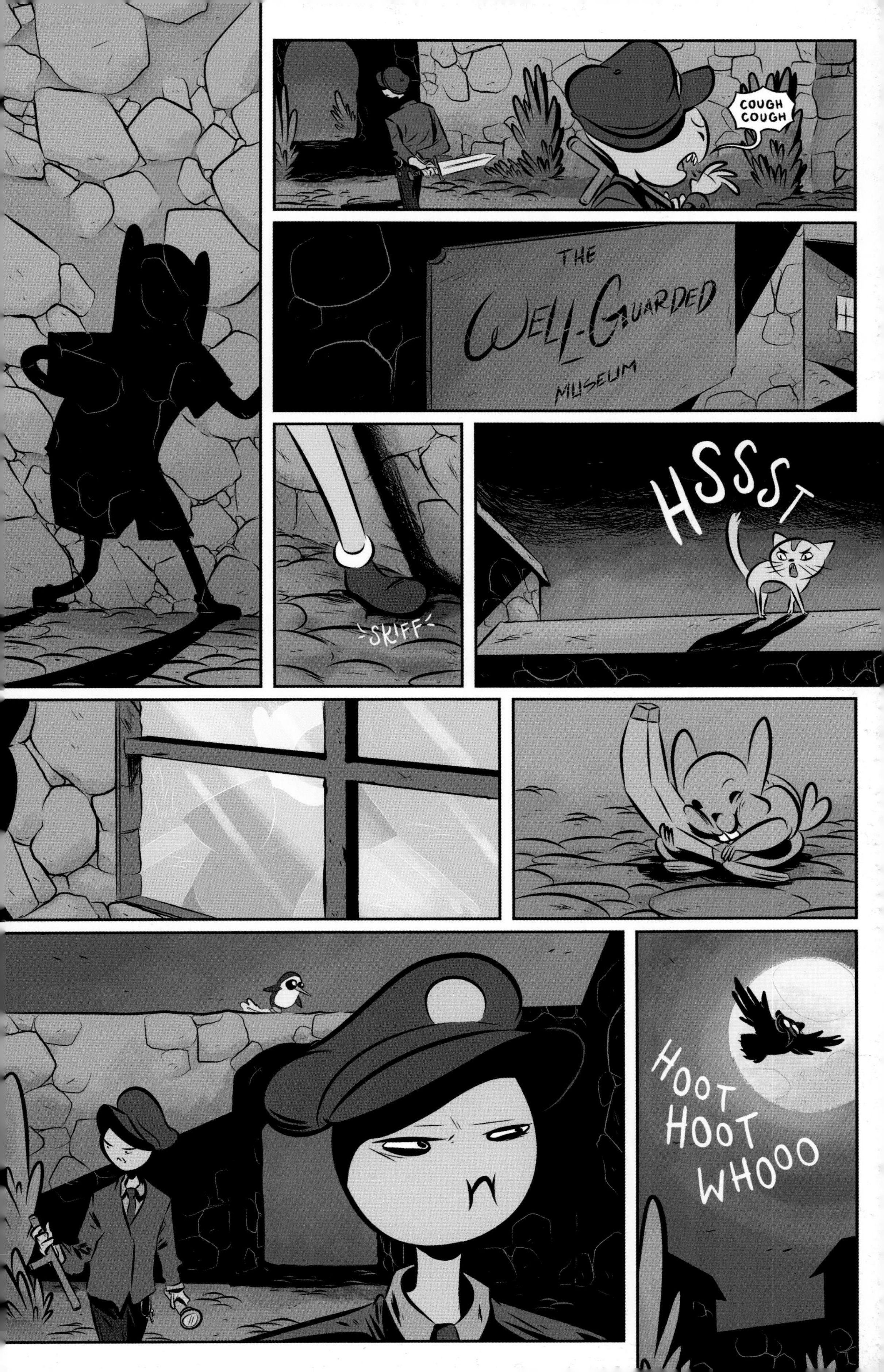
COUGH COUGH
THE WELL-GUARDED MUSEUM
SKIFF
HSSST
HOOT HOOT WHOOO

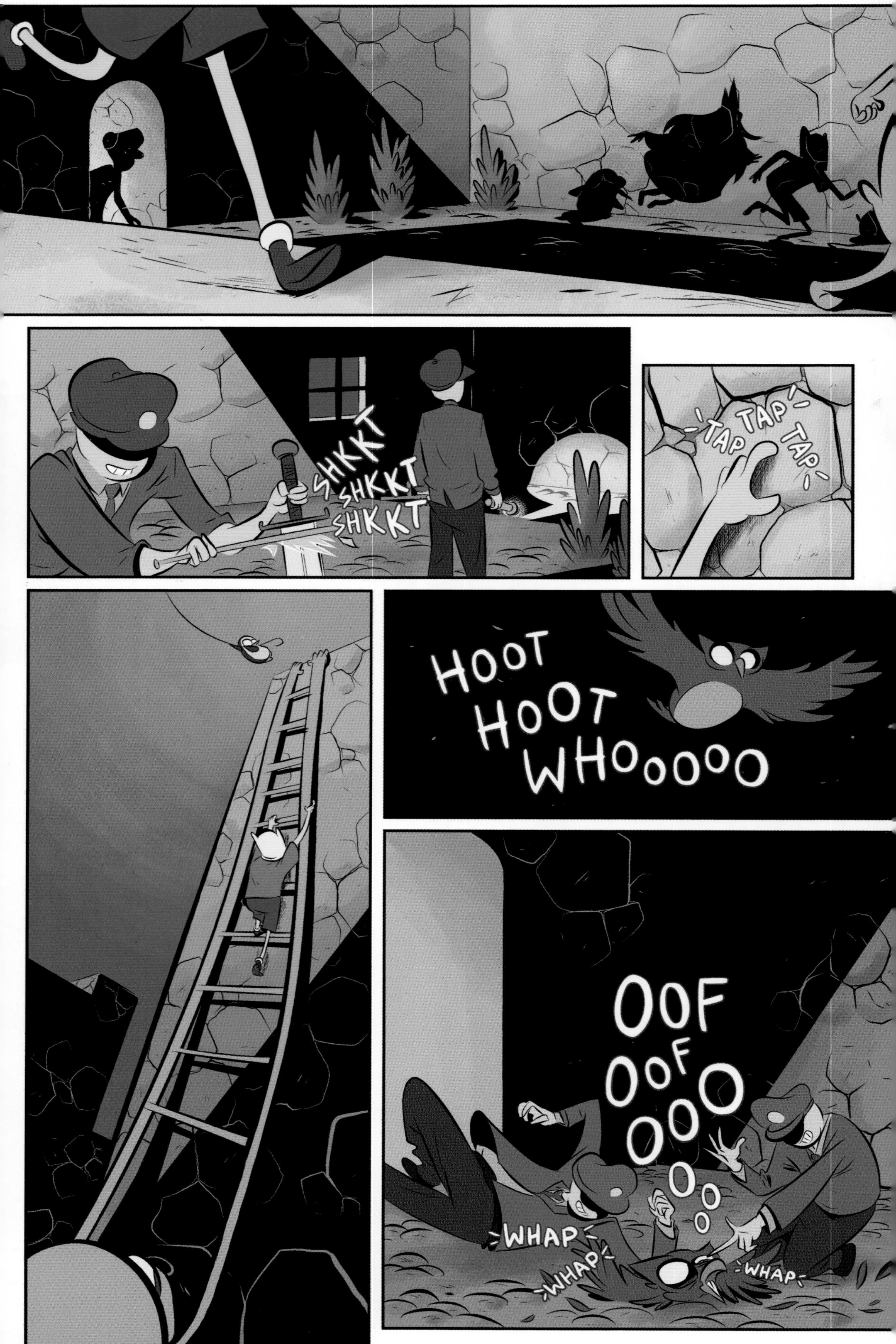
SHKKT
SHKKT
SHKKT
TAP
TAP
TAP
HOOT
HOOT
WHOooooo
OOF
OOF
OOOOOoo
WHAP
WHAP
WHAP

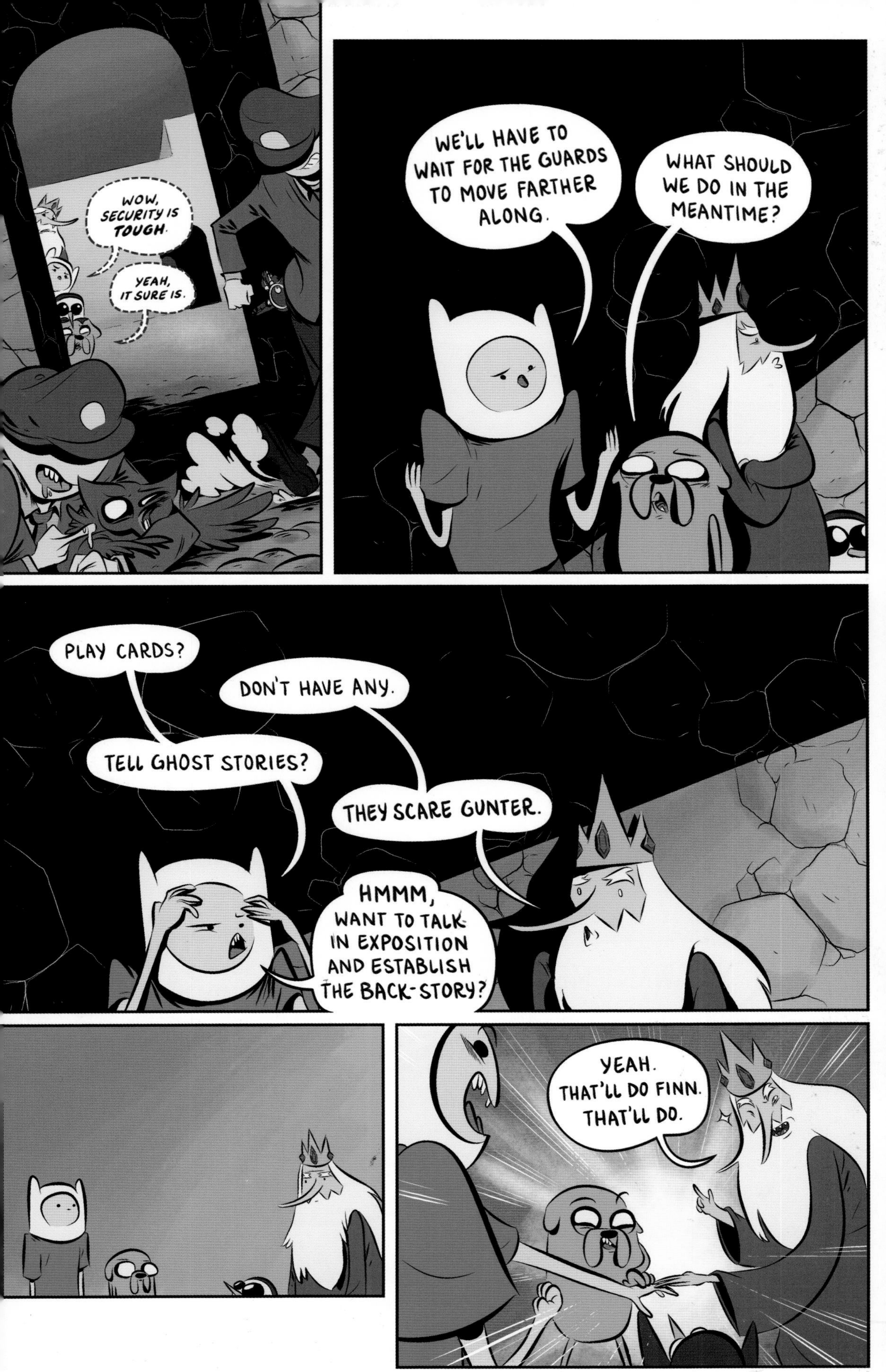
WOW, SECURITY IS TOUGH.
YEAH, IT SURE IS.
WE'LL HAVE TO WAIT FOR THE GUARDS TO MOVE FARTHER ALONG.
WHAT SHOULD WE DO IN THE MEANTIME?
PLAY CARDS?
DON'T HAVE ANY.
TELL GHOST STORIES?
THEY SCARE GUNTER.
HMMM, WANT TO TALK IN EXPOSITION AND ESTABLISH THE BACK-STORY?
YEAH. THAT'LL DO FINN. THAT'LL DO.

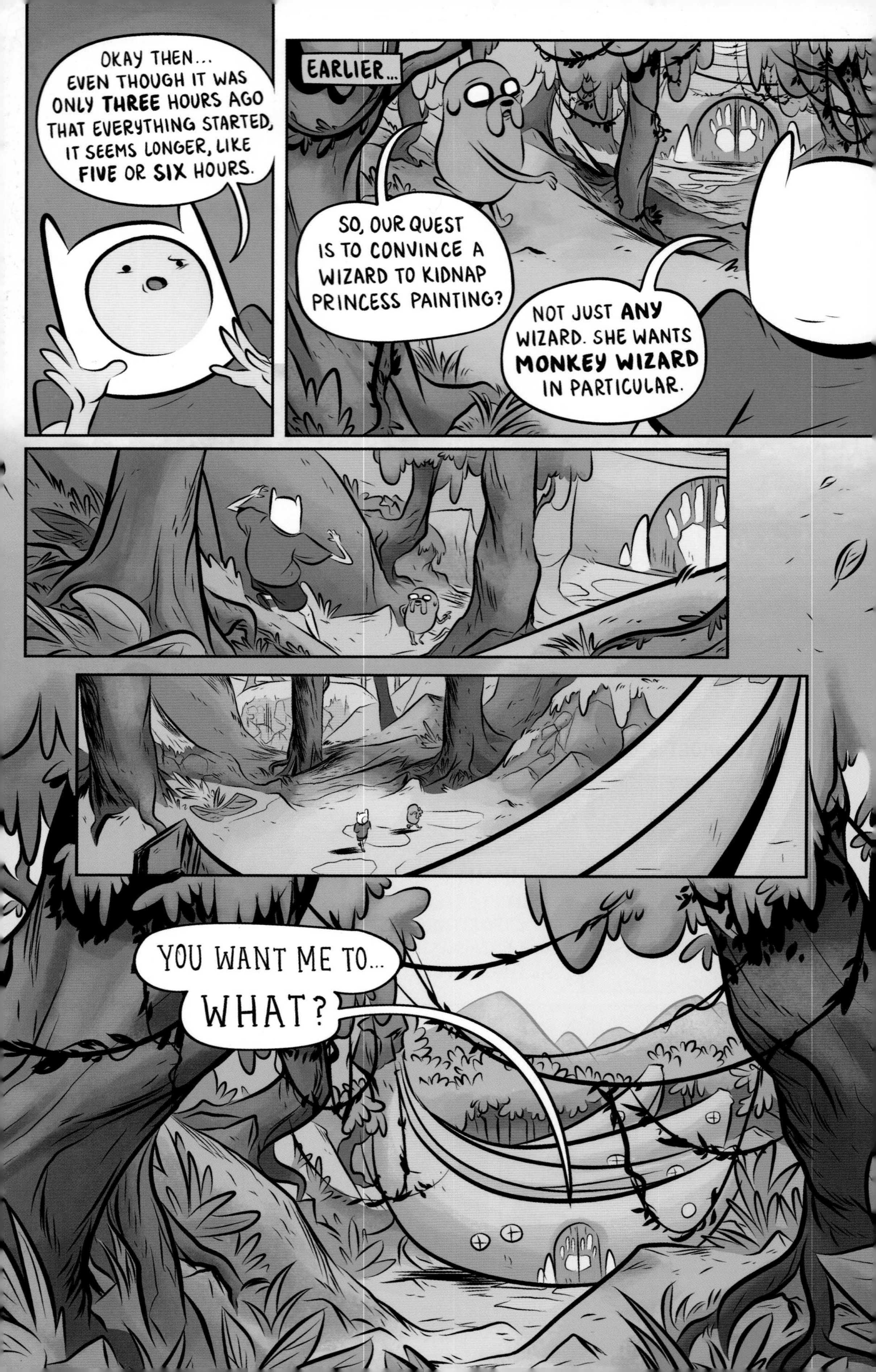
OKAY THEN... EVEN THOUGH IT WAS ONLY THREE HOURS AGO THAT EVERYTHING STARTED, IT SEEMS LONGER, LIKE FIVE OR SIX HOURS.
EARLIER...
SO, OUR QUEST IS TO CONVINCE A WIZARD TO KIDNAP PRINCESS PAINTING?
NOT JUST ANY WIZARD. SHE WANTS MONKEY WIZARD IN PARTICULAR.
YOU WANT ME TO... WHAT?

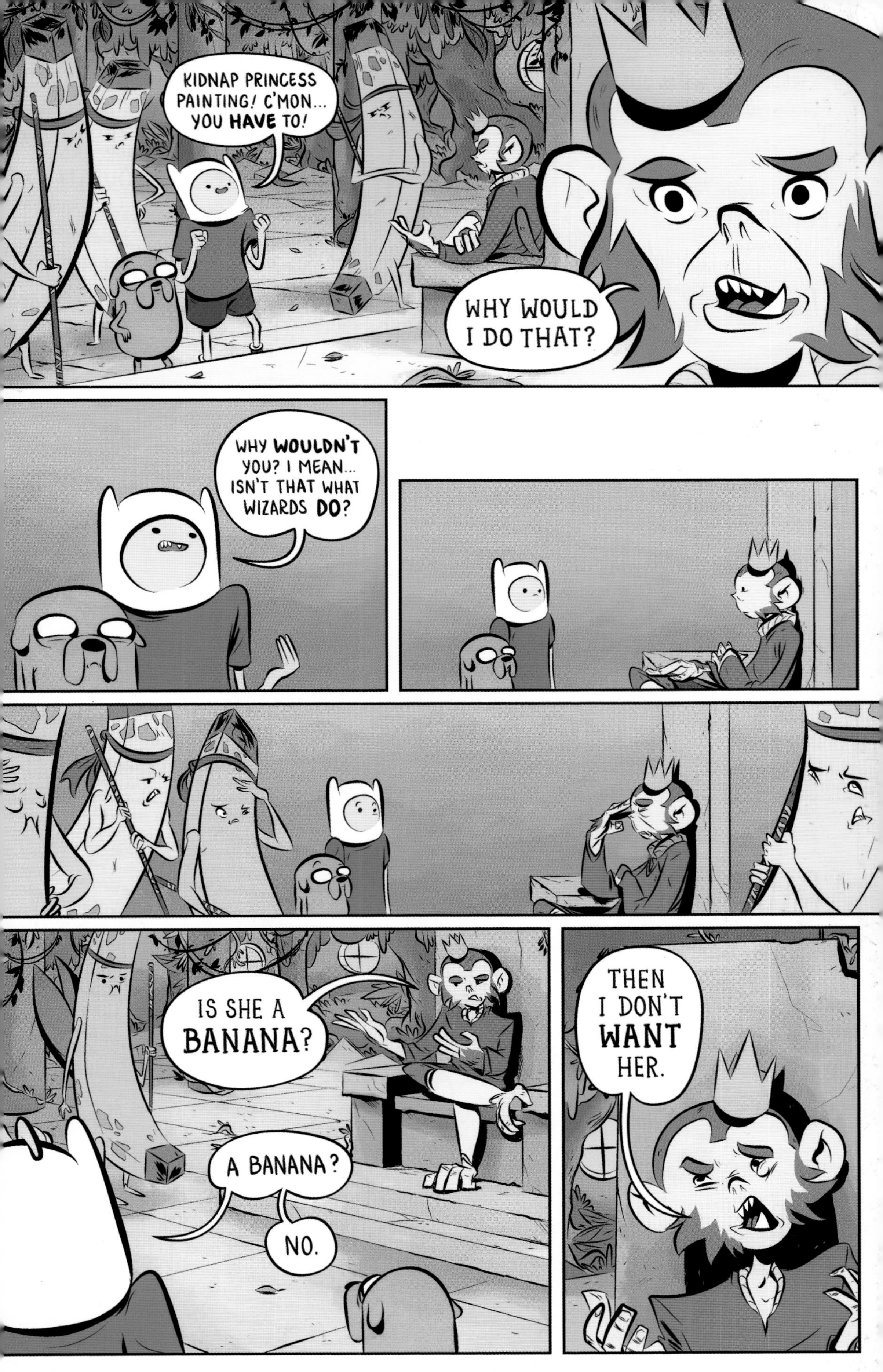
KIDNAP PRINCESS PAINTING! C'MON... YOU **HAVE** TO!
WHY WOULD I DO THAT?
WHY **WOULDN'T** YOU? I MEAN... ISN'T THAT WHAT WIZARDS **DO**?
IS SHE A **BANANA**?
A BANANA?
NO.
THEN I DON'T **WANT** HER.

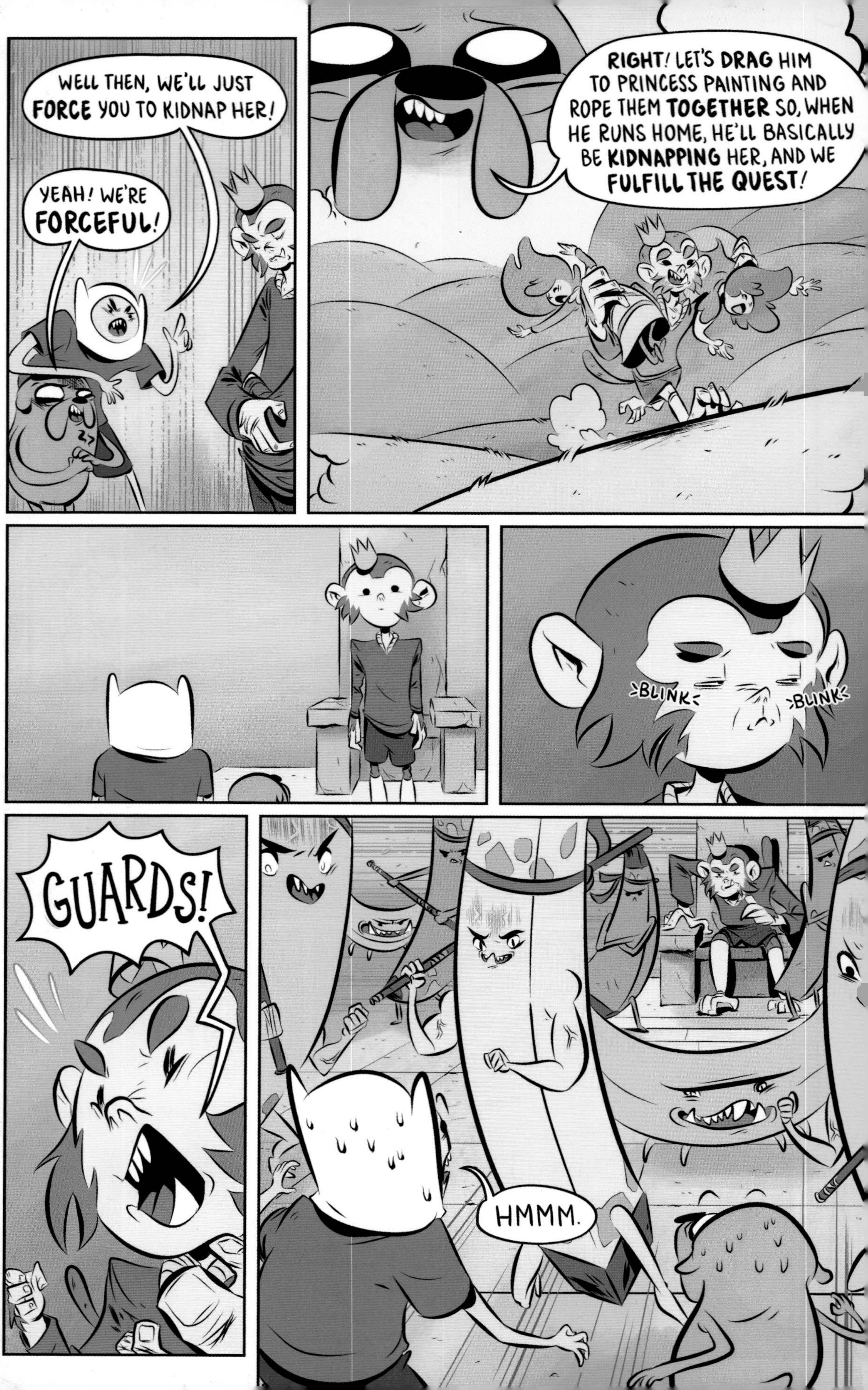
WELL THEN, WE'LL JUST **FORCE** YOU TO KIDNAP HER!
YEAH! WE'RE **FORCEFUL**!
RIGHT! LET'S **DRAG** HIM TO PRINCESS PAINTING AND ROPE THEM **TOGETHER** SO, WHEN HE RUNS HOME, HE'LL BASICALLY BE **KIDNAPPING** HER, AND WE **FULFILL THE QUEST**!
BLINK
BLINK
GUARDS!
HMMM.

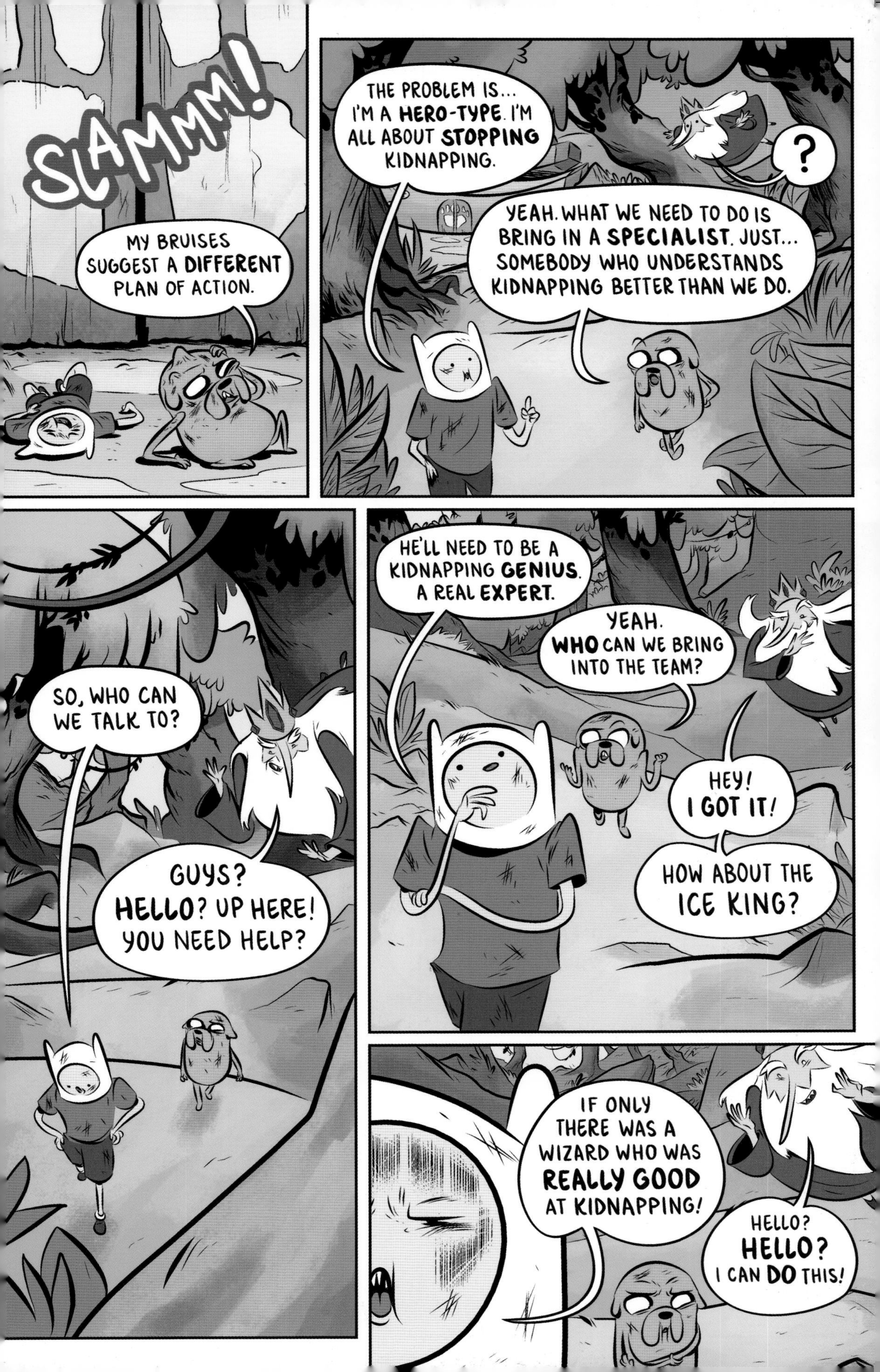
SLAMMM!
MY BRUISES SUGGEST A DIFFERENT PLAN OF ACTION.
THE PROBLEM IS... I'M A HERO-TYPE. I'M ALL ABOUT STOPPING KIDNAPPING.
?
YEAH. WHAT WE NEED TO DO IS BRING IN A SPECIALIST. JUST... SOMEBODY WHO UNDERSTANDS KIDNAPPING BETTER THAN WE DO.
SO, WHO CAN WE TALK TO?
GUYS? HELLO? UP HERE! YOU NEED HELP?
HE'LL NEED TO BE A KIDNAPPING GENIUS. A REAL EXPERT.
YEAH. WHO CAN WE BRING INTO THE TEAM?
HEY! I GOT IT!
HOW ABOUT THE ICE KING?
IF ONLY THERE WAS A WIZARD WHO WAS REALLY GOOD AT KIDNAPPING!
HELLO? HELLO? I CAN DO THIS!

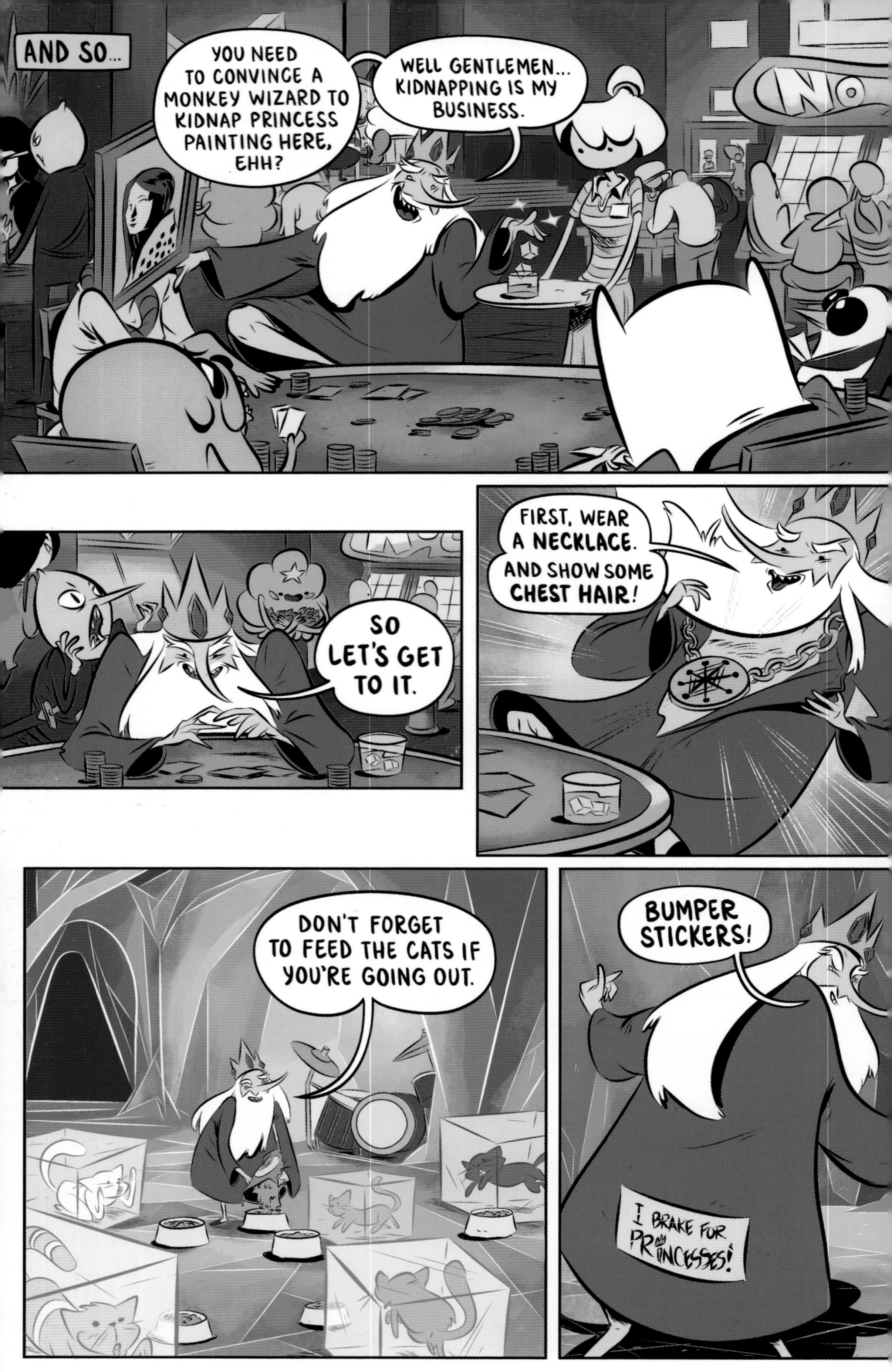
AND SO...
YOU NEED TO CONVINCE A MONKEY WIZARD TO KIDNAP PRINCESS PAINTING HERE, EHH?
WELL GENTLEMEN... KIDNAPPING IS MY BUSINESS.
SO LET'S GET TO IT.
FIRST, WEAR A NECKLACE. AND SHOW SOME CHEST HAIR!
DON'T FORGET TO FEED THE CATS IF YOU'RE GOING OUT.
BUMPER STICKERS!
I BRAKE FOR PRINCESSES!

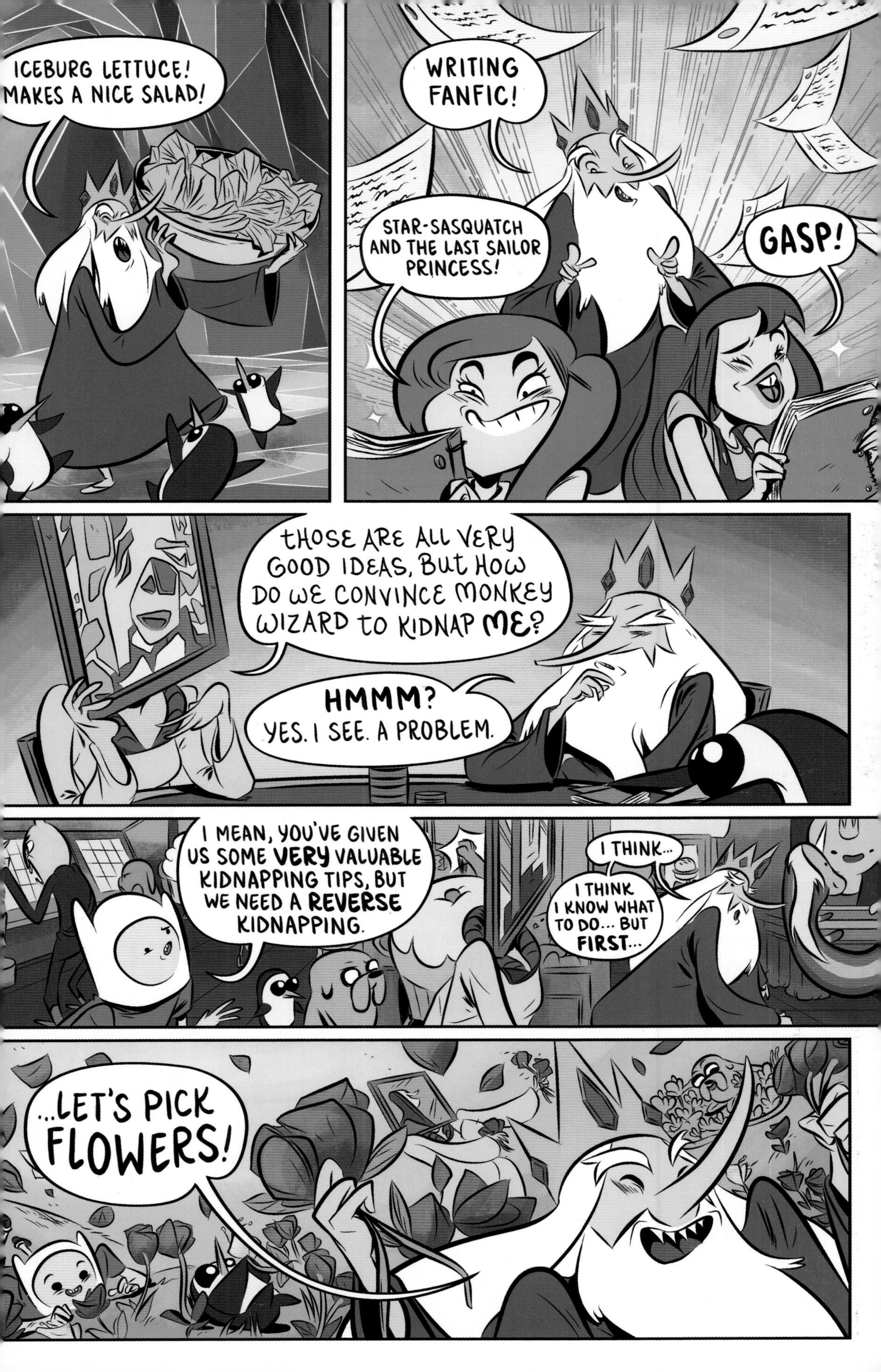
ICEBURG LETTUCE! MAKES A NICE SALAD!
WRITING FANFIC!
STAR-SASQUATCH AND THE LAST SAILOR PRINCESS!
GASP!
THOSE ARE ALL VERY GOOD IDEAS, BUT HOW DO WE CONVINCE MONKEY WIZARD TO KIDNAP ME?
HMMM? YES. I SEE. A PROBLEM.
I MEAN, YOU'VE GIVEN US SOME VERY VALUABLE KIDNAPPING TIPS, BUT WE NEED A REVERSE KIDNAPPING.
I THINK...
I THINK I KNOW WHAT TO DO... BUT FIRST...
...LET'S PICK FLOWERS!

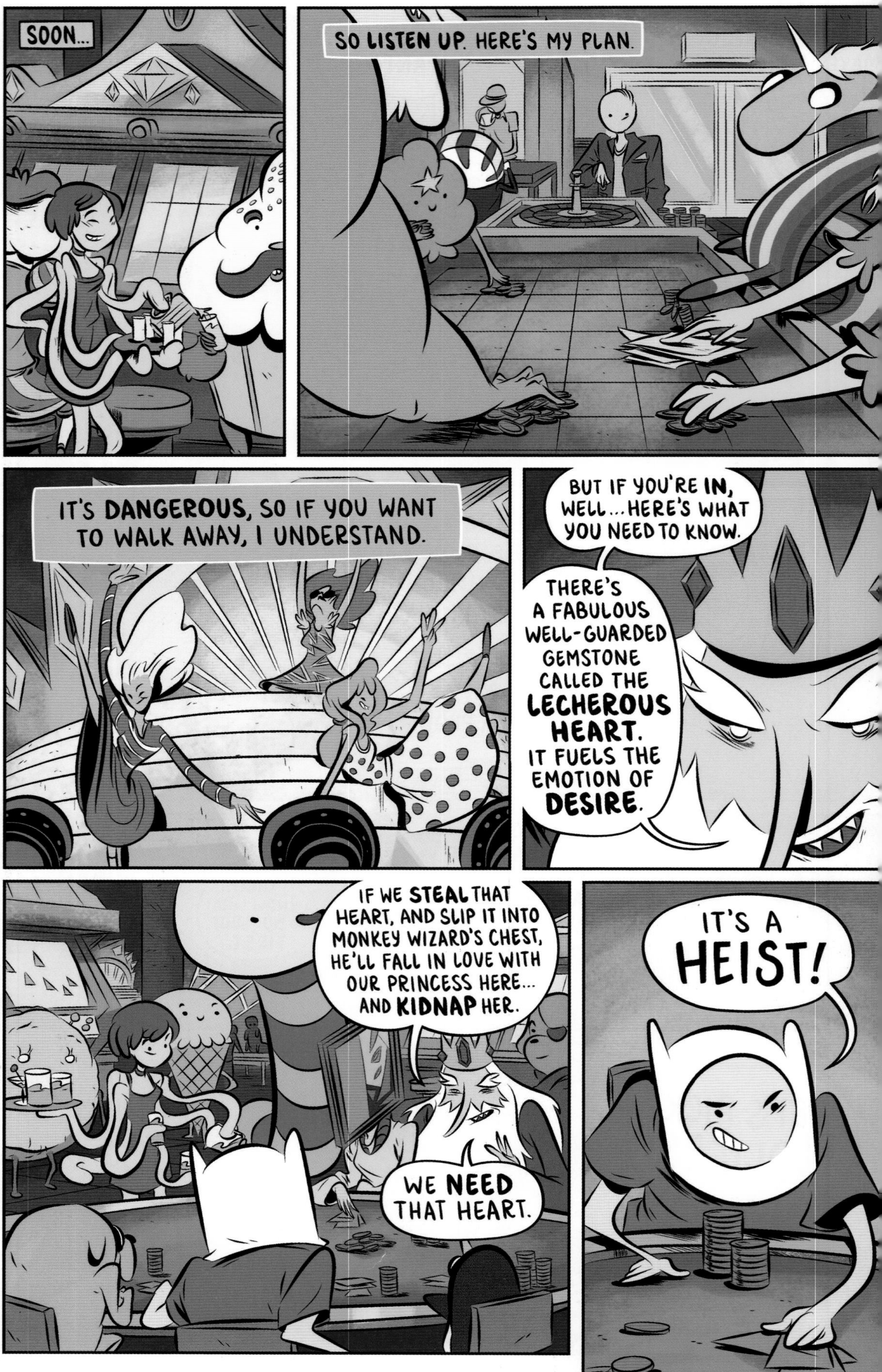
SOON...
SO LISTEN UP. HERE'S MY PLAN.
IT'S DANGEROUS, SO IF YOU WANT TO WALK AWAY, I UNDERSTAND.
BUT IF YOU'RE IN, WELL... HERE'S WHAT YOU NEED TO KNOW.
THERE'S A FABULOUS WELL-GUARDED GEMSTONE CALLED THE LECHEROUS HEART. IT FUELS THE EMOTION OF DESIRE.
IF WE STEAL THAT HEART, AND SLIP IT INTO MONKEY WIZARD'S CHEST, HE'LL FALL IN LOVE WITH OUR PRINCESS HERE... AND KIDNAP HER.
WE NEED THAT HEART.
IT'S A HEIST!

YEAH. A HEIST.

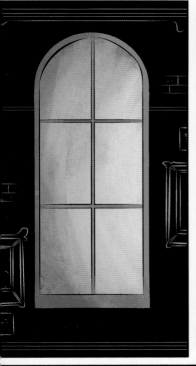

SKIFF

SKIFF

SKUFF

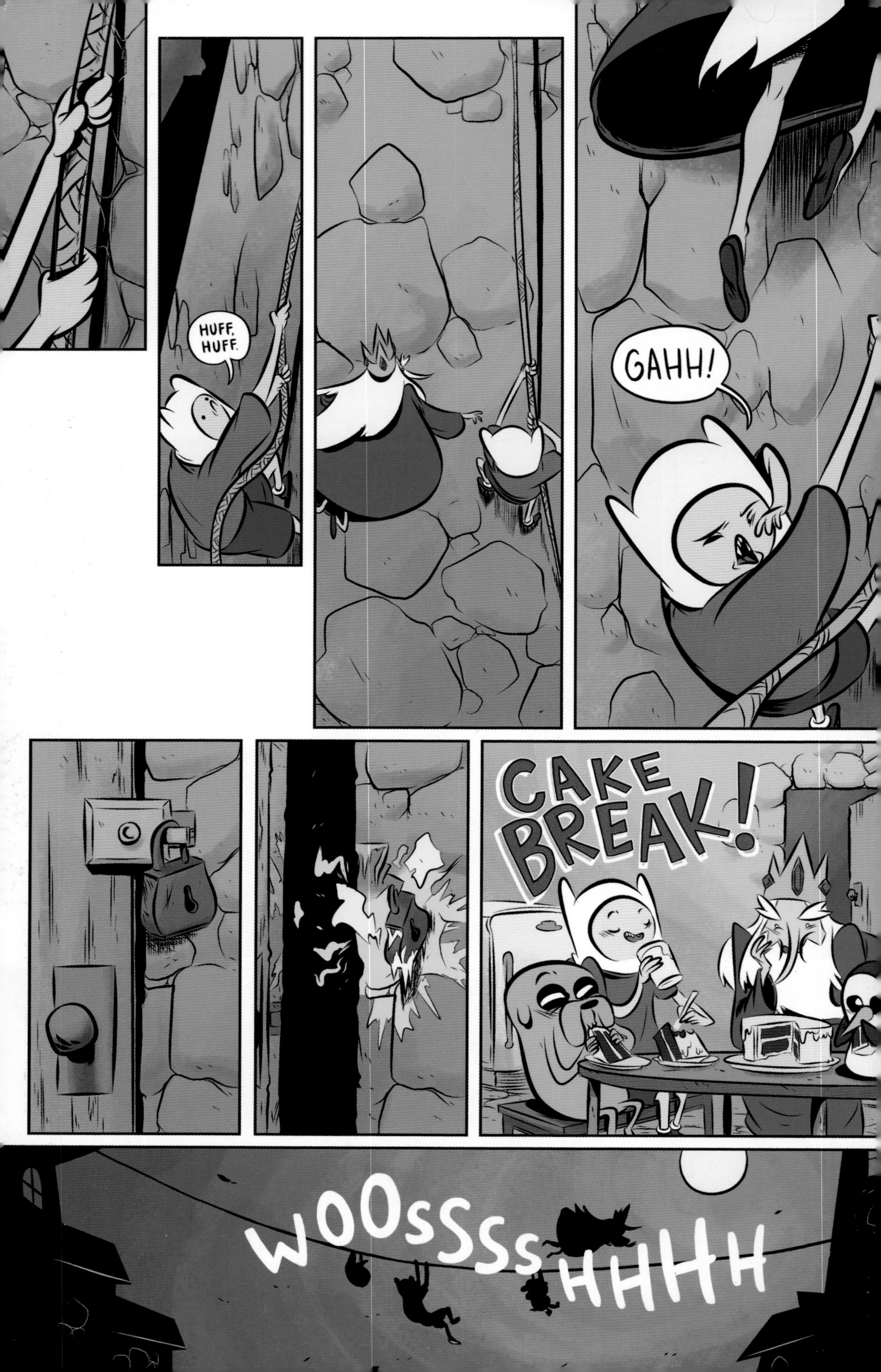
HUFF, HUFF.
GAHH!
CAKE BREAK!
WOOSSSSHHHHH

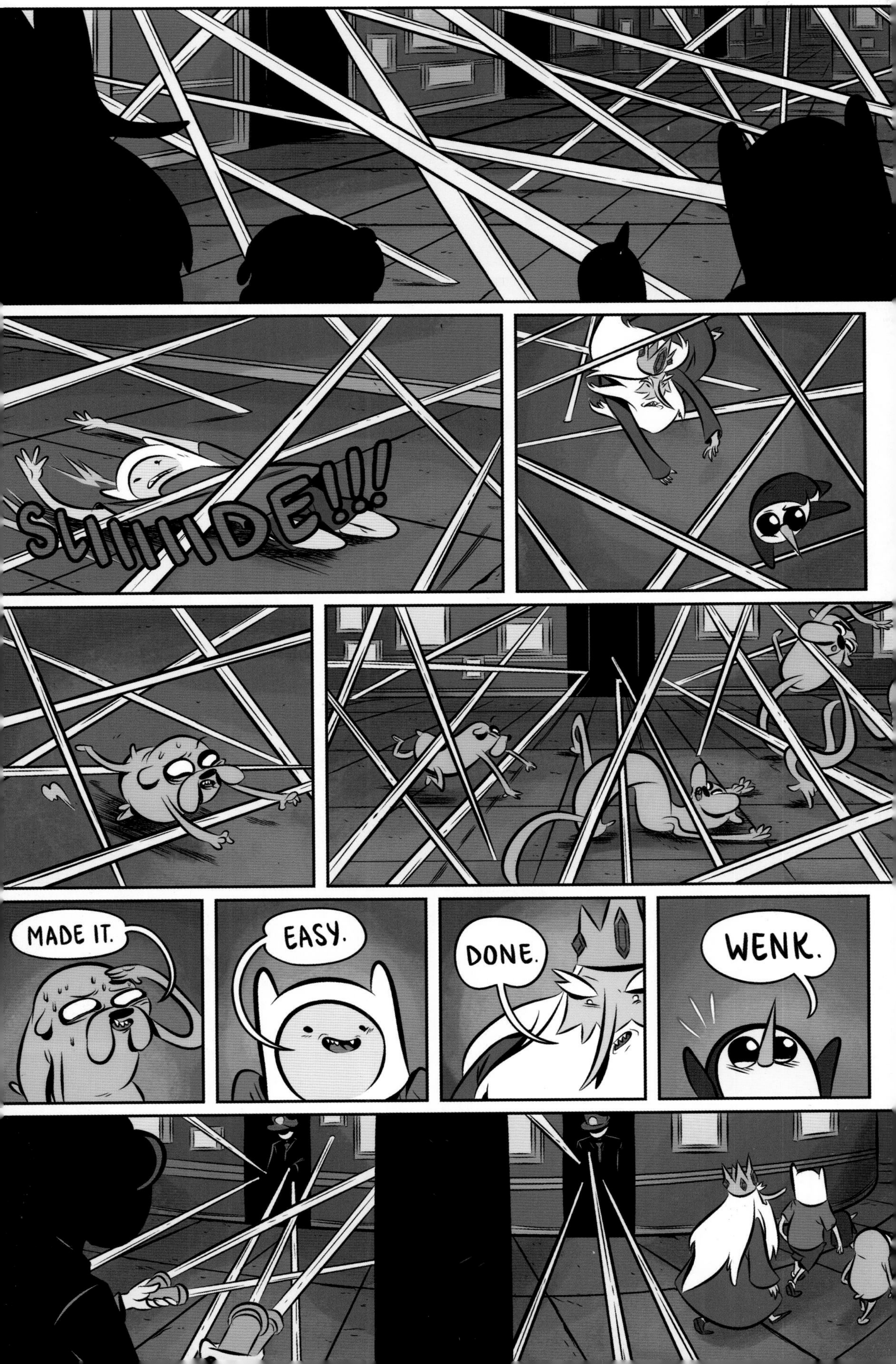
SLIIIIIDE!!!
MADE IT.
EASY.
DONE.
WENK.

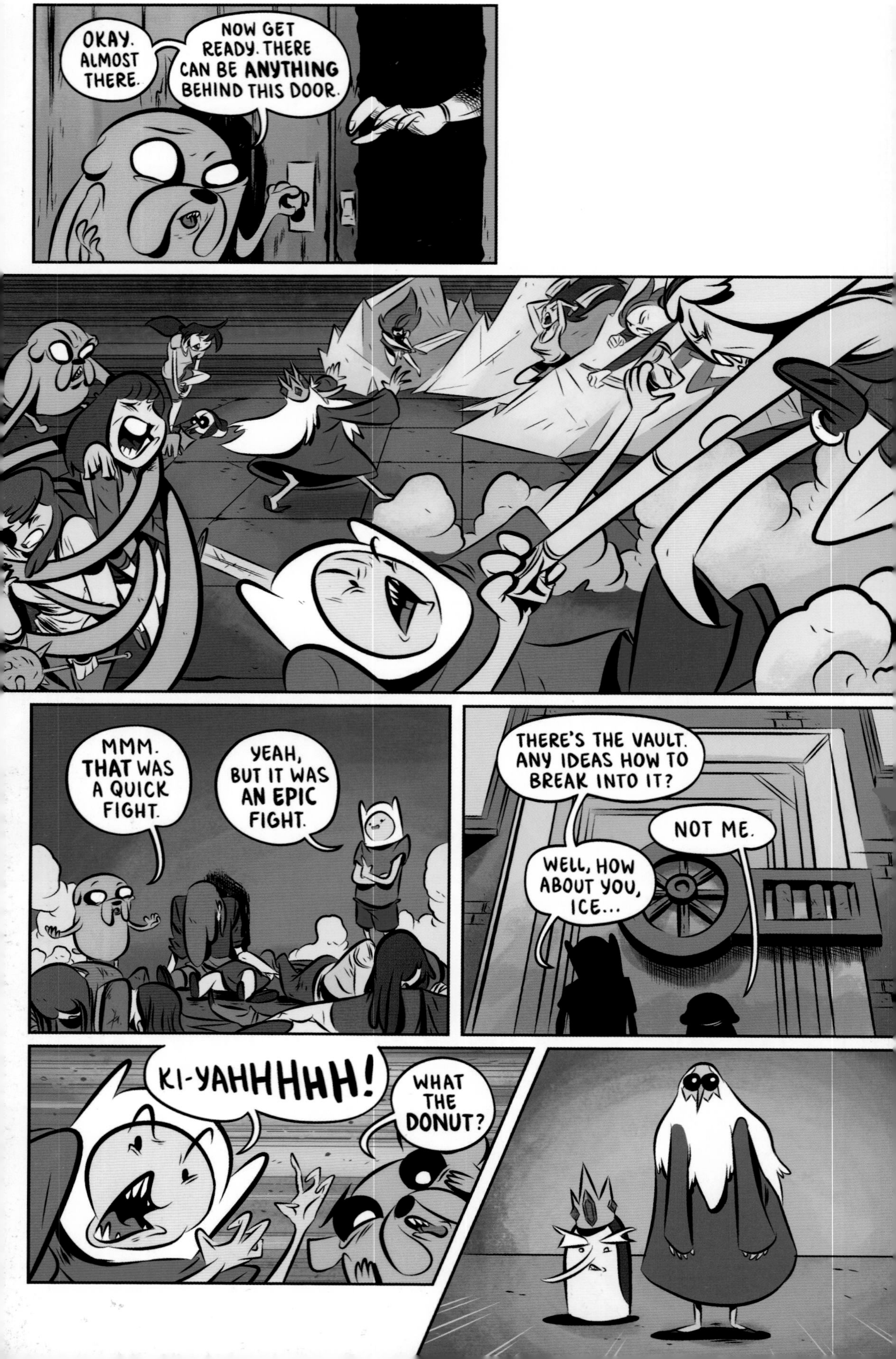
OKAY. ALMOST THERE.
NOW GET READY. THERE CAN BE ANYTHING BEHIND THIS DOOR.
MMM. THAT WAS A QUICK FIGHT.
YEAH, BUT IT WAS AN EPIC FIGHT.
THERE'S THE VAULT. ANY IDEAS HOW TO BREAK INTO IT?
NOT ME.
WELL, HOW ABOUT YOU, ICE...
KI-YAHHHHH!
WHAT THE DONUT?

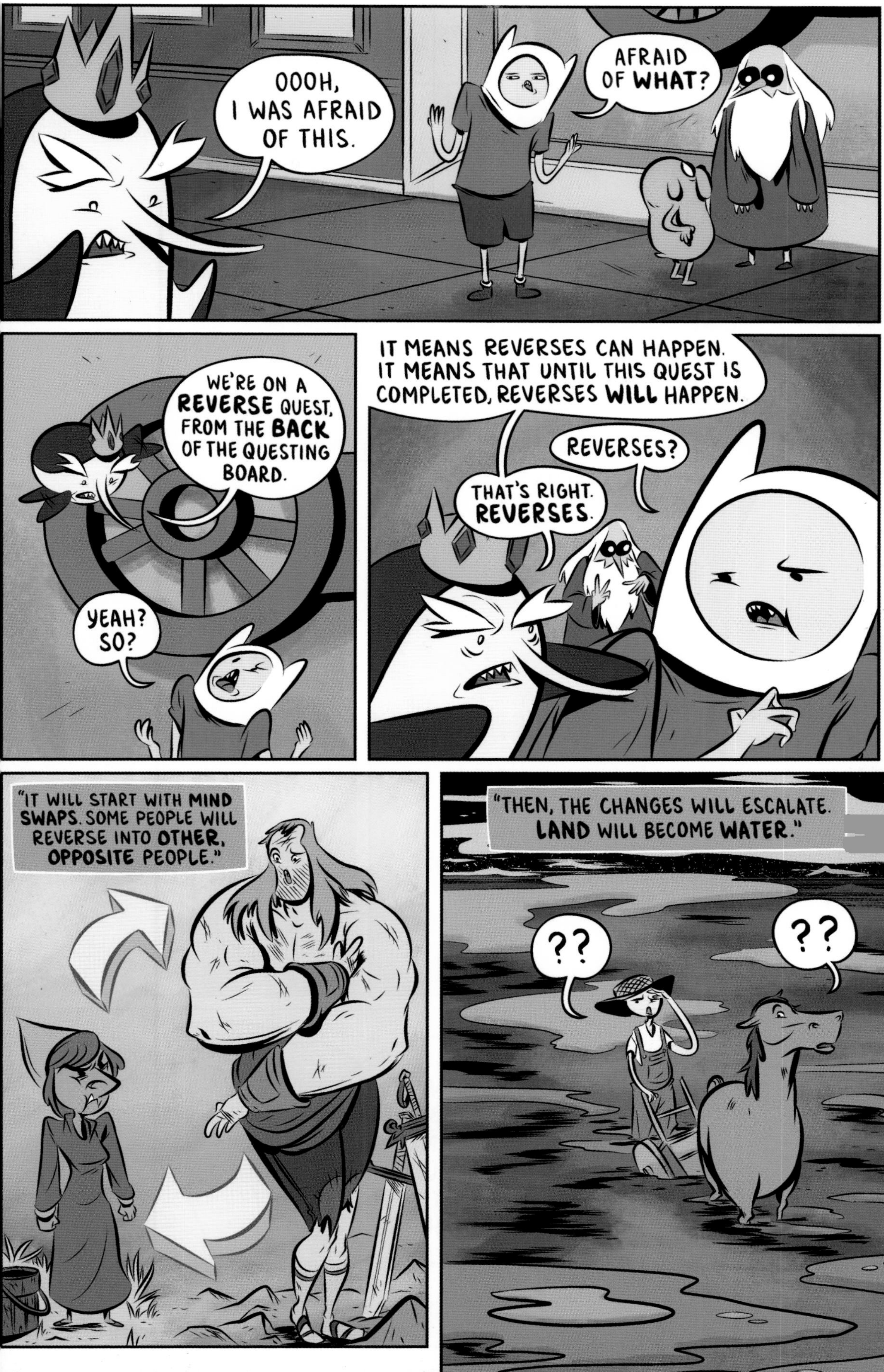
OOOH, I WAS AFRAID OF THIS.
AFRAID OF WHAT?
WE'RE ON A REVERSE QUEST, FROM THE BACK OF THE QUESTING BOARD.
YEAH? SO?
IT MEANS REVERSES CAN HAPPEN. IT MEANS THAT UNTIL THIS QUEST IS COMPLETED, REVERSES WILL HAPPEN.
REVERSES?
THAT'S RIGHT. REVERSES.
"IT WILL START WITH MIND SWAPS. SOME PEOPLE WILL REVERSE INTO OTHER, OPPOSITE PEOPLE."
"THEN, THE CHANGES WILL ESCALATE. LAND WILL BECOME WATER."
??
??

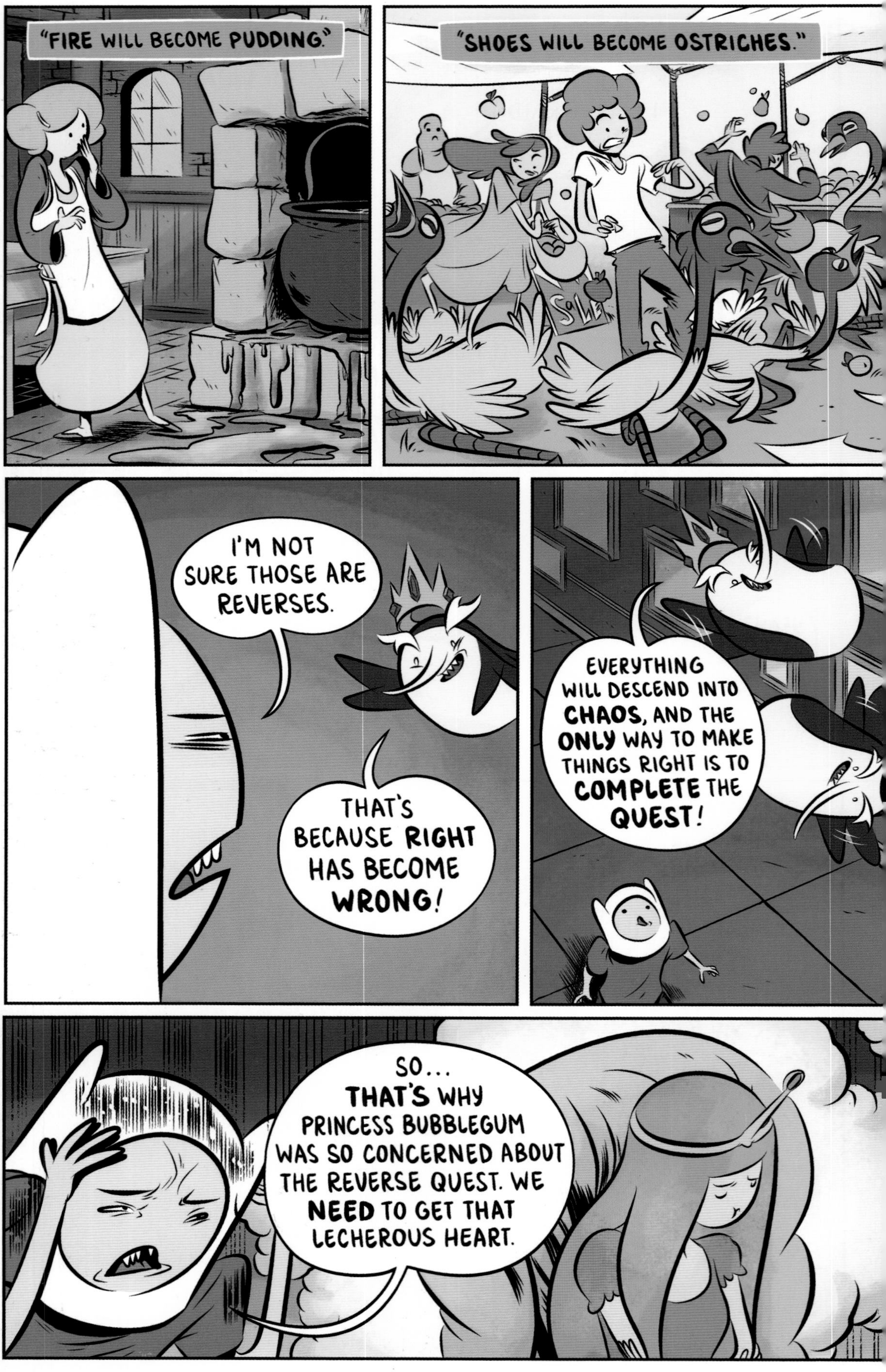
"FIRE WILL BECOME PUDDING."
"SHOES WILL BECOME OSTRICHES."
SALE
I'M NOT SURE THOSE ARE REVERSES.
THAT'S BECAUSE RIGHT HAS BECOME WRONG!
EVERYTHING WILL DESCEND INTO CHAOS, AND THE ONLY WAY TO MAKE THINGS RIGHT IS TO COMPLETE THE QUEST!
SO... THAT'S WHY PRINCESS BUBBLEGUM WAS SO CONCERNED ABOUT THE REVERSE QUEST. WE NEED TO GET THAT LECHEROUS HEART.

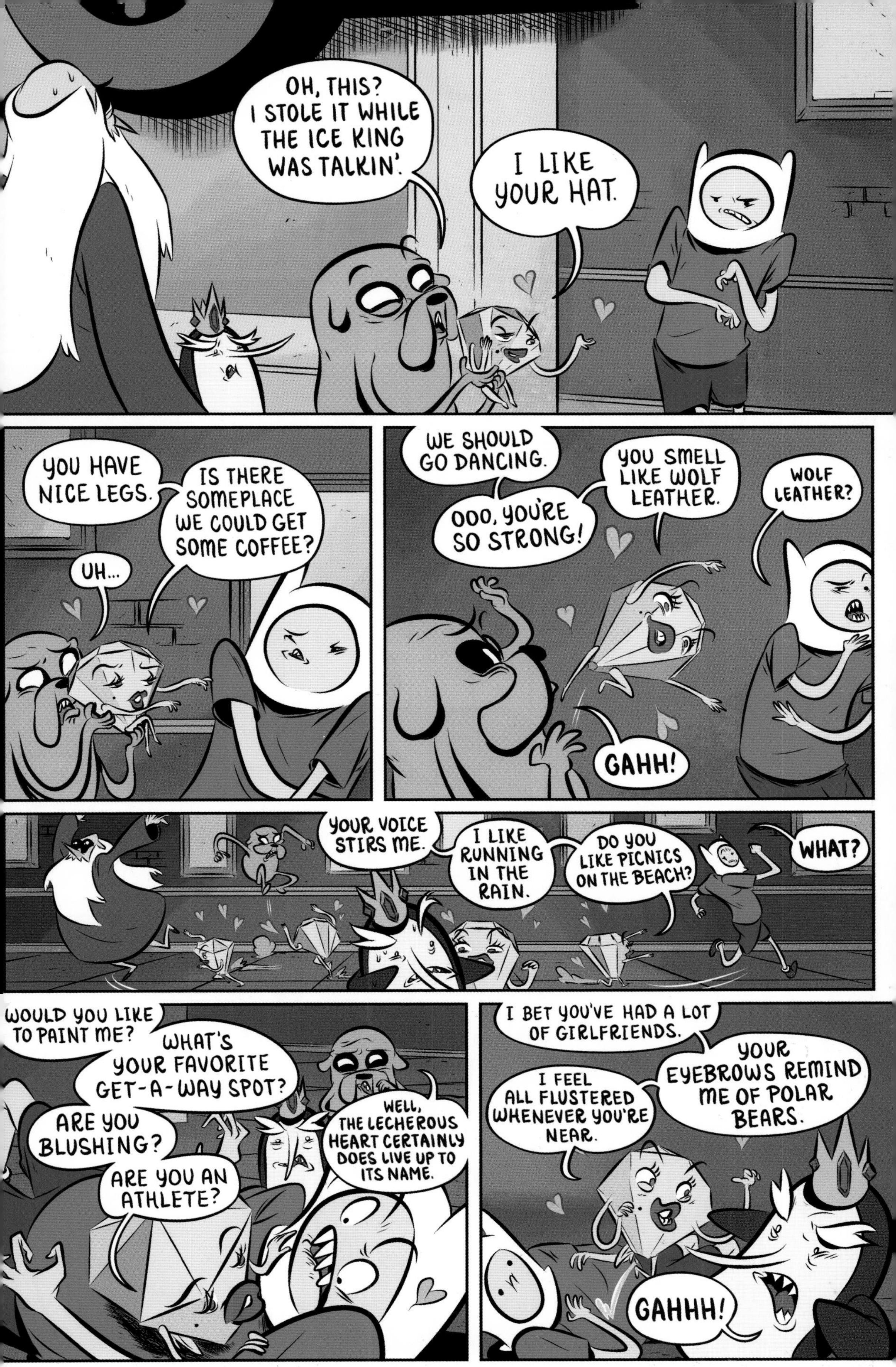
OH, THIS? I STOLE IT WHILE THE ICE KING WAS TALKIN'.
I LIKE YOUR HAT.
YOU HAVE NICE LEGS.
IS THERE SOMEPLACE WE COULD GET SOME COFFEE?
UH...
WE SHOULD GO DANCING.
OOO, YOU'RE SO STRONG!
YOU SMELL LIKE WOLF LEATHER.
WOLF LEATHER?
GAHH!
YOUR VOICE STIRS ME.
I LIKE RUNNING IN THE RAIN.
DO YOU LIKE PICNICS ON THE BEACH?
WHAT?
WOULD YOU LIKE TO PAINT ME?
WHAT'S YOUR FAVORITE GET-A-WAY SPOT?
ARE YOU BLUSHING?
ARE YOU AN ATHLETE?
WELL, THE LECHEROUS HEART CERTAINLY DOES LIVE UP TO ITS NAME.
I BET YOU'VE HAD A LOT OF GIRLFRIENDS.
YOUR EYEBROWS REMIND ME OF POLAR BEARS.
I FEEL ALL FLUSTERED WHENEVER YOU'RE NEAR.
GAHHH!

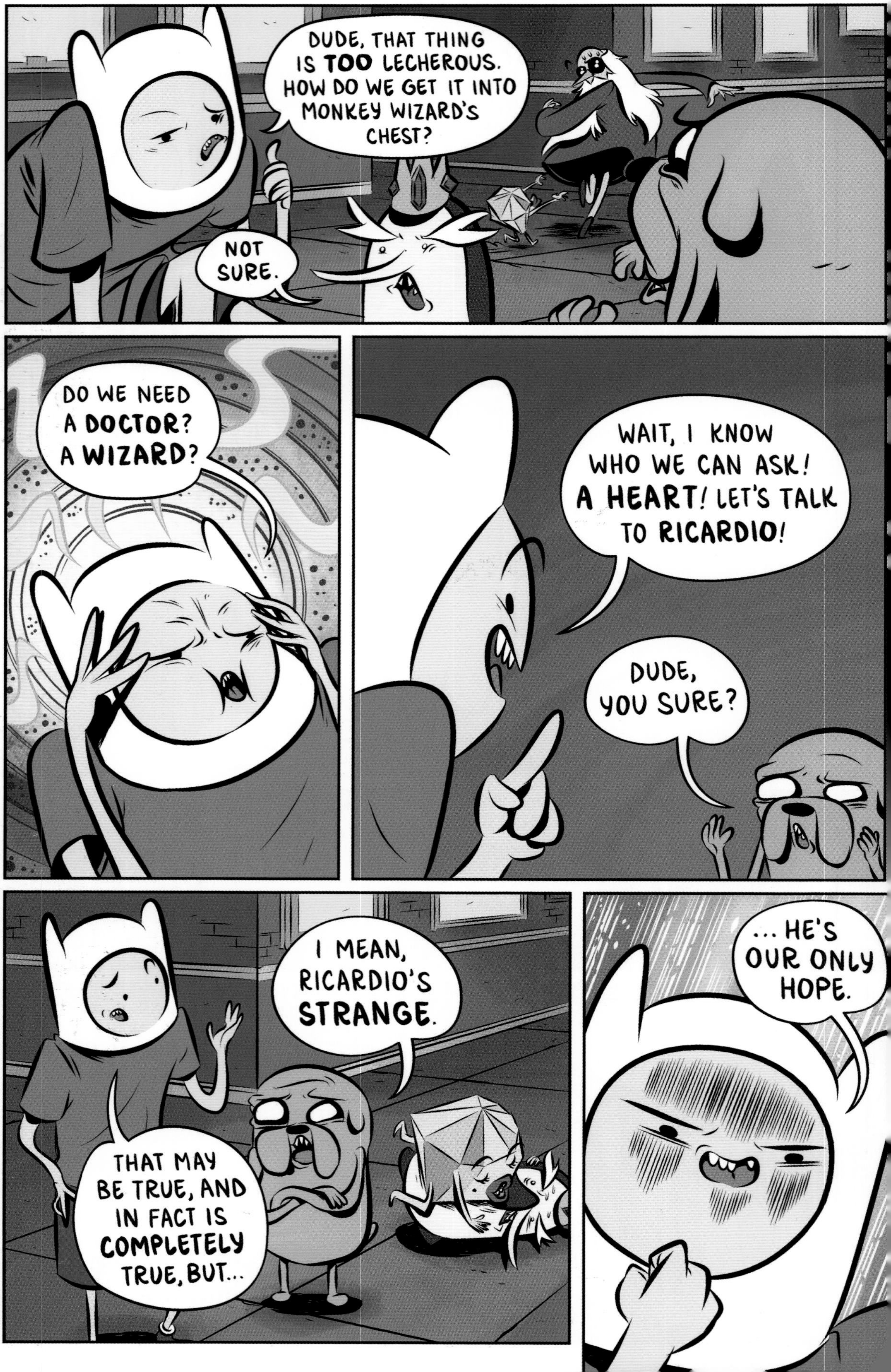
DUDE, THAT THING IS TOO LECHEROUS. HOW DO WE GET IT INTO MONKEY WIZARD'S CHEST?
NOT SURE.
DO WE NEED A DOCTOR? A WIZARD?
WAIT, I KNOW WHO WE CAN ASK! A HEART! LET'S TALK TO RICARDIO!
DUDE, YOU SURE?
I MEAN, RICARDIO'S STRANGE.
THAT MAY BE TRUE, AND IN FACT IS COMPLETELY TRUE, BUT...
... HE'S OUR ONLY HOPE.

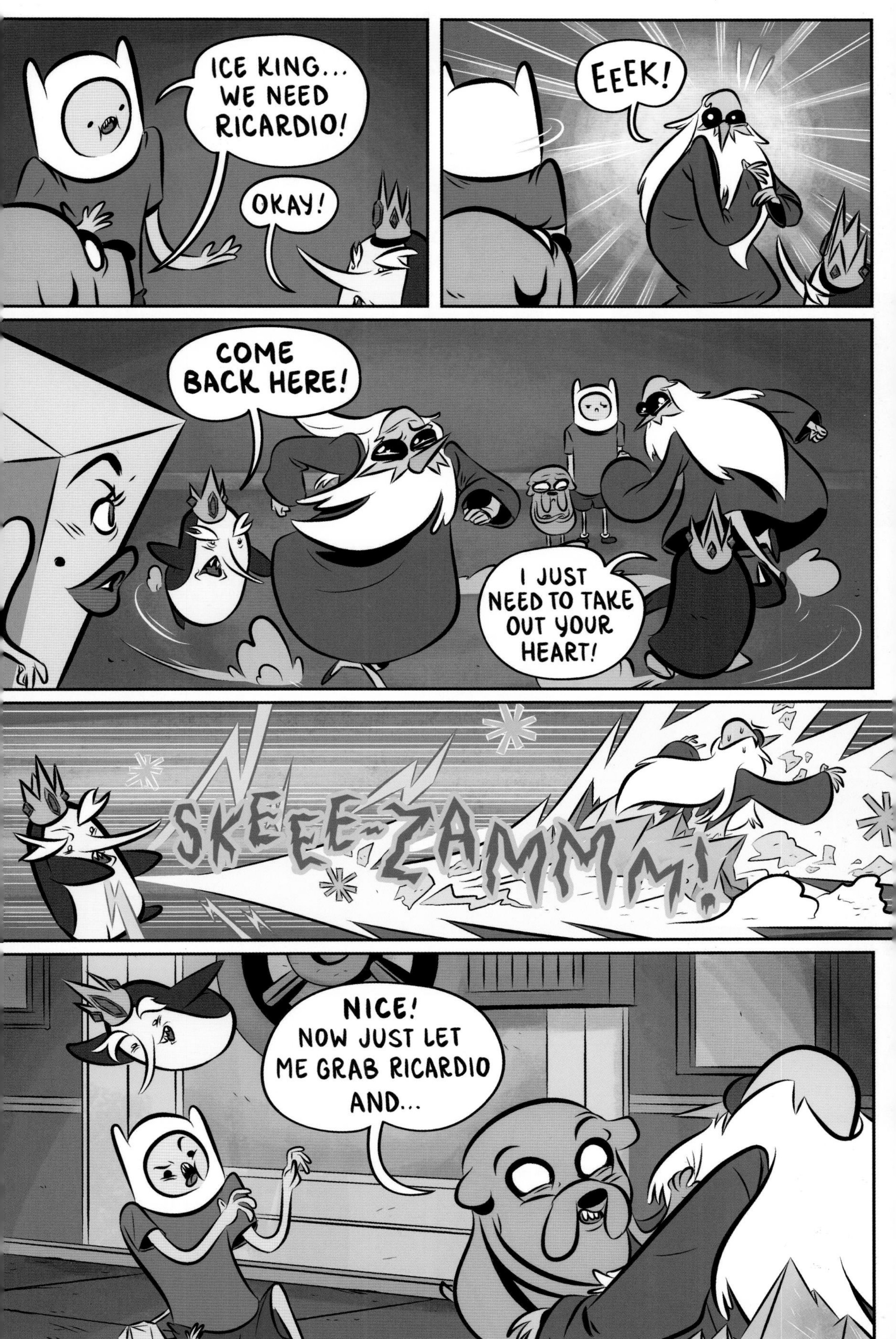
ICE KING... WE NEED RICARDIO!
OKAY!
EEEK!
COME BACK HERE!
I JUST NEED TO TAKE OUT YOUR HEART!
SKEEE-ZAMMM!
NICE! NOW JUST LET ME GRAB RICARDIO AND...

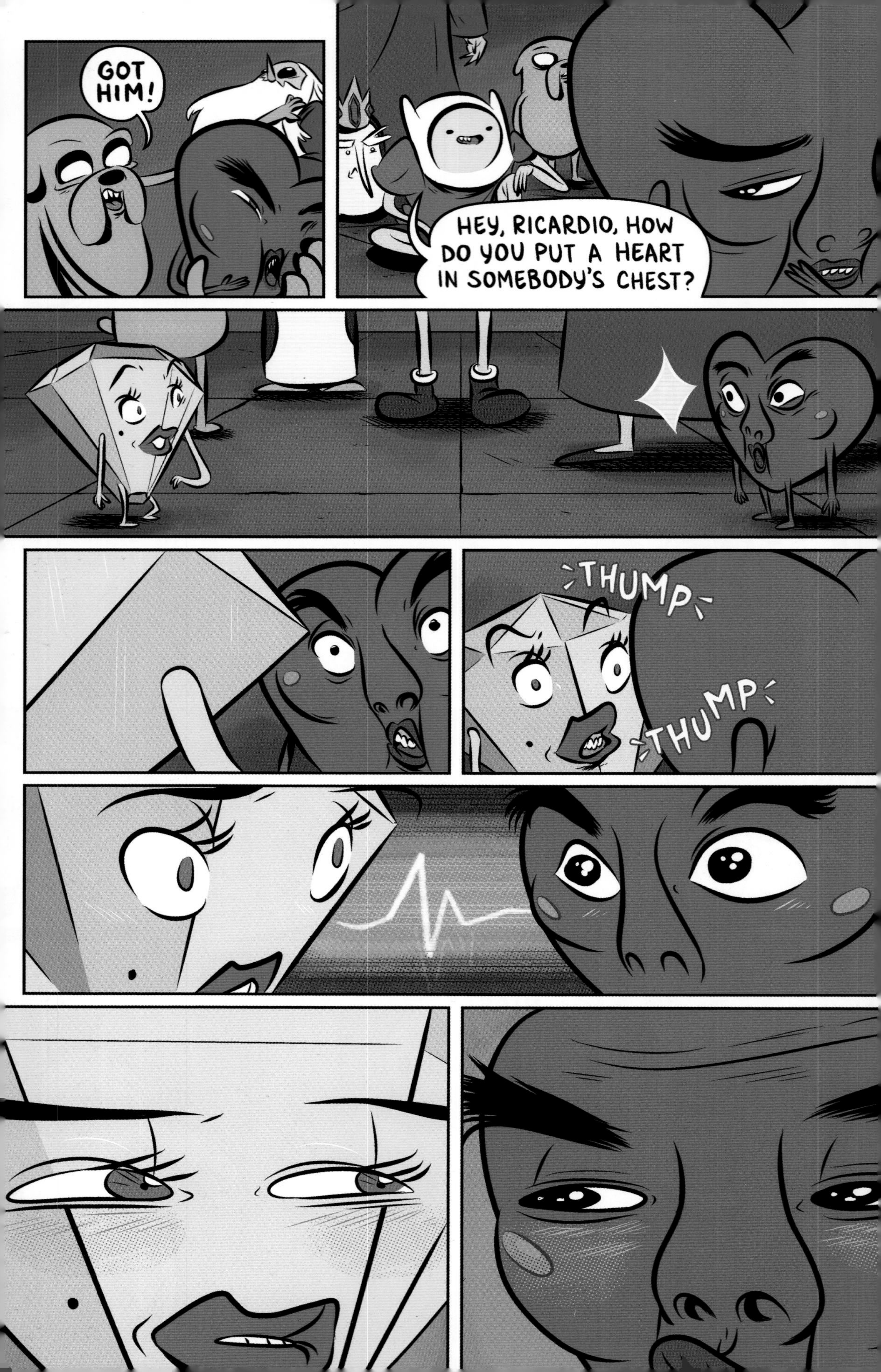
GOT HIM!
HEY, RICARDIO, HOW DO YOU PUT A HEART IN SOMEBODY'S CHEST?
THUMP
THUMP

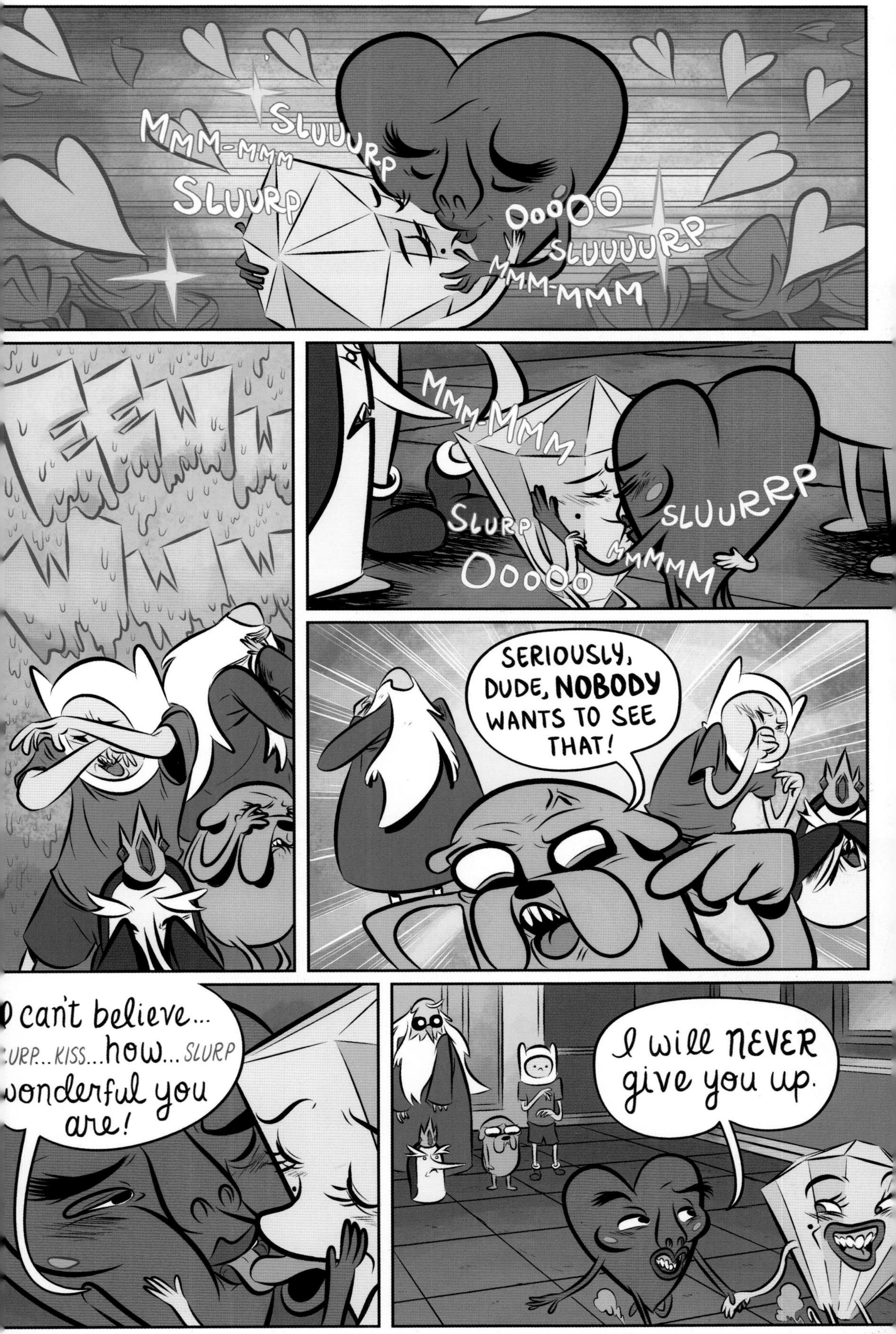
MMM-MMM
SLUUURP
SLUURP
OooOO
SLUUUURP
MMM-MMM
EEWWWWW
MMM-MMM
SLURP
SLUURRP
MMMMM
OoooO
SERIOUSLY, DUDE, NOBODY WANTS TO SEE THAT!
I can't believe... SLURP... KISS... how... SLURP wonderful you are!
I will NEVER give you up.

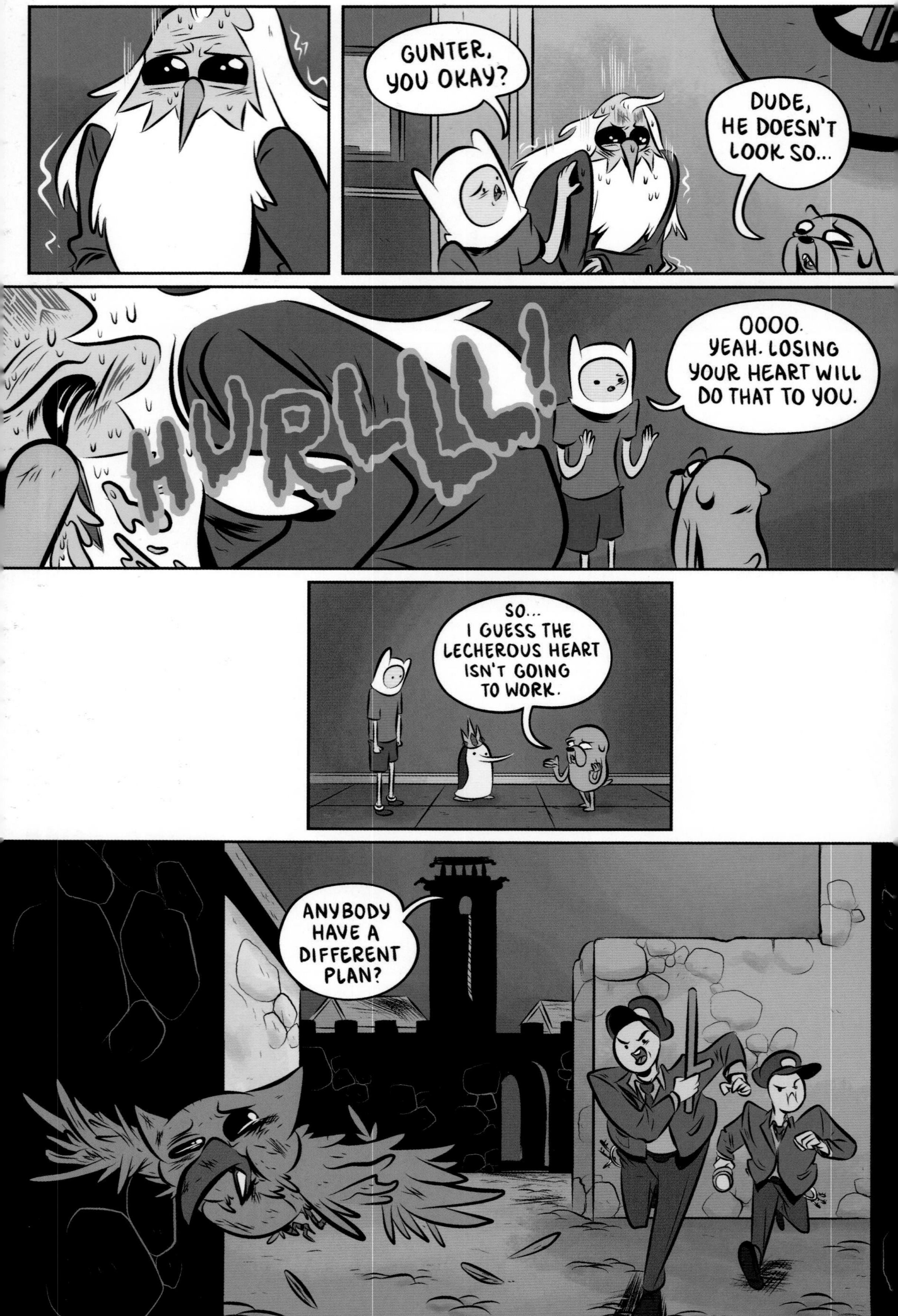
GUNTER, YOU OKAY?
DUDE, HE DOESN'T LOOK SO...
HURLLL!
OOOO. YEAH. LOSING YOUR HEART WILL DO THAT TO YOU.
SO... I GUESS THE LECHEROUS HEART ISN'T GOING TO WORK.
ANYBODY HAVE A DIFFERENT PLAN?

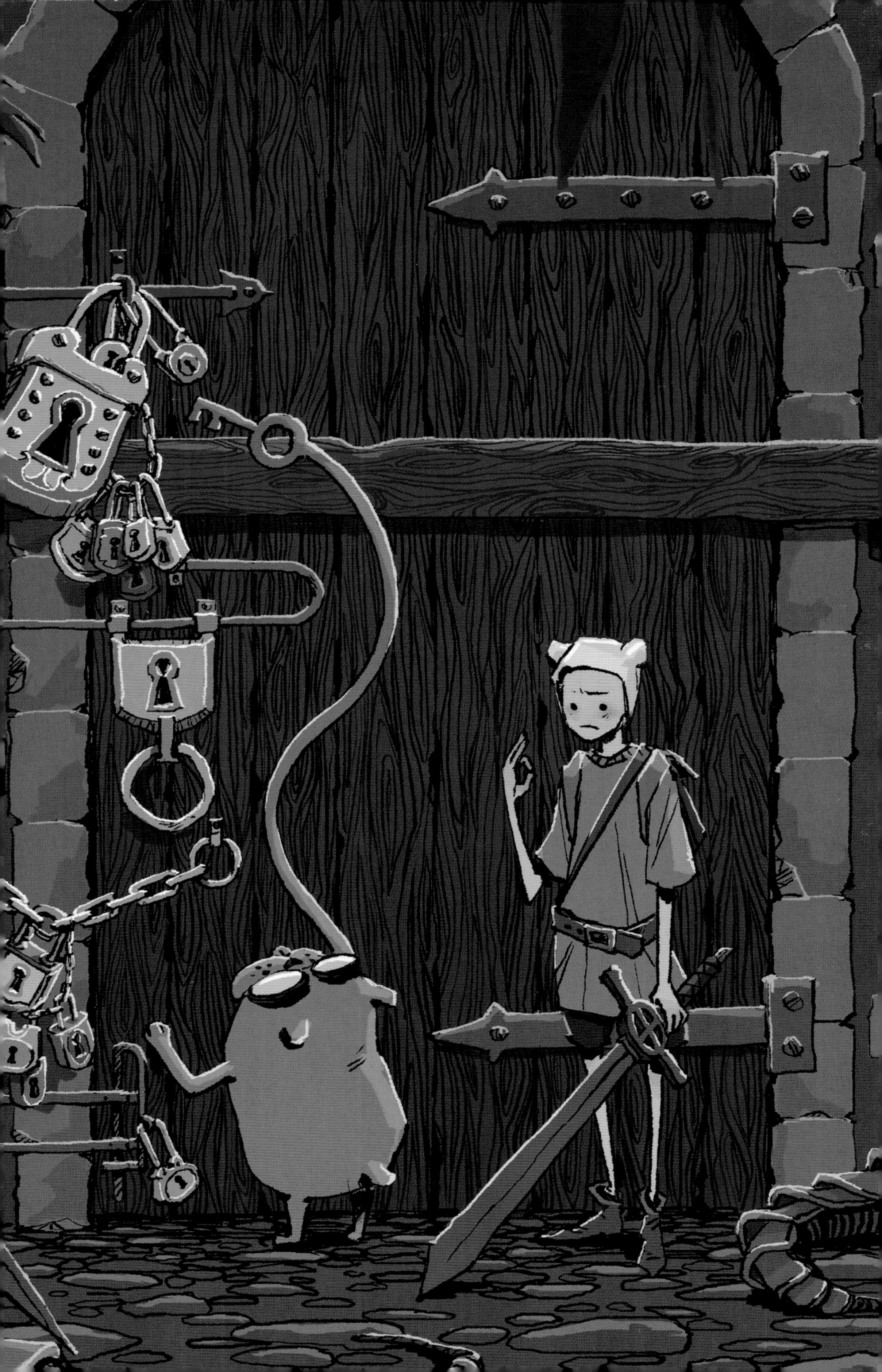

CHAPTER THREE

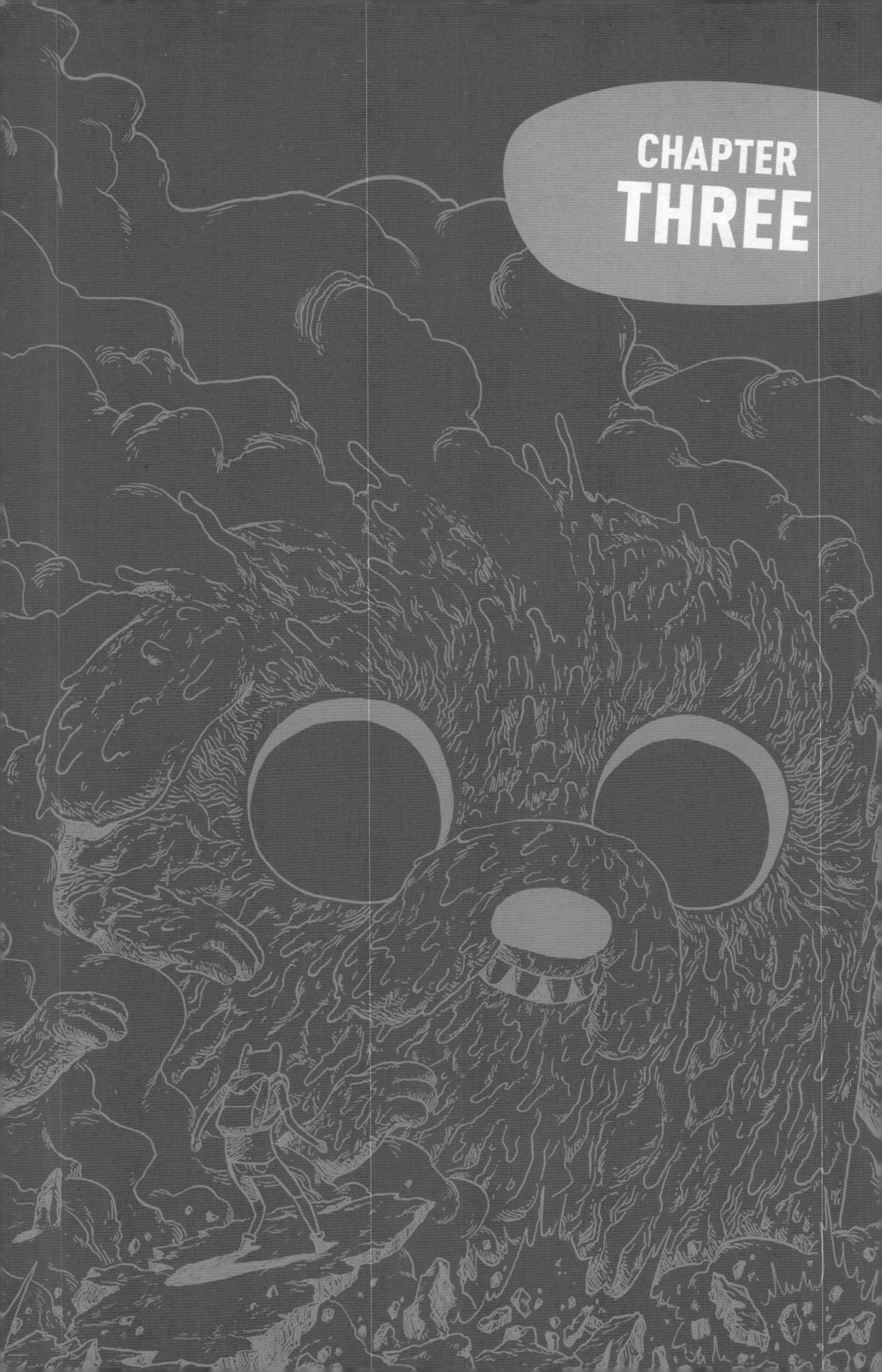

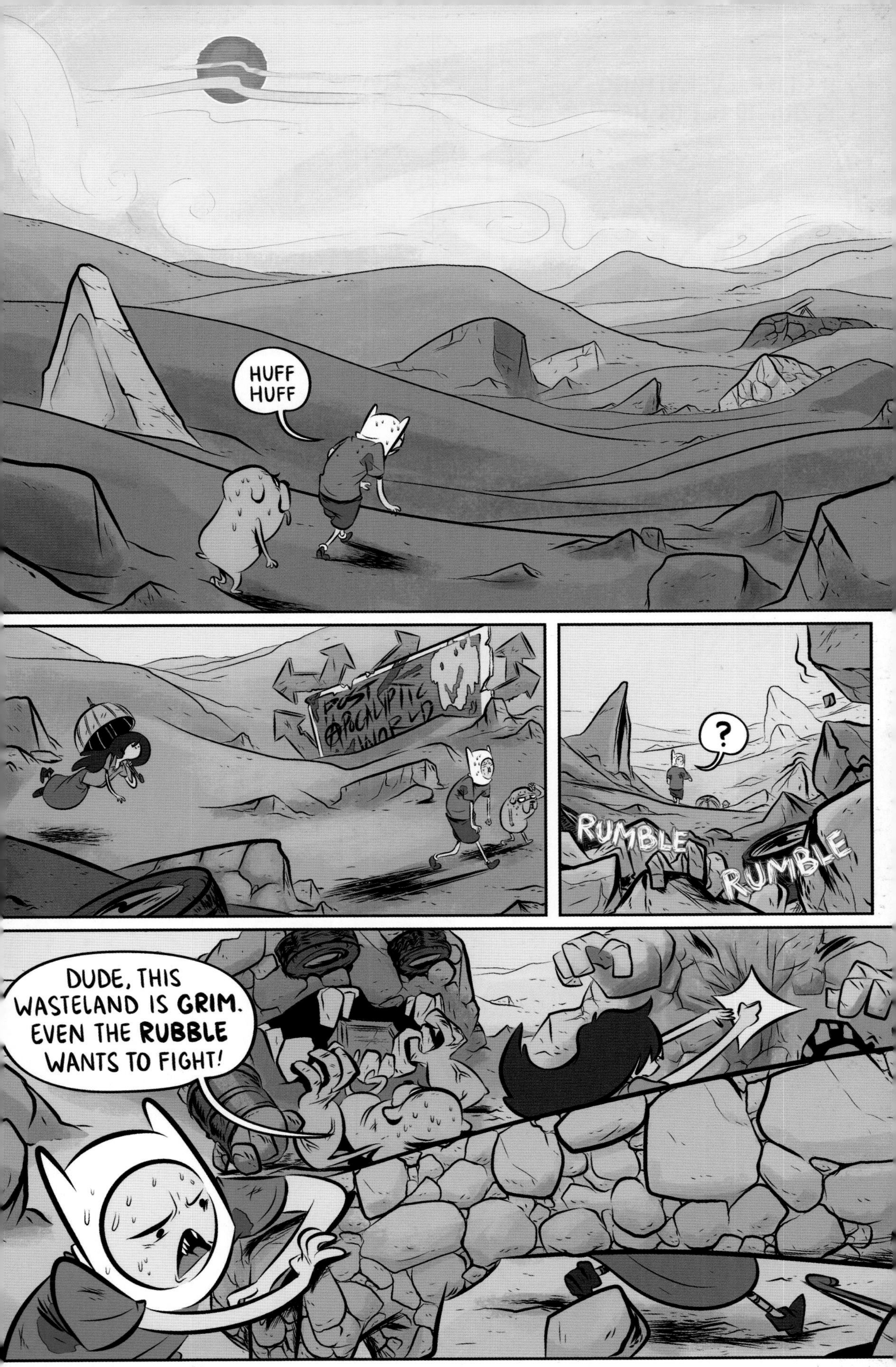
HUFF
HUFF
POST APOCALYPTIC WORLD
?
RUMBLE
RUMBLE
DUDE, THIS WASTELAND IS GRIM. EVEN THE RUBBLE WANTS TO FIGHT!

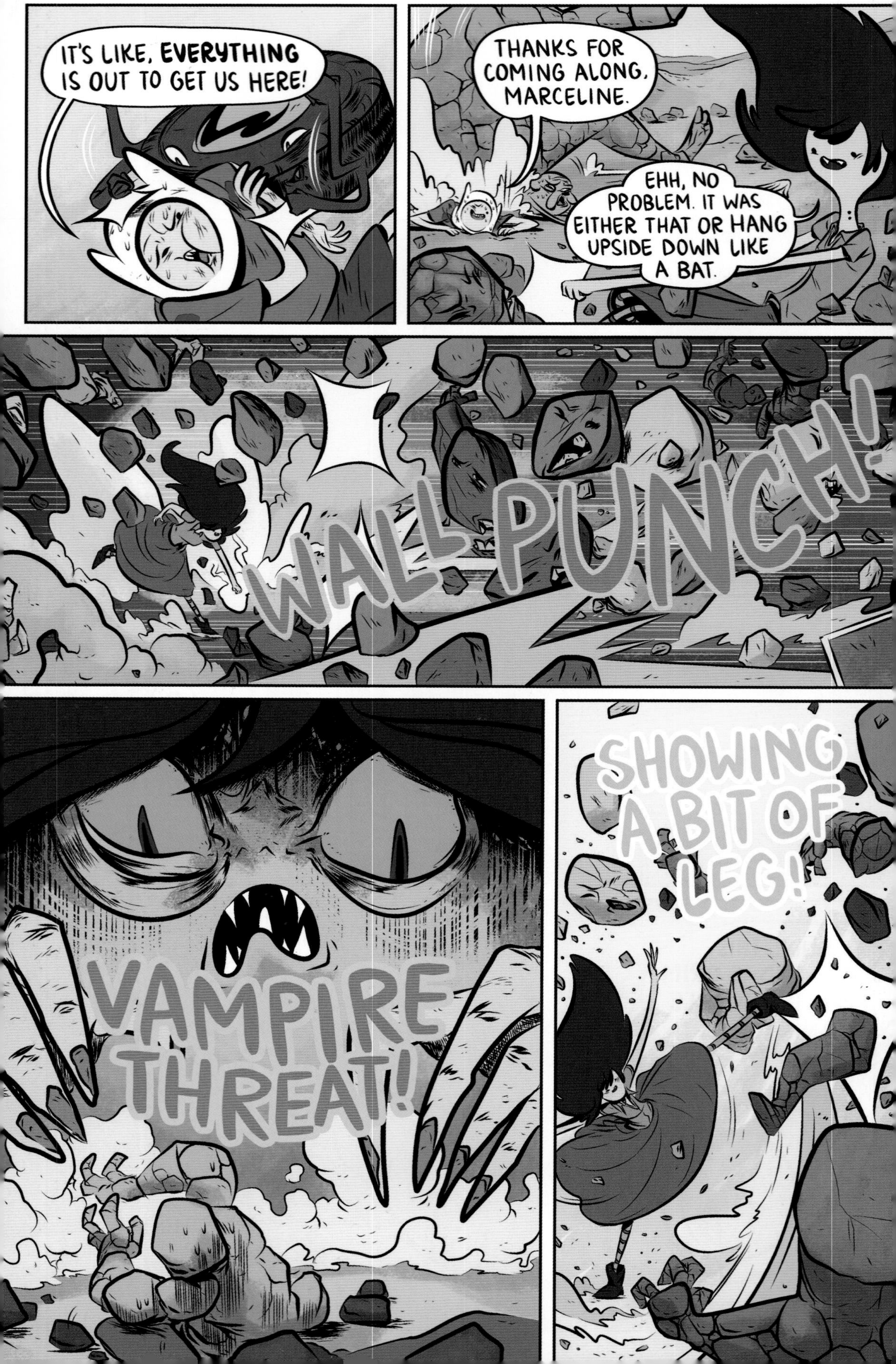
IT'S LIKE, EVERYTHING IS OUT TO GET US HERE!
THANKS FOR COMING ALONG, MARCELINE.
EHH, NO PROBLEM. IT WAS EITHER THAT OR HANG UPSIDE DOWN LIKE A BAT.
WALL PUNCH!
VAMPIRE THREAT!
SHOWING A BIT OF LEG!

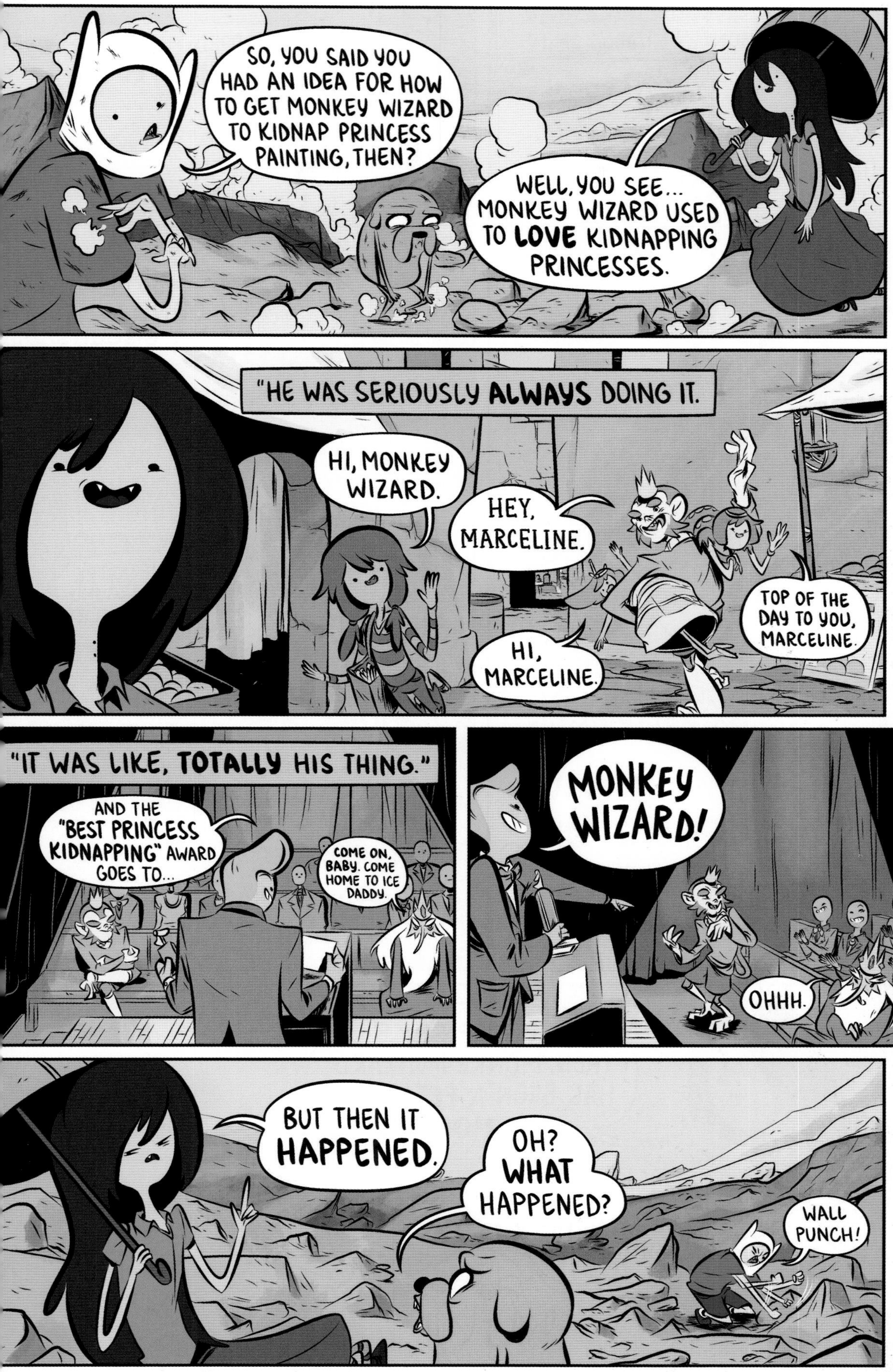
SO, YOU SAID YOU HAD AN IDEA FOR HOW TO GET MONKEY WIZARD TO KIDNAP PRINCESS PAINTING, THEN?
WELL, YOU SEE... MONKEY WIZARD USED TO LOVE KIDNAPPING PRINCESSES.
"HE WAS SERIOUSLY ALWAYS DOING IT.
HI, MONKEY WIZARD.
HEY, MARCELINE.
HI, MARCELINE.
TOP OF THE DAY TO YOU, MARCELINE.
"IT WAS LIKE, TOTALLY HIS THING."
AND THE "BEST PRINCESS KIDNAPPING" AWARD GOES TO...
COME ON, BABY. COME HOME TO ICE DADDY.
MONKEY WIZARD!
OHHH.
BUT THEN IT HAPPENED.
OH? WHAT HAPPENED?
WALL PUNCH!

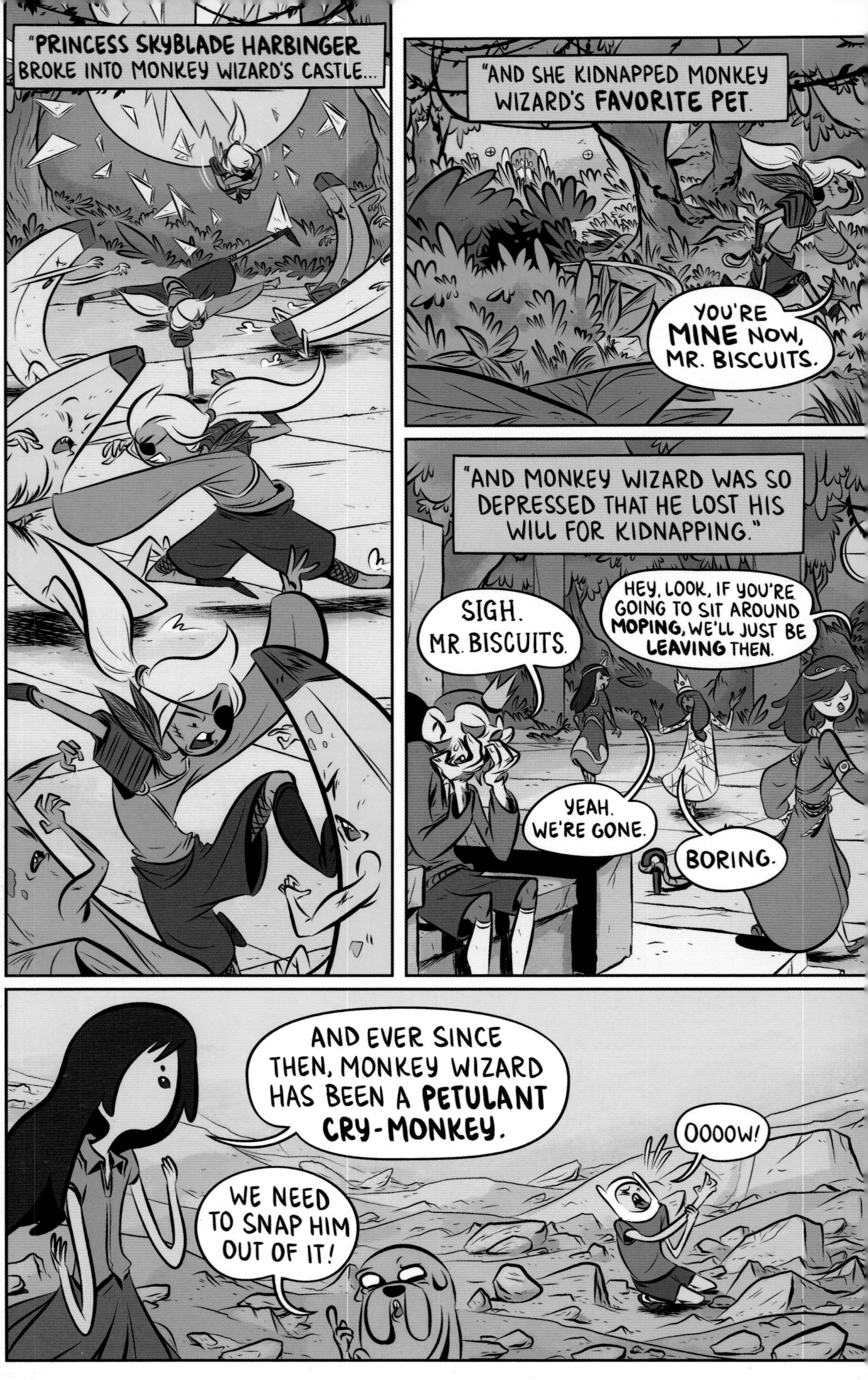

"PRINCESS SKYBLADE HARBINGER BROKE INTO MONKEY WIZARD'S CASTLE...
"AND SHE KIDNAPPED MONKEY WIZARD'S FAVORITE PET.
YOU'RE MINE NOW, MR. BISCUITS.
"AND MONKEY WIZARD WAS SO DEPRESSED THAT HE LOST HIS WILL FOR KIDNAPPING."
SIGH. MR. BISCUITS.
HEY, LOOK, IF YOU'RE GOING TO SIT AROUND MOPING, WE'LL JUST BE LEAVING THEN.
YEAH. WE'RE GONE.
BORING.
AND EVER SINCE THEN, MONKEY WIZARD HAS BEEN A PETULANT CRY-MONKEY.
OOOOW!
WE NEED TO SNAP HIM OUT OF IT!

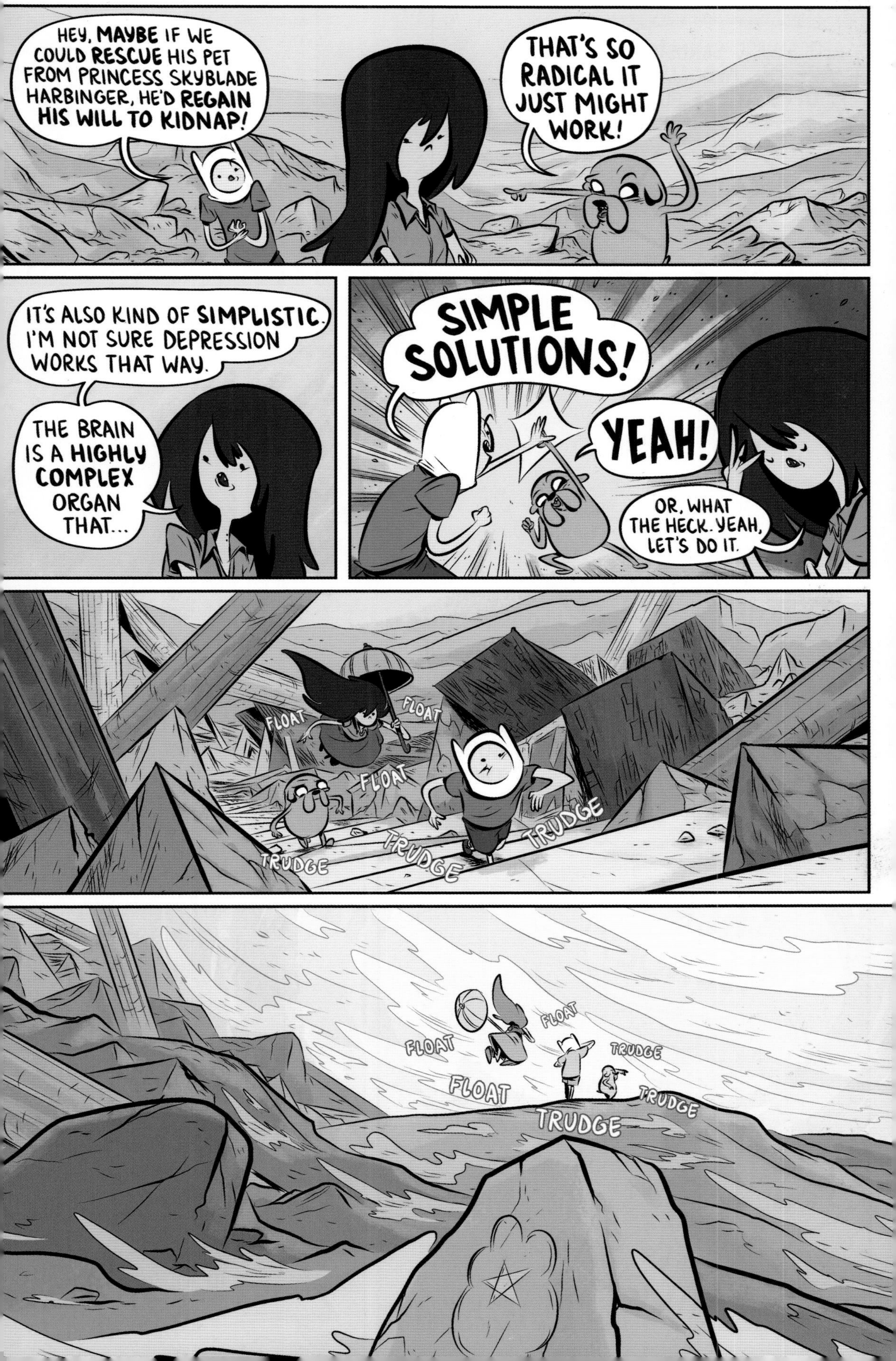
HEY, MAYBE IF WE COULD RESCUE HIS PET FROM PRINCESS SKYBLADE HARBINGER, HE'D REGAIN HIS WILL TO KIDNAP!
THAT'S SO RADICAL IT JUST MIGHT WORK!
IT'S ALSO KIND OF SIMPLISTIC. I'M NOT SURE DEPRESSION WORKS THAT WAY.
THE BRAIN IS A HIGHLY COMPLEX ORGAN THAT...
SIMPLE SOLUTIONS!
YEAH!
OR, WHAT THE HECK. YEAH, LET'S DO IT.
FLOAT
FLOAT
FLOAT
TRUDGE
TRUDGE
TRUDGE
FLOAT
FLOAT
FLOAT
TRUDGE
TRUDGE
TRUDGE

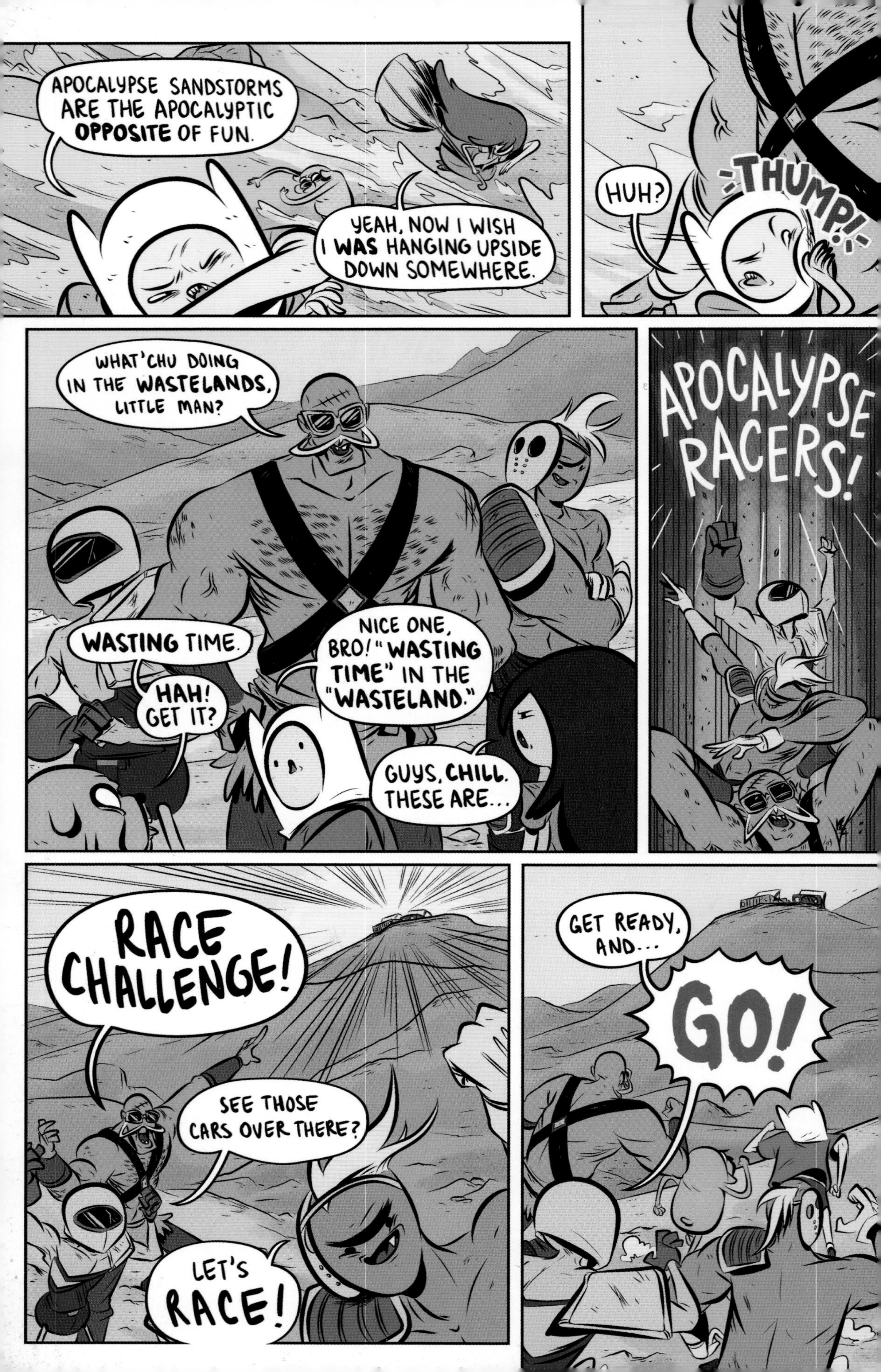
APOCALYPSE SANDSTORMS ARE THE APOCALYPTIC **OPPOSITE** OF FUN.
YEAH, NOW I WISH I **WAS** HANGING UPSIDE DOWN SOMEWHERE.
HUH?
THUMP!
WHAT'CHU DOING IN THE **WASTELANDS**, LITTLE MAN?
WASTING TIME.
HAH! GET IT?
NICE ONE, BRO! "**WASTING TIME**" IN THE "**WASTELAND**."
GUYS, **CHILL**. THESE ARE...
APOCALYPSE RACERS!
RACE CHALLENGE!
SEE THOSE CARS OVER THERE?
LET'S RACE!
GET READY, AND...
GO!

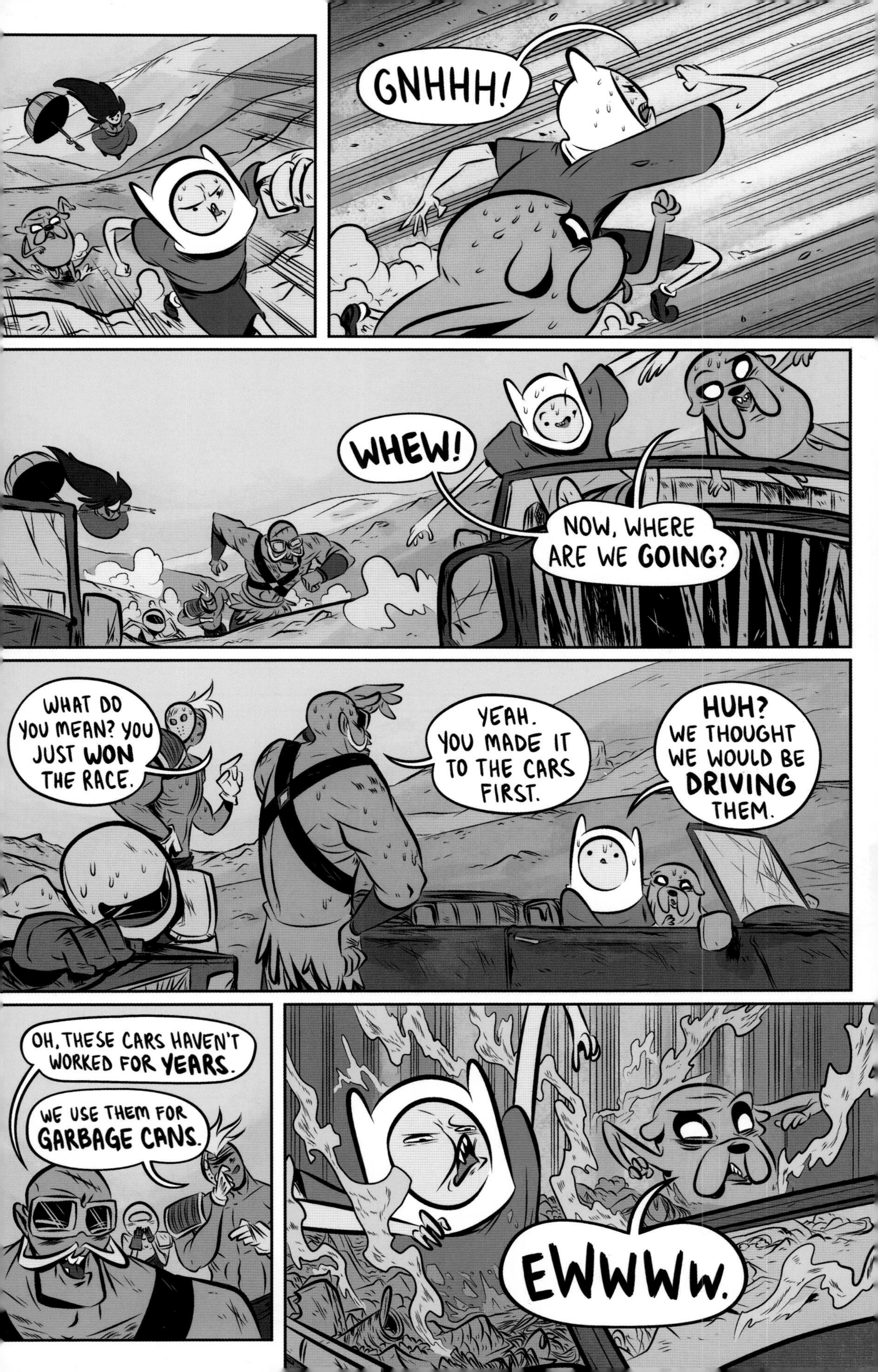
GNHHH!
WHEW!
NOW, WHERE ARE WE GOING?
WHAT DO YOU MEAN? YOU JUST WON THE RACE.
YEAH. YOU MADE IT TO THE CARS FIRST.
HUH? WE THOUGHT WE WOULD BE DRIVING THEM.
OH, THESE CARS HAVEN'T WORKED FOR YEARS.
WE USE THEM FOR GARBAGE CANS.
EWWWW.

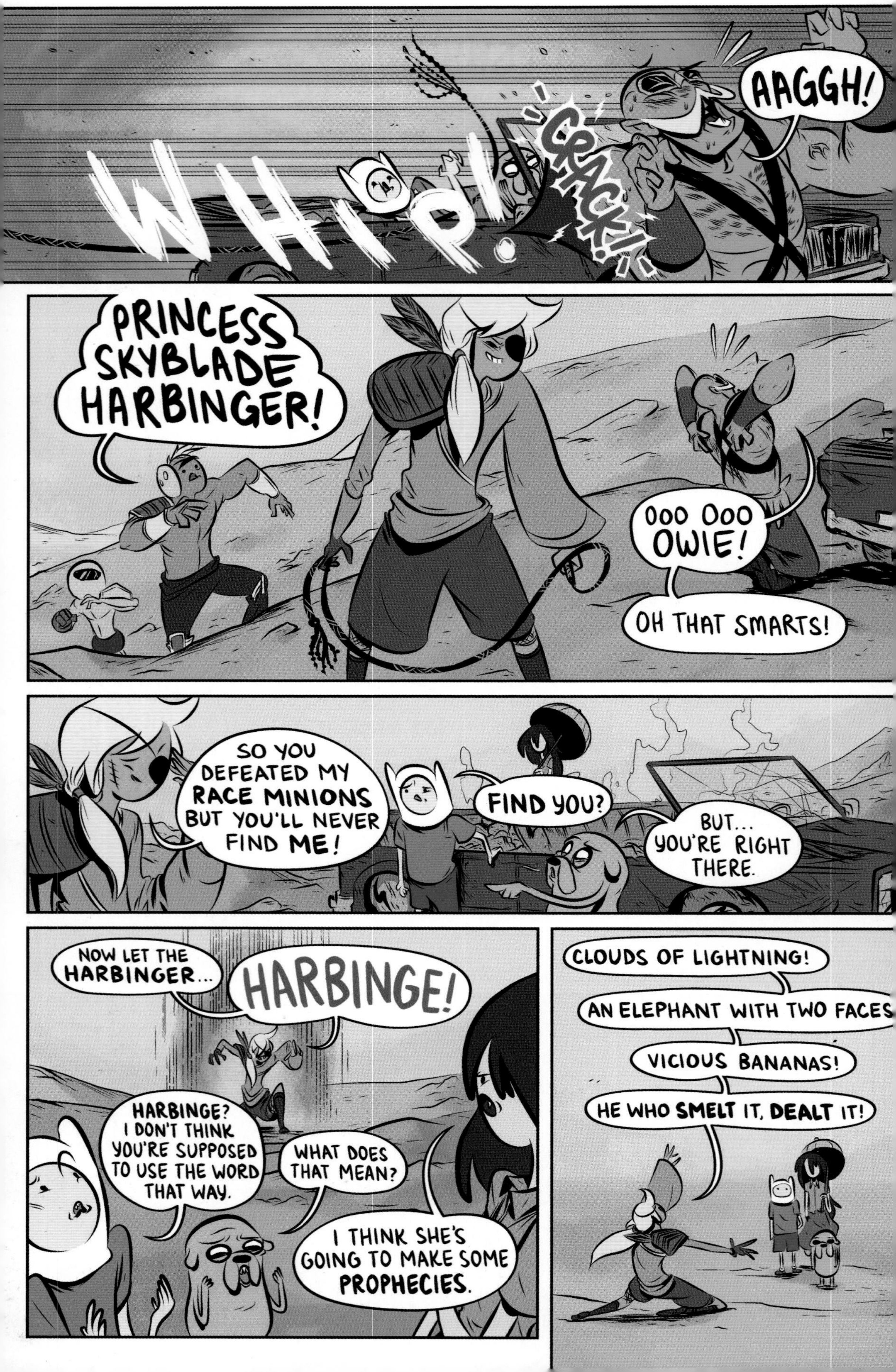

WHIP!
CRACK!
AAGGH!
PRINCESS SKYBLADE HARBINGER!
OOO OOO OWIE!
OH THAT SMARTS!
SO YOU DEFEATED MY RACE MINIONS BUT YOU'LL NEVER FIND ME!
FIND YOU?
BUT... YOU'RE RIGHT THERE.
NOW LET THE HARBINGER...
HARBINGE!
HARBINGE? I DON'T THINK YOU'RE SUPPOSED TO USE THE WORD THAT WAY.
WHAT DOES THAT MEAN?
I THINK SHE'S GOING TO MAKE SOME PROPHECIES.
CLOUDS OF LIGHTNING!
AN ELEPHANT WITH TWO FACES
VICIOUS BANANAS!
HE WHO SMELT IT, DEALT IT!

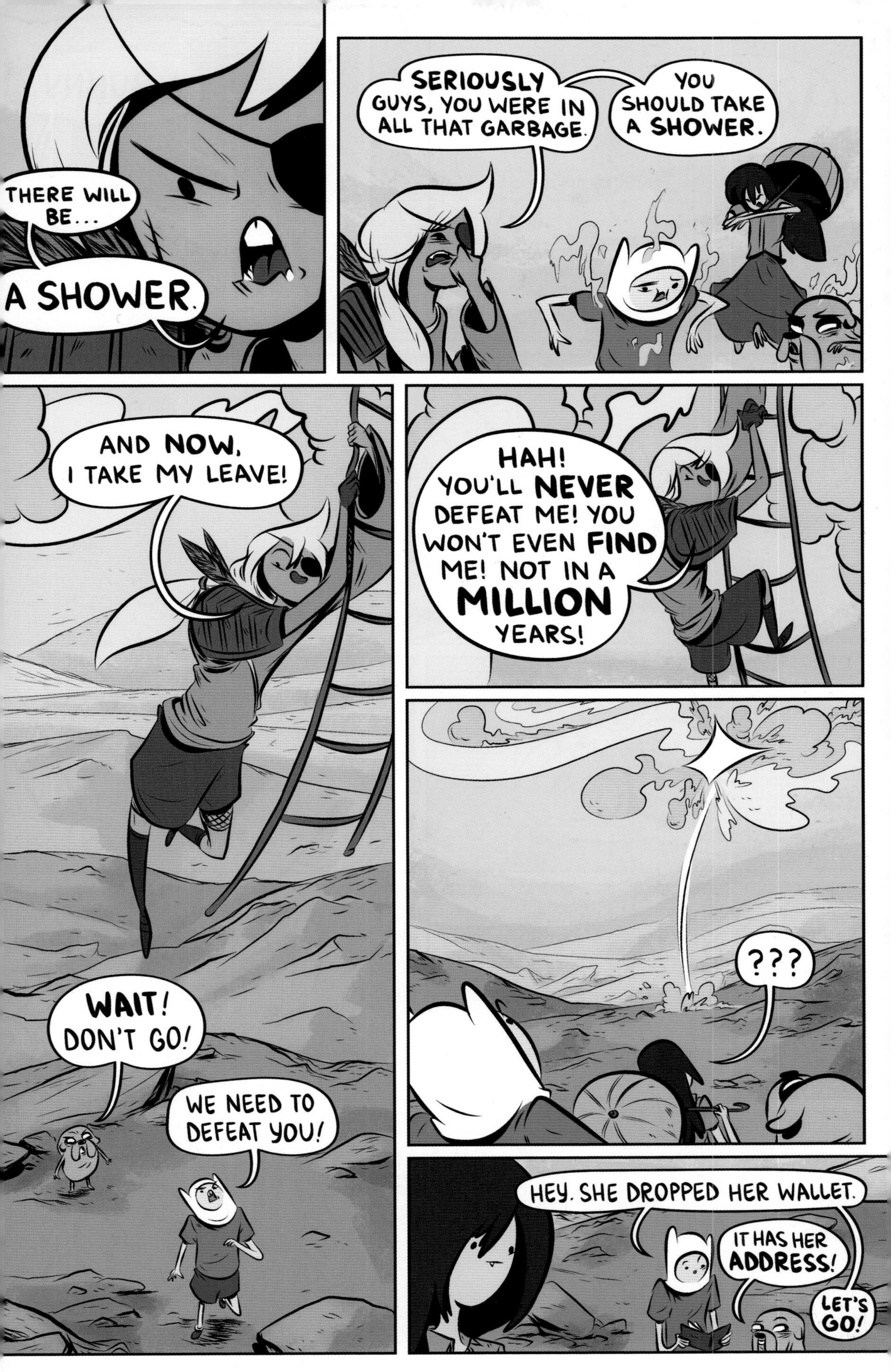
THERE WILL BE...
A SHOWER.
SERIOUSLY GUYS, YOU WERE IN ALL THAT GARBAGE.
YOU SHOULD TAKE A SHOWER.
AND NOW, I TAKE MY LEAVE!
HAH! YOU'LL NEVER DEFEAT ME! YOU WON'T EVEN FIND ME! NOT IN A MILLION YEARS!
WAIT! DON'T GO!
WE NEED TO DEFEAT YOU!
???
HEY. SHE DROPPED HER WALLET.
IT HAS HER ADDRESS!
LET'S GO!

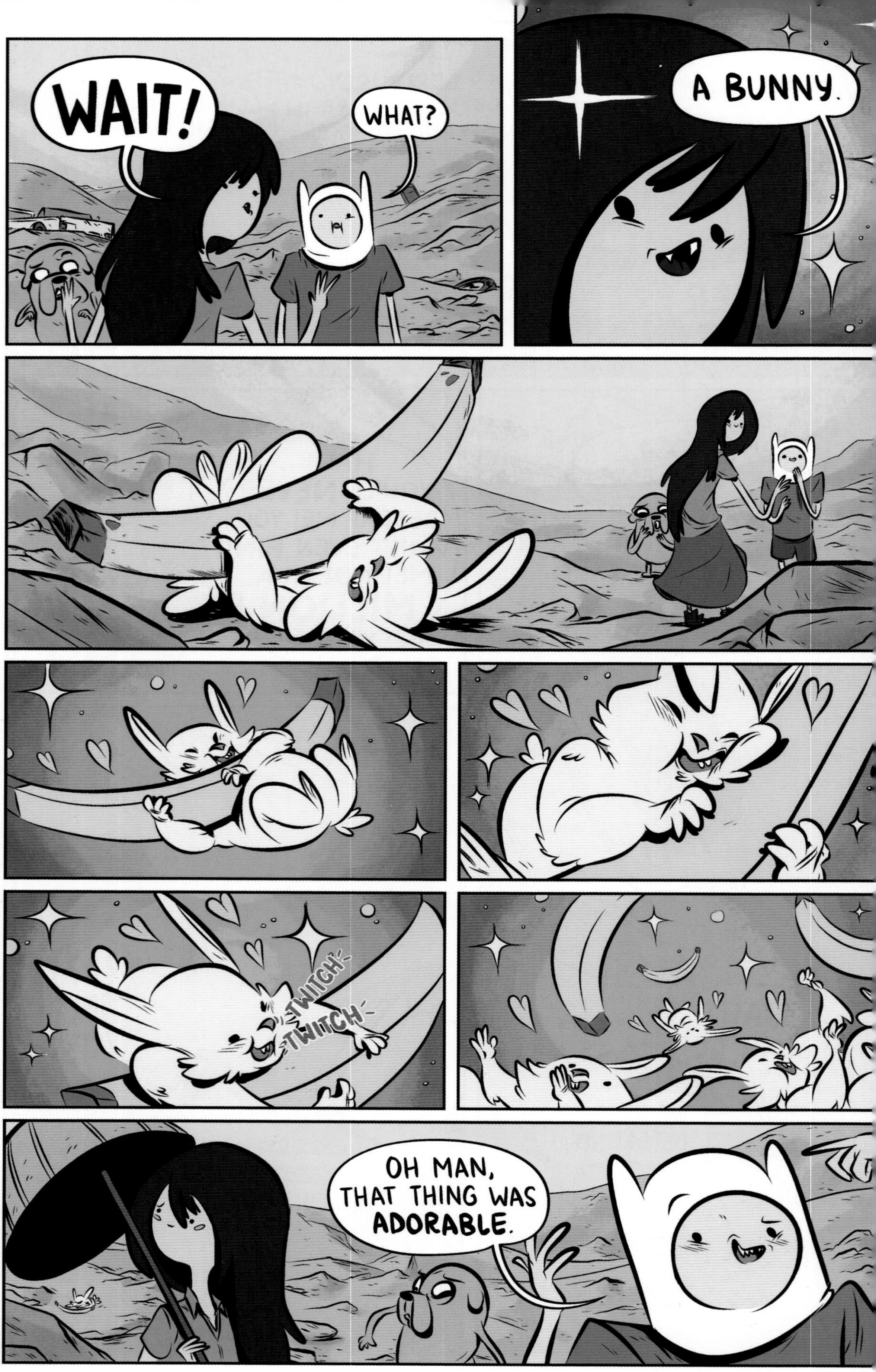
WAIT!
WHAT?
A BUNNY.
TWITCH
TWITCH
OH MAN, THAT THING WAS ADORABLE.

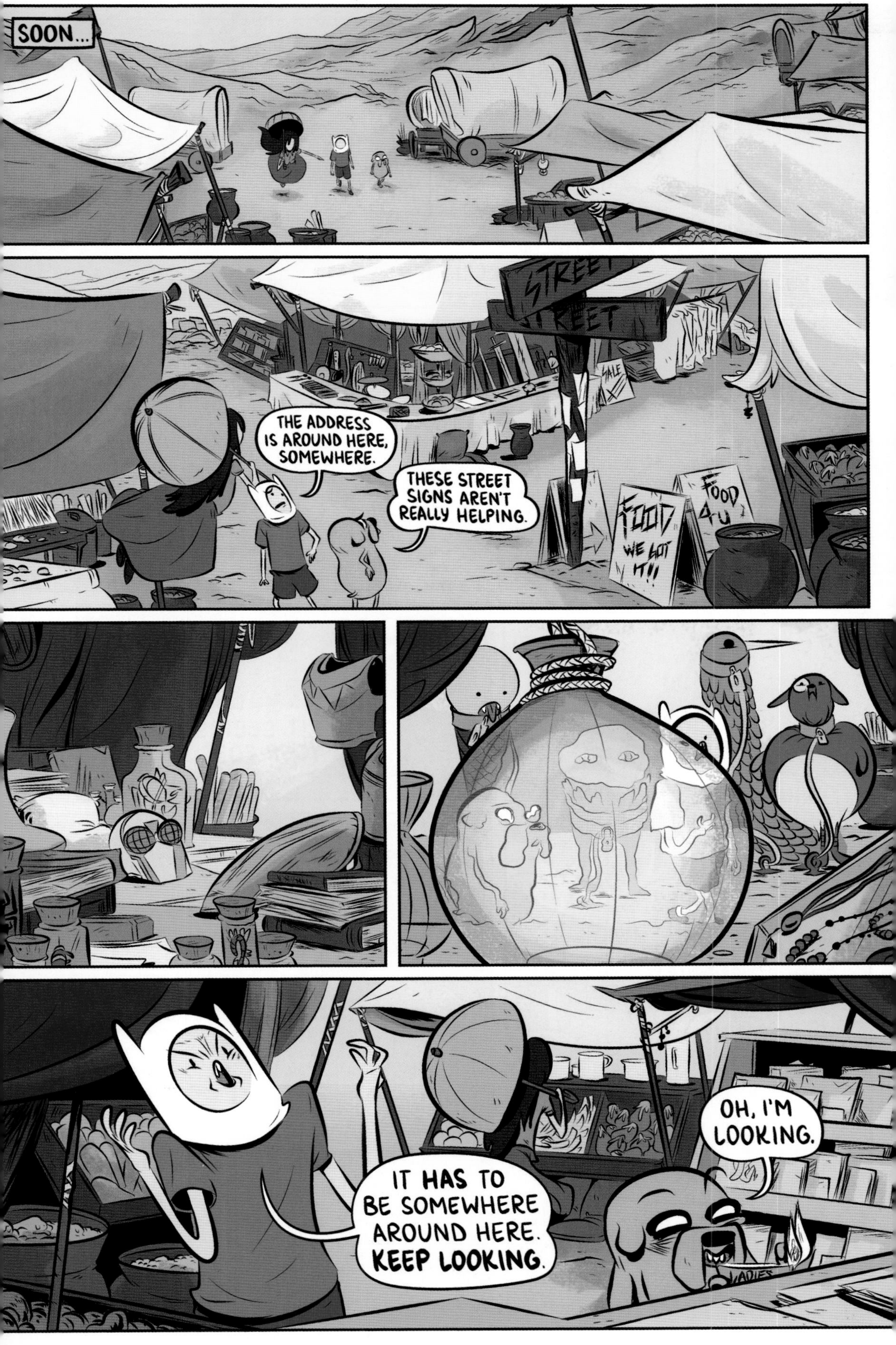
SOON...
STREET
STREET
SALE
THE ADDRESS IS AROUND HERE, SOMEWHERE.
THESE STREET SIGNS AREN'T REALLY HELPING.
FOOD WE GOT IT!!
FOOD 4 U
IT HAS TO BE SOMEWHERE AROUND HERE. KEEP LOOKING.
OH, I'M LOOKING.

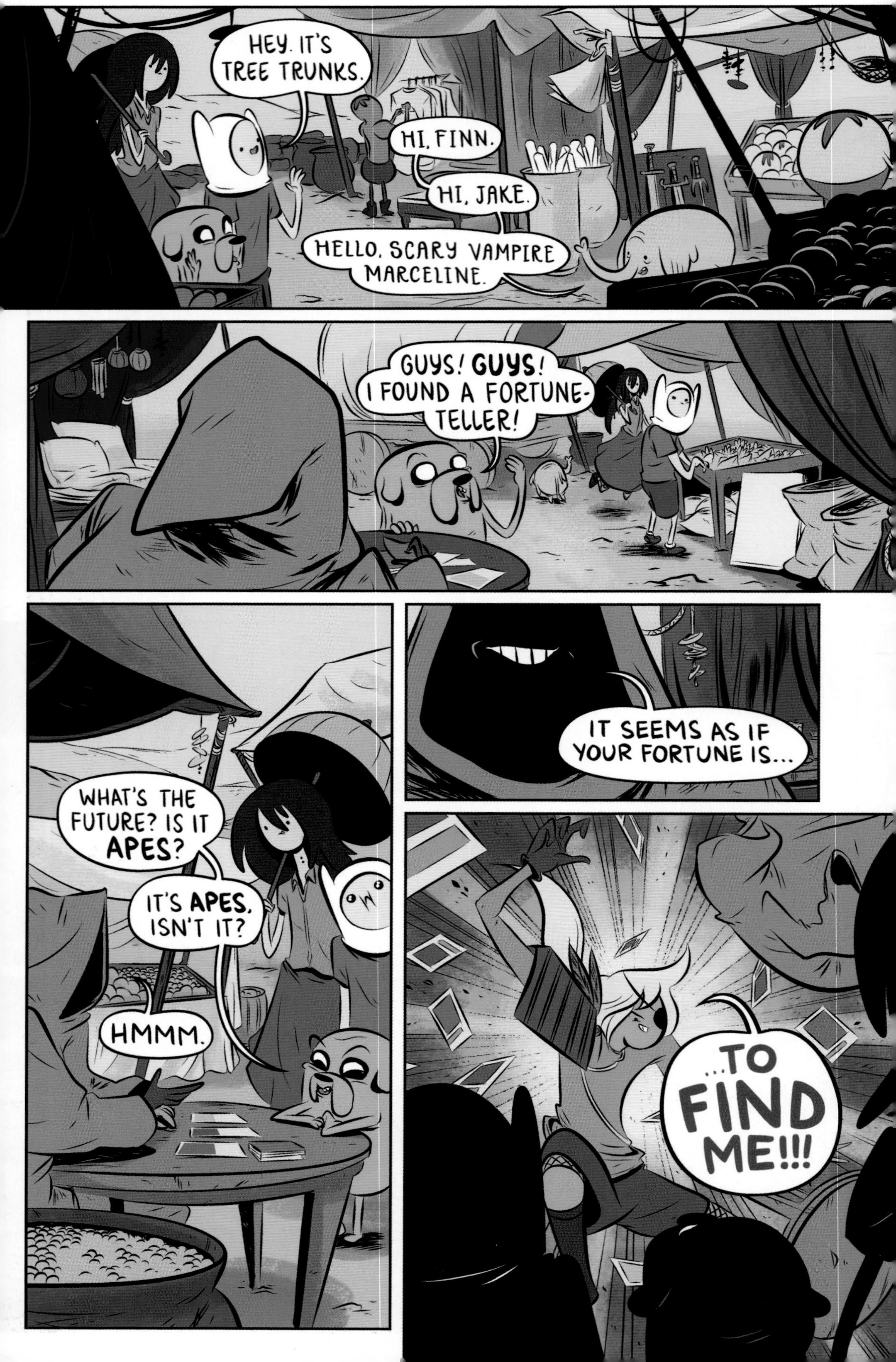
HEY. IT'S TREE TRUNKS.
HI, FINN.
HI, JAKE.
HELLO, SCARY VAMPIRE MARCELINE.
GUYS! **GUYS**! I FOUND A FORTUNE-TELLER!
WHAT'S THE FUTURE? IS IT **APES**?
IT'S **APES**, ISN'T IT?
HMMM.
IT SEEMS AS IF YOUR FORTUNE IS...
...TO FIND ME!!!

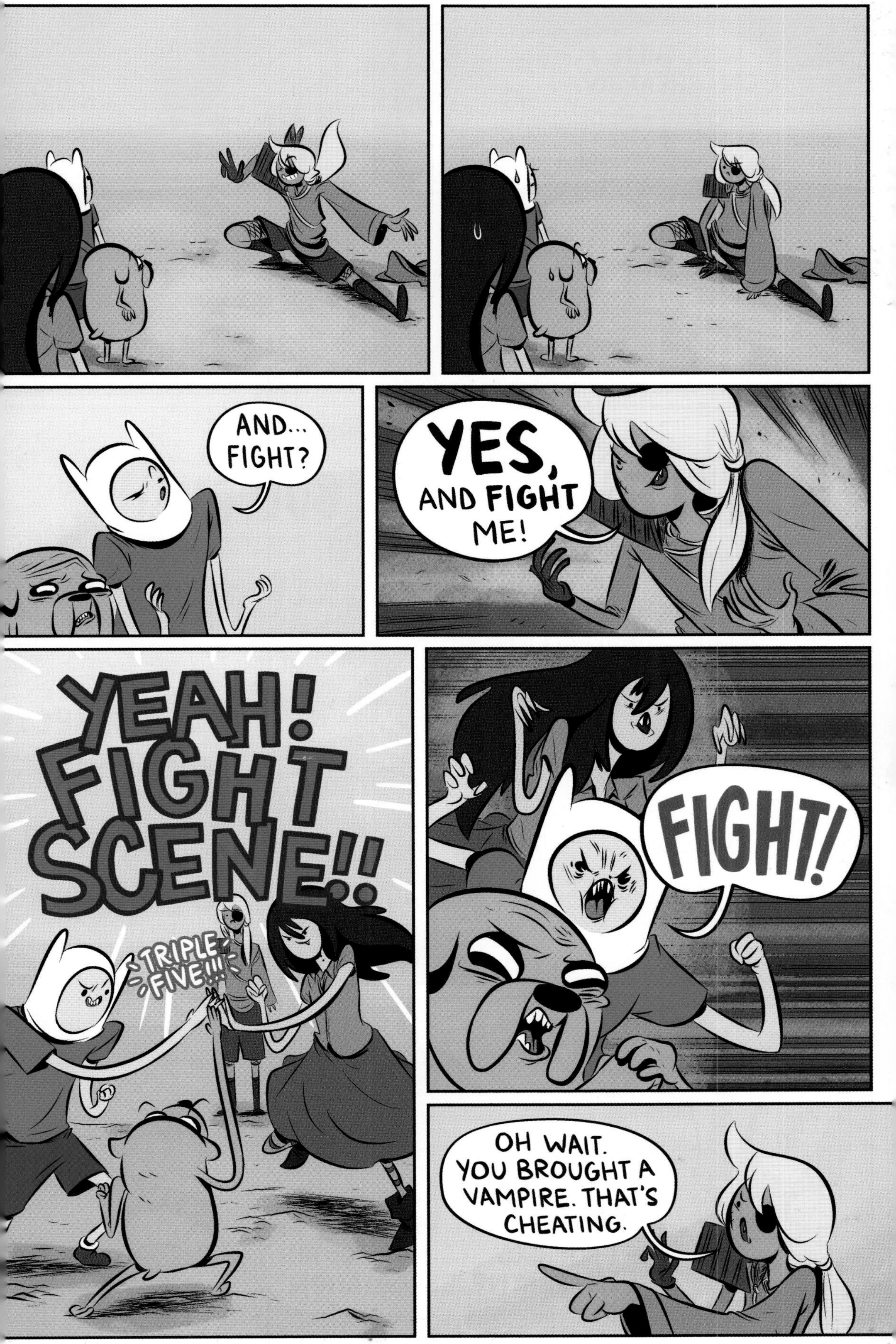
AND... FIGHT?
YES, AND FIGHT ME!
YEAH! FIGHT SCENE!!
TRIPLE FIVE!!!
FIGHT!
OH WAIT. YOU BROUGHT A VAMPIRE. THAT'S CHEATING.

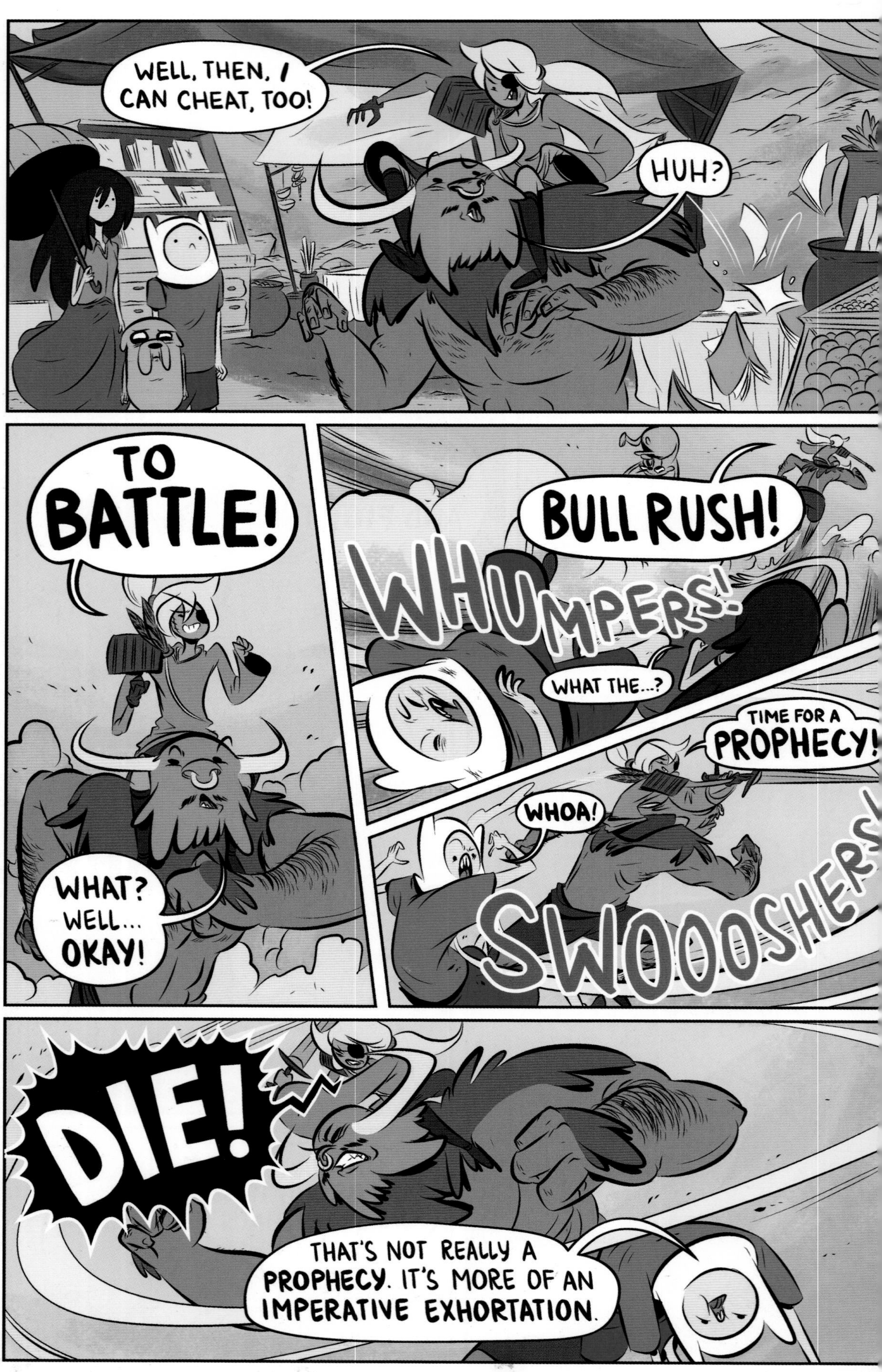
WELL, THEN, I CAN CHEAT, TOO!
HUH?
TO BATTLE!
WHAT? WELL... OKAY!
BULL RUSH!
WHUMPERS!
WHAT THE...?
TIME FOR A PROPHECY!
WHOA!
SWOOOSHERS!
DIE!
THAT'S NOT REALLY A PROPHECY. IT'S MORE OF AN IMPERATIVE EXHORTATION.

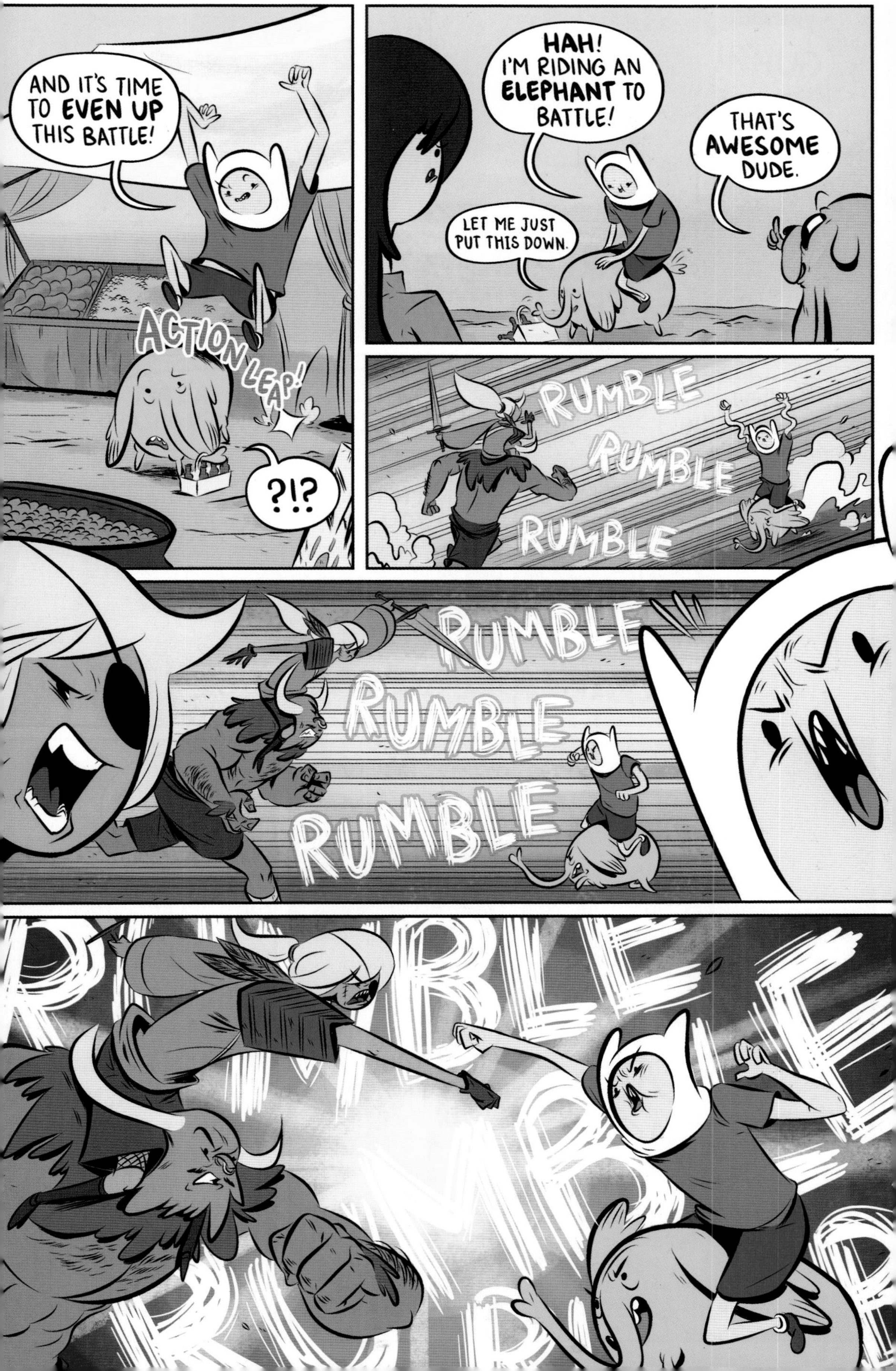

AND IT'S TIME TO **EVEN UP** THIS BATTLE!
ACTION LEAP!
?!?
HAH! I'M RIDING AN **ELEPHANT** TO BATTLE!
LET ME JUST PUT THIS DOWN.
THAT'S **AWESOME** DUDE.
RUMBLE
RUMBLE
RUMBLE
RUMBLE
RUMBLE
RUMBLE

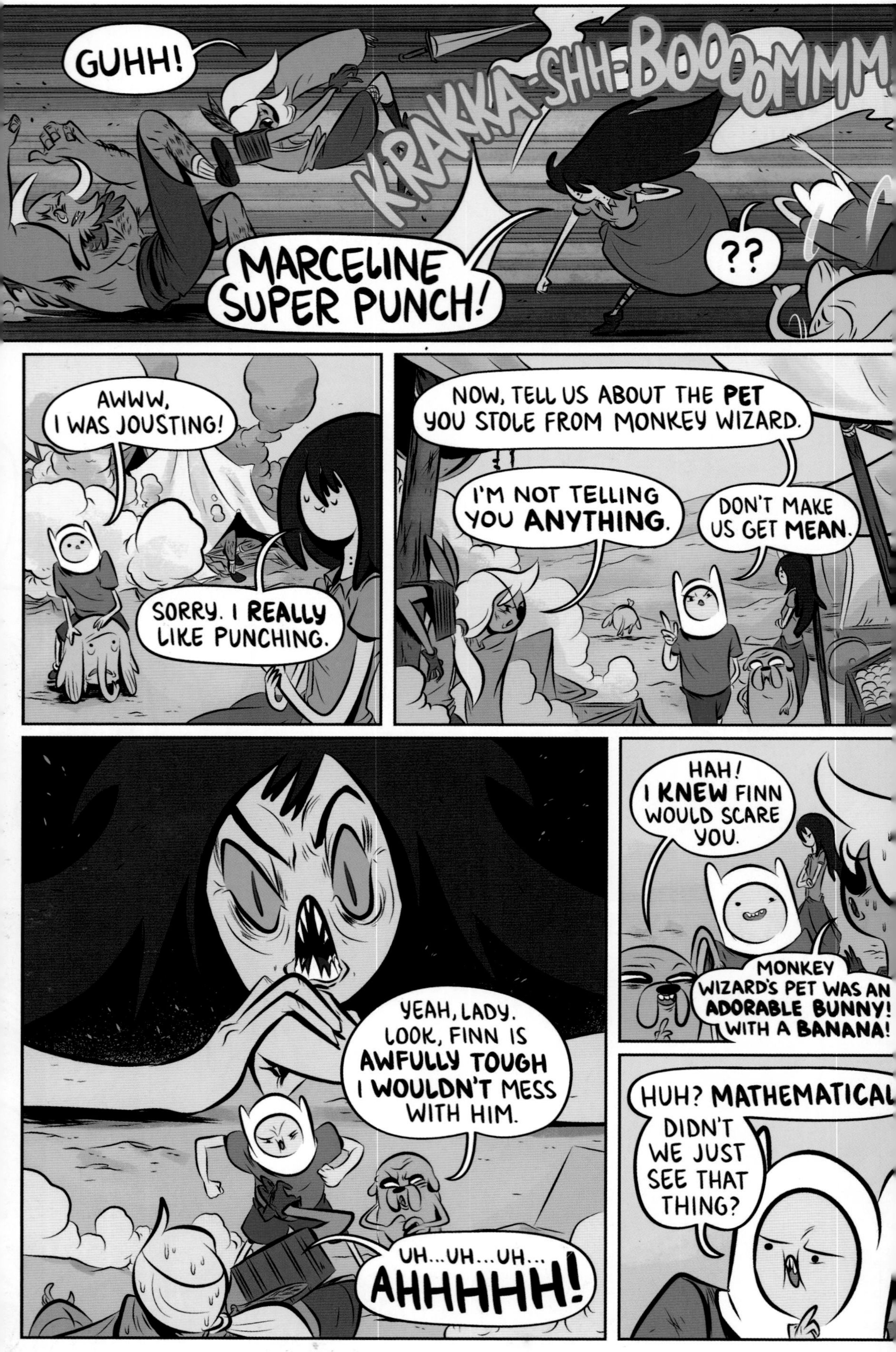
GUHH!
KRAKKA-SHH-BOOOOMMM
MARCELINE SUPER PUNCH!
??
AWWW, I WAS JOUSTING!
SORRY. I REALLY LIKE PUNCHING.
NOW, TELL US ABOUT THE PET YOU STOLE FROM MONKEY WIZARD.
I'M NOT TELLING YOU ANYTHING.
DON'T MAKE US GET MEAN.
YEAH, LADY. LOOK, FINN IS AWFULLY TOUGH I WOULDN'T MESS WITH HIM.
UH...UH...UH... AHHHHH!
HAH! I KNEW FINN WOULD SCARE YOU.
MONKEY WIZARD'S PET WAS AN ADORABLE BUNNY! WITH A BANANA!
HUH? MATHEMATICAL
DIDN'T WE JUST SEE THAT THING?

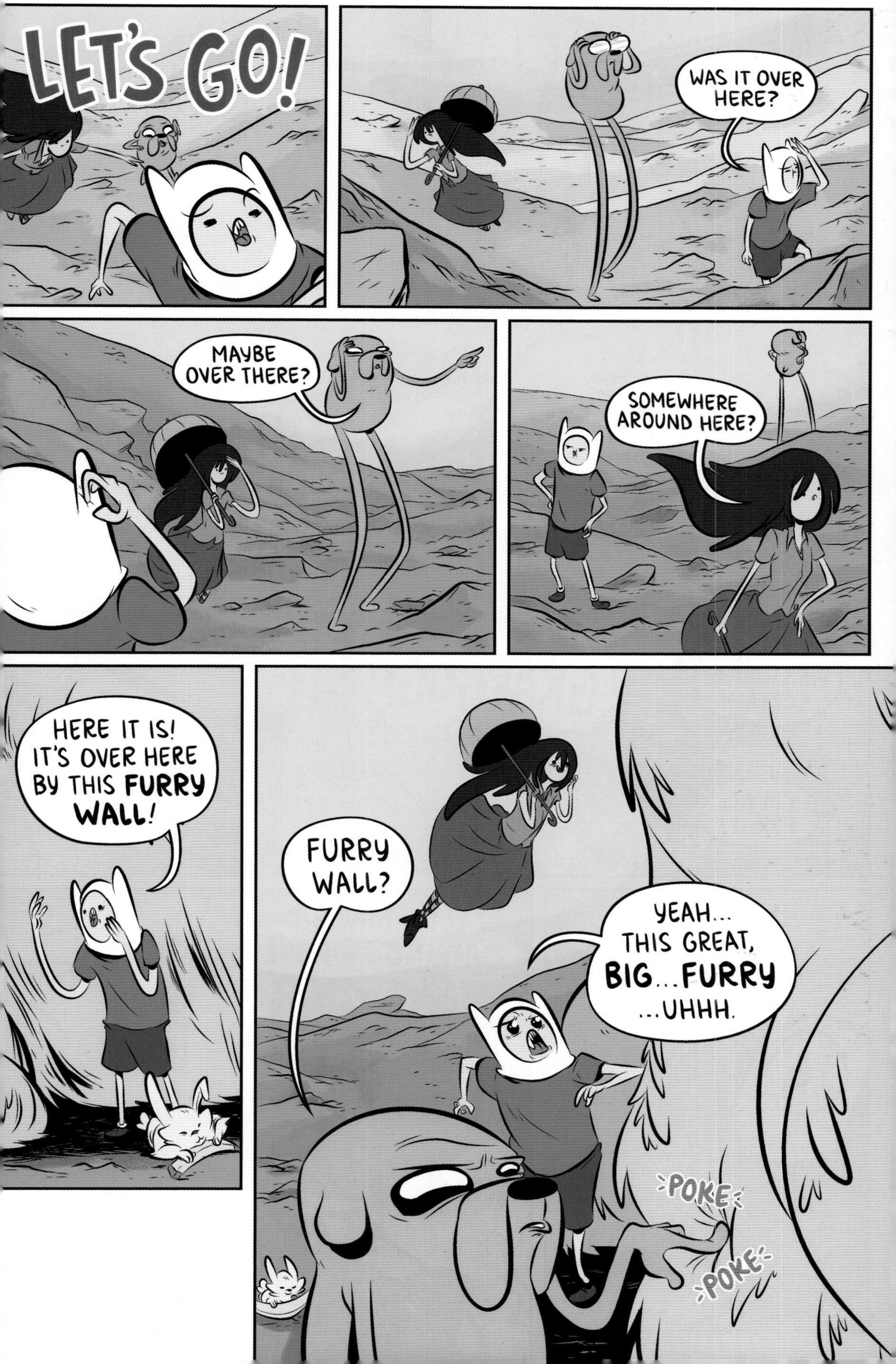

LET'S GO!
WAS IT OVER HERE?
MAYBE OVER THERE?
SOMEWHERE AROUND HERE?
HERE IT IS! IT'S OVER HERE BY THIS **FURRY WALL**!
FURRY WALL?
YEAH... THIS GREAT, **BIG**...**FURRY** ...UHHH.
POKE
POKE

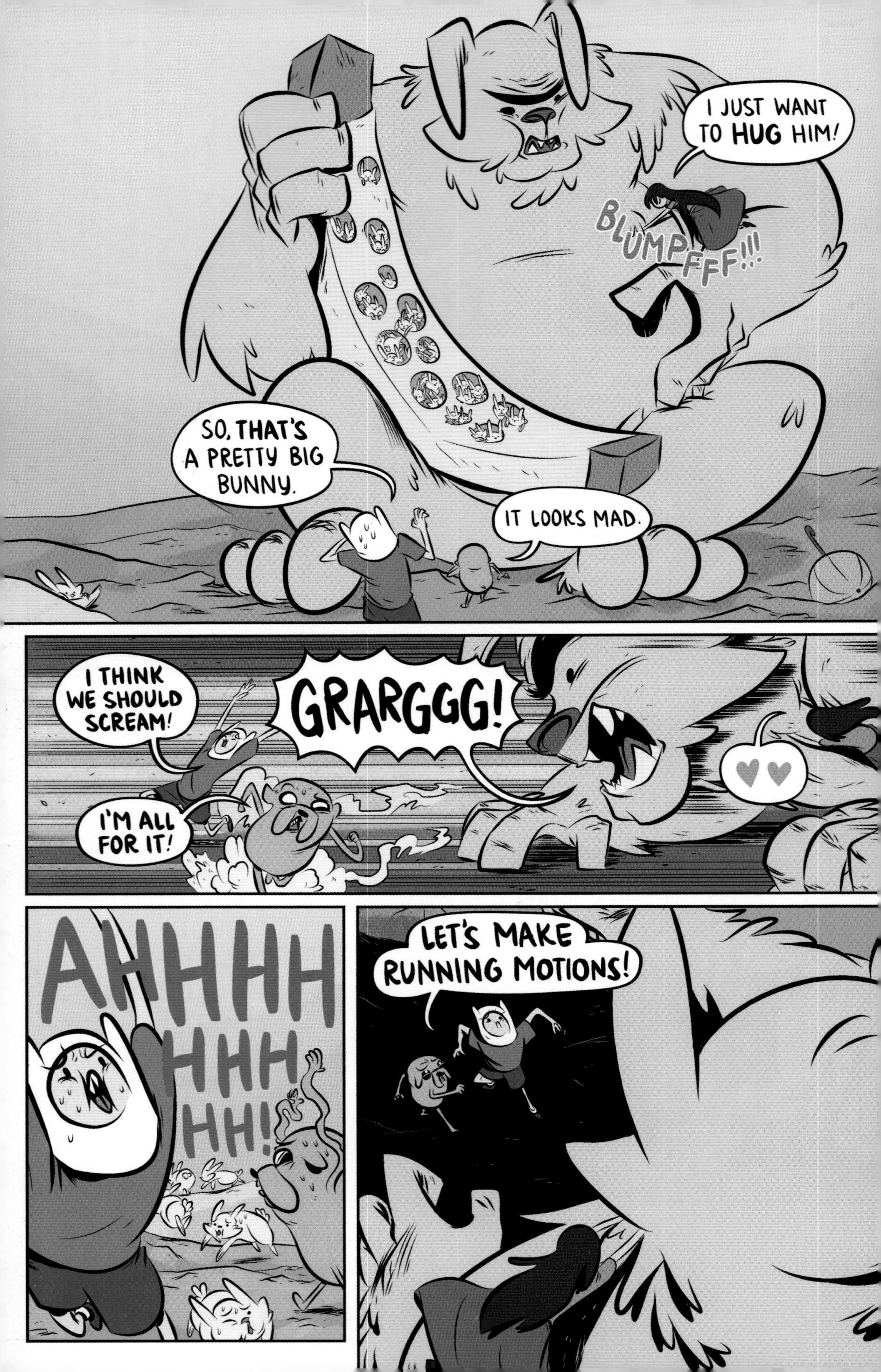
I JUST WANT TO HUG HIM!
BLUMPFFF!!!
SO, THAT'S A PRETTY BIG BUNNY.
IT LOOKS MAD.
I THINK WE SHOULD SCREAM!
GRARGGG!
I'M ALL FOR IT!
AHHHHHHHHH!
LET'S MAKE RUNNING MOTIONS!

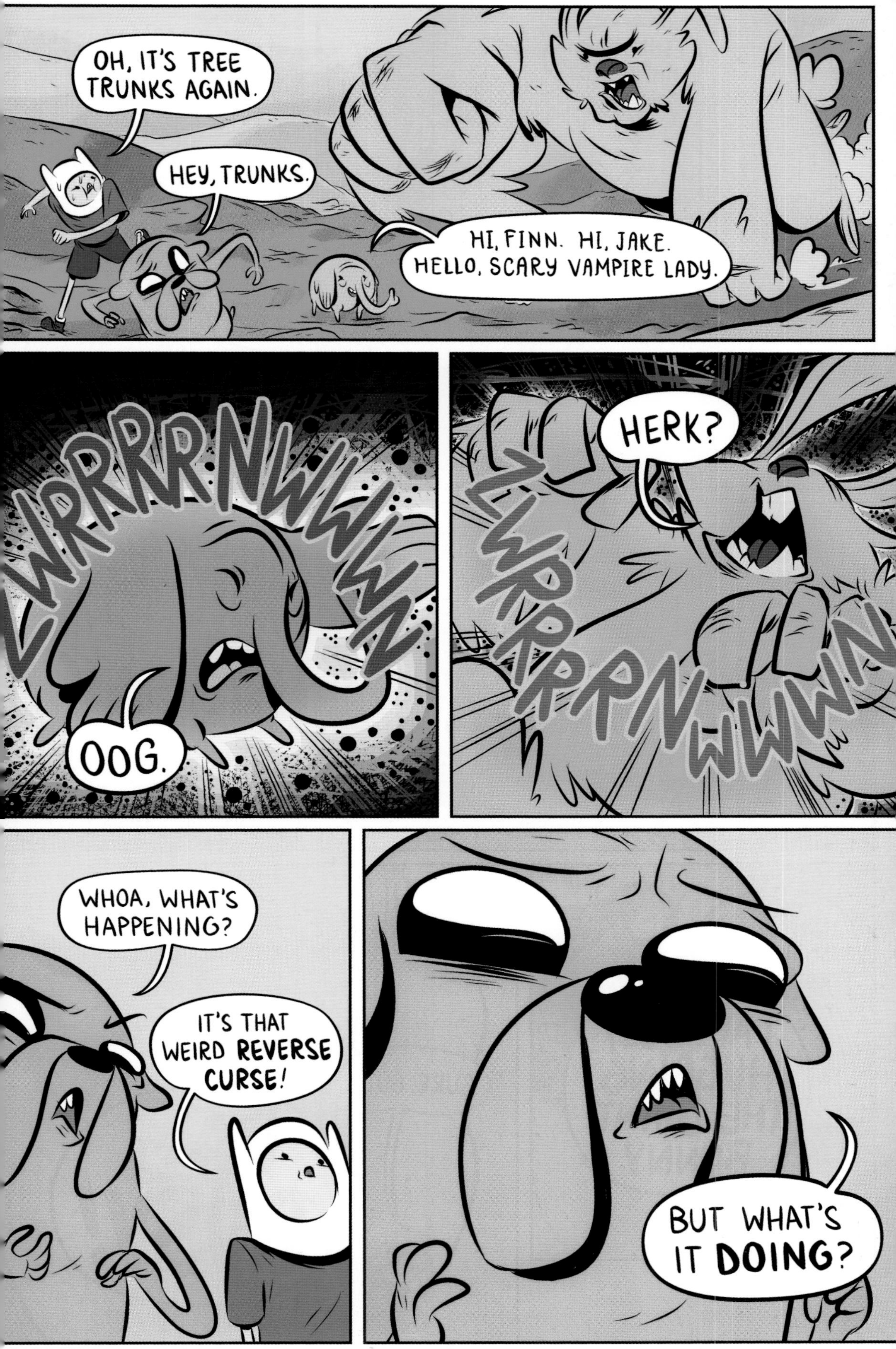
OH, IT'S TREE TRUNKS AGAIN.
HEY, TRUNKS.
HI, FINN. HI, JAKE. HELLO, SCARY VAMPIRE LADY.
ZWRRRRNWWWWN
OOG.
HERK?
ZWRRRRNWWWWN
WHOA, WHAT'S HAPPENING?
IT'S THAT WEIRD **REVERSE CURSE**!
BUT WHAT'S IT **DOING**?

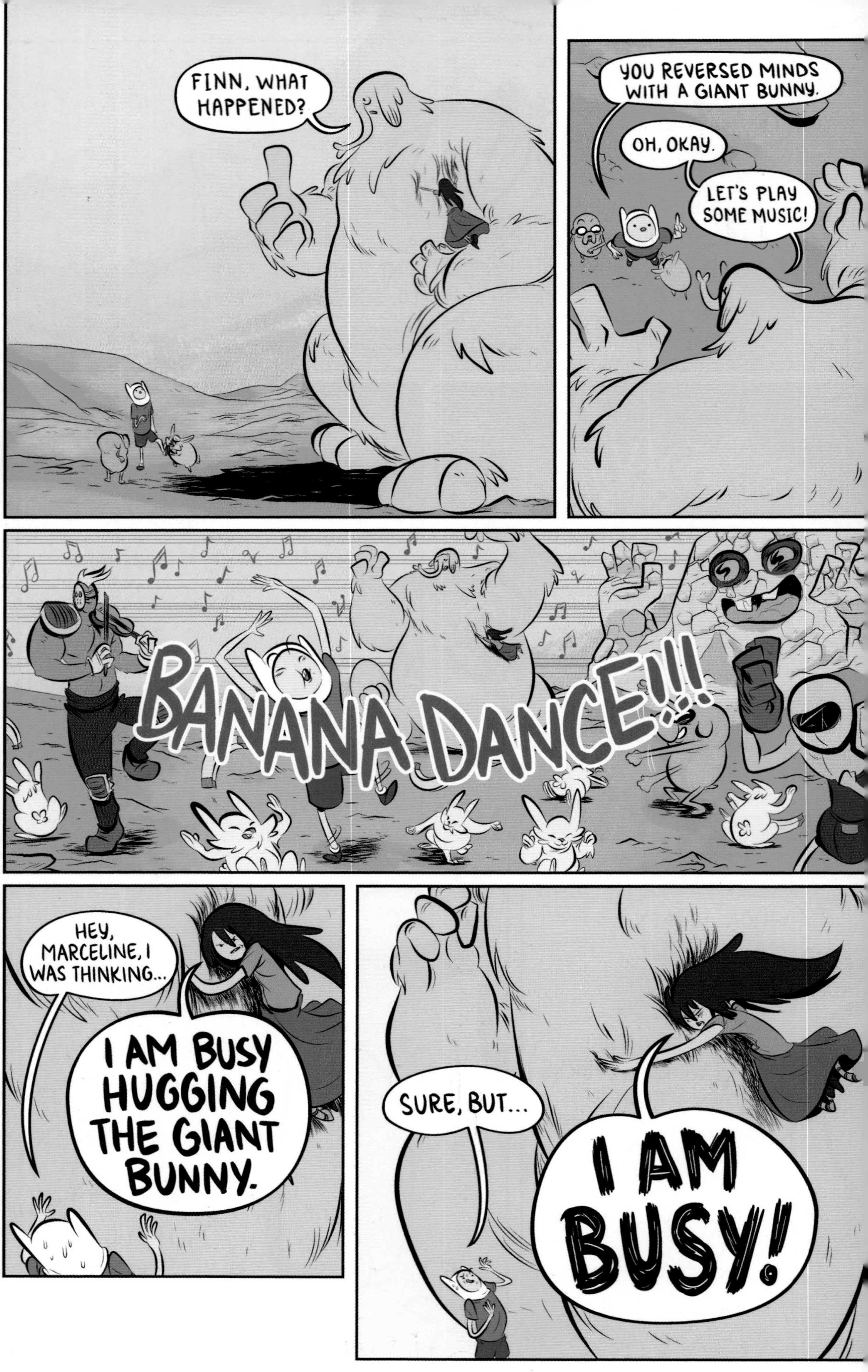
FINN, WHAT HAPPENED?
YOU REVERSED MINDS WITH A GIANT BUNNY.
OH, OKAY.
LET'S PLAY SOME MUSIC!
BANANA DANCE!!!
HEY, MARCELINE, I WAS THINKING...
I AM BUSY HUGGING THE GIANT BUNNY.
SURE, BUT...
I AM BUSY!

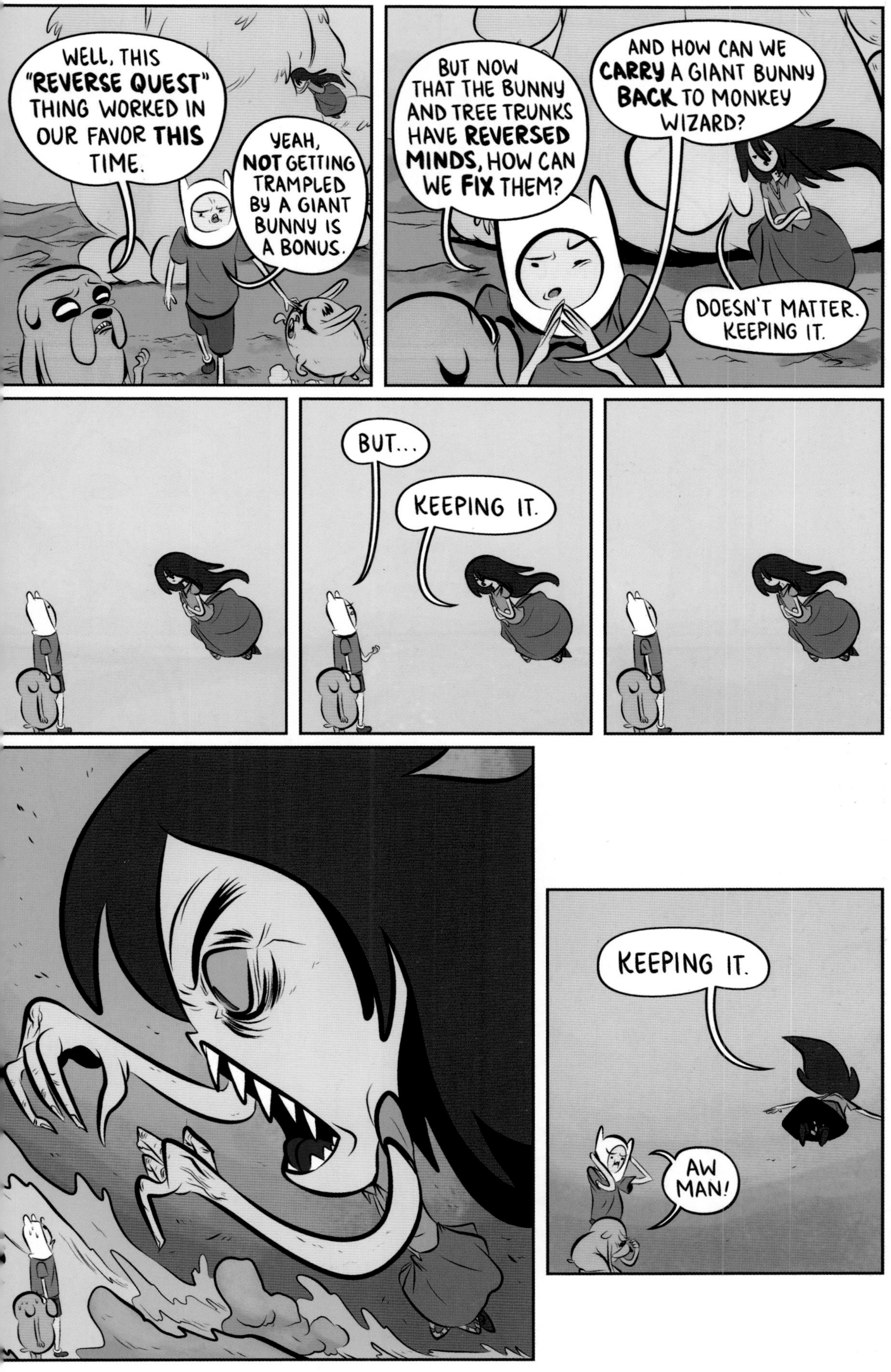
WELL, THIS "REVERSE QUEST" THING WORKED IN OUR FAVOR THIS TIME.
YEAH, NOT GETTING TRAMPLED BY A GIANT BUNNY IS A BONUS.
BUT NOW THAT THE BUNNY AND TREE TRUNKS HAVE REVERSED MINDS, HOW CAN WE FIX THEM?
AND HOW CAN WE CARRY A GIANT BUNNY BACK TO MONKEY WIZARD?
DOESN'T MATTER. KEEPING IT.
BUT...
KEEPING IT.
KEEPING IT.
AW MAN!

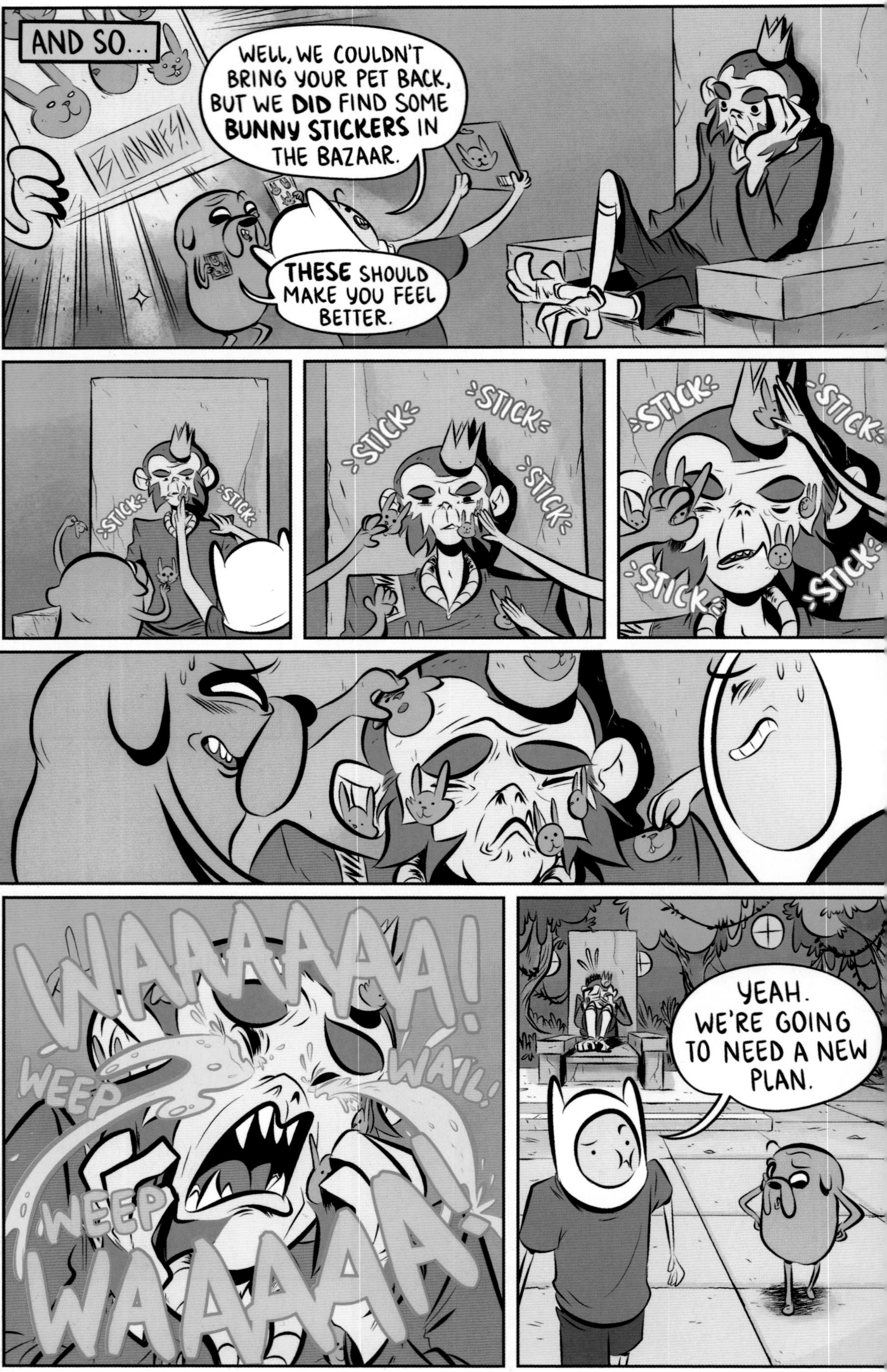
AND SO...
BUNNIES!
WELL, WE COULDN'T BRING YOUR PET BACK, BUT WE **DID** FIND SOME **BUNNY STICKERS** IN THE BAZAAR.
THESE SHOULD MAKE YOU FEEL BETTER.
STICK
STICK
STICK
STICK
STICK
STICK
STICK
STICK
STICK
WAAAAAA!
WEEP
WAIL!
WEEP
WAAAAA
YEAH. WE'RE GOING TO NEED A NEW PLAN.

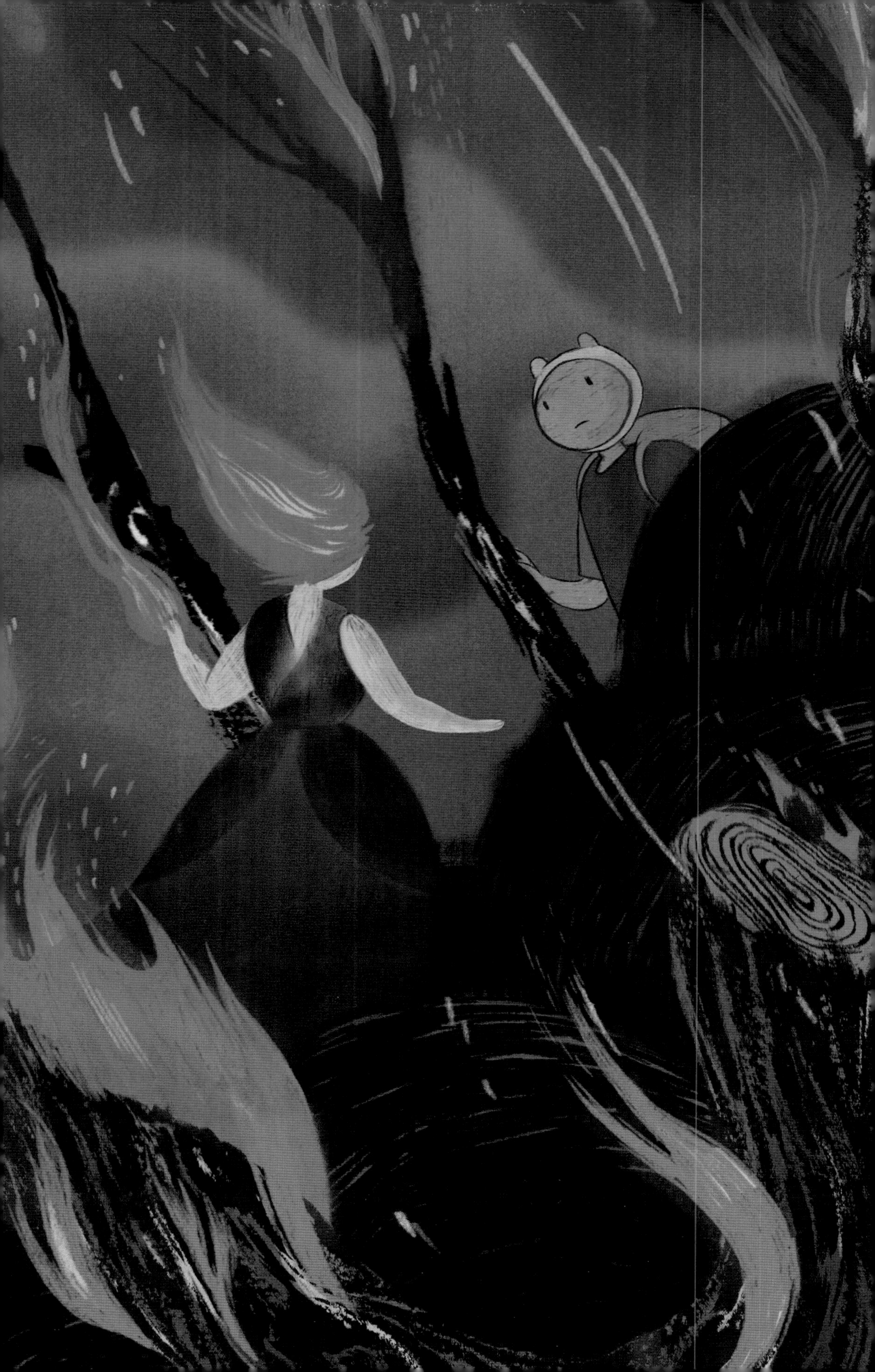

CHAPTER FOUR

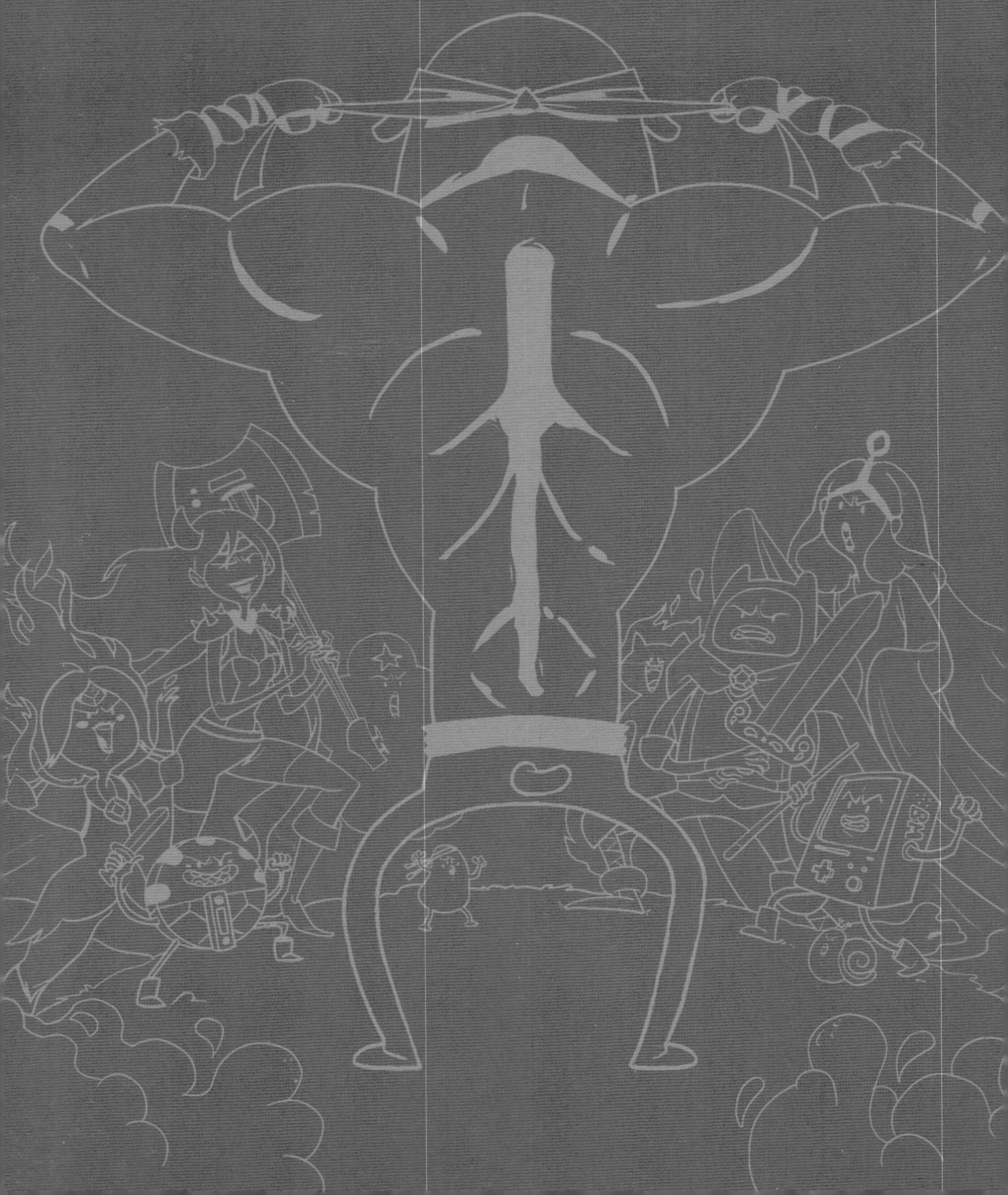
BMO

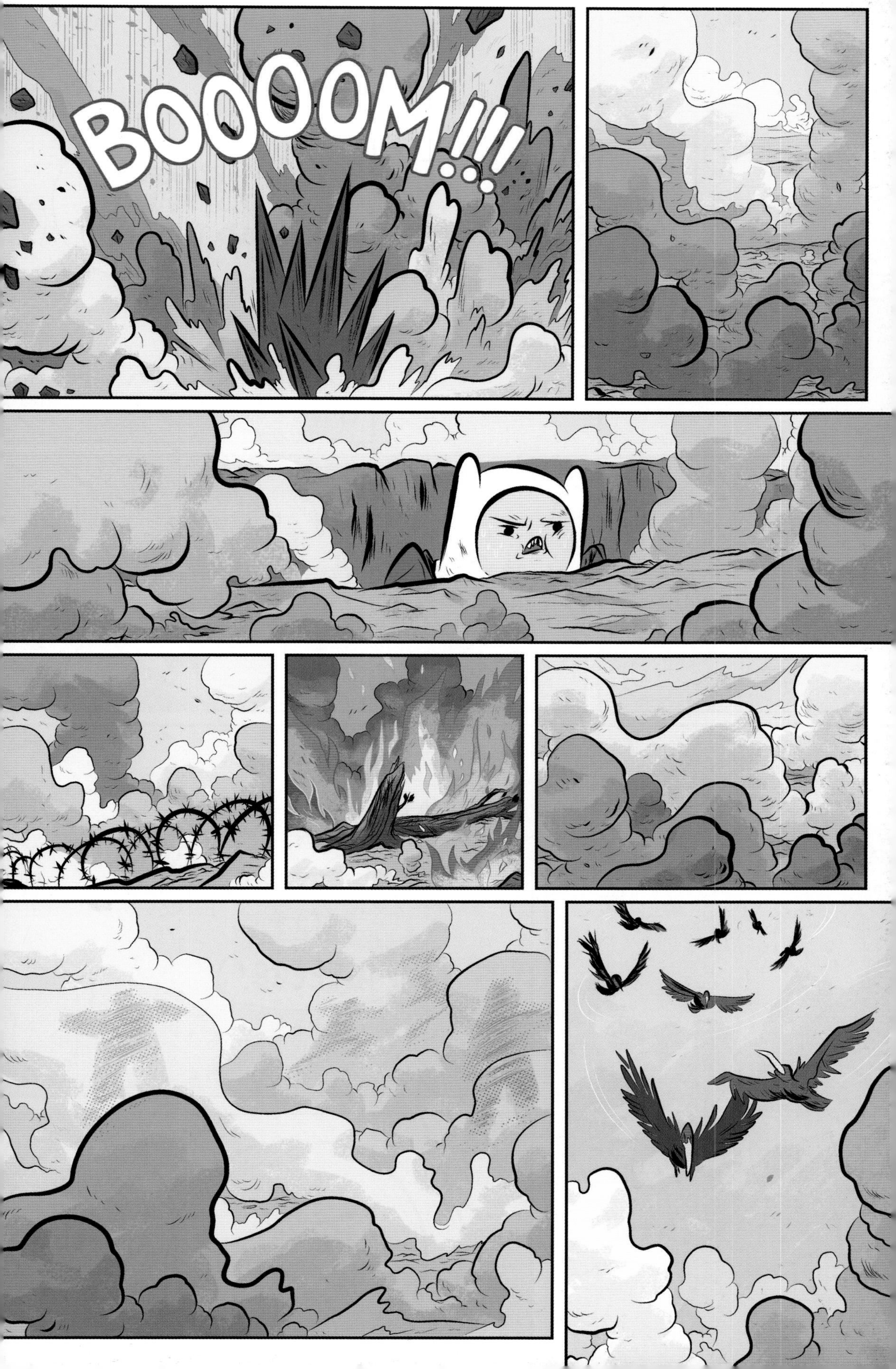
BOOOOM...!!!

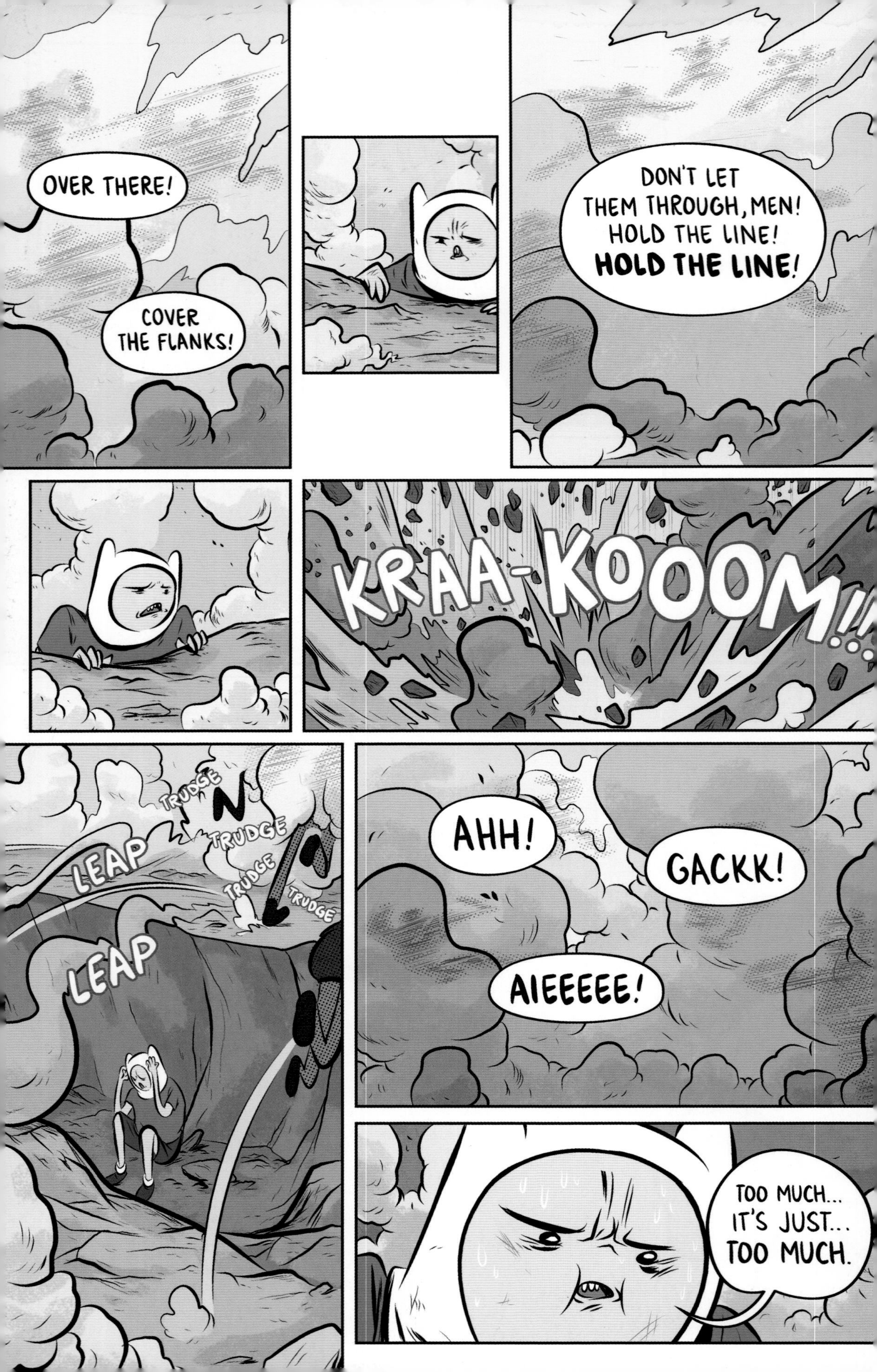
OVER THERE!
COVER THE FLANKS!
DON'T LET THEM THROUGH, MEN! HOLD THE LINE! **HOLD THE LINE**!
KRAA-KOOOM!!!
LEAP
TRUDGE
N
TRUDGE
TRUDGE
TRUDGE
LEAP
AHH!
GACKK!
AIEEEEE!
TOO MUCH... IT'S JUST... TOO MUCH.

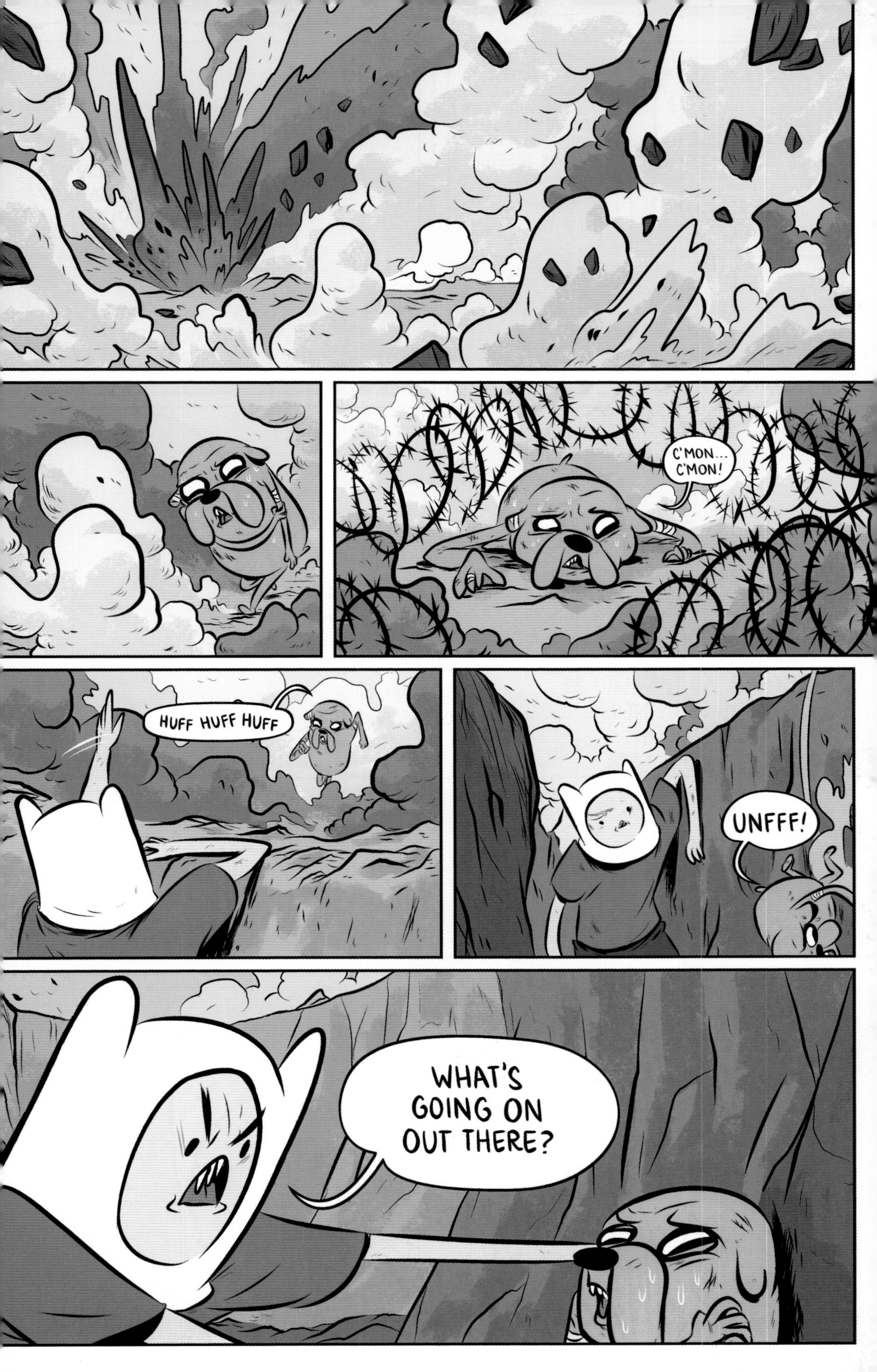
C'MON... C'MON!
HUFF HUFF HUFF
UNFFF!
WHAT'S GOING ON OUT THERE?

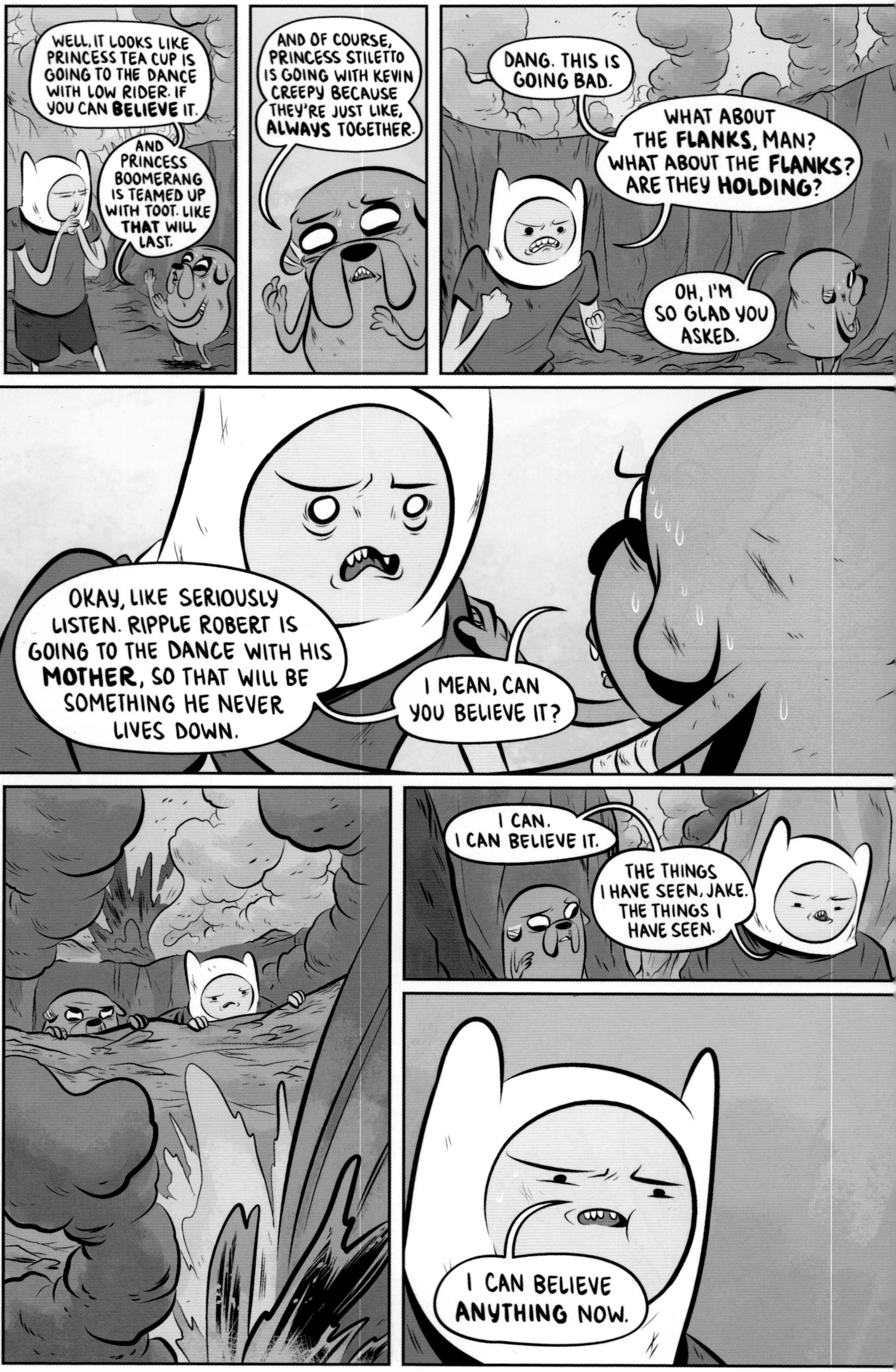
WELL, IT LOOKS LIKE PRINCESS TEA CUP IS GOING TO THE DANCE WITH LOW RIDER. IF YOU CAN BELIEVE IT.
AND PRINCESS BOOMERANG IS TEAMED UP WITH TOOT. LIKE THAT WILL LAST.
AND OF COURSE, PRINCESS STILETTO IS GOING WITH KEVIN CREEPY BECAUSE THEY'RE JUST LIKE, ALWAYS TOGETHER.
DANG. THIS IS GOING BAD.
WHAT ABOUT THE FLANKS, MAN? WHAT ABOUT THE FLANKS? ARE THEY HOLDING?
OH, I'M SO GLAD YOU ASKED.
OKAY, LIKE SERIOUSLY LISTEN. RIPPLE ROBERT IS GOING TO THE DANCE WITH HIS MOTHER, SO THAT WILL BE SOMETHING HE NEVER LIVES DOWN.
I MEAN, CAN YOU BELIEVE IT?
I CAN. I CAN BELIEVE IT.
THE THINGS I HAVE SEEN, JAKE. THE THINGS I HAVE SEEN.
I CAN BELIEVE ANYTHING NOW.

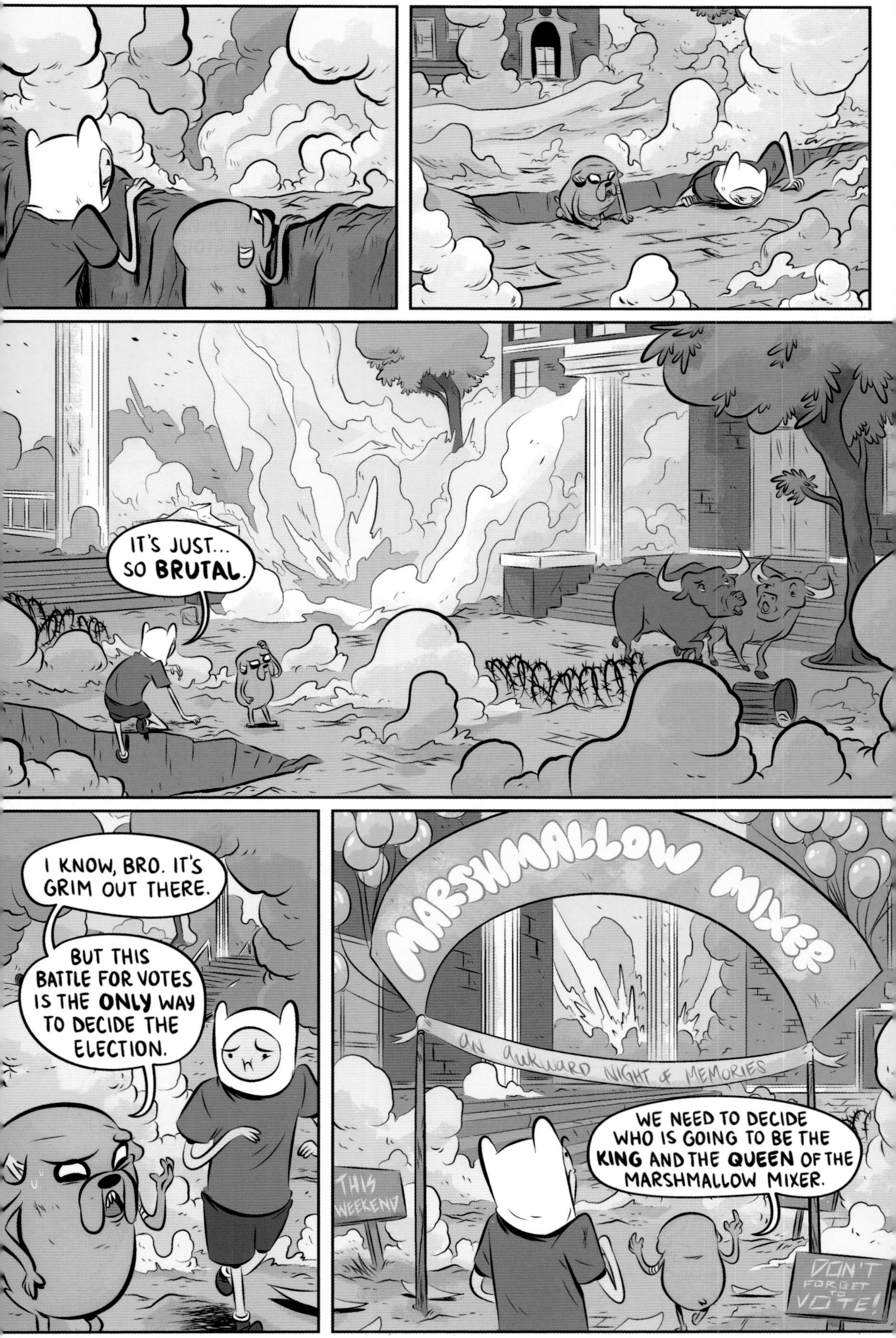

IT'S JUST... SO BRUTAL.
I KNOW, BRO. IT'S GRIM OUT THERE.
BUT THIS BATTLE FOR VOTES IS THE ONLY WAY TO DECIDE THE ELECTION.
MARSHMALLOW MIXER
AN AWKWARD NIGHT OF MEMORIES
THIS WEEKEND
WE NEED TO DECIDE WHO IS GOING TO BE THE KING AND THE QUEEN OF THE MARSHMALLOW MIXER.
DON'T FORGET TO VOTE!

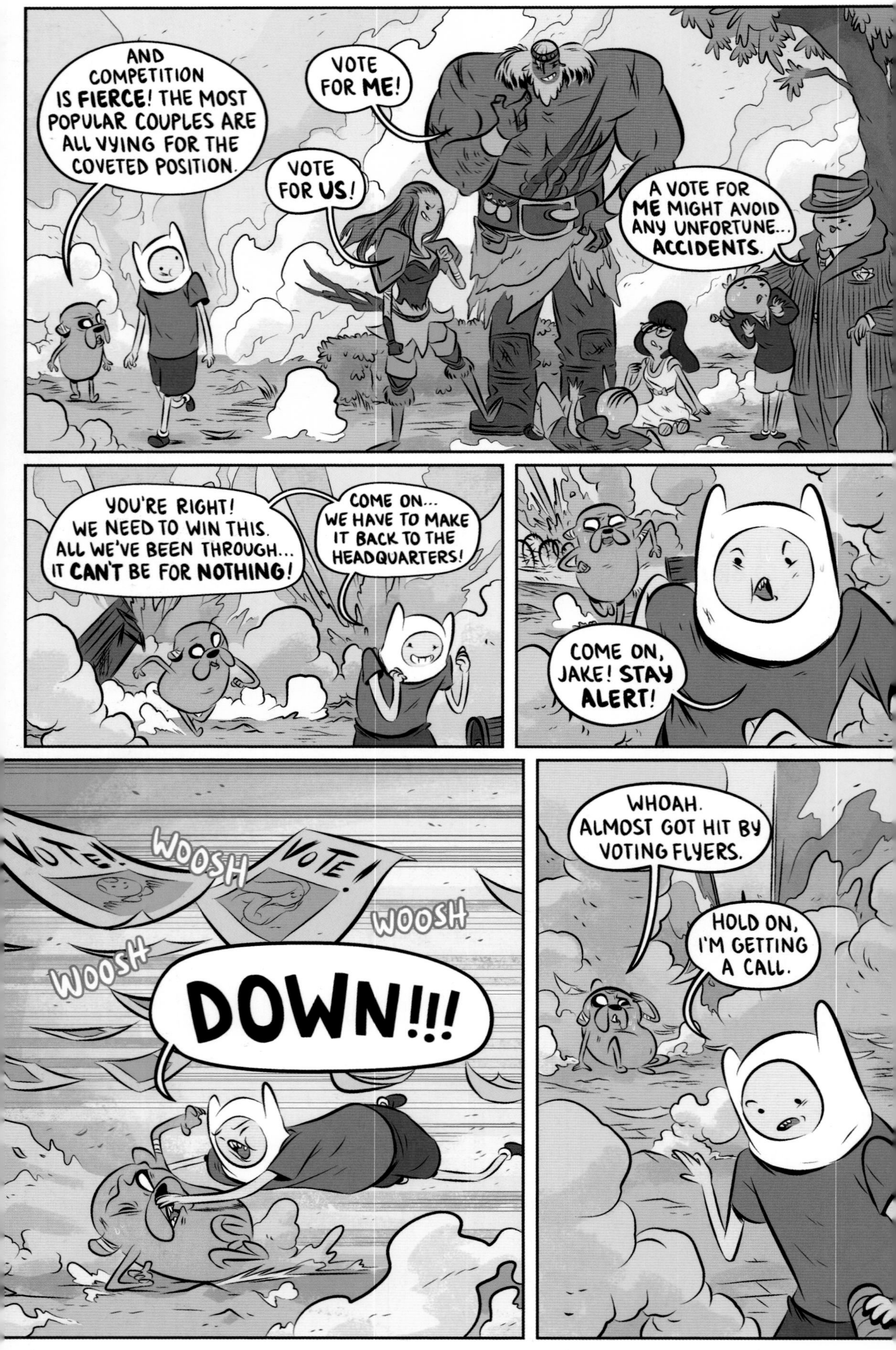

AND COMPETITION IS FIERCE! THE MOST POPULAR COUPLES ARE ALL VYING FOR THE COVETED POSITION.
VOTE FOR ME!
VOTE FOR US!
A VOTE FOR ME MIGHT AVOID ANY UNFORTUNE... ACCIDENTS.
YOU'RE RIGHT! WE NEED TO WIN THIS. ALL WE'VE BEEN THROUGH... IT CAN'T BE FOR NOTHING!
COME ON... WE HAVE TO MAKE IT BACK TO THE HEADQUARTERS!
COME ON, JAKE! STAY ALERT!
VOTE!
WOOSH
VOTE!
WOOSH
WOOSH
DOWN!!!
WHOAH. ALMOST GOT HIT BY VOTING FLYERS.
HOLD ON, I'M GETTING A CALL.

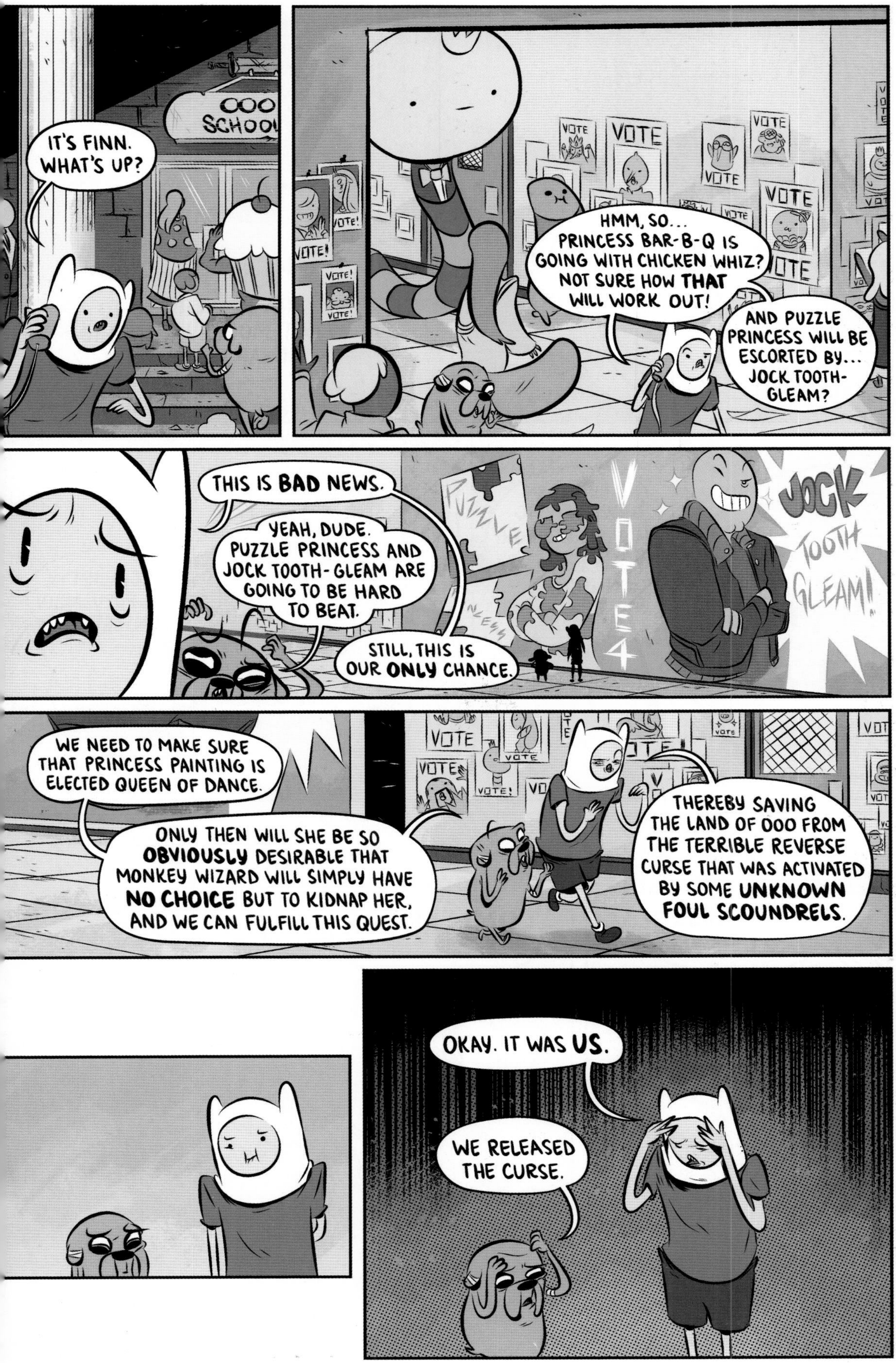
OOO SCHOO
IT'S FINN. WHAT'S UP?
HMM, SO... PRINCESS BAR-B-Q IS GOING WITH CHICKEN WHIZ? NOT SURE HOW **THAT** WILL WORK OUT!
AND PUZZLE PRINCESS WILL BE ESCORTED BY... JOCK TOOTH-GLEAM?
THIS IS **BAD** NEWS.
YEAH, DUDE. PUZZLE PRINCESS AND JOCK TOOTH-GLEAM ARE GOING TO BE HARD TO BEAT.
STILL, THIS IS OUR **ONLY** CHANCE.
PUZZLE
VOTE 4
JOCK TOOTH GLEAM!
WE NEED TO MAKE SURE THAT PRINCESS PAINTING IS ELECTED QUEEN OF DANCE.
ONLY THEN WILL SHE BE SO **OBVIOUSLY** DESIRABLE THAT MONKEY WIZARD WILL SIMPLY HAVE **NO CHOICE** BUT TO KIDNAP HER, AND WE CAN FULFILL THIS QUEST.
THEREBY SAVING THE LAND OF OOO FROM THE TERRIBLE REVERSE CURSE THAT WAS ACTIVATED BY SOME **UNKNOWN FOUL SCOUNDRELS**.
OKAY. IT WAS **US**.
WE RELEASED THE CURSE.

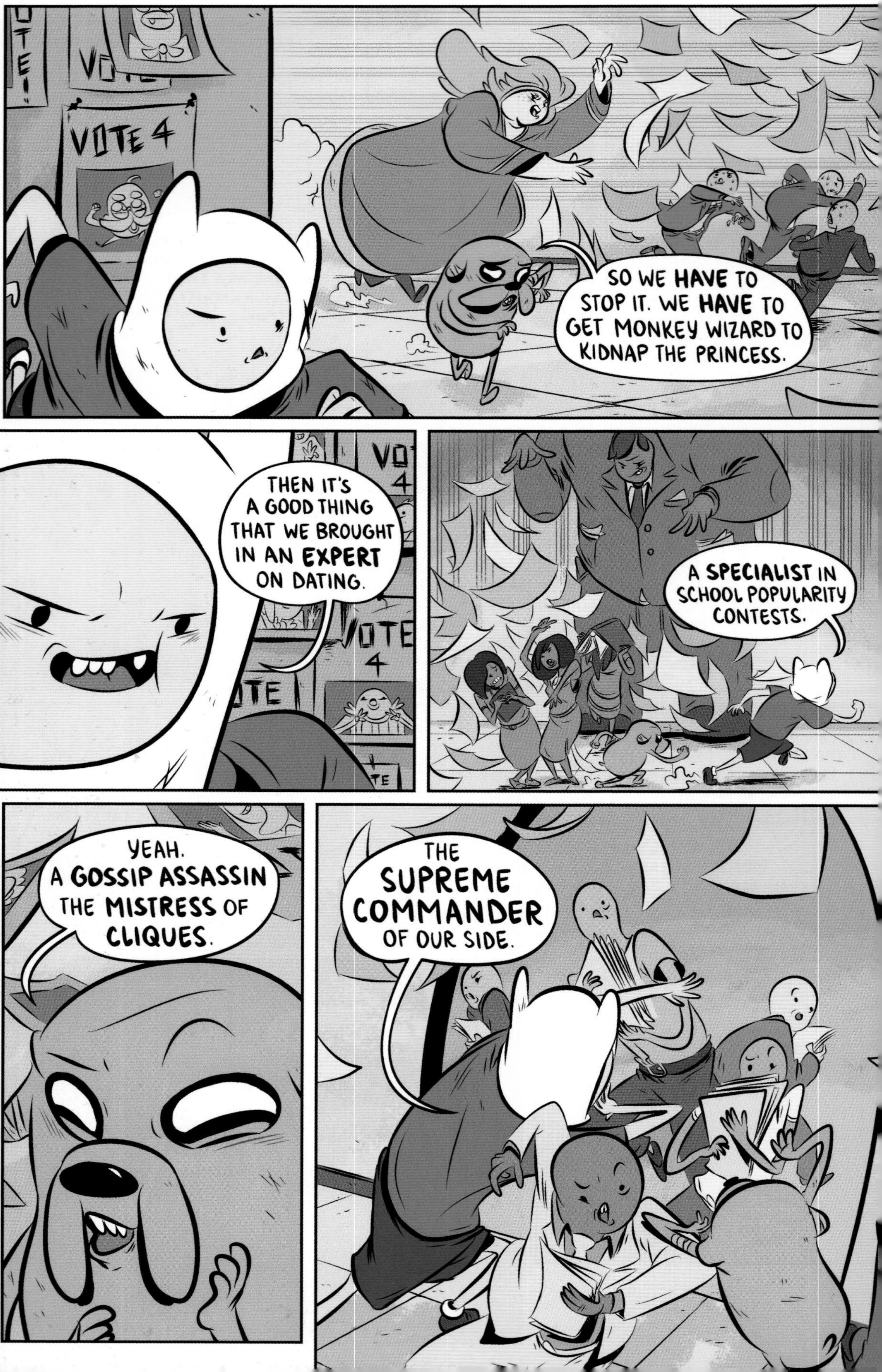
VOTE!!
VOTE
VOTE 4
SO WE HAVE TO STOP IT. WE HAVE TO GET MONKEY WIZARD TO KIDNAP THE PRINCESS.
VOTE 4
THEN IT'S A GOOD THING THAT WE BROUGHT IN AN EXPERT ON DATING.
VOTE 4
A SPECIALIST IN SCHOOL POPULARITY CONTESTS.
YEAH. A GOSSIP ASSASSIN THE MISTRESS OF CLIQUES.
THE SUPREME COMMANDER OF OUR SIDE.

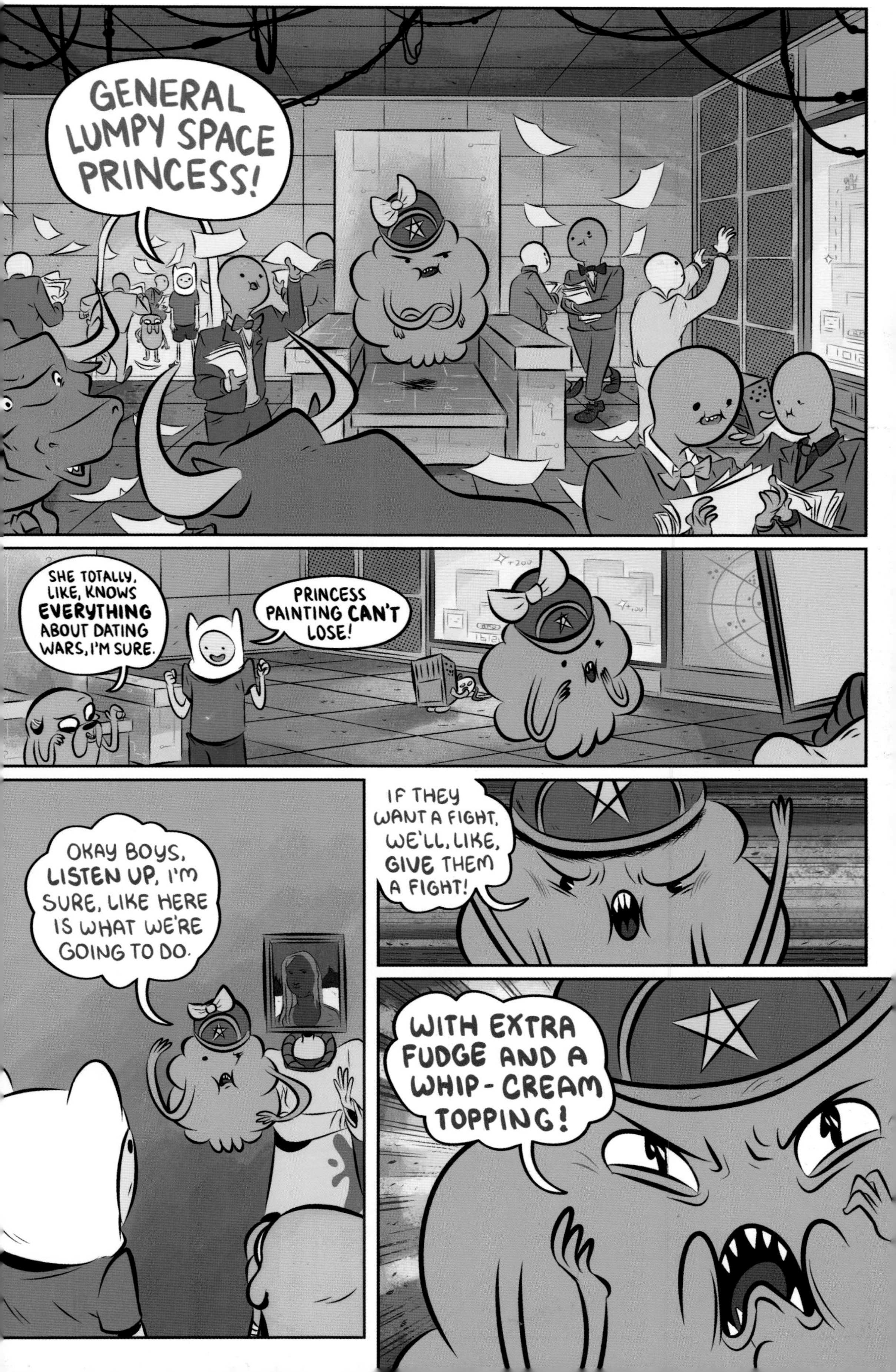
GENERAL LUMPY SPACE PRINCESS!
SHE TOTALLY, LIKE, KNOWS EVERYTHING ABOUT DATING WARS, I'M SURE.
PRINCESS PAINTING CAN'T LOSE!
OKAY BOYS, LISTEN UP, I'M SURE, LIKE HERE IS WHAT WE'RE GOING TO DO.
IF THEY WANT A FIGHT, WE'LL, LIKE, GIVE THEM A FIGHT!
WITH EXTRA FUDGE AND A WHIP-CREAM TOPPING!

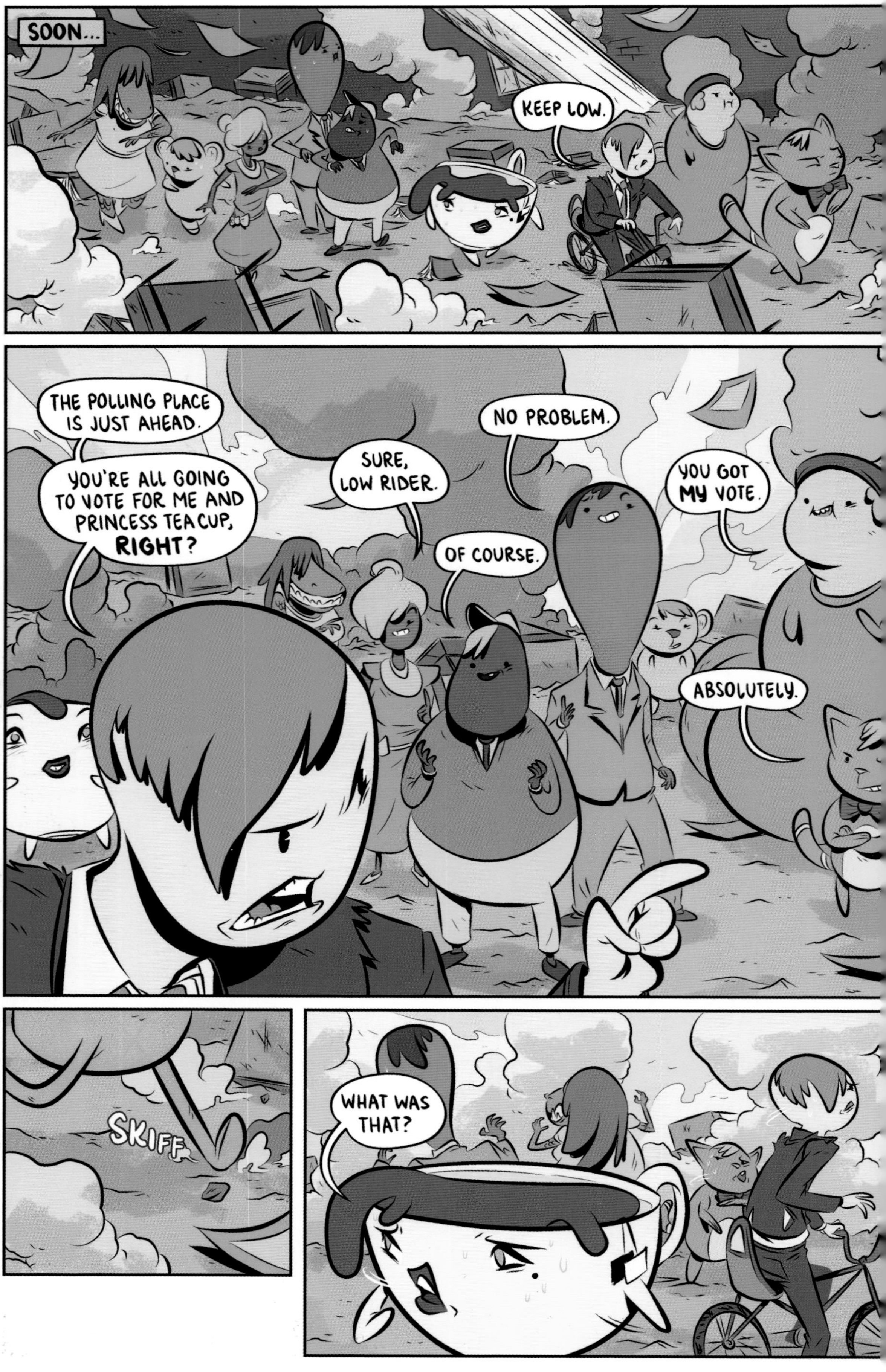
SOON...
KEEP LOW.
THE POLLING PLACE IS JUST AHEAD.
YOU'RE ALL GOING TO VOTE FOR ME AND PRINCESS TEA CUP, RIGHT?
SURE, LOW RIDER.
NO PROBLEM.
OF COURSE.
YOU GOT MY VOTE.
ABSOLUTELY.
SKIFF
WHAT WAS THAT?

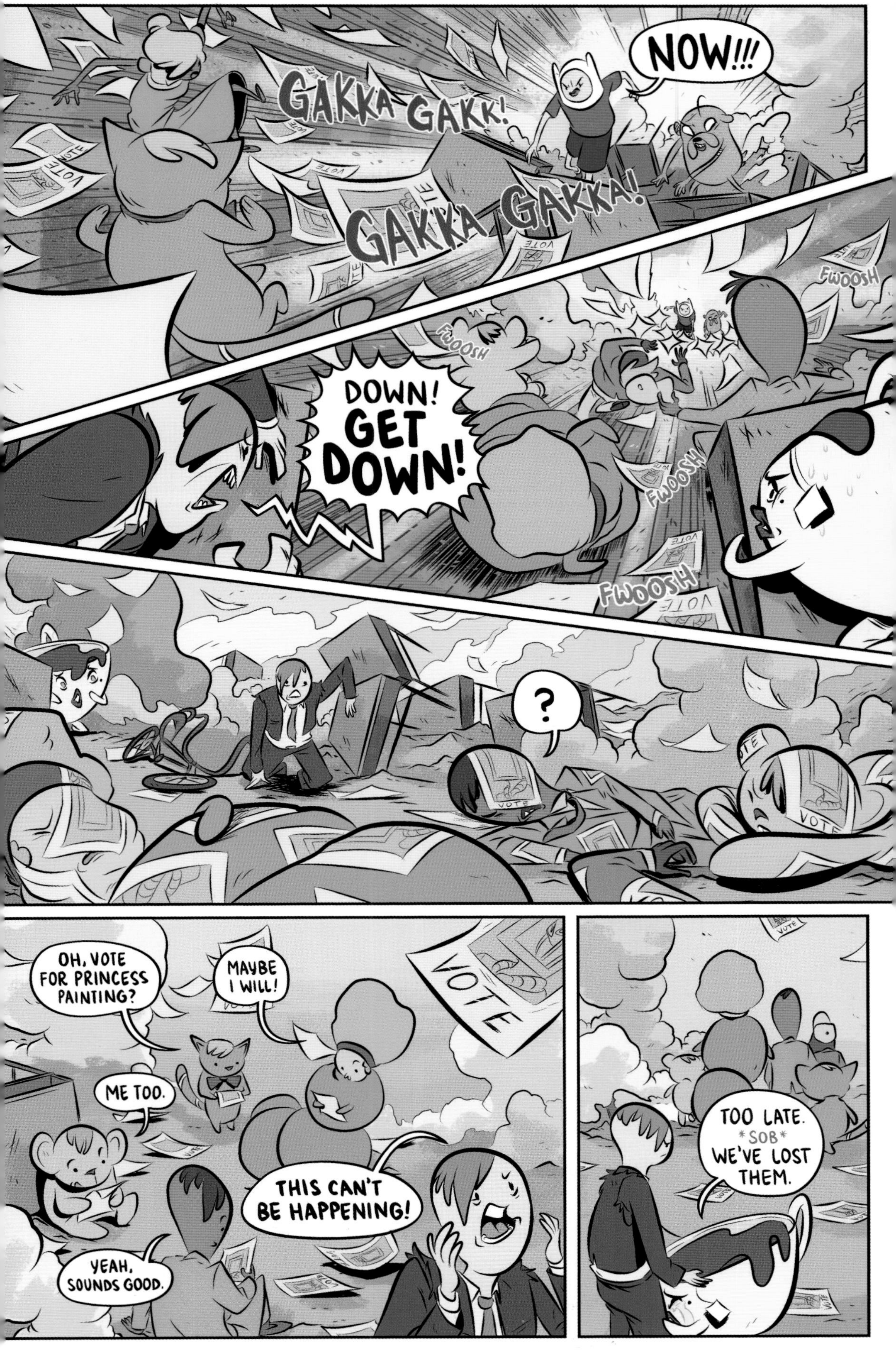
GAKKA GAKK!
NOW!!!
GAKKA GAKKA!
FWOOSH
FWOOSH
DOWN! GET DOWN!
FWOOSH
FWOOSH
?
OH, VOTE FOR PRINCESS PAINTING?
MAYBE I WILL!
ME TOO.
THIS CAN'T BE HAPPENING!
YEAH, SOUNDS GOOD.
TOO LATE. *SOB* WE'VE LOST THEM.

RING
RING
RING

SOUNDS LIKE GENERAL LUMPY SPACE PRINCESS IS CALLING.

HELLO?

FINN! THERE'S LIKE, TOTALLY TWO CANDIDATES TRAVELING SECTOR SEVEN, LIKE FOR SURE OH MY GLOB!

"GOT IT, GENERAL LUMPY SPACE PRINCESS. JAKE AND I ARE **ON** IT. THEY WON'T KNOW WHAT HIT THEM."

KEEP YOUR HEADS DOWN. THE GYM IS DANGEROUS.

SO DANGEROUS THAT THEY **HOPEFULLY** WON'T EXPECT US TO BE CROSSING HERE.

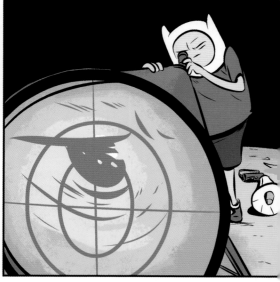

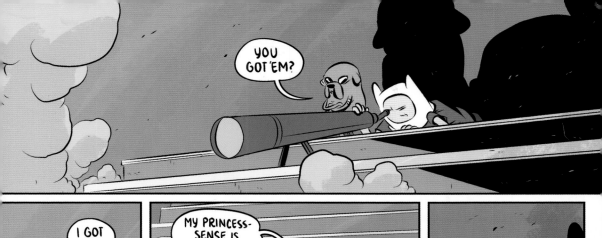

YOU GOT 'EM?

I GOT 'EM.

MY PRINCESS-SENSE IS SPARKLING!

SOMETHING IS WRONG!

NOW!

OH NO, GOSSIP!!

HEY! PUZZLE PRINCESS IS MISSING PIECES!

WHAT? I DO NOT! THAT'S A LIE!

AND JOCK TOOTH-GLEAM HAS FALSE TEETH!

HMMM. MAYBE I'LL VOTE FOR PRINCESS PAINTING.

GAHH! THEY GOT US!

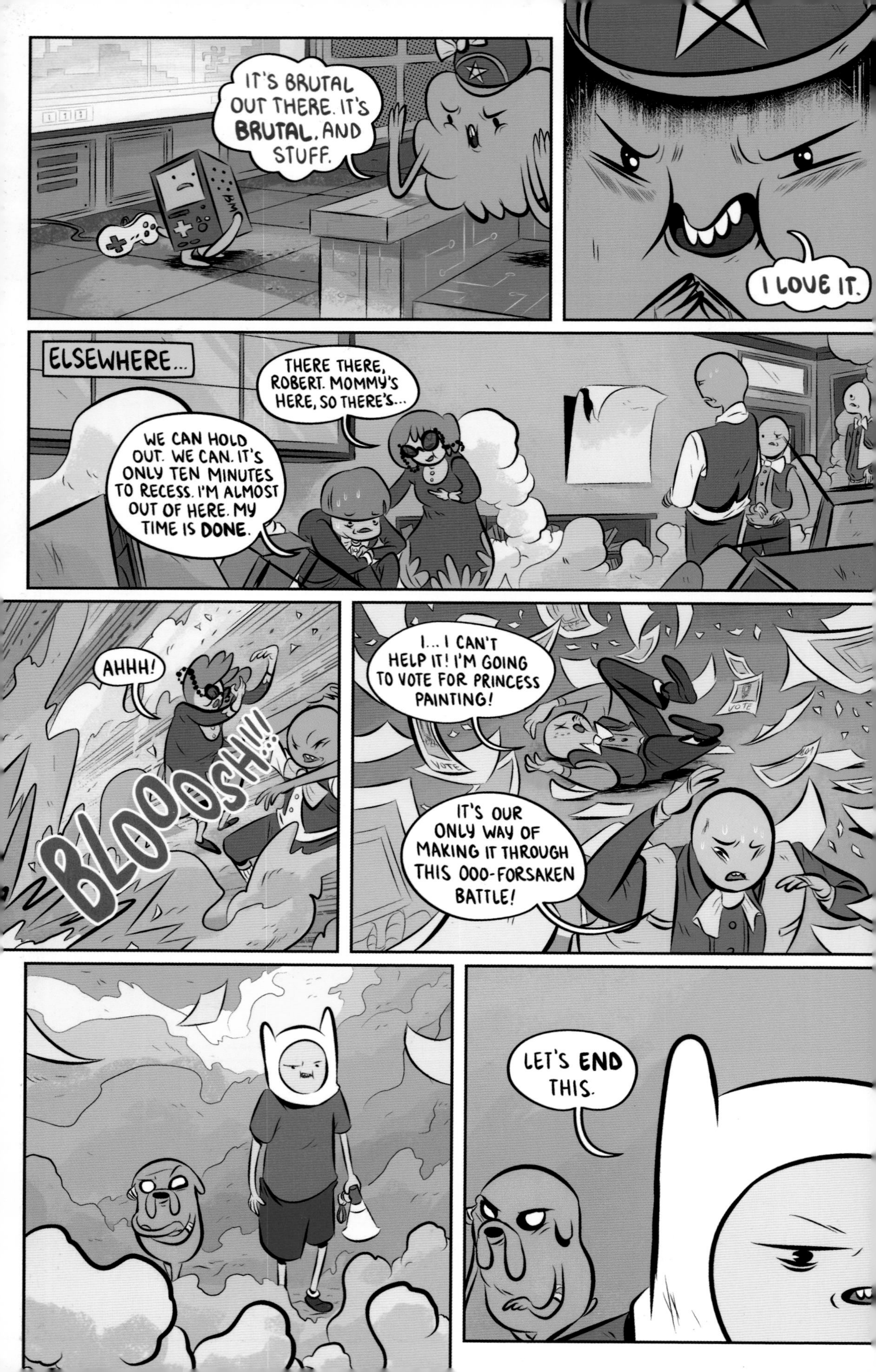
IT'S BRUTAL OUT THERE. IT'S BRUTAL. AND STUFF.
I LOVE IT.
ELSEWHERE...
THERE THERE, ROBERT. MOMMY'S HERE, SO THERE'S...
WE CAN HOLD OUT. WE CAN. IT'S ONLY TEN MINUTES TO RECESS. I'M ALMOST OUT OF HERE. MY TIME IS DONE.
AHHH!
BLOOOSH!!!
I... I CAN'T HELP IT! I'M GOING TO VOTE FOR PRINCESS PAINTING!
IT'S OUR ONLY WAY OF MAKING IT THROUGH THIS OOO-FORSAKEN BATTLE!
LET'S END THIS.

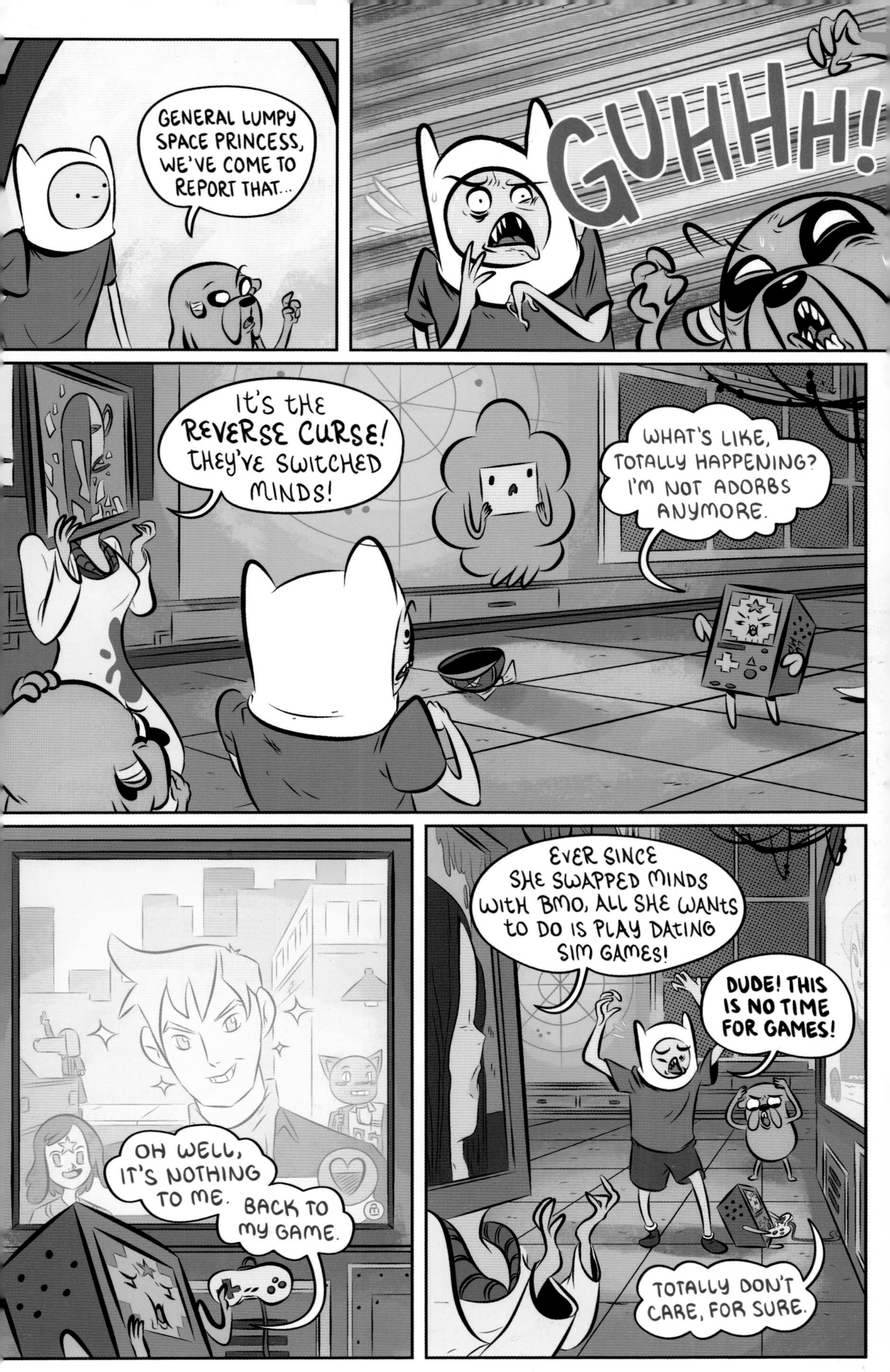
GENERAL LUMPY SPACE PRINCESS, WE'VE COME TO REPORT THAT...
GUHHH!
IT'S THE REVERSE CURSE! THEY'VE SWITCHED MINDS!
WHAT'S LIKE, TOTALLY HAPPENING? I'M NOT ADORBS ANYMORE.
OH WELL, IT'S NOTHING TO ME.
BACK TO MY GAME.
EVER SINCE SHE SWAPPED MINDS WITH BMO, ALL SHE WANTS TO DO IS PLAY DATING SIM GAMES!
DUDE! THIS IS NO TIME FOR GAMES!
TOTALLY DON'T CARE, FOR SURE.

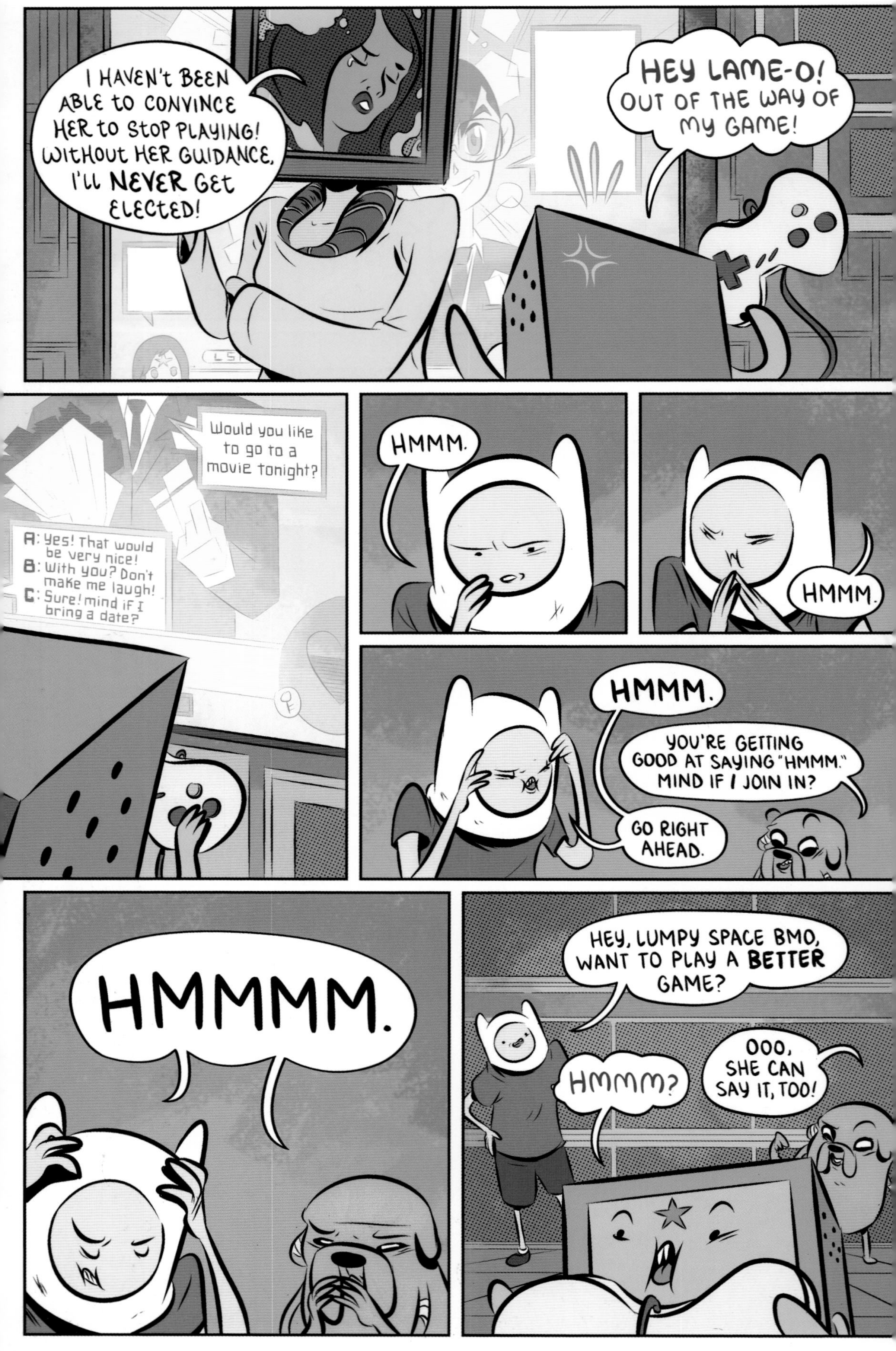
I HAVEN'T BEEN ABLE TO CONVINCE HER TO STOP PLAYING! WITHOUT HER GUIDANCE, I'LL NEVER GET ELECTED!
HEY LAME-O! OUT OF THE WAY OF MY GAME!
Would you like to go to a movie tonight?
A: Yes! That would be very nice!
B: With you? Don't make me laugh!
C: Sure! mind if I bring a date?
HMMM.
HMMM.
HMMM.
YOU'RE GETTING GOOD AT SAYING "HMMM." MIND IF I JOIN IN?
GO RIGHT AHEAD.
HMMMM.
HEY, LUMPY SPACE BMO, WANT TO PLAY A BETTER GAME?
HMMM?
OOO, SHE CAN SAY IT, TOO!

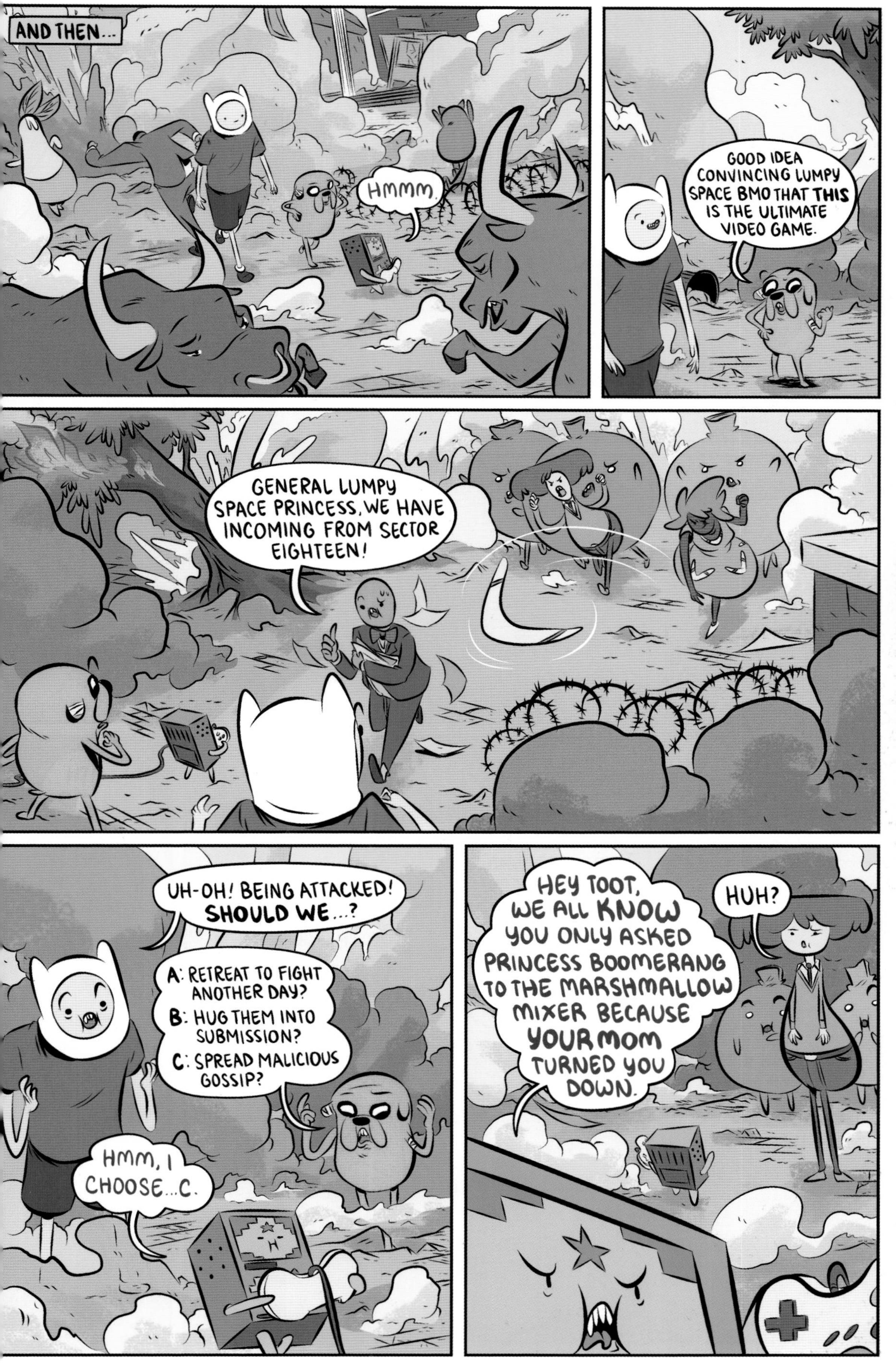
AND THEN...
HMMM.
GOOD IDEA CONVINCING LUMPY SPACE BMO THAT THIS IS THE ULTIMATE VIDEO GAME.
GENERAL LUMPY SPACE PRINCESS, WE HAVE INCOMING FROM SECTOR EIGHTEEN!
UH-OH! BEING ATTACKED! SHOULD WE...?
A: RETREAT TO FIGHT ANOTHER DAY?
B: HUG THEM INTO SUBMISSION?
C: SPREAD MALICIOUS GOSSIP?
HMM, I CHOOSE...C.
HEY TOOT, WE ALL KNOW YOU ONLY ASKED PRINCESS BOOMERANG TO THE MARSHMALLOW MIXER BECAUSE YOUR MOM TURNED YOU DOWN.
HUH?

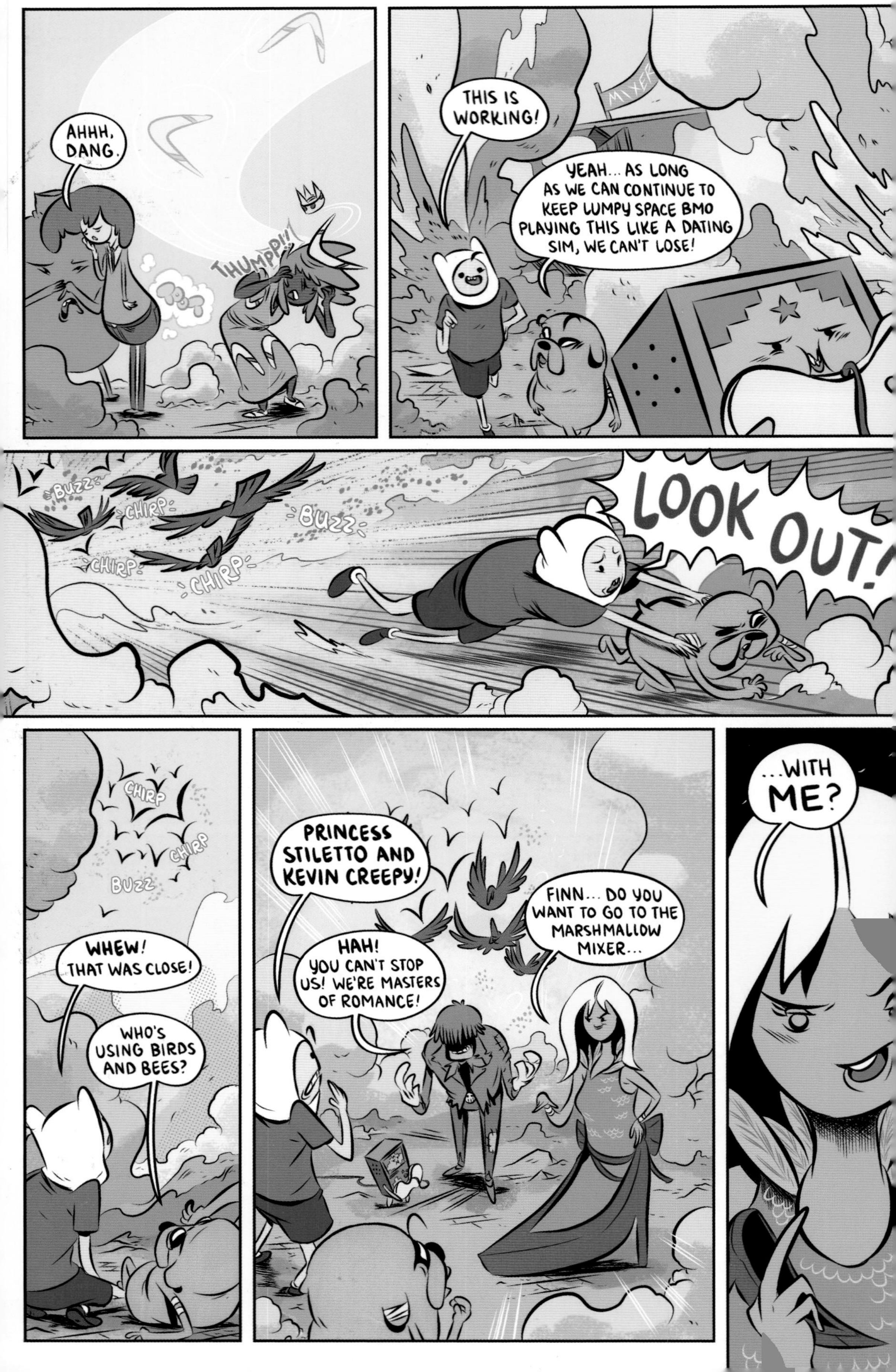
AHHH, DANG.
THUMPP!!
THIS IS WORKING!
MIXER
YEAH... AS LONG AS WE CAN CONTINUE TO KEEP LUMPY SPACE BMO PLAYING THIS LIKE A DATING SIM, WE CAN'T LOSE!
BUZZ
CHIRP
BUZZ
CHIRP
CHIRP
LOOK OUT!
CHIRP
CHIRP
BUZZ
WHEW! THAT WAS CLOSE!
WHO'S USING BIRDS AND BEES?
PRINCESS STILETTO AND KEVIN CREEPY!
HAH! YOU CAN'T STOP US! WE'RE MASTERS OF ROMANCE!
FINN... DO YOU WANT TO GO TO THE MARSHMALLOW MIXER...
...WITH ME?

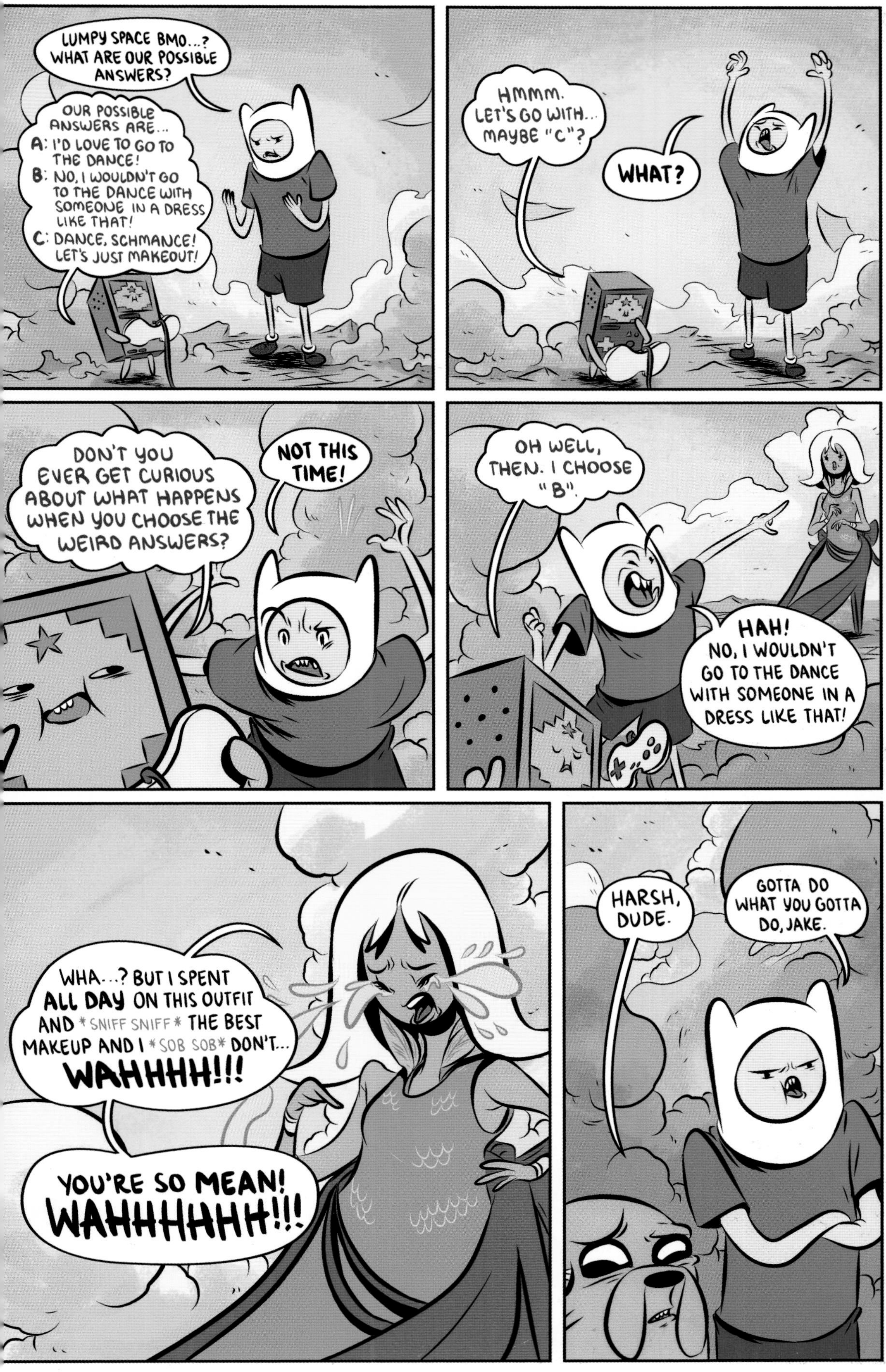
LUMPY SPACE BMO...? WHAT ARE OUR POSSIBLE ANSWERS?
OUR POSSIBLE ANSWERS ARE...
A: I'D LOVE TO GO TO THE DANCE!
B: NO, I WOULDN'T GO TO THE DANCE WITH SOMEONE IN A DRESS LIKE THAT!
C: DANCE, SCHMANCE! LET'S JUST MAKEOUT!
HMMM. LET'S GO WITH... MAYBE "C"?
WHAT?
DON'T YOU EVER GET CURIOUS ABOUT WHAT HAPPENS WHEN YOU CHOOSE THE WEIRD ANSWERS?
NOT THIS TIME!
OH WELL, THEN. I CHOOSE "B".
HAH! NO, I WOULDN'T GO TO THE DANCE WITH SOMEONE IN A DRESS LIKE THAT!
WHA...? BUT I SPENT ALL DAY ON THIS OUTFIT AND *SNIFF SNIFF* THE BEST MAKEUP AND I *SOB SOB* DON'T... WAHHHH!!!
YOU'RE SO MEAN! WAHHHHHH!!!
HARSH, DUDE.
GOTTA DO WHAT YOU GOTTA DO, JAKE.

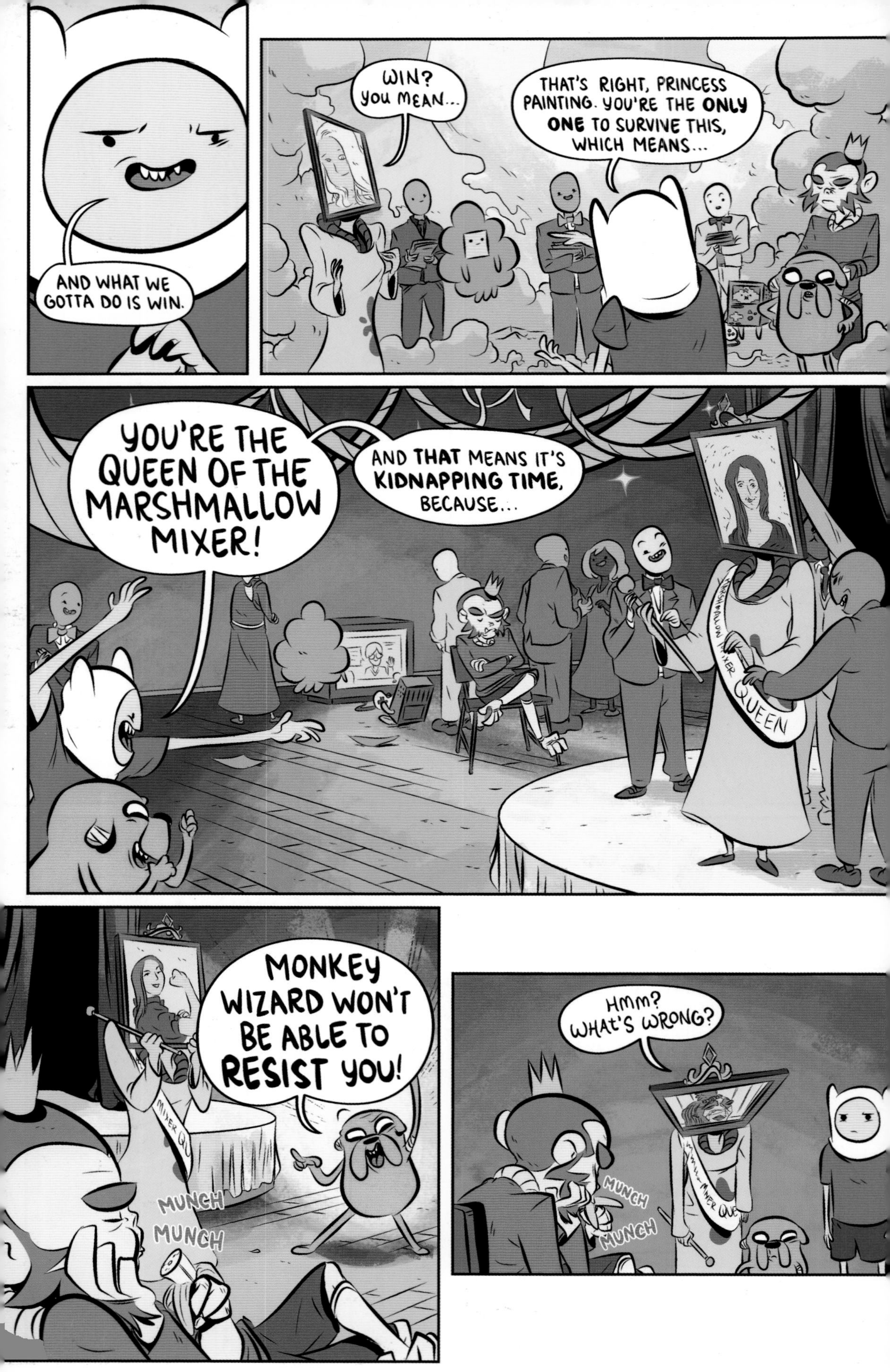

AND WHAT WE GOTTA DO IS WIN.
WIN? YOU MEAN...
THAT'S RIGHT, PRINCESS PAINTING. YOU'RE THE **ONLY ONE** TO SURVIVE THIS, WHICH MEANS...
YOU'RE THE QUEEN OF THE MARSHMALLOW MIXER!
AND **THAT** MEANS IT'S **KIDNAPPING TIME,** BECAUSE...
MARSHMALLOW MIXER QUEEN
MONKEY WIZARD WON'T BE ABLE TO **RESIST** YOU!
MUNCH
MUNCH
HMM? WHAT'S WRONG?
MUNCH
MUNCH

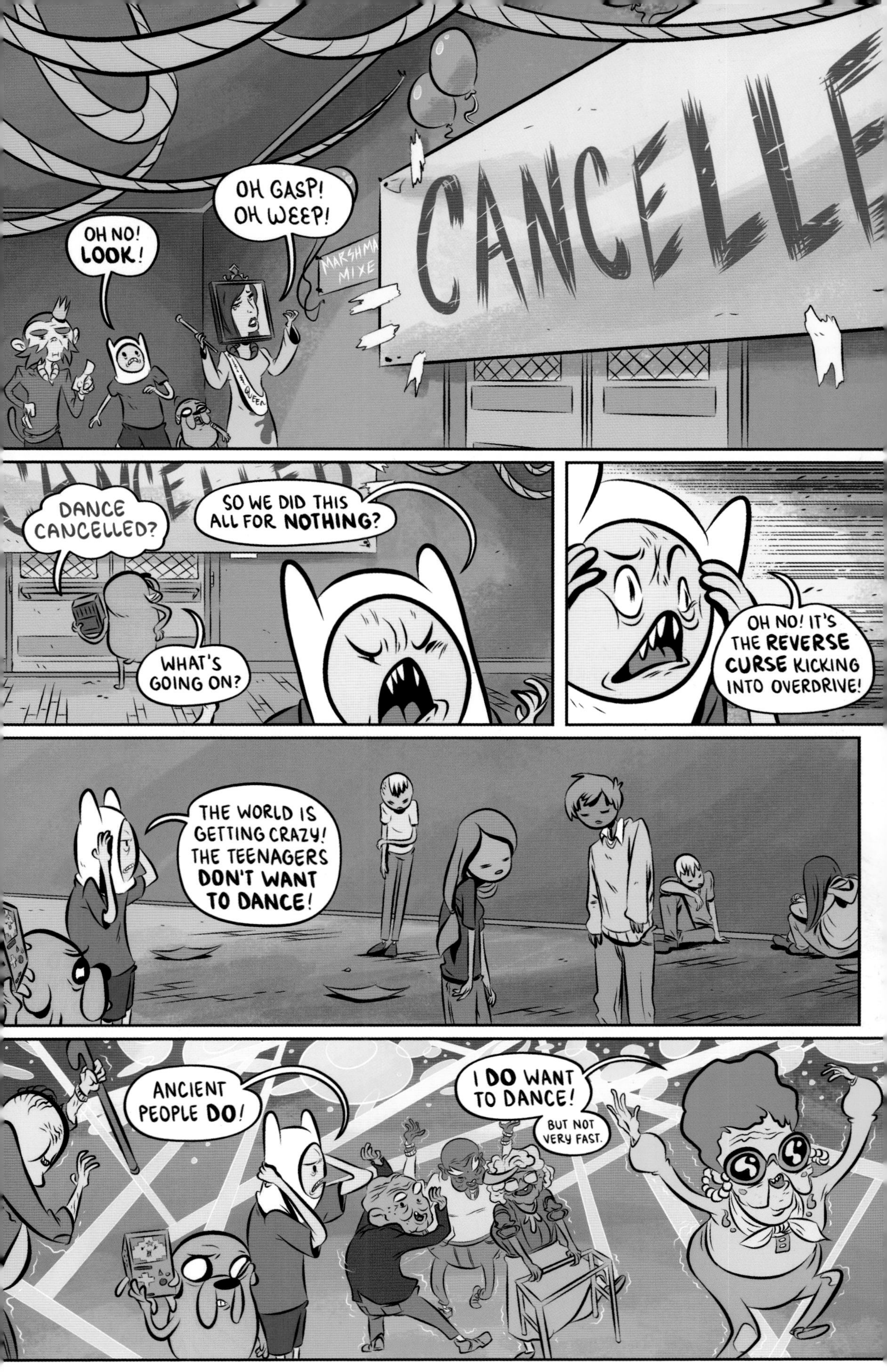
CANCELLE
MARSHMA
MIXE
OH NO! LOOK!
OH GASP! OH WEEP!
QUEEN
DANCE CANCELLED?
SO WE DID THIS ALL FOR NOTHING?
WHAT'S GOING ON?
OH NO! IT'S THE REVERSE CURSE KICKING INTO OVERDRIVE!
THE WORLD IS GETTING CRAZY! THE TEENAGERS DON'T WANT TO DANCE!
ANCIENT PEOPLE DO!
I DO WANT TO DANCE!
BUT NOT VERY FAST.

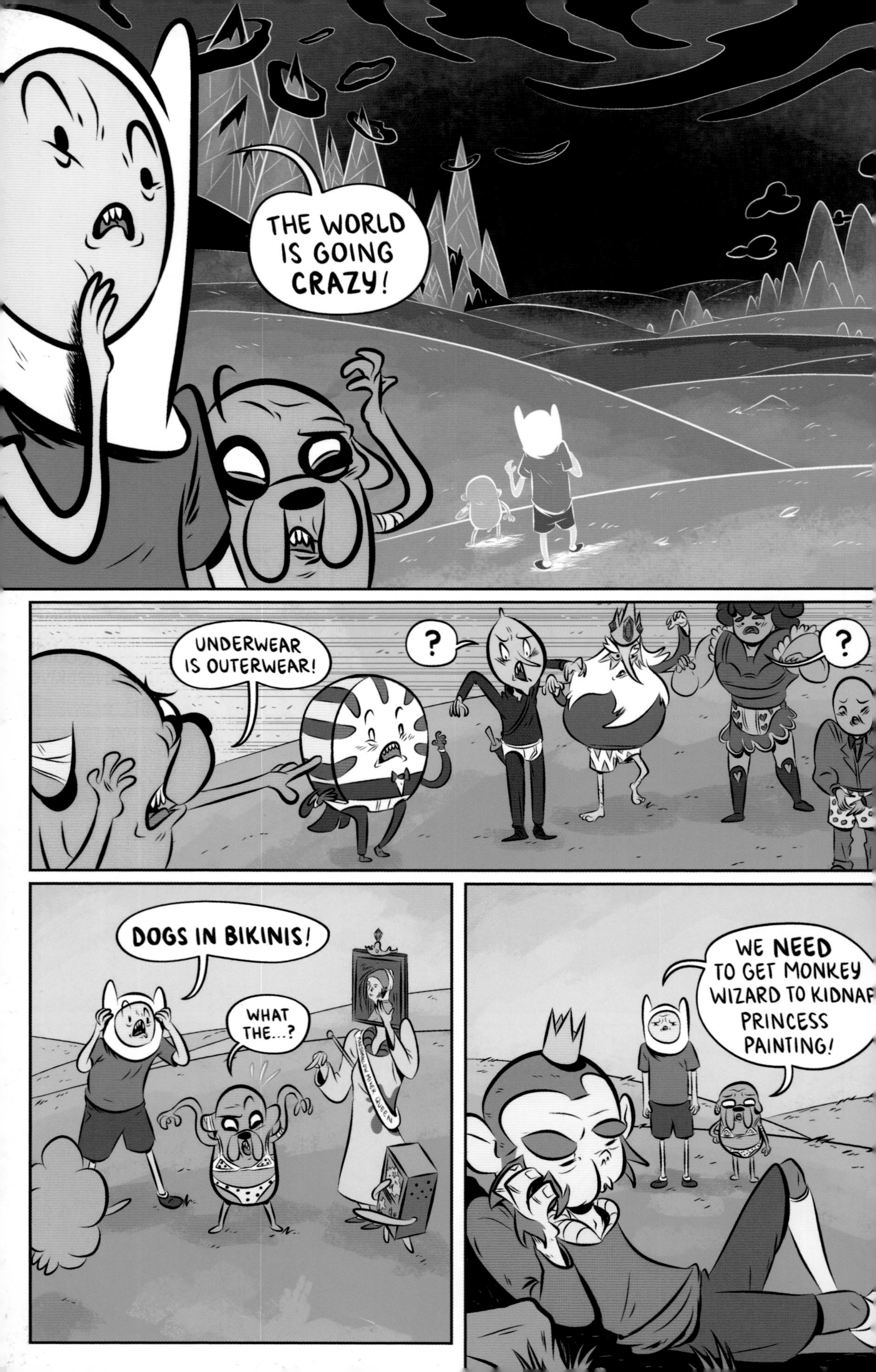
THE WORLD IS GOING CRAZY!
UNDERWEAR IS OUTERWEAR!
?
?
DOGS IN BIKINIS!
WHAT THE...?
MARSHMALLOW MINER QUEEN
WE NEED TO GET MONKEY WIZARD TO KIDNAP PRINCESS PAINTING!

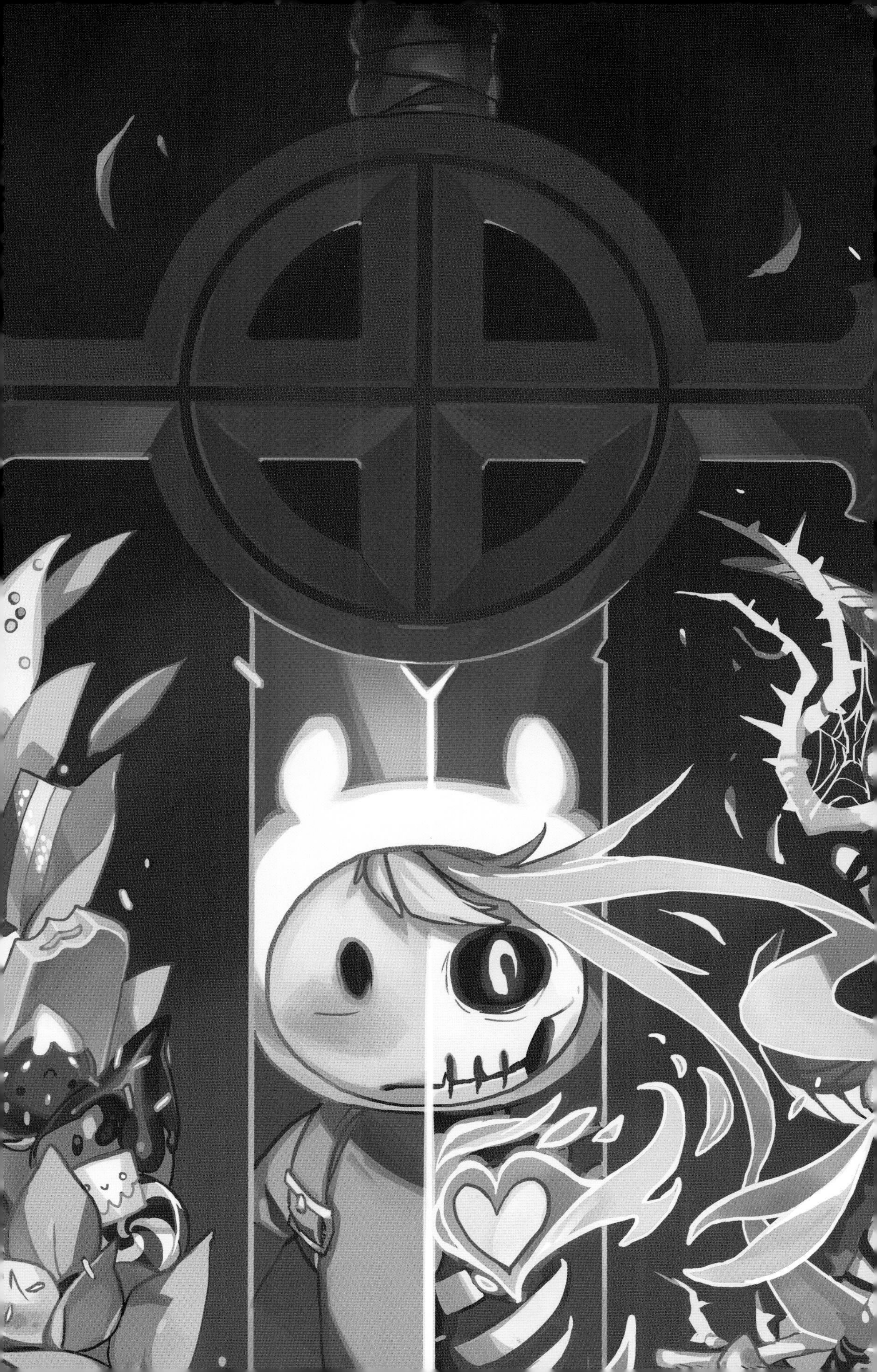

CHAPTER FIVE

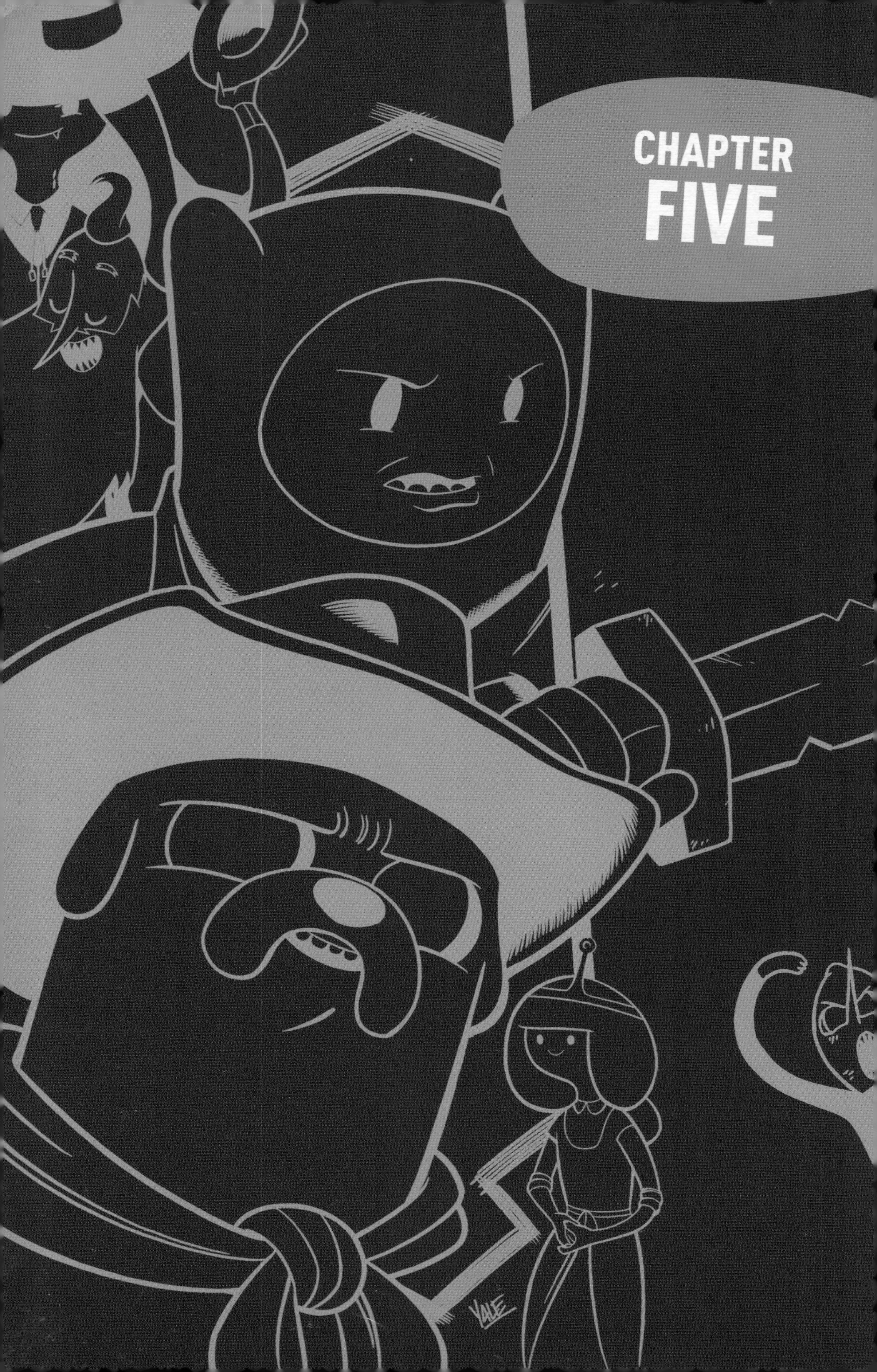

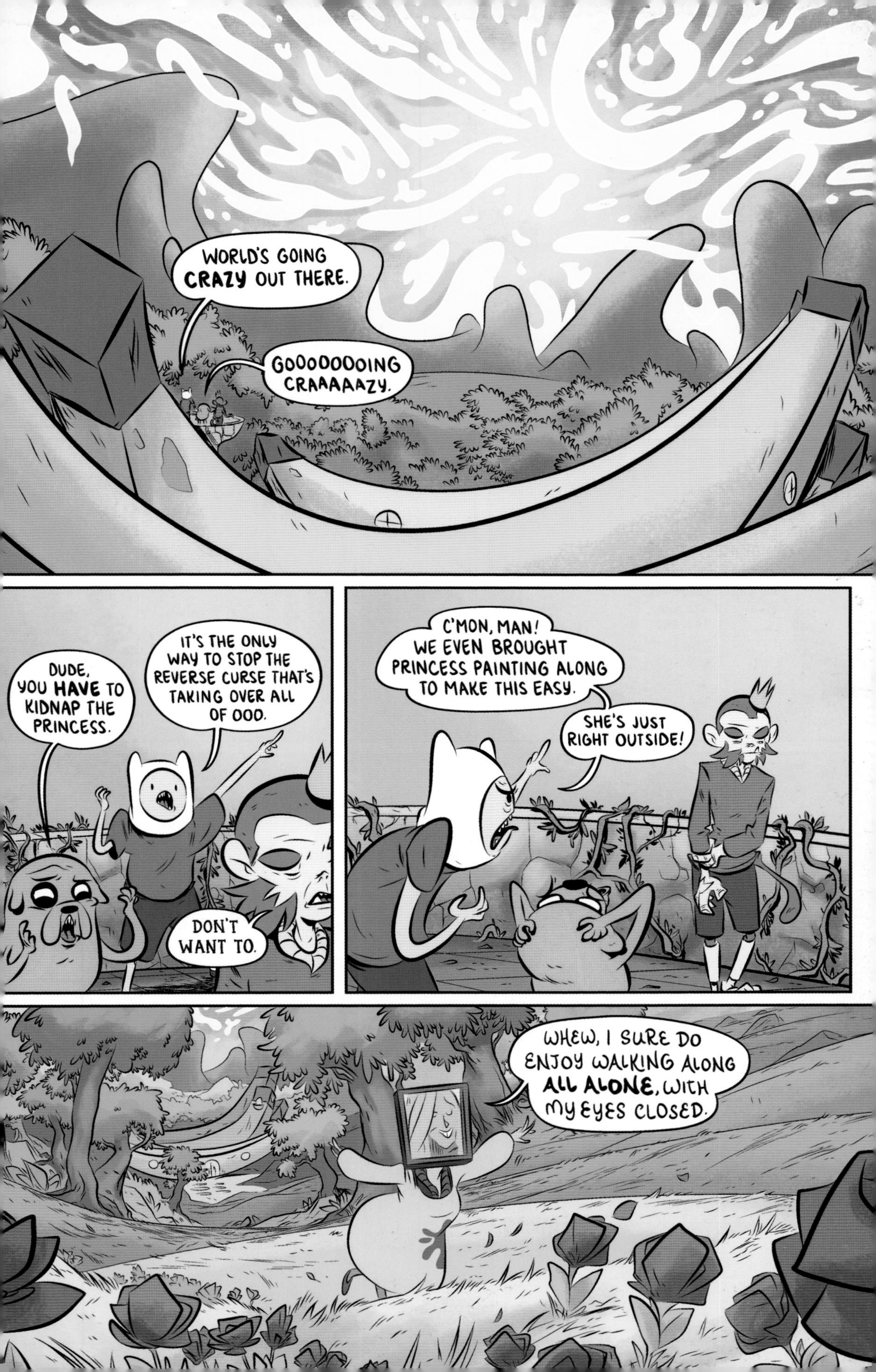
WORLD'S GOING CRAZY OUT THERE.
GOOOOOOOING CRAAAAAZY.
DUDE, YOU HAVE TO KIDNAP THE PRINCESS.
IT'S THE ONLY WAY TO STOP THE REVERSE CURSE THAT'S TAKING OVER ALL OF OOO.
DON'T WANT TO.
C'MON, MAN! WE EVEN BROUGHT PRINCESS PAINTING ALONG TO MAKE THIS EASY.
SHE'S JUST RIGHT OUTSIDE!
WHEW, I SURE DO ENJOY WALKING ALONG ALL ALONE, WITH MY EYES CLOSED.

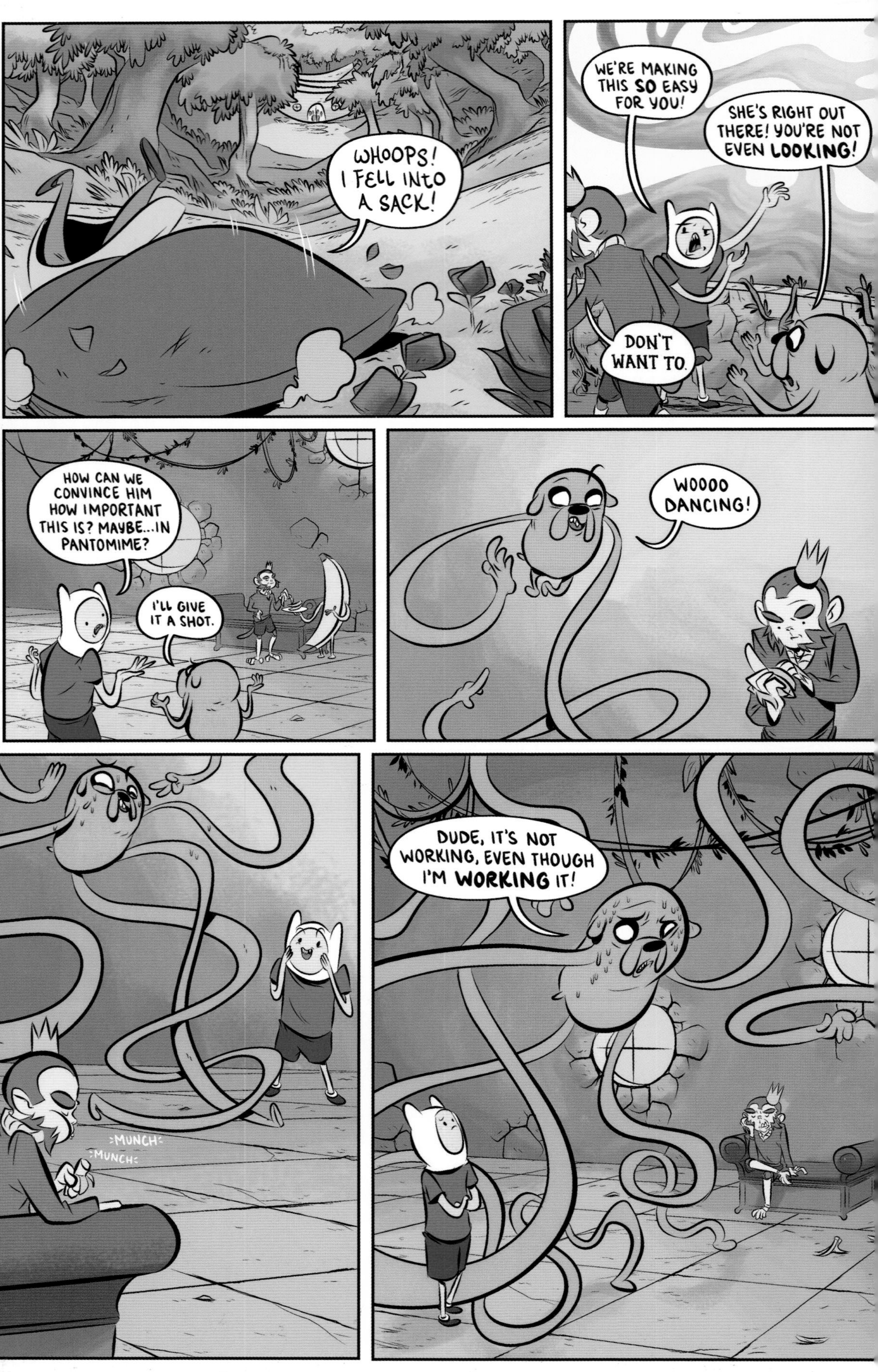
WHOOPS! I FELL INTO A SACK!
WE'RE MAKING THIS SO EASY FOR YOU!
SHE'S RIGHT OUT THERE! YOU'RE NOT EVEN LOOKING!
DON'T WANT TO.
HOW CAN WE CONVINCE HIM HOW IMPORTANT THIS IS? MAYBE...IN PANTOMIME?
I'LL GIVE IT A SHOT.
WOOOO DANCING!
MUNCH
MUNCH
DUDE, IT'S NOT WORKING, EVEN THOUGH I'M WORKING IT!

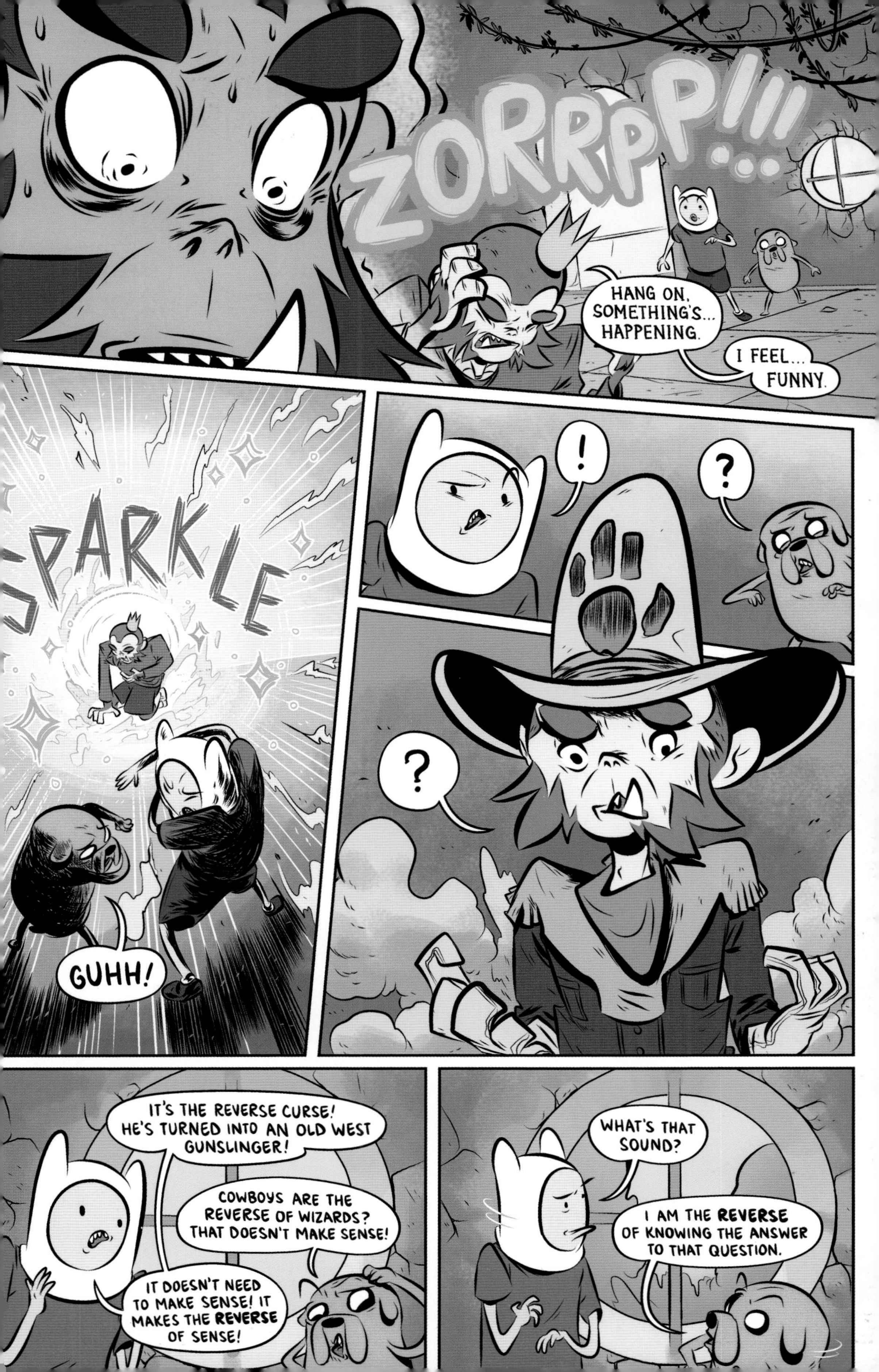
ZORRPP!!!...
HANG ON, SOMETHING'S... HAPPENING.
I FEEL... FUNNY.
SPARKLE
GUHH!
!
?
?
IT'S THE REVERSE CURSE! HE'S TURNED INTO AN OLD WEST GUNSLINGER!
COWBOYS ARE THE REVERSE OF WIZARDS? THAT DOESN'T MAKE SENSE!
IT DOESN'T NEED TO MAKE SENSE! IT MAKES THE REVERSE OF SENSE!
WHAT'S THAT SOUND?
I AM THE REVERSE OF KNOWING THE ANSWER TO THAT QUESTION.

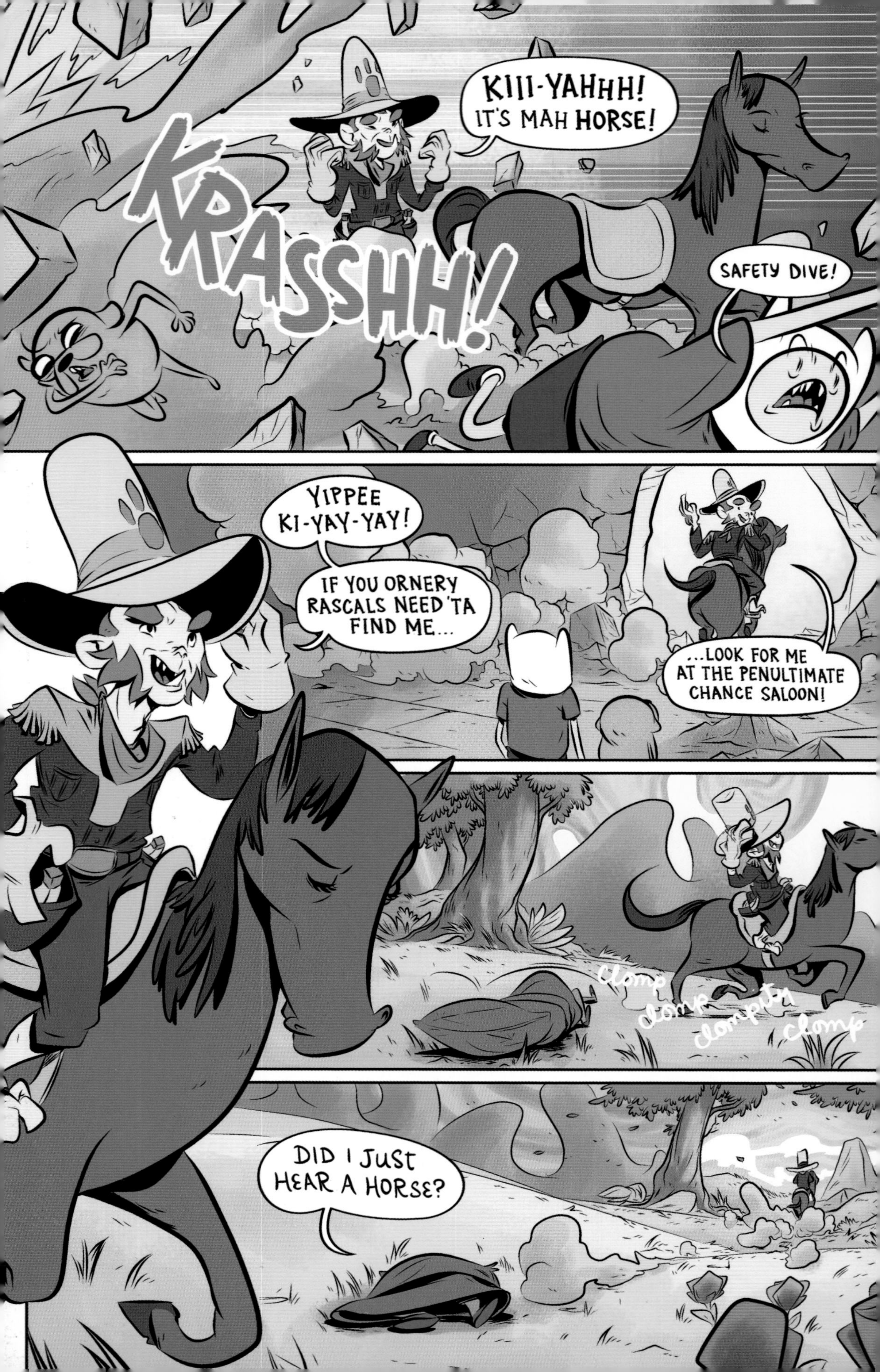
KRASSHH!
KIII-YAHHH! IT'S MAH HORSE!
SAFETY DIVE!
YIPPEE KI-YAY-YAY!
IF YOU ORNERY RASCALS NEED 'TA FIND ME...
...LOOK FOR ME AT THE PENULTIMATE CHANCE SALOON!
clomp clomp clompity clomp
DID I JUST HEAR A HORSE?

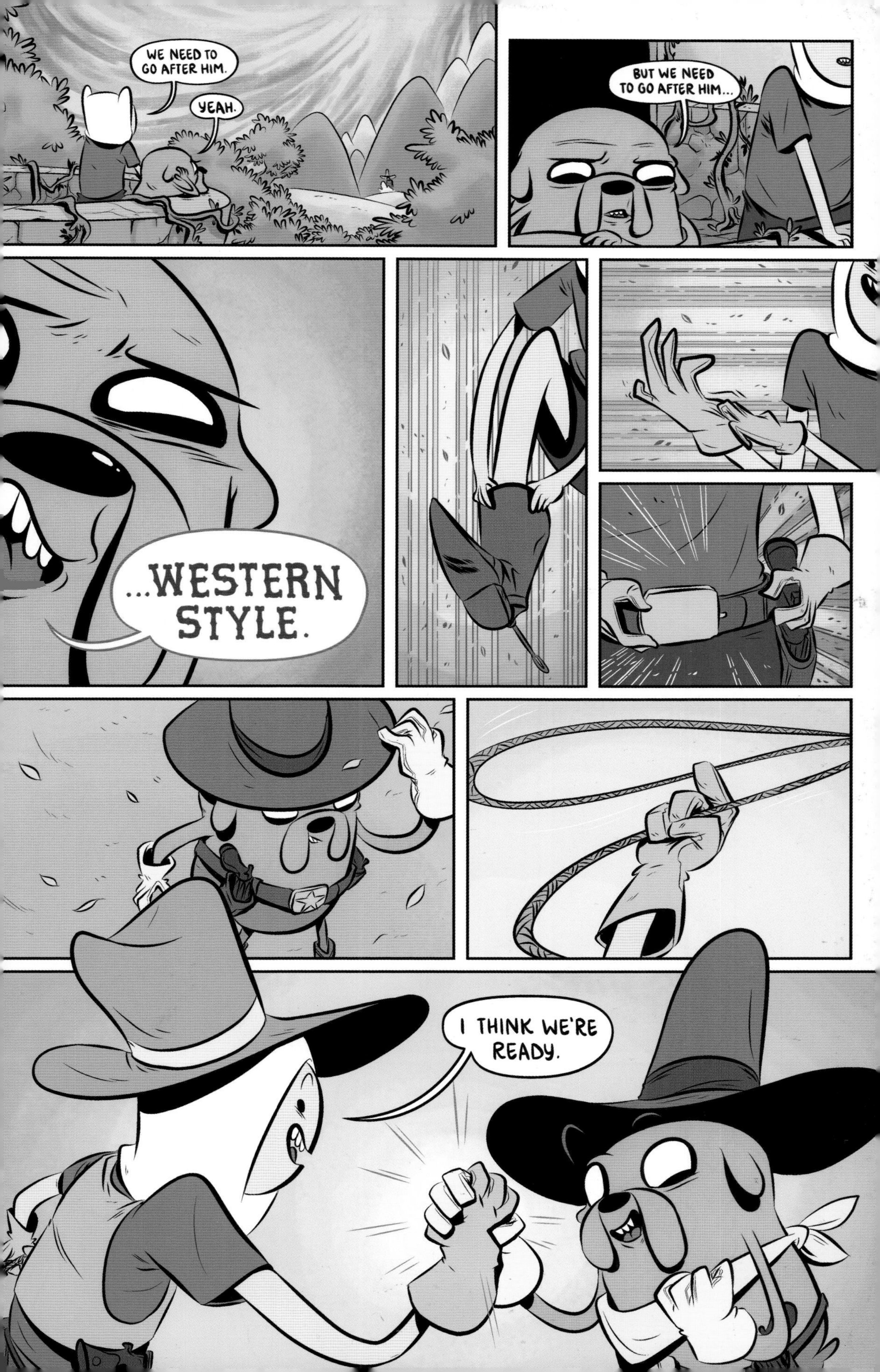
WE NEED TO GO AFTER HIM.
YEAH.
BUT WE NEED TO GO AFTER HIM...
...WESTERN STYLE.
I THINK WE'RE READY.

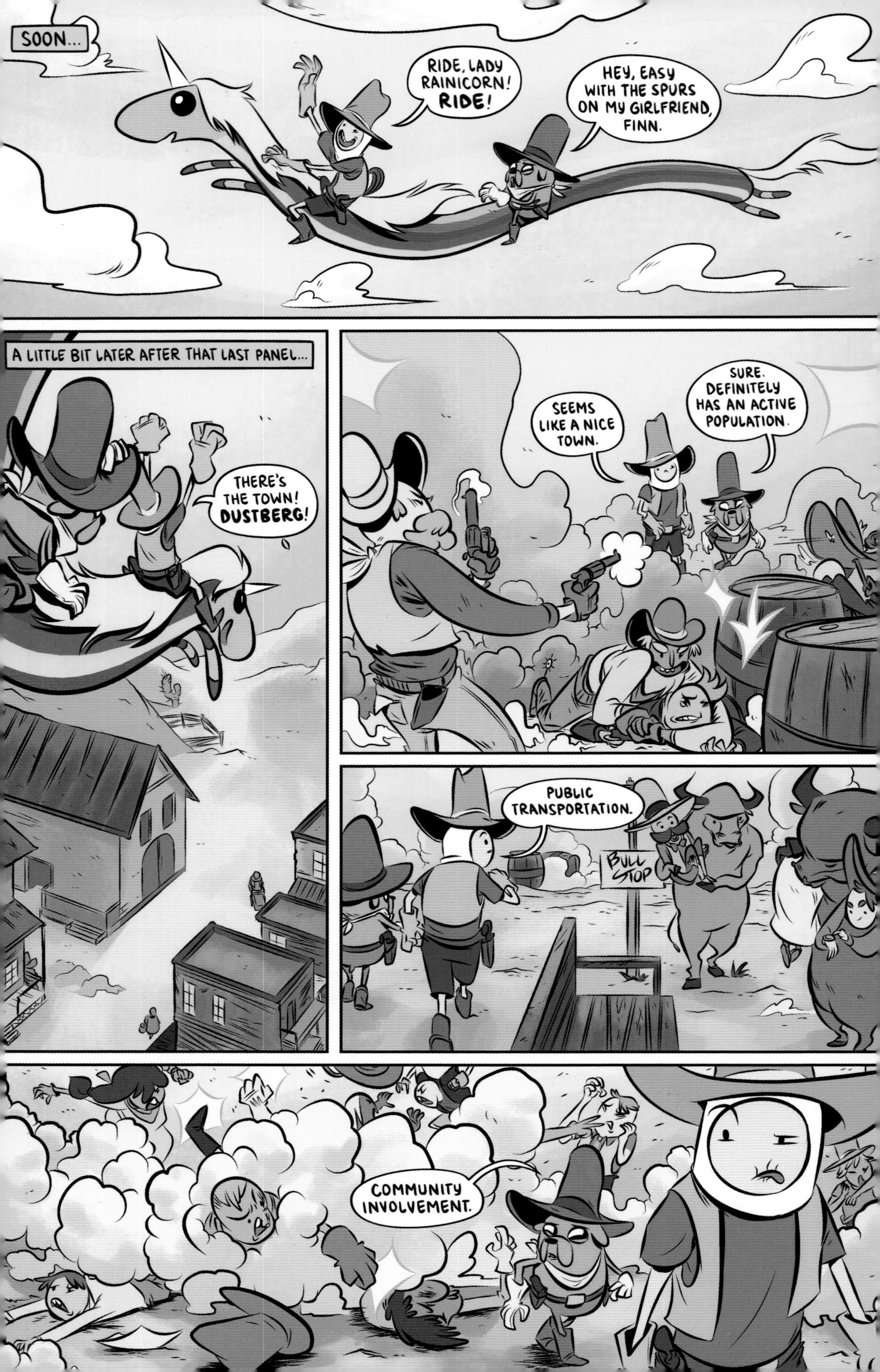
SOON...
RIDE, LADY RAINICORN! RIDE!
HEY, EASY WITH THE SPURS ON MY GIRLFRIEND, FINN.
A LITTLE BIT LATER AFTER THAT LAST PANEL...
THERE'S THE TOWN! DUSTBERG!
SEEMS LIKE A NICE TOWN.
SURE. DEFINITELY HAS AN ACTIVE POPULATION.
PUBLIC TRANSPORTATION.
BULL STOP
COMMUNITY INVOLVEMENT.

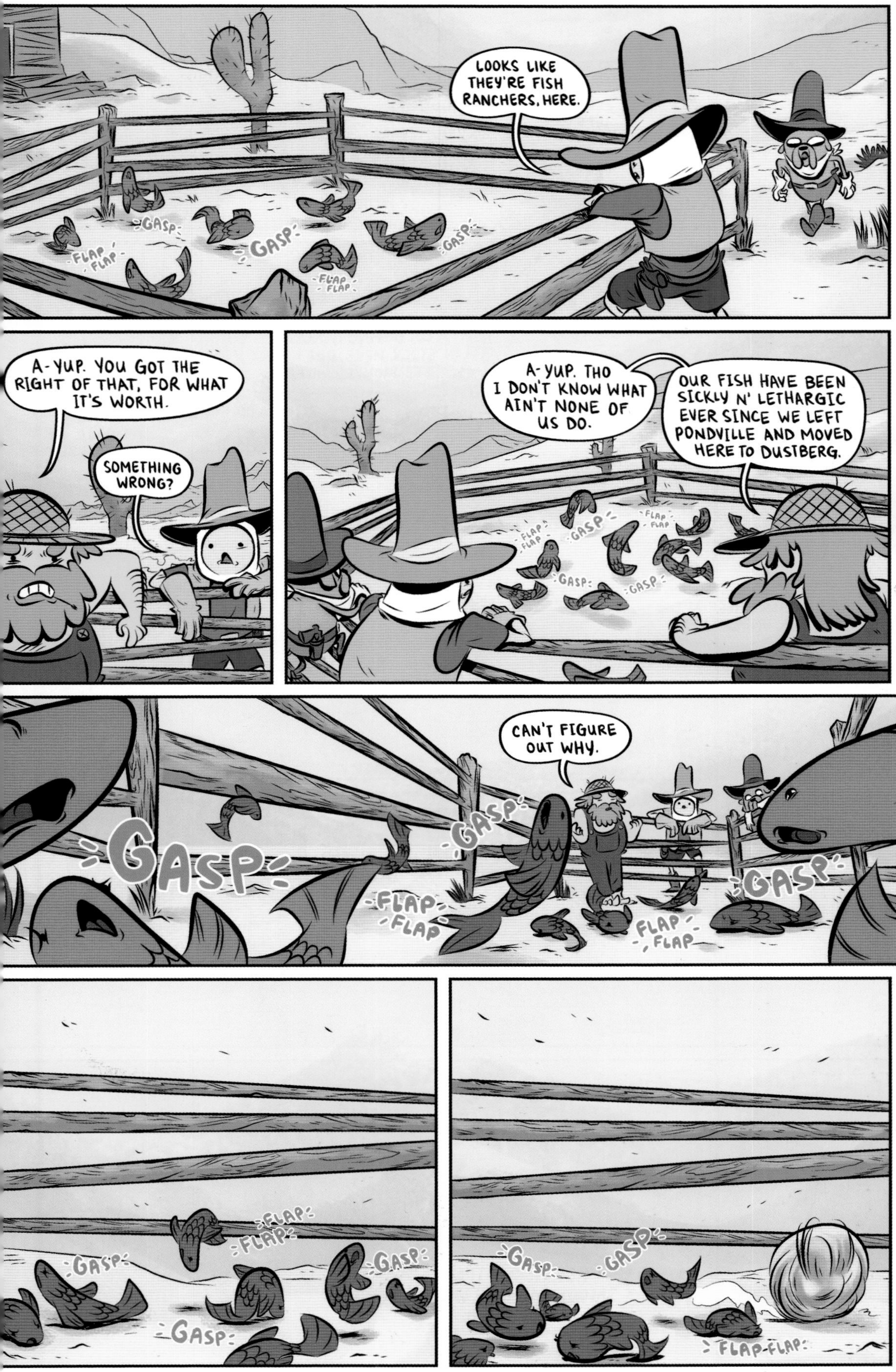
LOOKS LIKE THEY'RE FISH RANCHERS, HERE.
GASP
FLAP FLAP
GASP
GASP
FLAP FLAP
A-YUP. YOU GOT THE RIGHT OF THAT, FOR WHAT IT'S WORTH.
SOMETHING WRONG?
A-YUP. THO I DON'T KNOW WHAT AIN'T NONE OF US DO.
OUR FISH HAVE BEEN SICKLY N' LETHARGIC EVER SINCE WE LEFT PONDVILLE AND MOVED HERE TO DUSTBERG.
FLAP FLAP
GASP
FLAP FLAP
GASP
GASP
CAN'T FIGURE OUT WHY.
GASP
GASP
FLAP FLAP
FLAP FLAP
GASP
FLAP
FLAP
GASP
GASP
GASP
GASP
GASP
FLAP FLAP

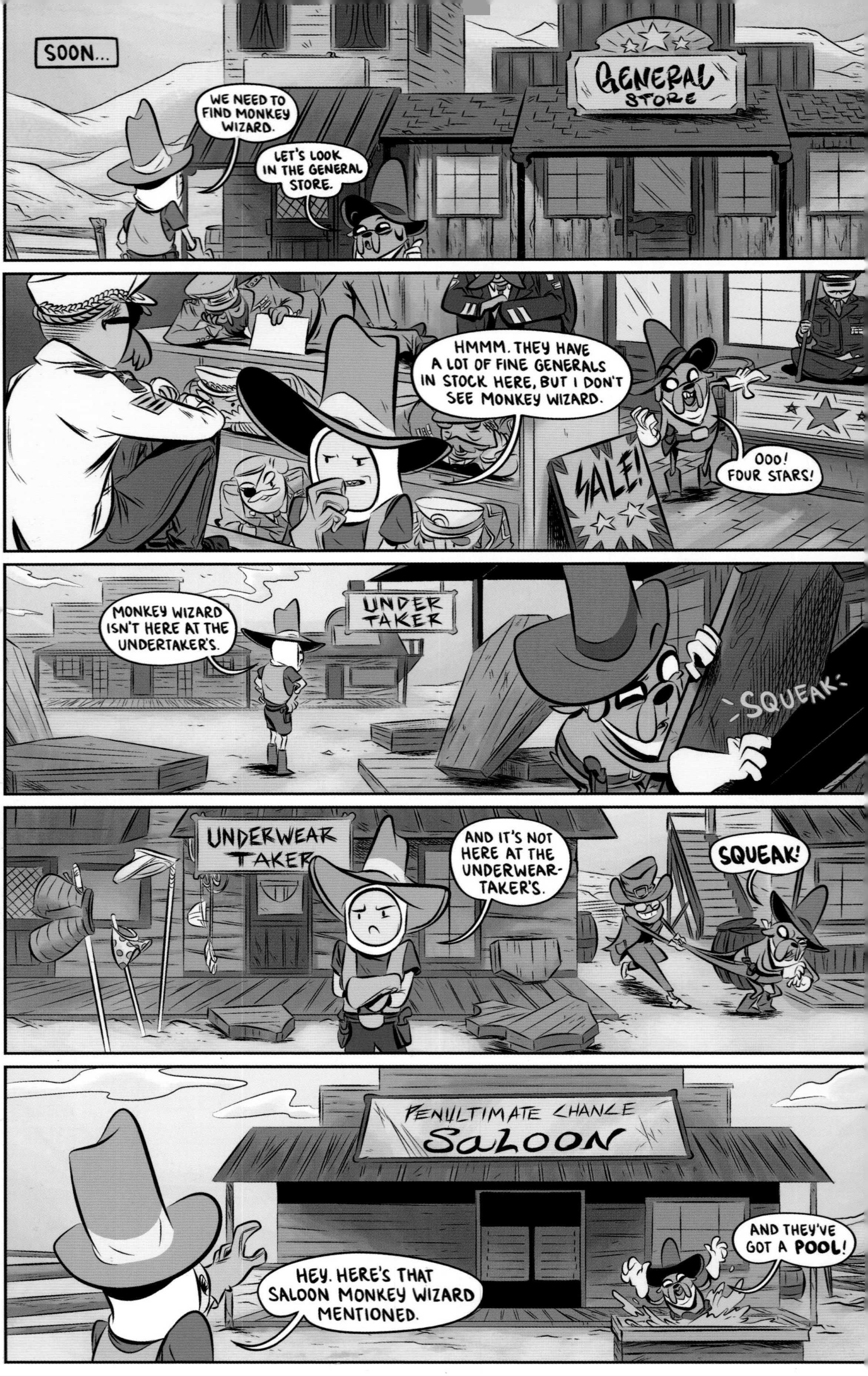
SOON...
GENERAL STORE
WE NEED TO FIND MONKEY WIZARD.
LET'S LOOK IN THE GENERAL STORE.
HMMM. THEY HAVE A LOT OF FINE GENERALS IN STOCK HERE, BUT I DON'T SEE MONKEY WIZARD.
SALE!
OOO! FOUR STARS!
UNDER TAKER
MONKEY WIZARD ISN'T HERE AT THE UNDERTAKER'S.
SQUEAK
UNDERWEAR TAKER
AND IT'S NOT HERE AT THE UNDERWEAR-TAKER'S.
SQUEAK!
PENULTIMATE CHANCE SALOON
HEY. HERE'S THAT SALOON MONKEY WIZARD MENTIONED.
AND THEY'VE GOT A **POOL**!

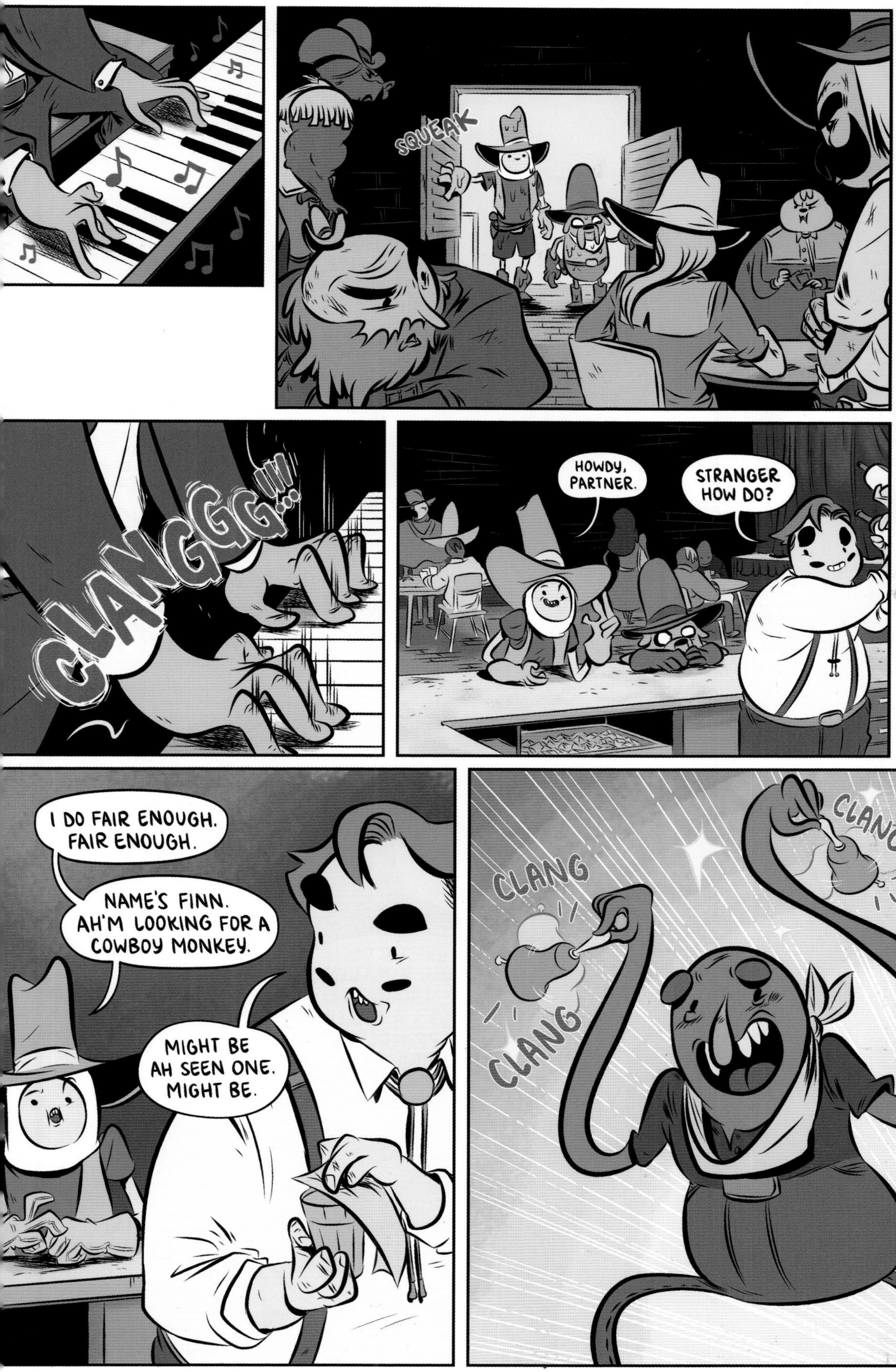
SQUEAK
CLANGGG!!!
HOWDY, PARTNER.
STRANGER HOW DO?
I DO FAIR ENOUGH. FAIR ENOUGH.
NAME'S FINN. AH'M LOOKING FOR A COWBOY MONKEY.
MIGHT BE AH SEEN ONE. MIGHT BE.
CLANG
CLANG
CLANG

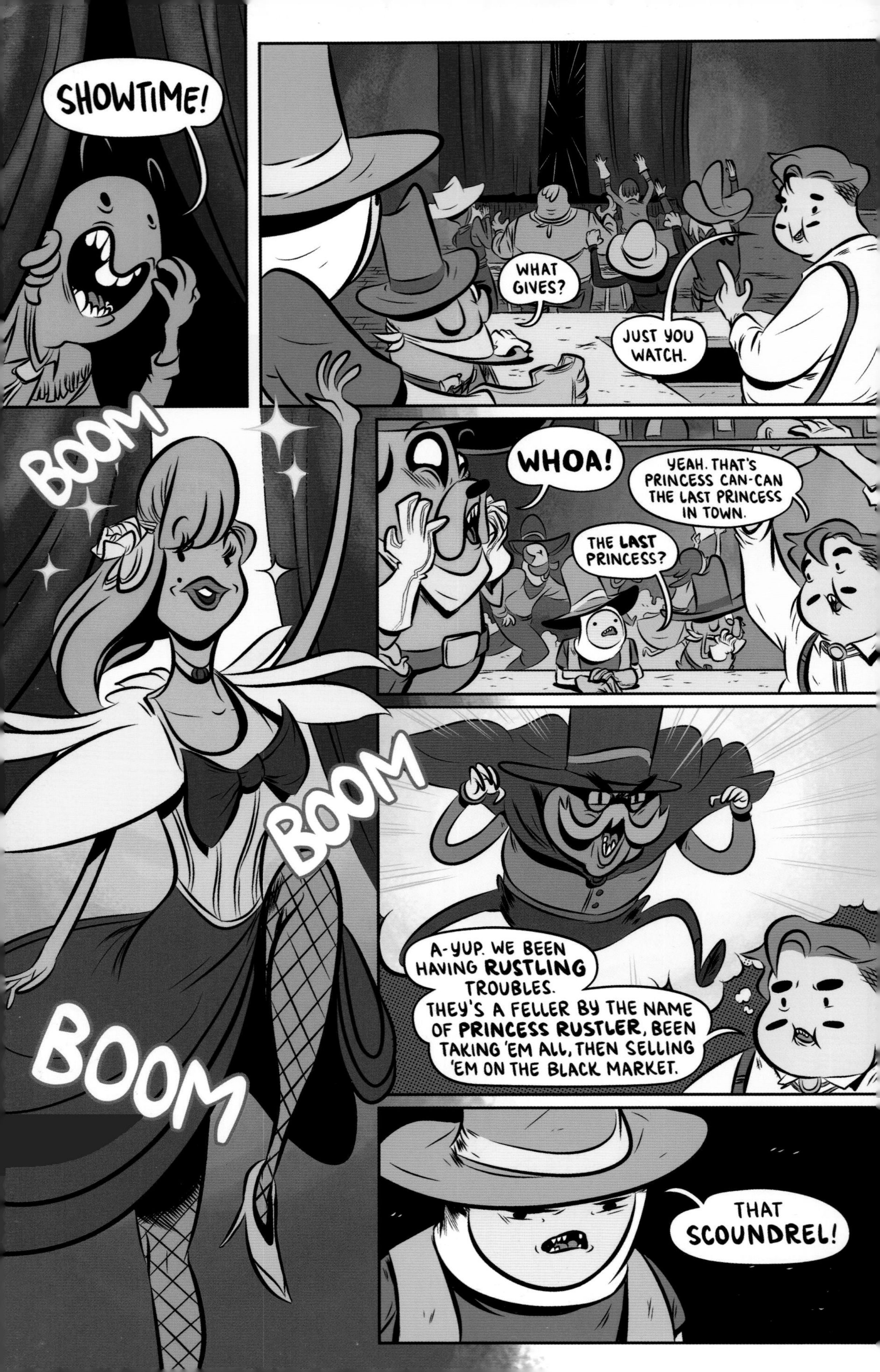
SHOWTIME!
WHAT GIVES?
JUST YOU WATCH.
BOOM
BOOM
BOOM
WHOA!
YEAH. THAT'S PRINCESS CAN-CAN THE LAST PRINCESS IN TOWN.
THE LAST PRINCESS?
A-YUP. WE BEEN HAVING RUSTLING TROUBLES. THEY'S A FELLER BY THE NAME OF PRINCESS RUSTLER, BEEN TAKING 'EM ALL, THEN SELLING 'EM ON THE BLACK MARKET.
THAT SCOUNDREL!

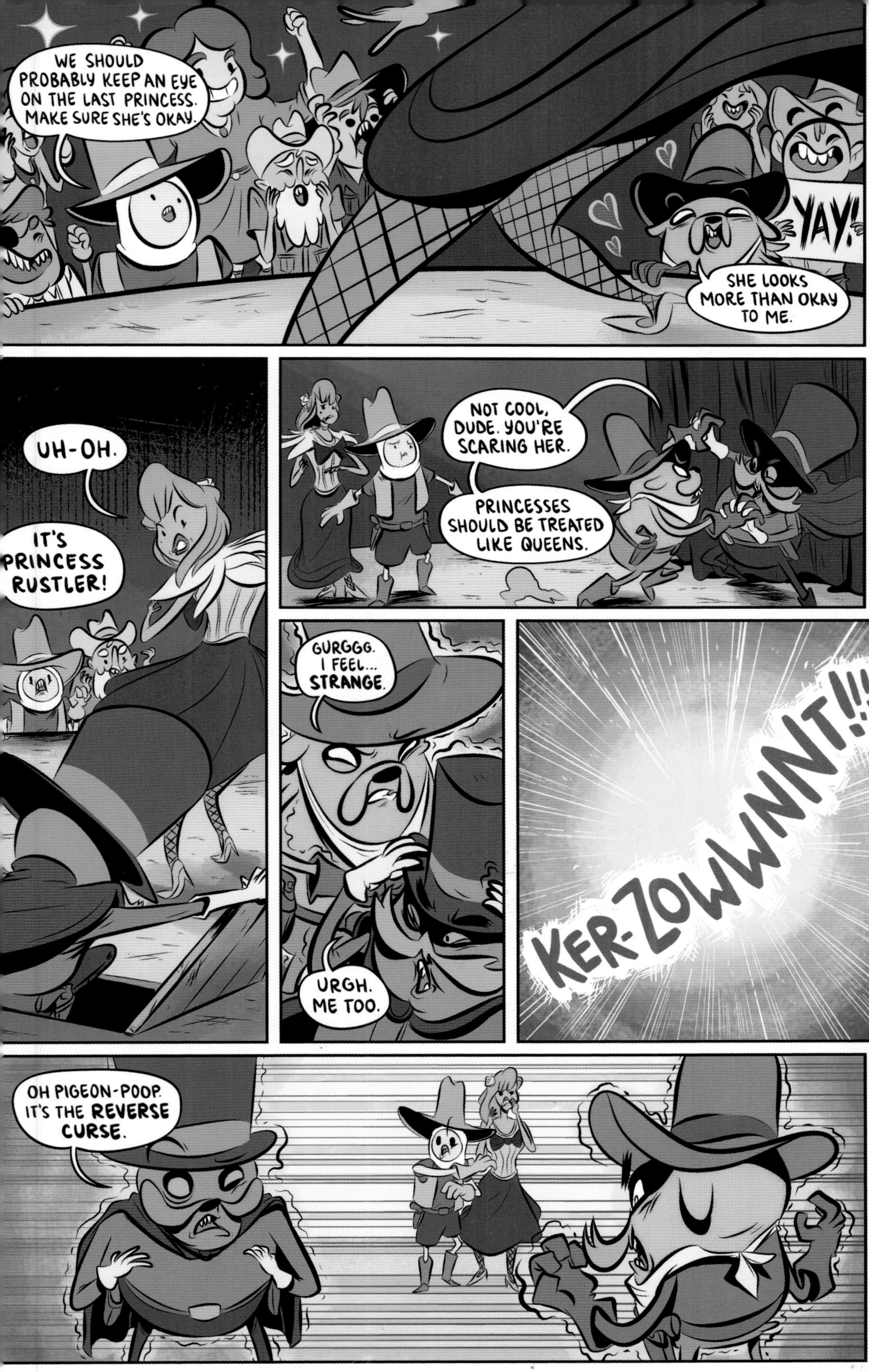
WE SHOULD PROBABLY KEEP AN EYE ON THE LAST PRINCESS. MAKE SURE SHE'S OKAY.
YAY!
SHE LOOKS MORE THAN OKAY TO ME.
UH-OH.
IT'S PRINCESS RUSTLER!
NOT COOL, DUDE. YOU'RE SCARING HER.
PRINCESSES SHOULD BE TREATED LIKE QUEENS.
GURGGG. I FEEL... STRANGE.
URGH. ME TOO.
KER-ZOWWNNT!!
OH PIGEON-POOP. IT'S THE REVERSE CURSE.

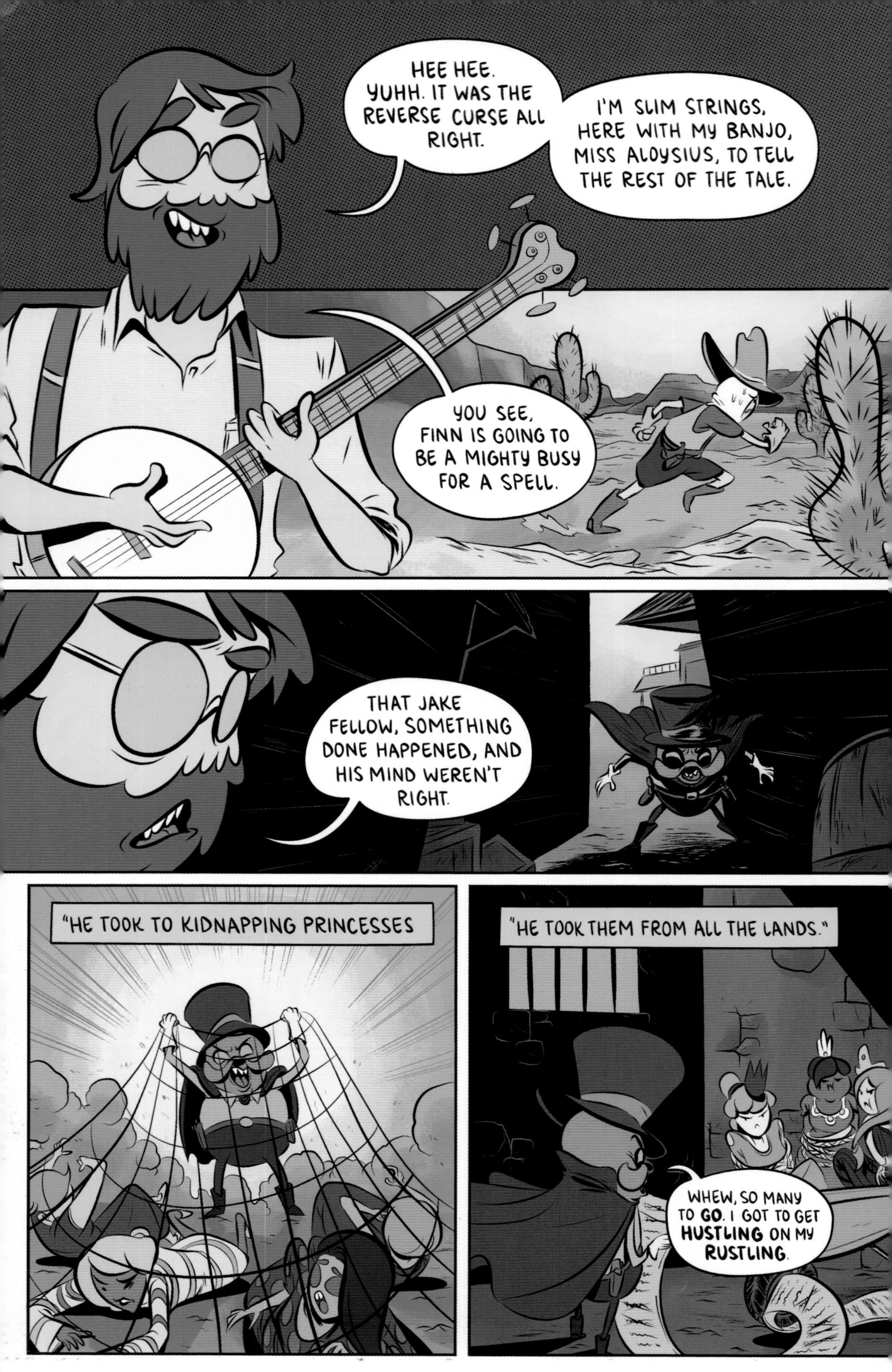

HEE HEE. YUHH. IT WAS THE REVERSE CURSE ALL RIGHT.
I'M SLIM STRINGS, HERE WITH MY BANJO, MISS ALOYSIUS, TO TELL THE REST OF THE TALE.
YOU SEE, FINN IS GOING TO BE A MIGHTY BUSY FOR A SPELL.
THAT JAKE FELLOW, SOMETHING DONE HAPPENED, AND HIS MIND WEREN'T RIGHT.
"HE TOOK TO KIDNAPPING PRINCESSES
"HE TOOK THEM FROM ALL THE LANDS."
WHEW, SO MANY TO **GO**. I GOT TO GET **HUSTLING** ON MY **RUSTLING**.

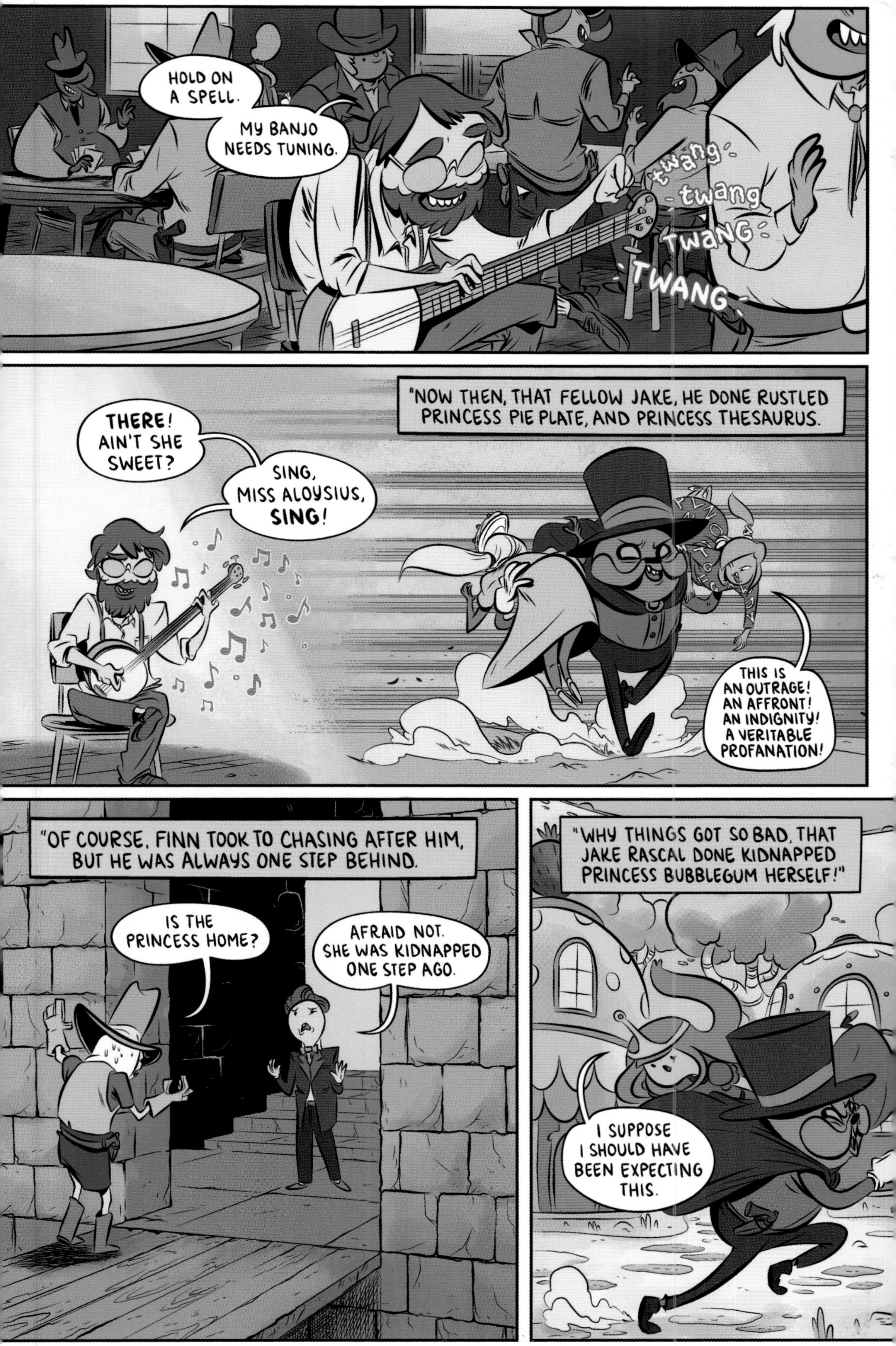
HOLD ON A SPELL.
MY BANJO NEEDS TUNING.
twang
twang
TWANG
TWANG
"NOW THEN, THAT FELLOW JAKE, HE DONE RUSTLED PRINCESS PIE PLATE, AND PRINCESS THESAURUS.
THERE! AIN'T SHE SWEET?
SING, MISS ALOYSIUS, SING!
THIS IS AN OUTRAGE! AN AFFRONT! AN INDIGNITY! A VERITABLE PROFANATION!
"OF COURSE, FINN TOOK TO CHASING AFTER HIM, BUT HE WAS ALWAYS ONE STEP BEHIND.
IS THE PRINCESS HOME?
AFRAID NOT. SHE WAS KIDNAPPED ONE STEP AGO.
"WHY THINGS GOT SO BAD, THAT JAKE RASCAL DONE KIDNAPPED PRINCESS BUBBLEGUM HERSELF!"
I SUPPOSE I SHOULD HAVE BEEN EXPECTING THIS.

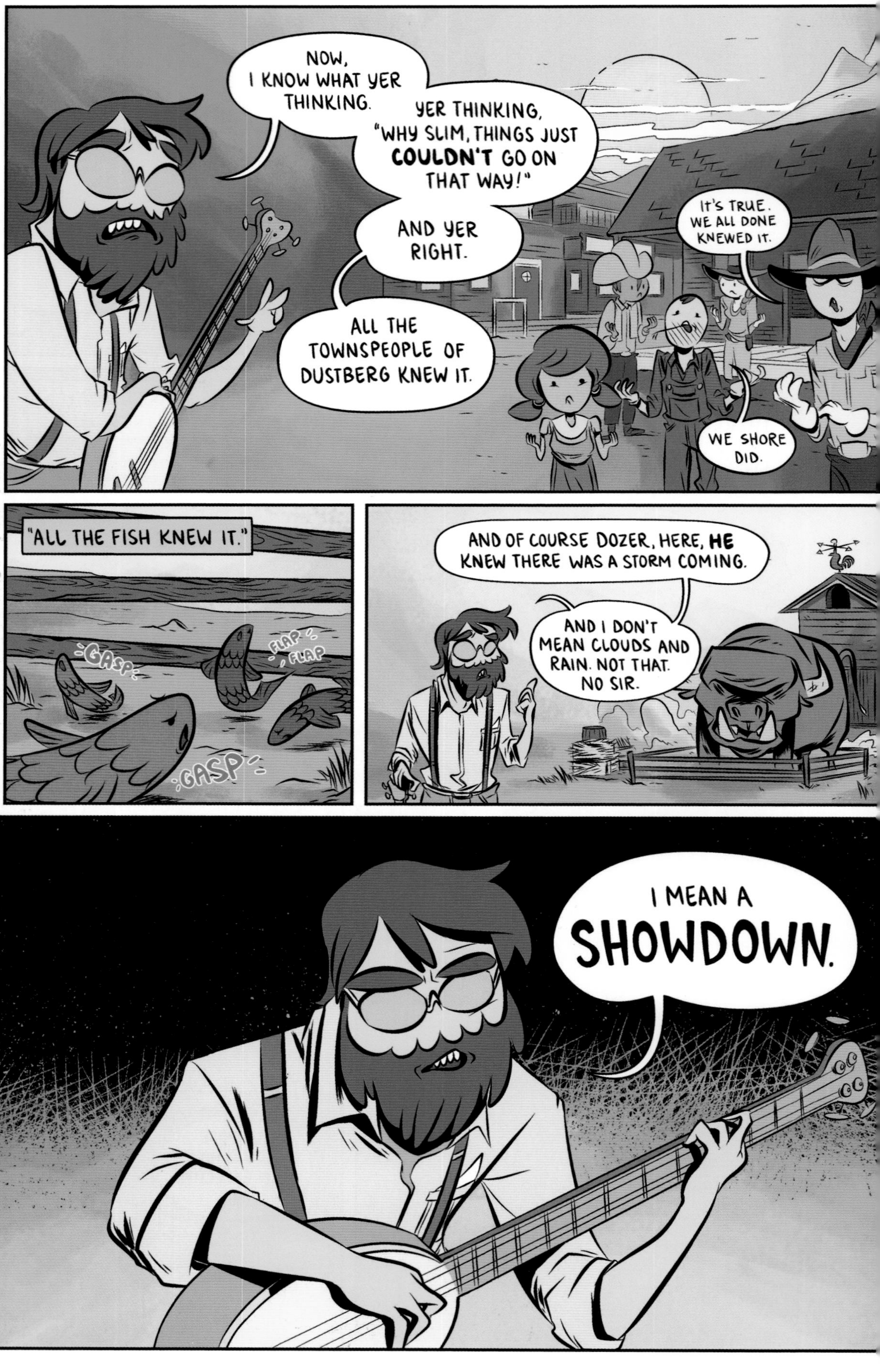
NOW, I KNOW WHAT YER THINKING.
YER THINKING, "WHY SLIM, THINGS JUST **COULDN'T** GO ON THAT WAY!"
AND YER RIGHT.
ALL THE TOWNSPEOPLE OF DUSTBERG KNEW IT.
IT'S TRUE. WE ALL DONE KNEWED IT.
WE SHORE DID.
"ALL THE FISH KNEW IT."
GASP
FLAP FLAP
GASP
AND OF COURSE DOZER, HERE, **HE** KNEW THERE WAS A STORM COMING.
AND I DON'T MEAN CLOUDS AND RAIN. NOT THAT. NO SIR.
I MEAN A SHOWDOWN.

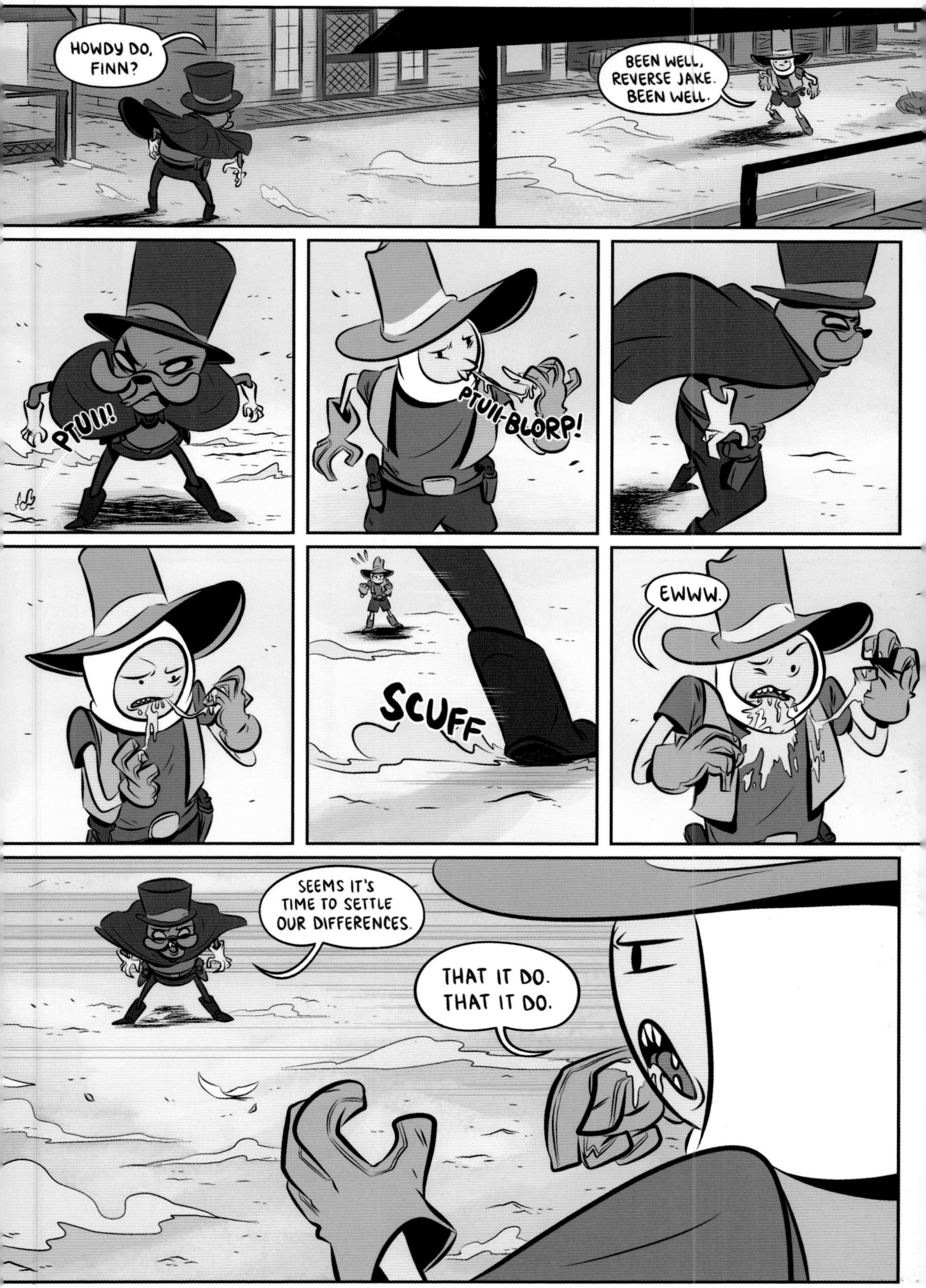
HOWDY DO, FINN?
BEEN WELL, REVERSE JAKE. BEEN WELL.
PTUII!
PTUII-BLORP!
SCUFF
EWWW.
SEEMS IT'S TIME TO SETTLE OUR DIFFERENCES.
THAT IT DO. THAT IT DO.

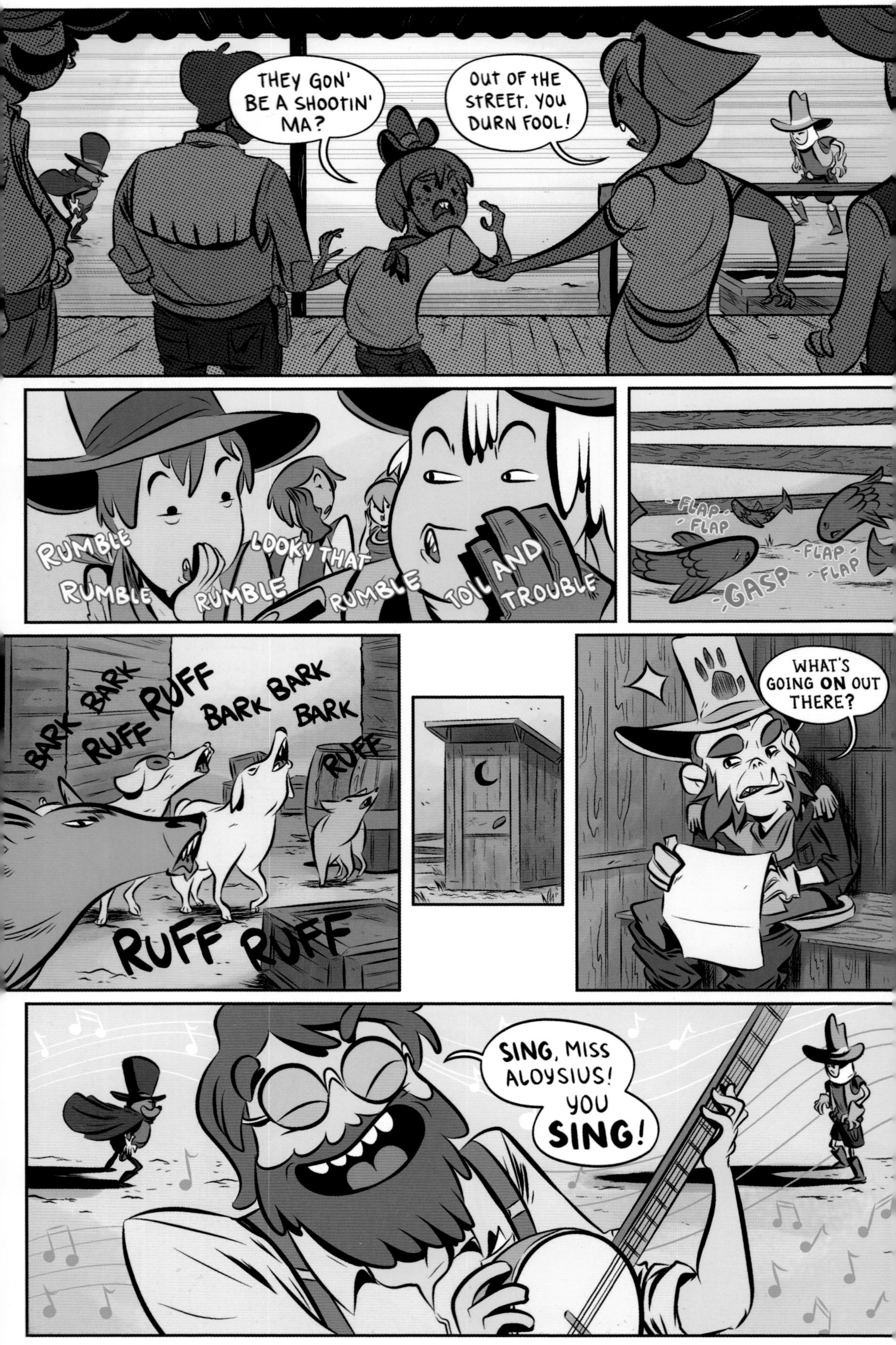
THEY GON' BE A SHOOTIN' MA?
OUT OF THE STREET, YOU DURN FOOL!
RUMBLE
RUMBLE
LOOKY THAT
RUMBLE
RUMBLE
TOIL AND TROUBLE
FLAP FLAP
FLAP FLAP
GASP
BARK
BARK
RUFF
RUFF
BARK BARK
BARK
RUFF
RUFF RUFF
WHAT'S GOING ON OUT THERE?
SING, MISS ALOYSIUS! YOU SING!

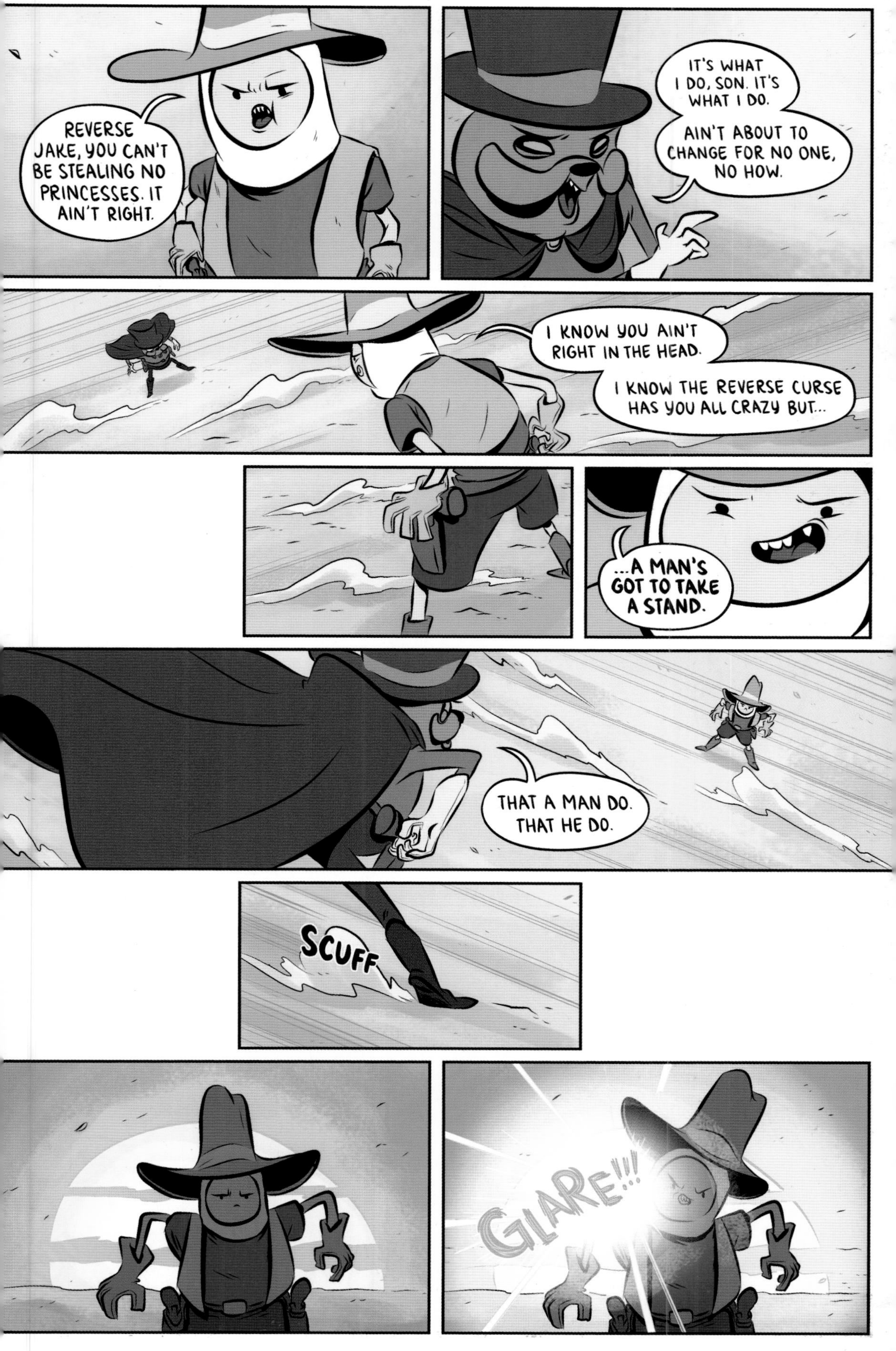
REVERSE JAKE, YOU CAN'T BE STEALING NO PRINCESSES. IT AIN'T RIGHT.
IT'S WHAT I DO, SON. IT'S WHAT I DO.
AIN'T ABOUT TO CHANGE FOR NO ONE, NO HOW.
I KNOW YOU AIN'T RIGHT IN THE HEAD.
I KNOW THE REVERSE CURSE HAS YOU ALL CRAZY BUT...
...A MAN'S GOT TO TAKE A STAND.
THAT A MAN DO. THAT HE DO.
SCUFF
GLARE!!!

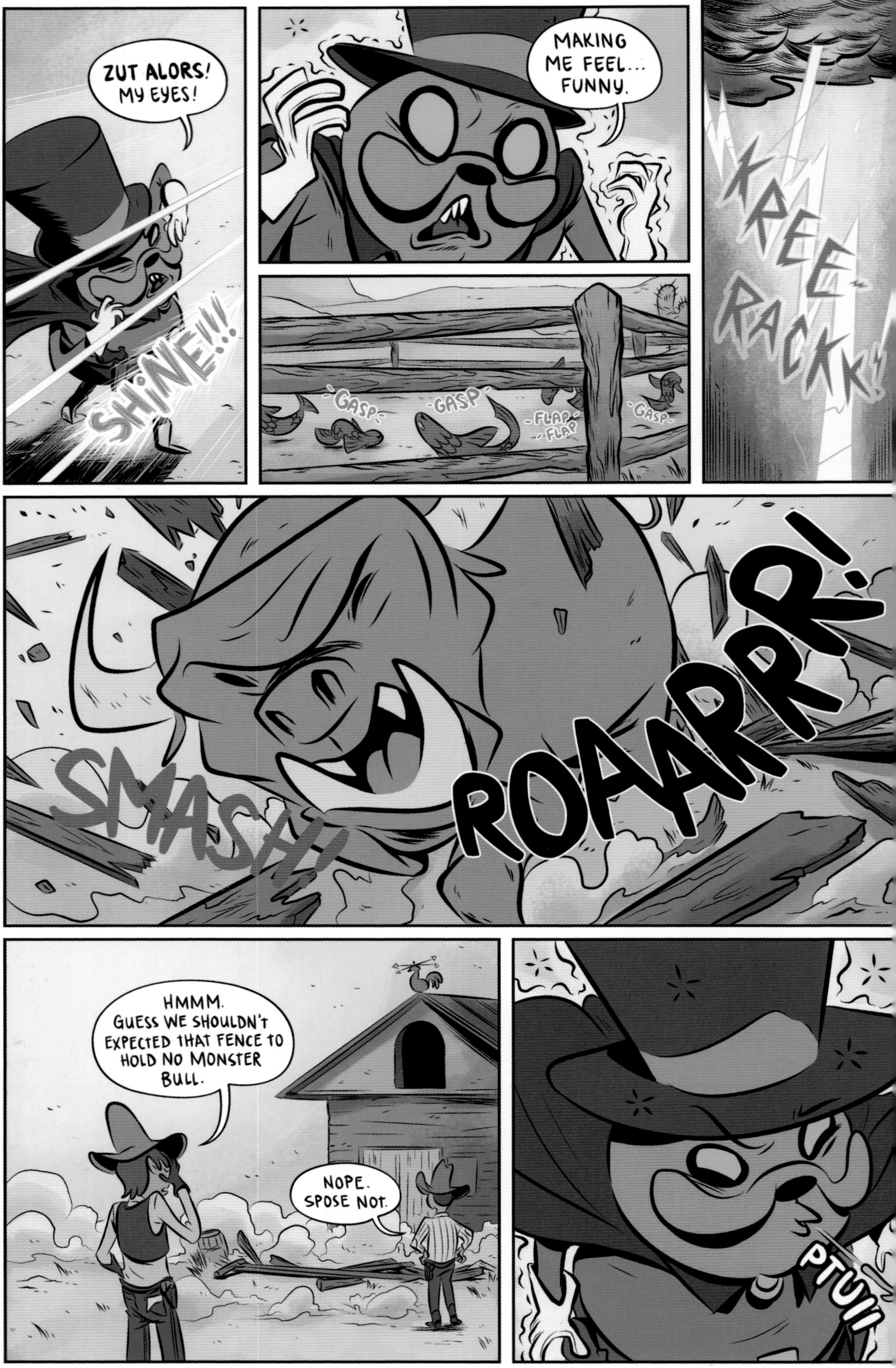

ZUT ALORS! MY EYES!
SHINE!!!
MAKING ME FEEL... FUNNY.
GASP
GASP
FLAP FLAP
GASP
KREE-RACKK!
SMASH!
ROAARRR!
HMMM. GUESS WE SHOULDN'T EXPECTED THAT FENCE TO HOLD NO MONSTER BULL.
NOPE. SPOSE NOT.
PTUI!!

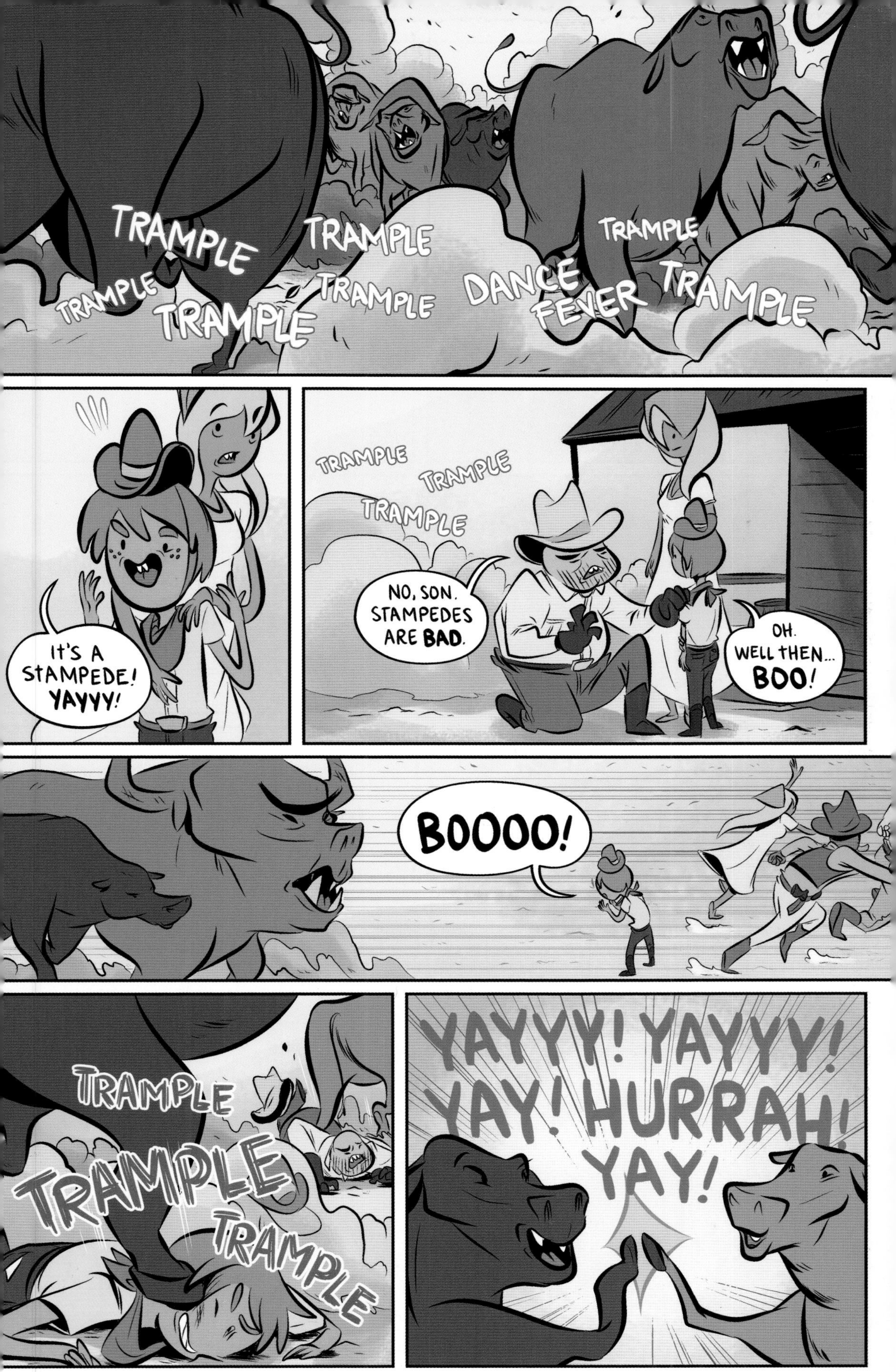
TRAMPLE
TRAMPLE
TRAMPLE
TRAMPLE
TRAMPLE
TRAMPLE
DANCE FEVER
TRAMPLE
IT'S A STAMPEDE! YAYYY!
TRAMPLE
TRAMPLE
TRAMPLE
NO, SON. STAMPEDES ARE BAD.
OH. WELL THEN... BOO!
BOOOO!
TRAMPLE
TRAMPLE
TRAMPLE
YAYYY! YAYYY! YAY! HURRAH! YAY!

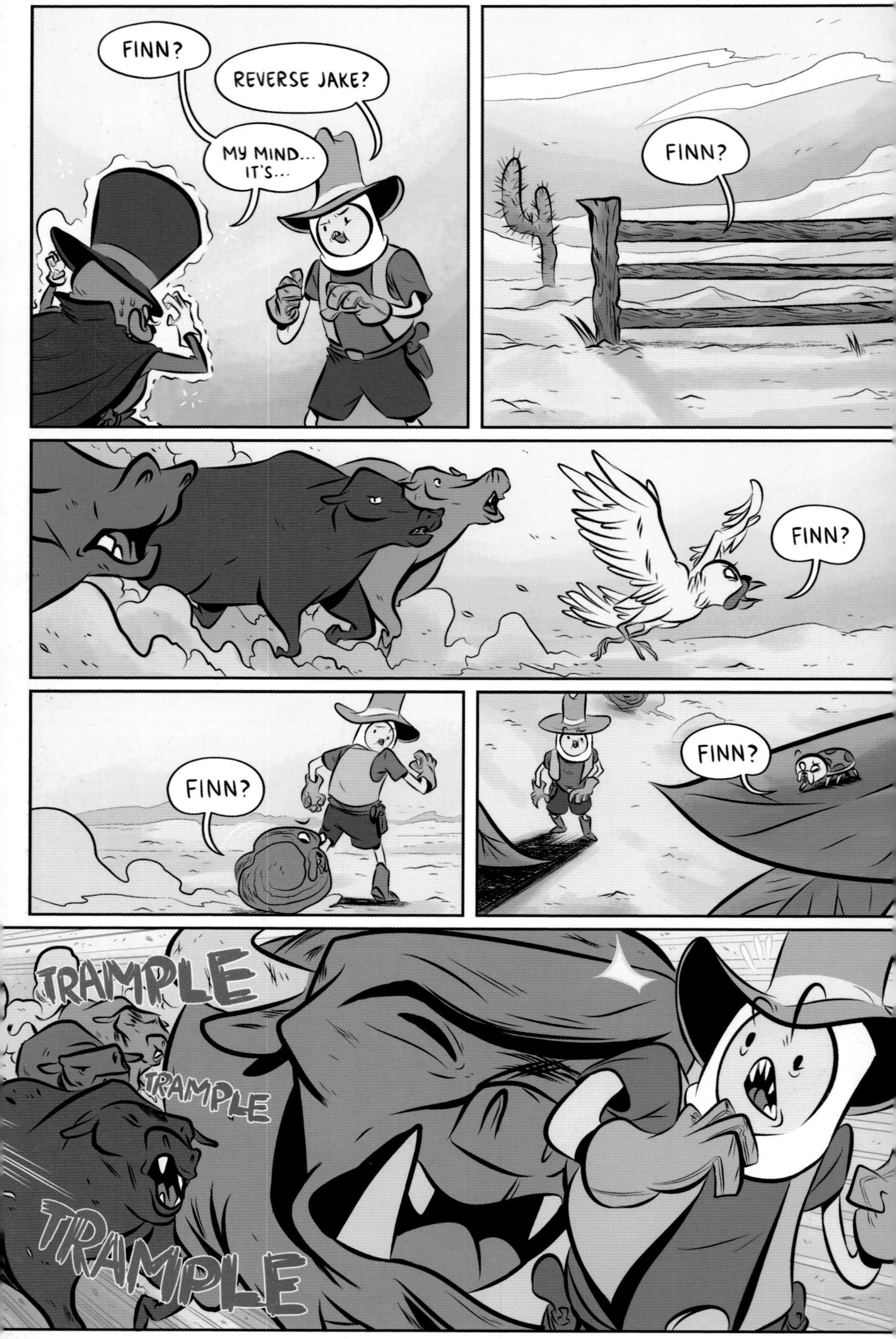
FINN?
REVERSE JAKE?
MY MIND... IT'S...
FINN?
FINN?
FINN?
FINN?
TRAMPLE
TRAMPLE
TRAMPLE

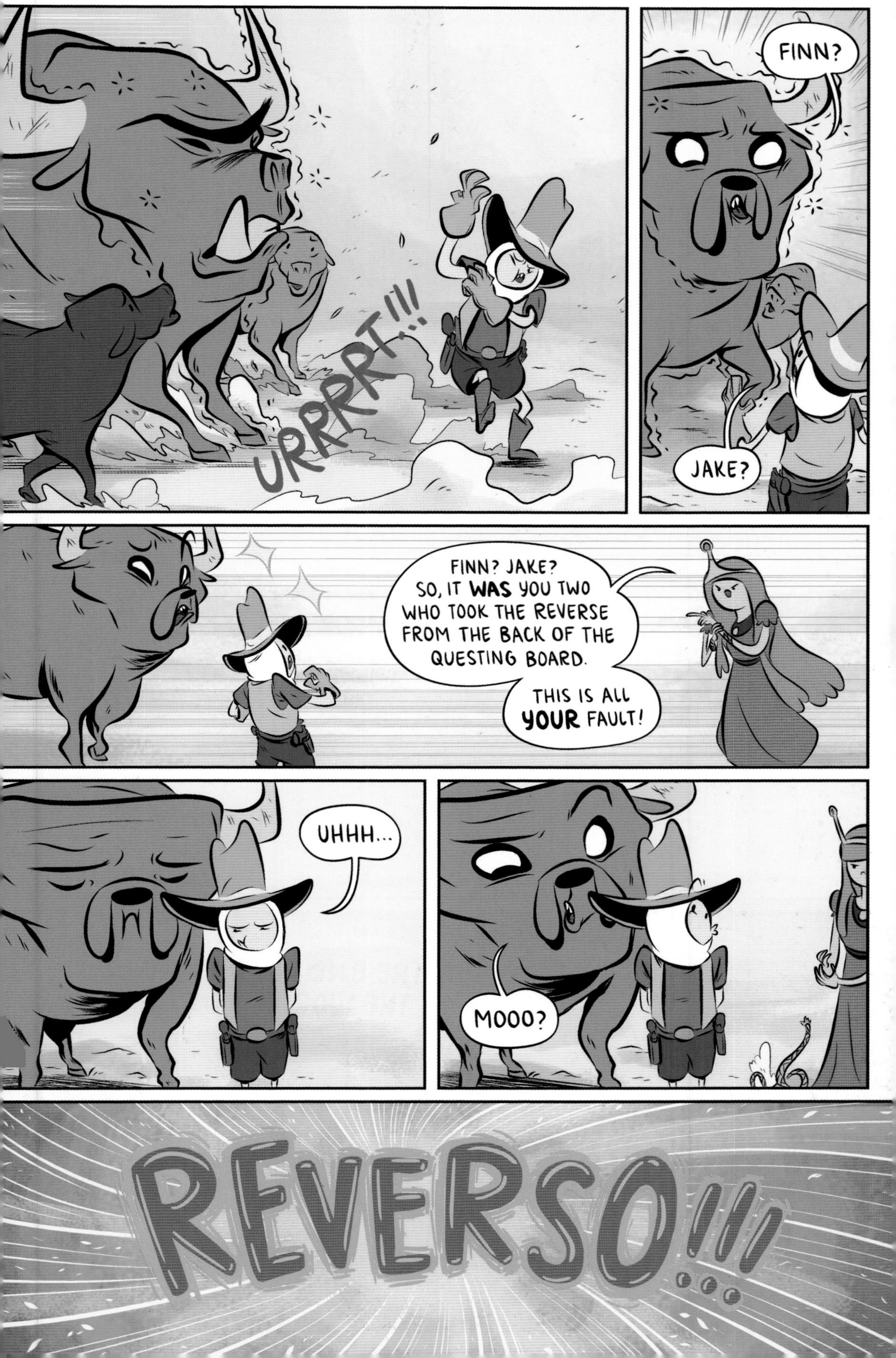
URRRRT!!!
FINN?
JAKE?
FINN? JAKE? SO, IT WAS YOU TWO WHO TOOK THE REVERSE FROM THE BACK OF THE QUESTING BOARD.
THIS IS ALL YOUR FAULT!
UHHH...
MOOO?
REVERSO!!!

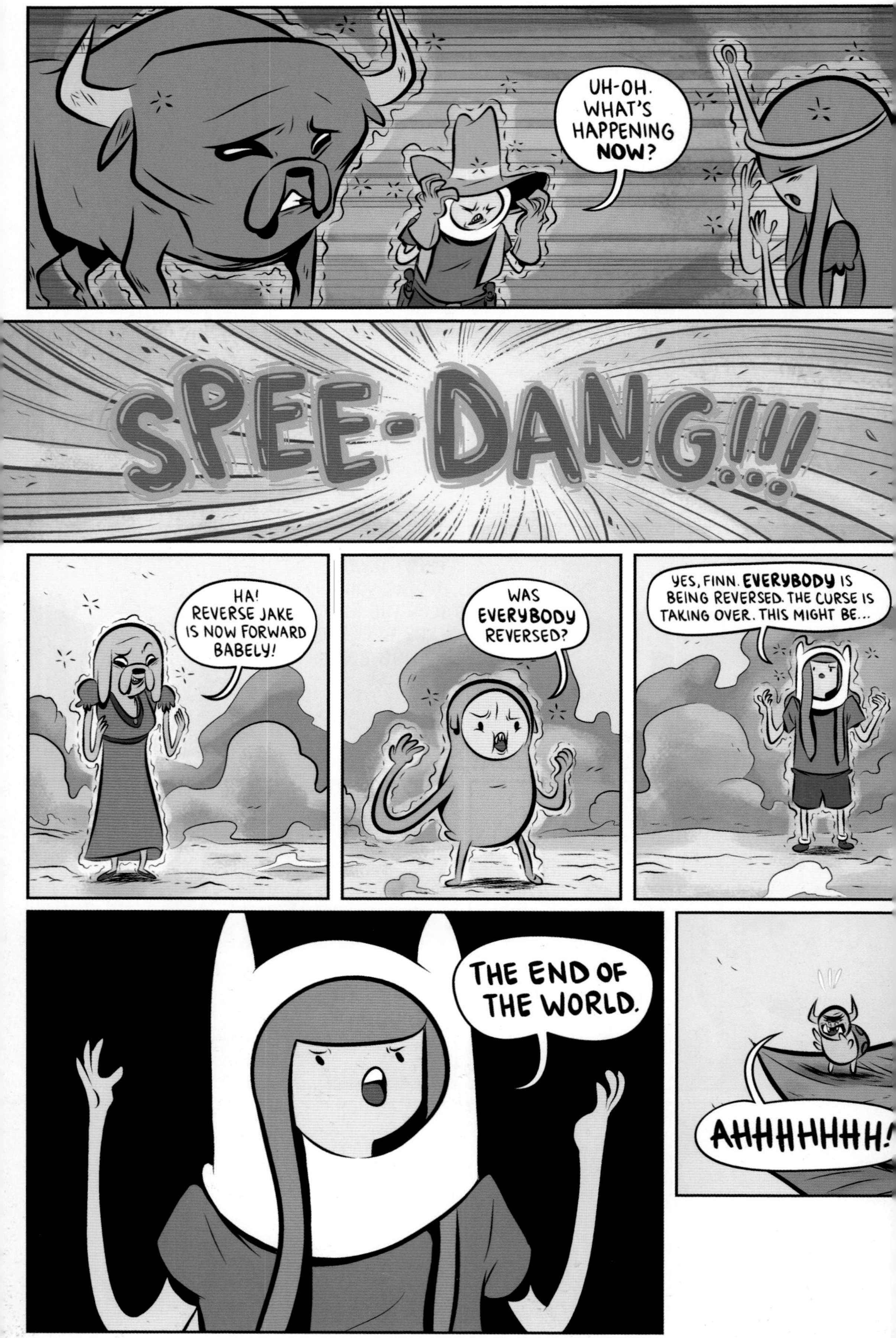

UH-OH. WHAT'S HAPPENING NOW?
SPEE-DANG!!!
HA! REVERSE JAKE IS NOW FORWARD BABELY!
WAS EVERYBODY REVERSED?
YES, FINN. EVERYBODY IS BEING REVERSED. THE CURSE IS TAKING OVER. THIS MIGHT BE...
THE END OF THE WORLD.
AHHHHHHH!

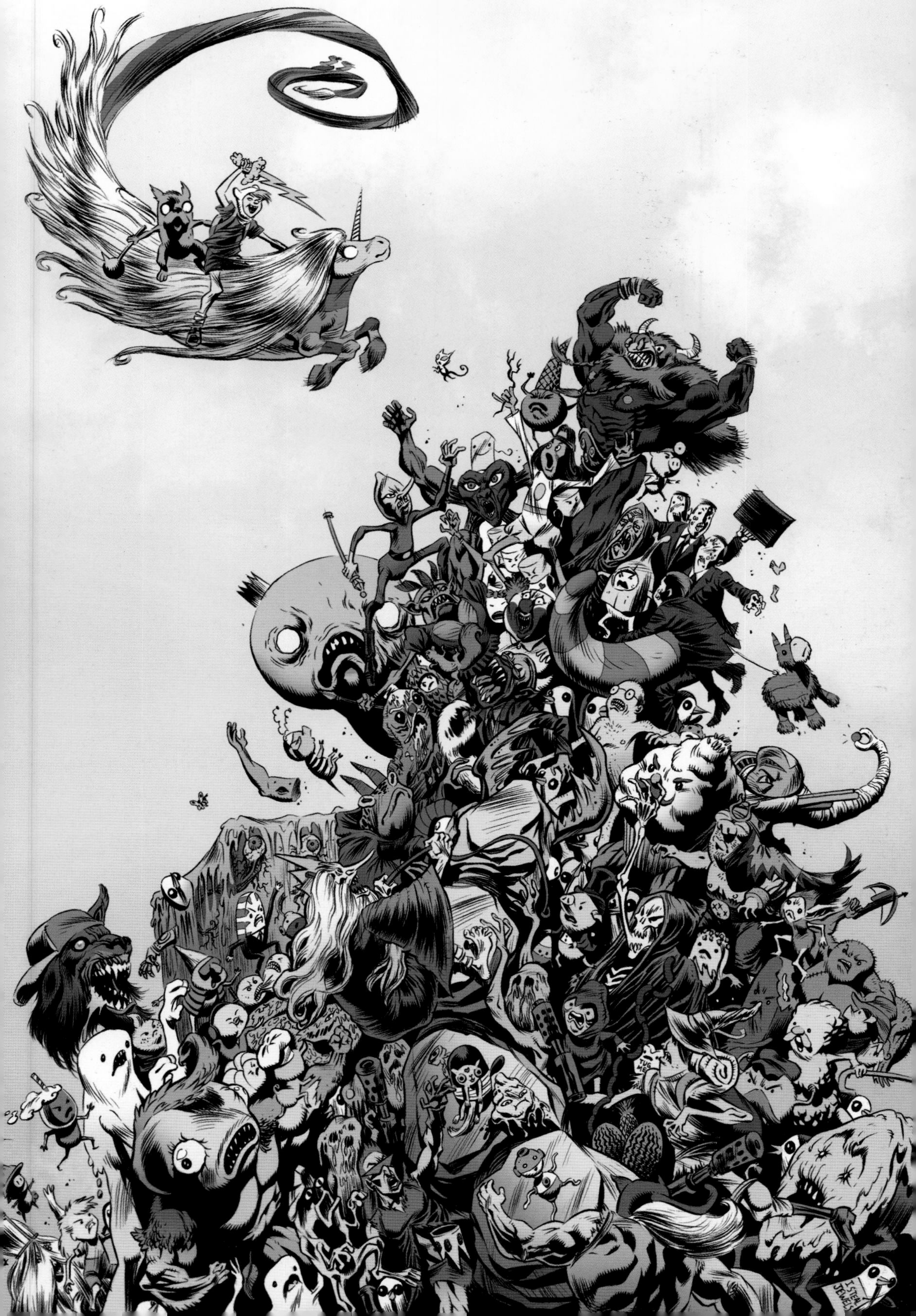
TUG ME
I STEAL JEWELS

CHAPTER SIX

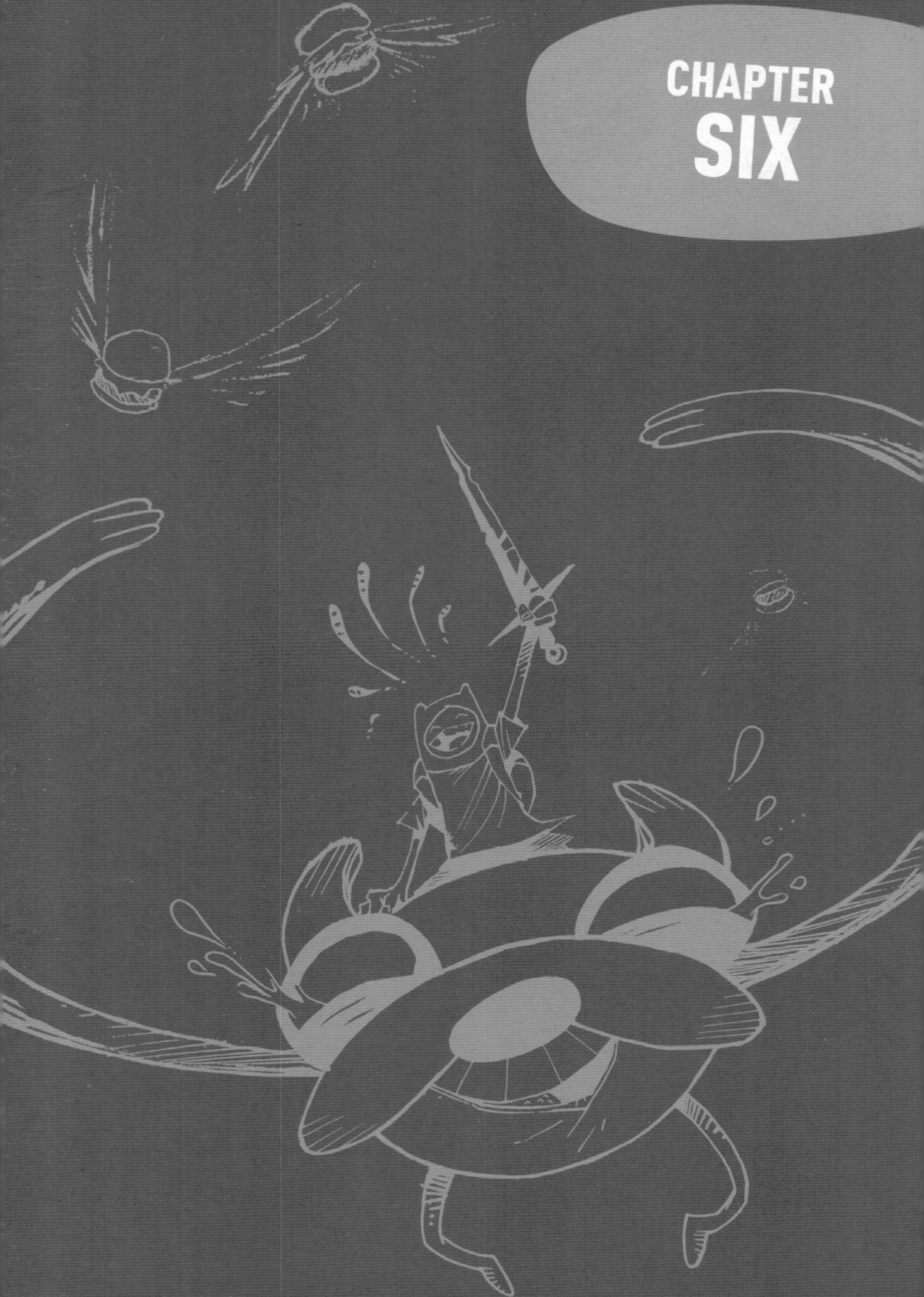

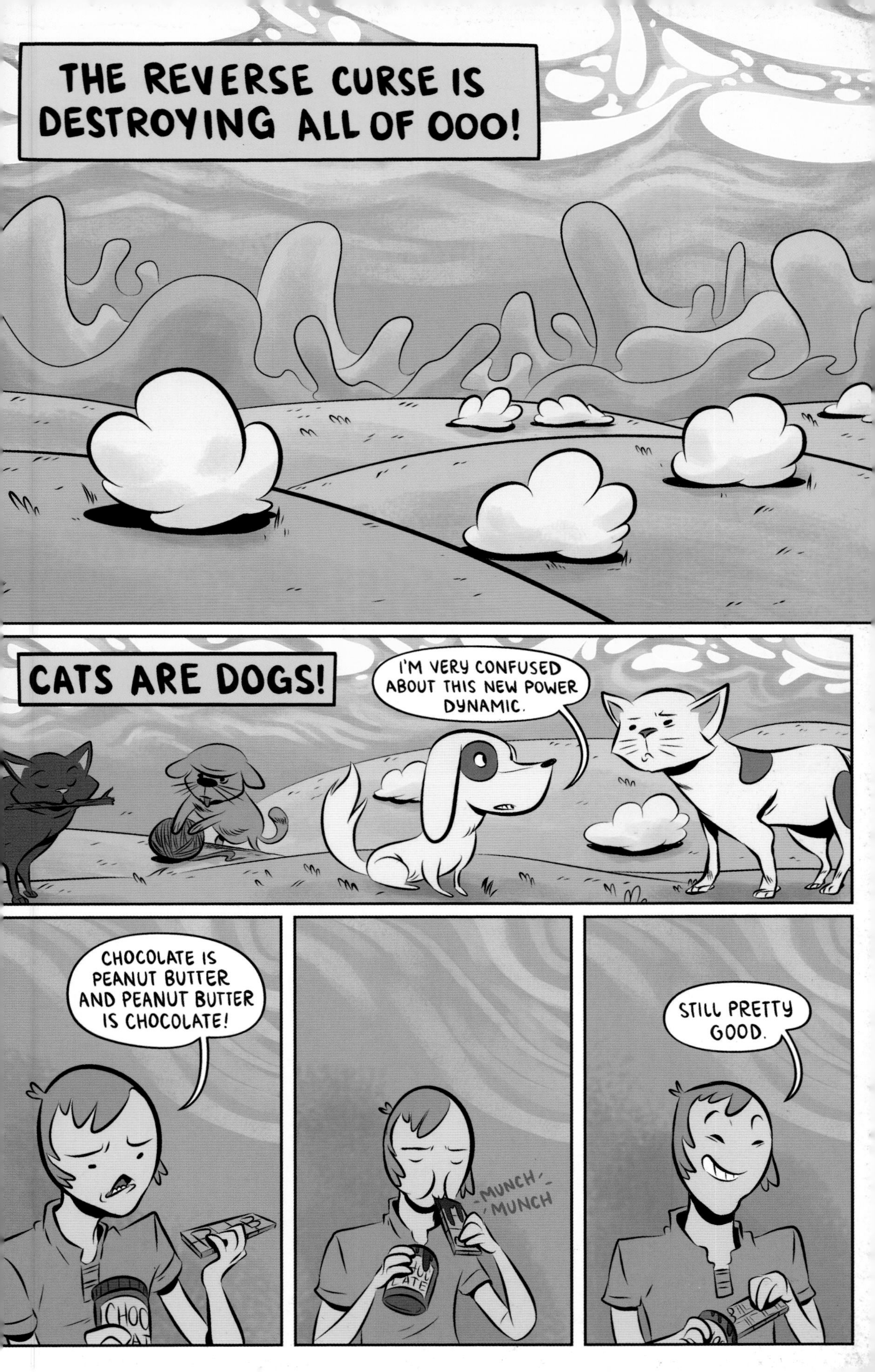
THE REVERSE CURSE IS DESTROYING ALL OF OOO!
CATS ARE DOGS!
I'M VERY CONFUSED ABOUT THIS NEW POWER DYNAMIC.
CHOCOLATE IS PEANUT BUTTER AND PEANUT BUTTER IS CHOCOLATE!
MUNCH MUNCH
STILL PRETTY GOOD.

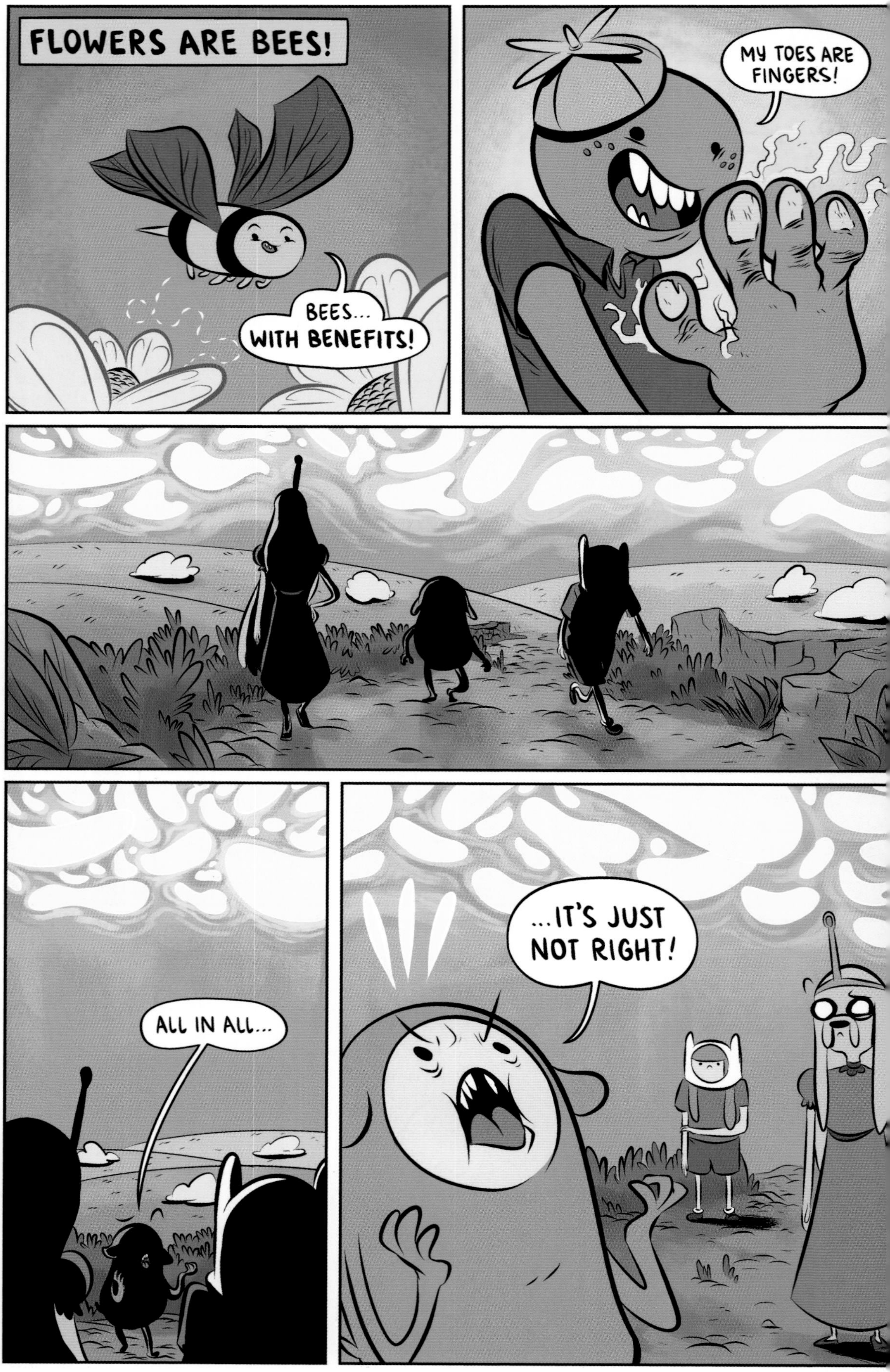
FLOWERS ARE BEES!
BEES... WITH BENEFITS!
MY TOES ARE FINGERS!
ALL IN ALL...
...IT'S JUST NOT RIGHT!

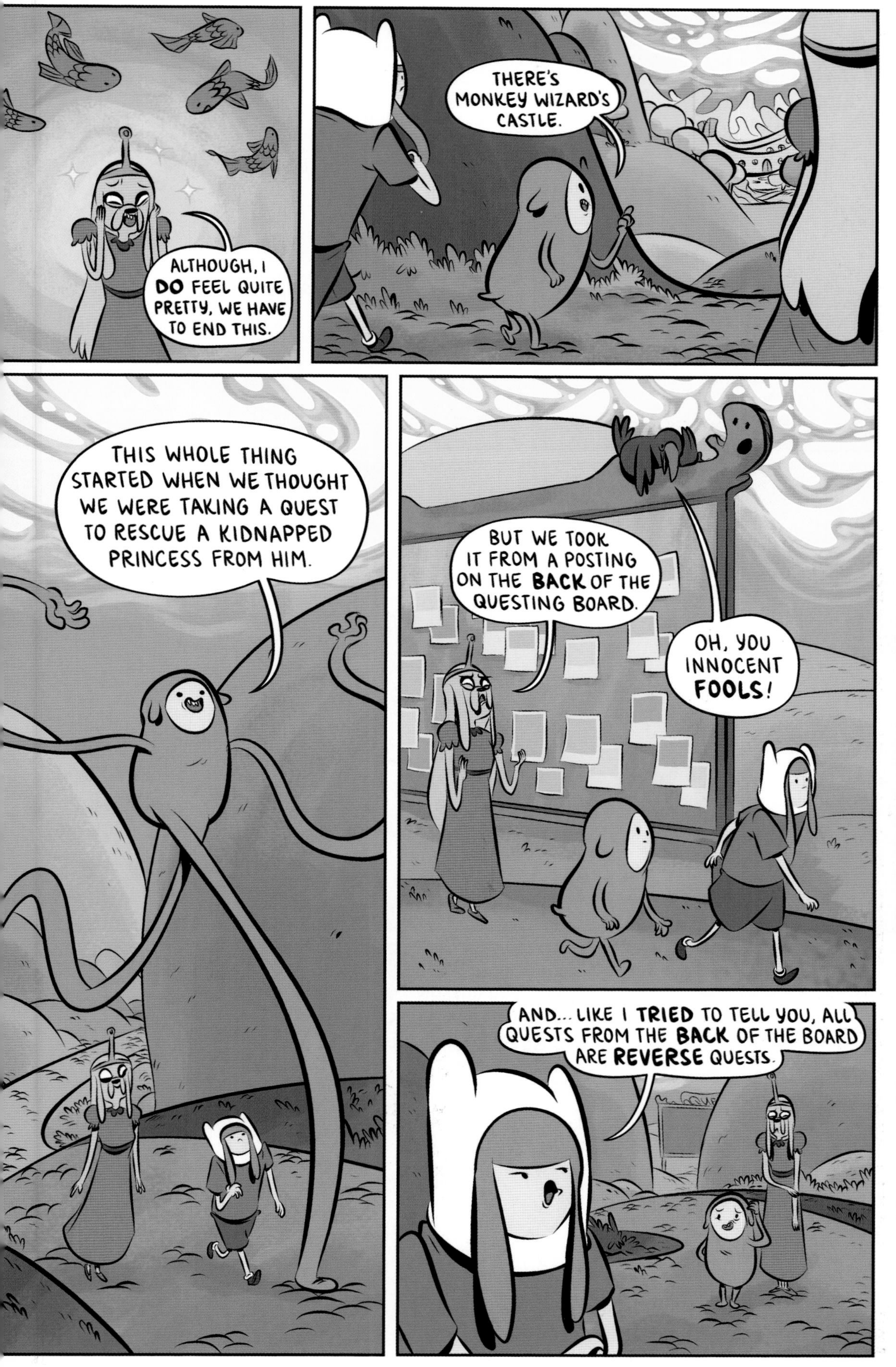
ALTHOUGH, I DO FEEL QUITE PRETTY, WE HAVE TO END THIS.
THERE'S MONKEY WIZARD'S CASTLE.
THIS WHOLE THING STARTED WHEN WE THOUGHT WE WERE TAKING A QUEST TO RESCUE A KIDNAPPED PRINCESS FROM HIM.
BUT WE TOOK IT FROM A POSTING ON THE BACK OF THE QUESTING BOARD.
OH, YOU INNOCENT FOOLS!
AND... LIKE I TRIED TO TELL YOU, ALL QUESTS FROM THE BACK OF THE BOARD ARE REVERSE QUESTS.

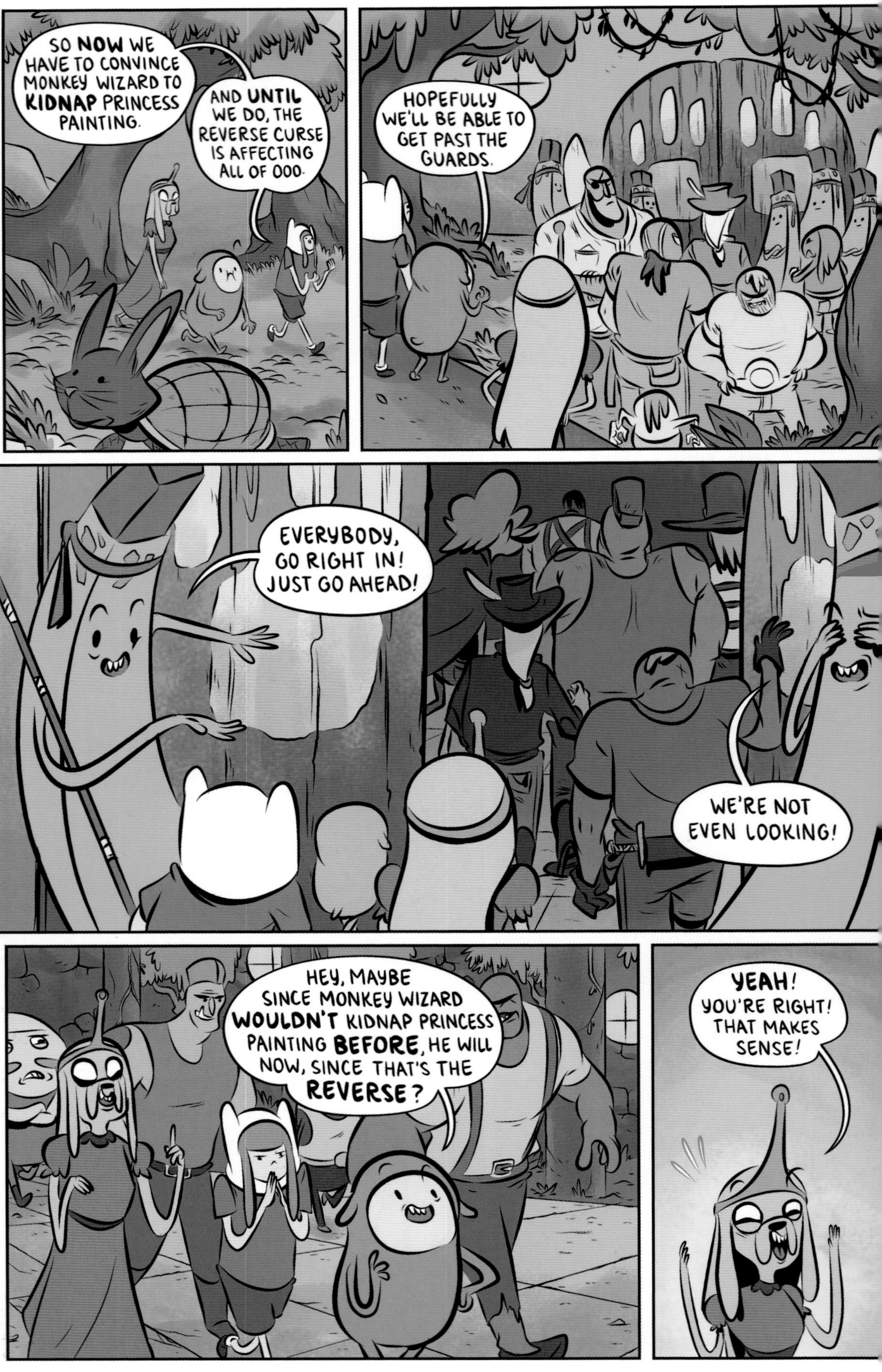
SO **NOW** WE HAVE TO CONVINCE MONKEY WIZARD TO **KIDNAP** PRINCESS PAINTING.
AND **UNTIL** WE DO, THE REVERSE CURSE IS AFFECTING ALL OF OOO.
HOPEFULLY WE'LL BE ABLE TO GET PAST THE GUARDS.
EVERYBODY, GO RIGHT IN! JUST GO AHEAD!
WE'RE NOT EVEN LOOKING!
HEY, MAYBE SINCE MONKEY WIZARD **WOULDN'T** KIDNAP PRINCESS PAINTING **BEFORE**, HE WILL NOW, SINCE THAT'S THE **REVERSE**?
YEAH! YOU'RE RIGHT! THAT MAKES SENSE!

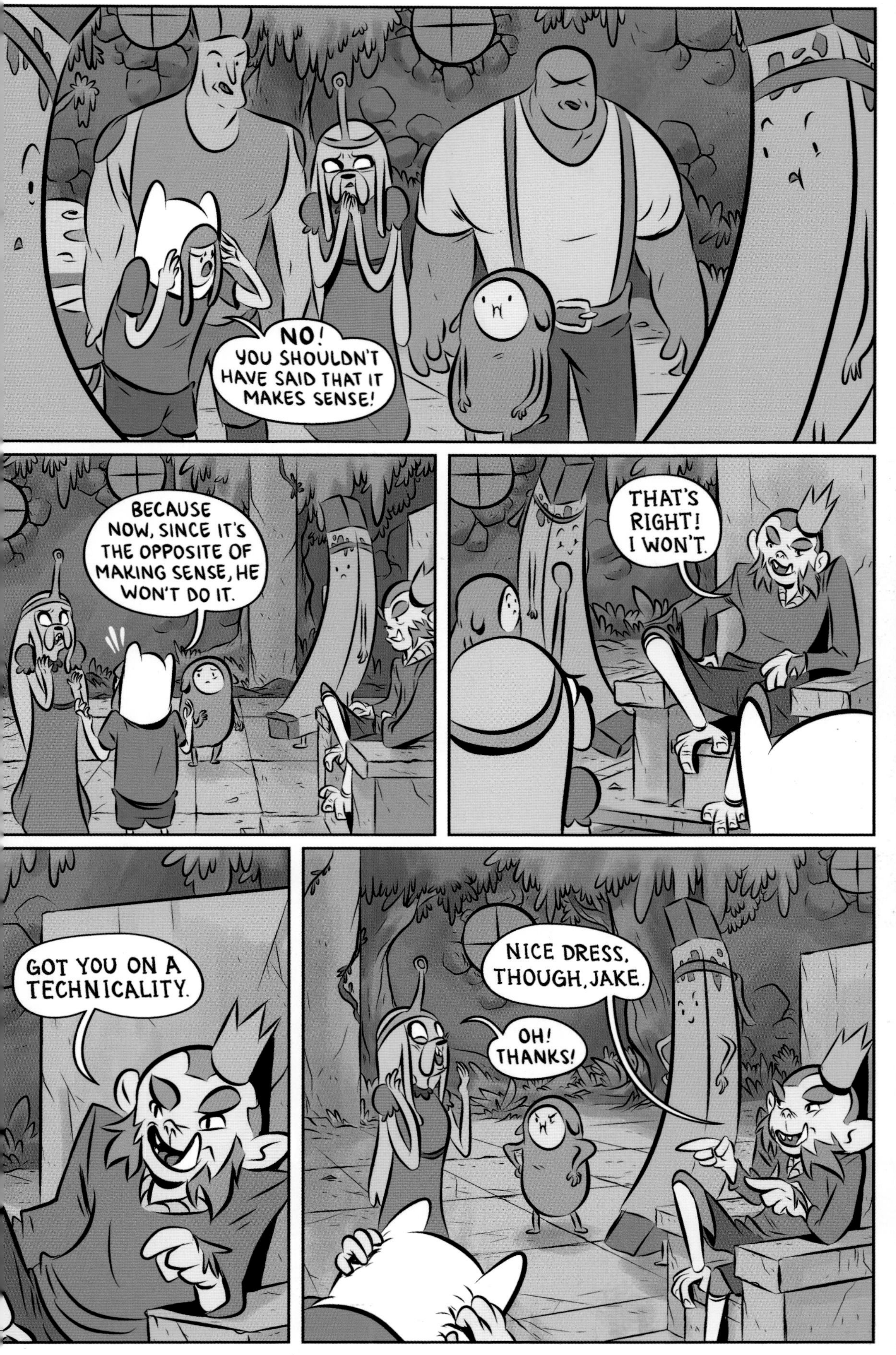
NO! YOU SHOULDN'T HAVE SAID THAT IT MAKES SENSE!
BECAUSE NOW, SINCE IT'S THE OPPOSITE OF MAKING SENSE, HE WON'T DO IT.
THAT'S RIGHT! I WON'T.
GOT YOU ON A TECHNICALITY.
NICE DRESS, THOUGH, JAKE.
OH! THANKS!

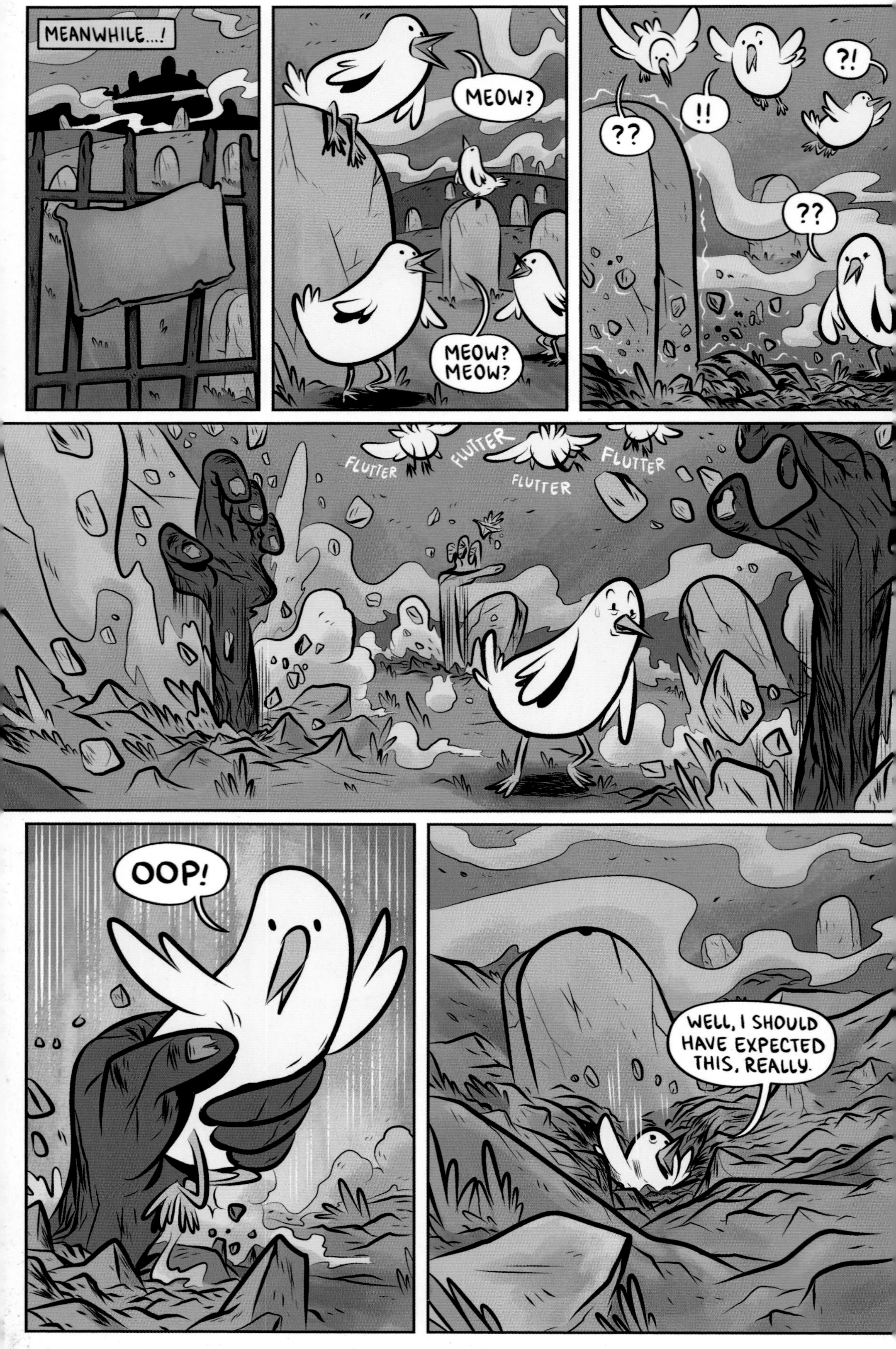
MEANWHILE...!
MEOW?
MEOW? MEOW?
??
!!
?!
??
FLUTTER
FLUTTER
FLUTTER
FLUTTER
OOP!
WELL, I SHOULD HAVE EXPECTED THIS, REALLY.

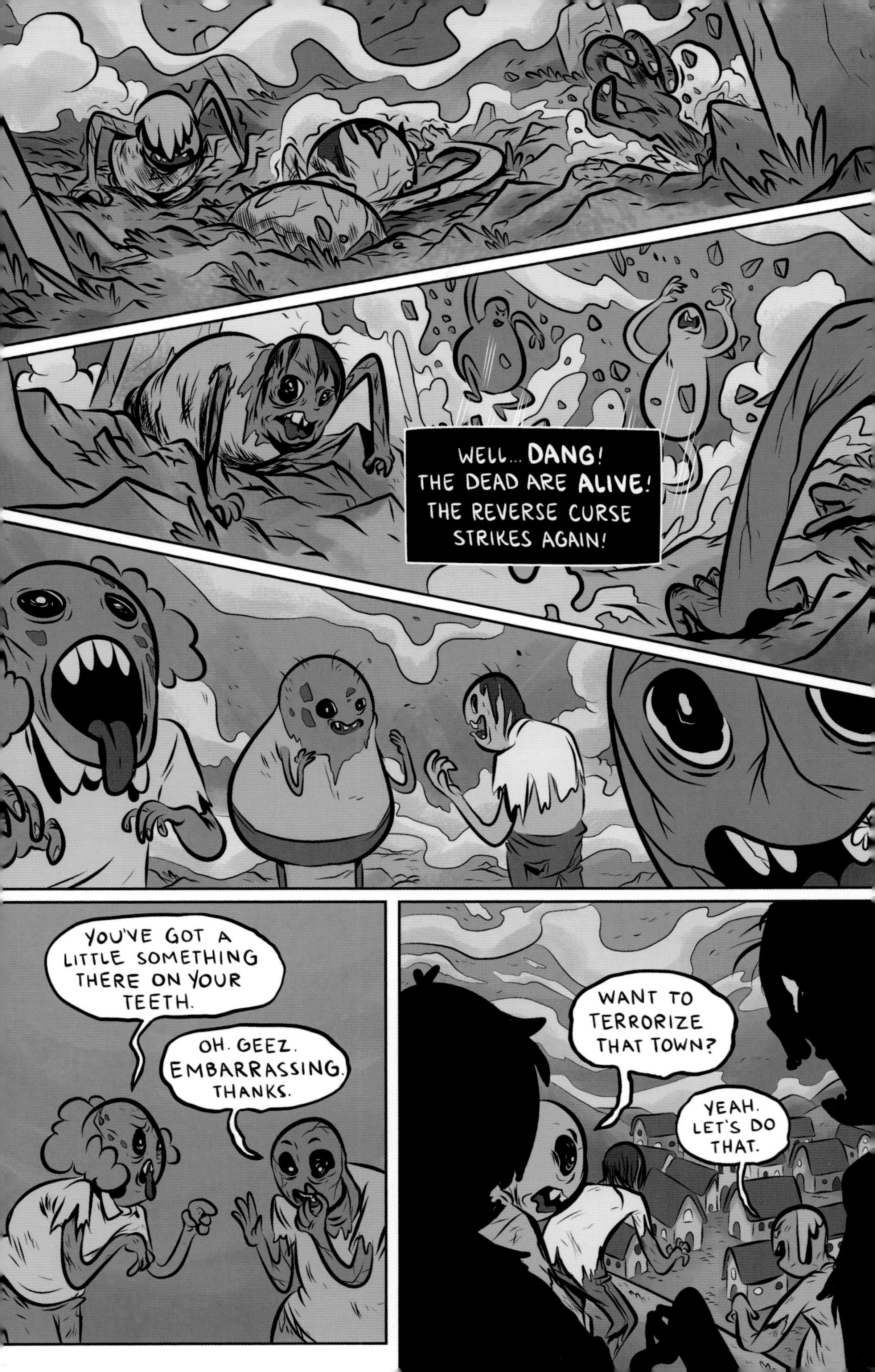
WELL... DANG! THE DEAD ARE ALIVE! THE REVERSE CURSE STRIKES AGAIN!
YOU'VE GOT A LITTLE SOMETHING THERE ON YOUR TEETH.
OH. GEEZ. EMBARRASSING. THANKS.
WANT TO TERRORIZE THAT TOWN?
YEAH. LET'S DO THAT.

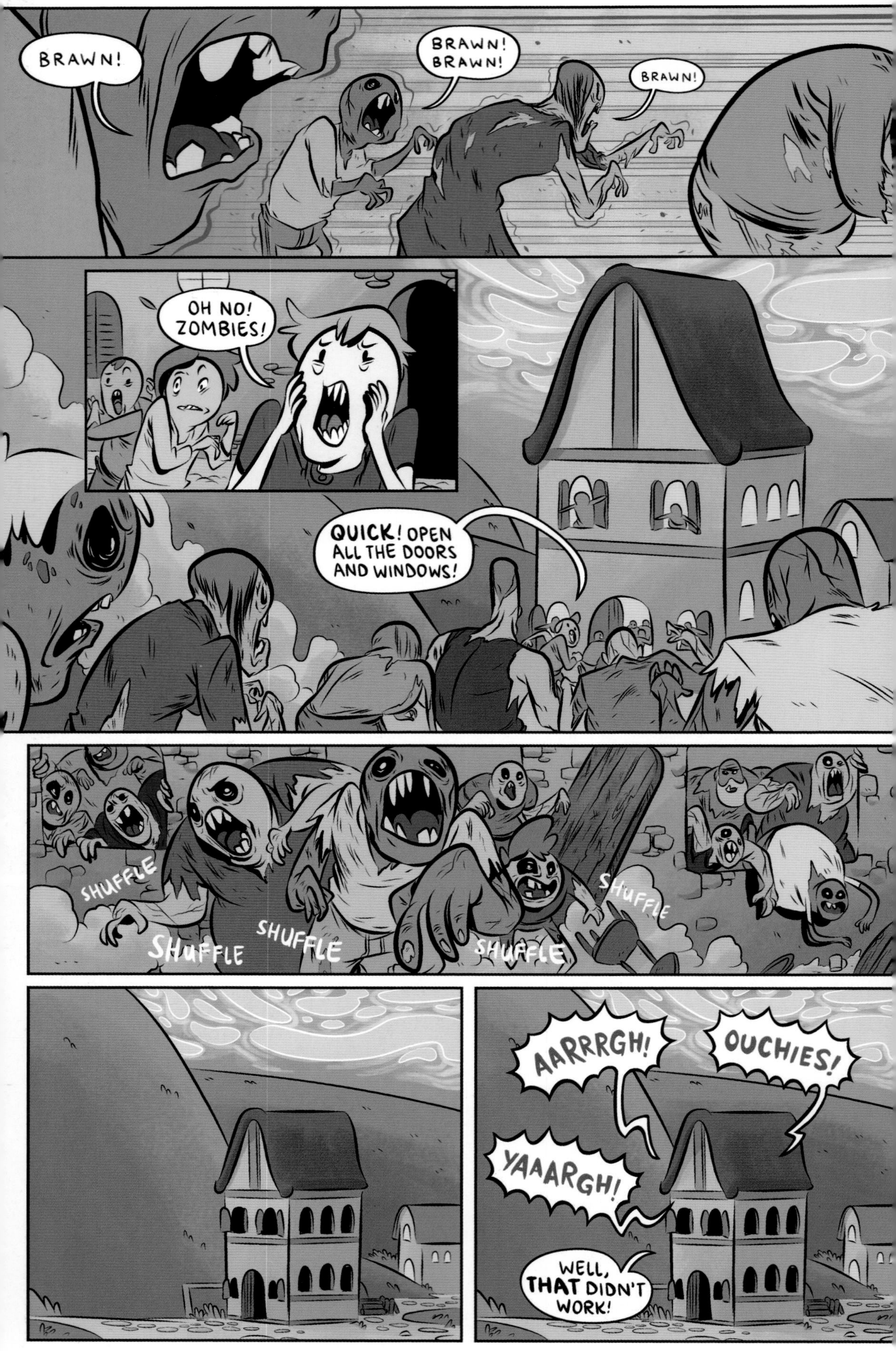
BRAWN!
BRAWN! BRAWN!
BRAWN!
OH NO! ZOMBIES!
QUICK! OPEN ALL THE DOORS AND WINDOWS!
SHUFFLE
SHUFFLE
SHUFFLE
SHUFFLE
SHUFFLE
AARRRGH!
OUCHIES!
YAAARGH!
WELL, THAT DIDN'T WORK!

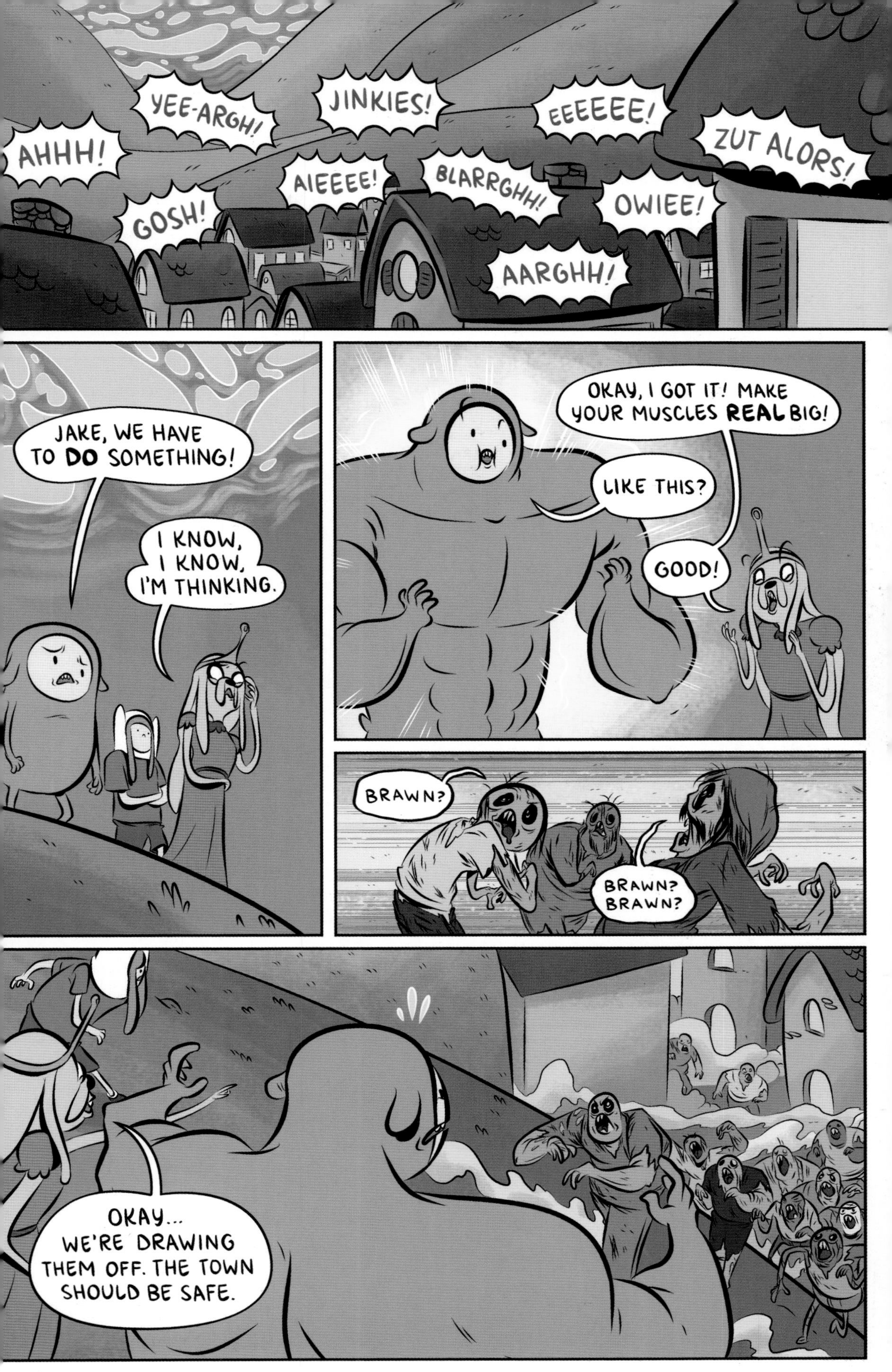
AHHH!
YEE-ARGH!
GOSH!
AIEEEE!
JINKIES!
BLARRGHH!
EEEEEE!
OWIEE!
AARGHH!
ZUT ALORS!
JAKE, WE HAVE TO DO SOMETHING!
I KNOW, I KNOW, I'M THINKING.
OKAY, I GOT IT! MAKE YOUR MUSCLES REAL BIG!
LIKE THIS?
GOOD!
BRAWN?
BRAWN? BRAWN?
OKAY... WE'RE DRAWING THEM OFF. THE TOWN SHOULD BE SAFE.

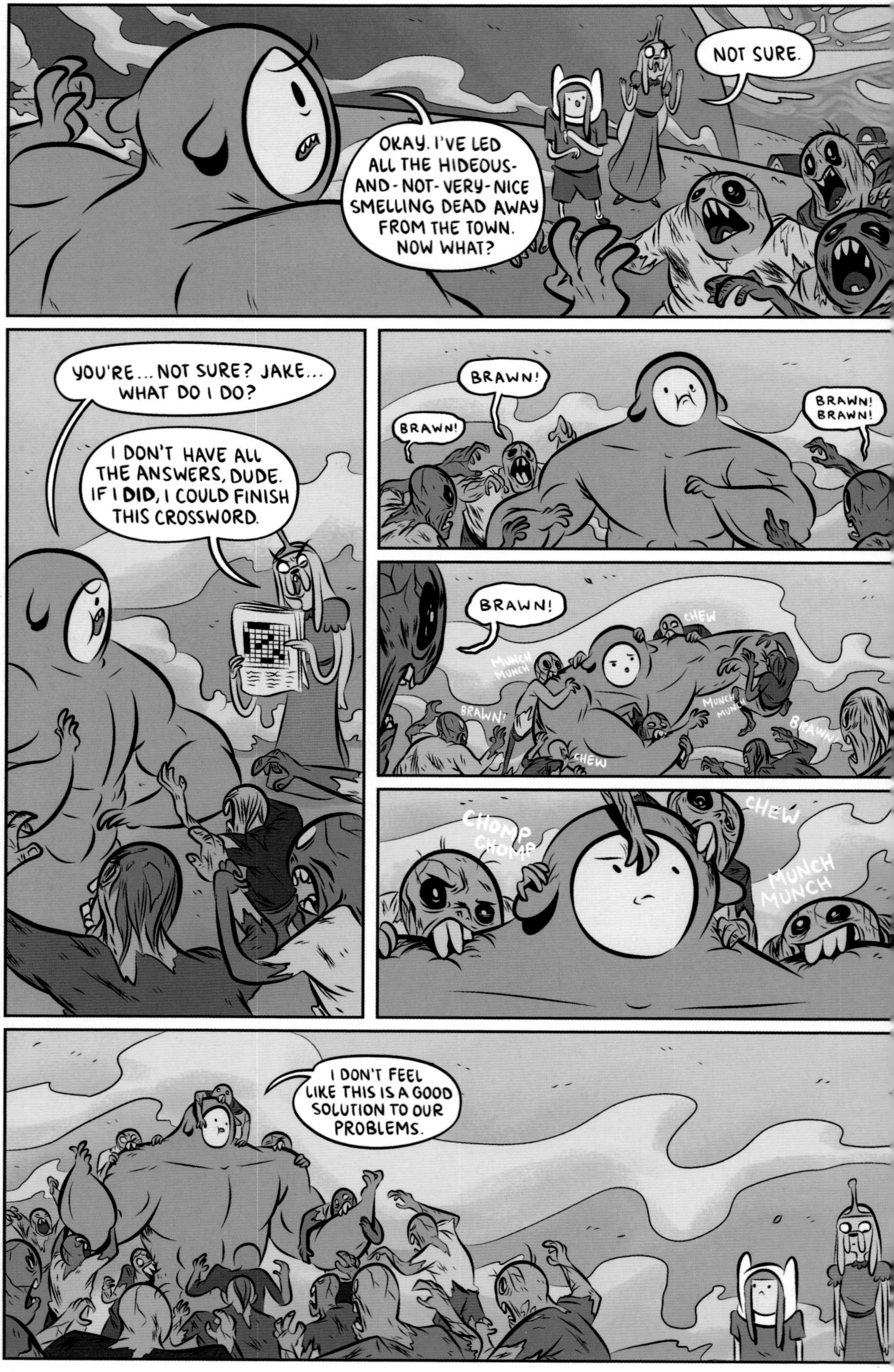
NOT SURE.
OKAY. I'VE LED ALL THE HIDEOUS-AND-NOT-VERY-NICE SMELLING DEAD AWAY FROM THE TOWN. NOW WHAT?
YOU'RE... NOT SURE? JAKE... WHAT DO I DO?
I DON'T HAVE ALL THE ANSWERS, DUDE. IF I **DID**, I COULD FINISH THIS CROSSWORD.
BRAWN!
BRAWN!
BRAWN! BRAWN!
BRAWN!
CHEW
MUNCH MUNCH
BRAWN!
MUNCH MUNCH
BRAWN!
CHEW
CHOMP CHOMP
CHEW
MUNCH MUNCH
I DON'T FEEL LIKE THIS IS A GOOD SOLUTION TO OUR PROBLEMS.

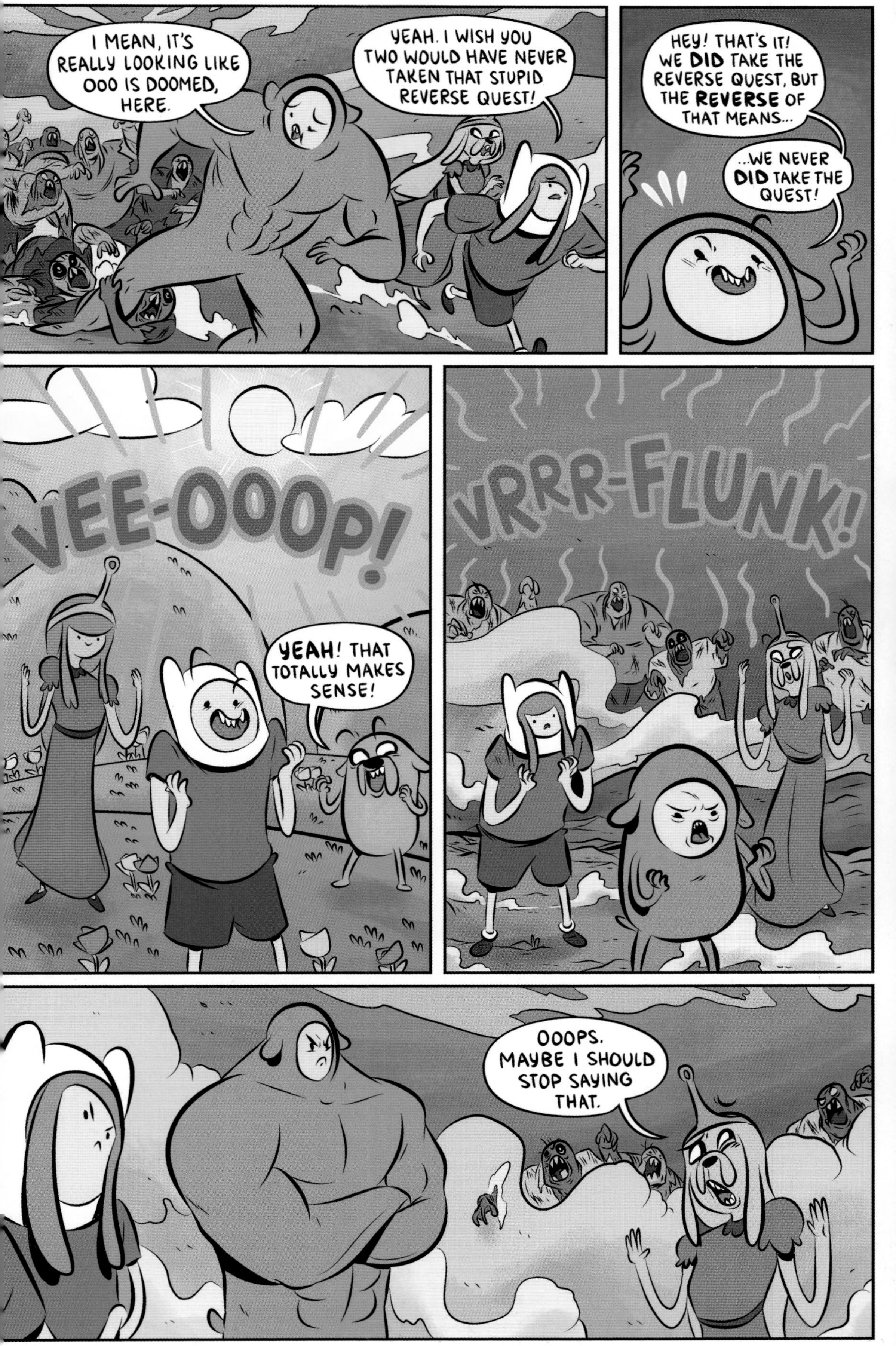
I MEAN, IT'S REALLY LOOKING LIKE OOO IS DOOMED, HERE.
YEAH. I WISH YOU TWO WOULD HAVE NEVER TAKEN THAT STUPID REVERSE QUEST!
HEY! THAT'S IT! WE DID TAKE THE REVERSE QUEST, BUT THE REVERSE OF THAT MEANS...
...WE NEVER DID TAKE THE QUEST!
VEE-OOOP!
YEAH! THAT TOTALLY MAKES SENSE!
VRRR-FLUNK!
OOOPS. MAYBE I SHOULD STOP SAYING THAT.

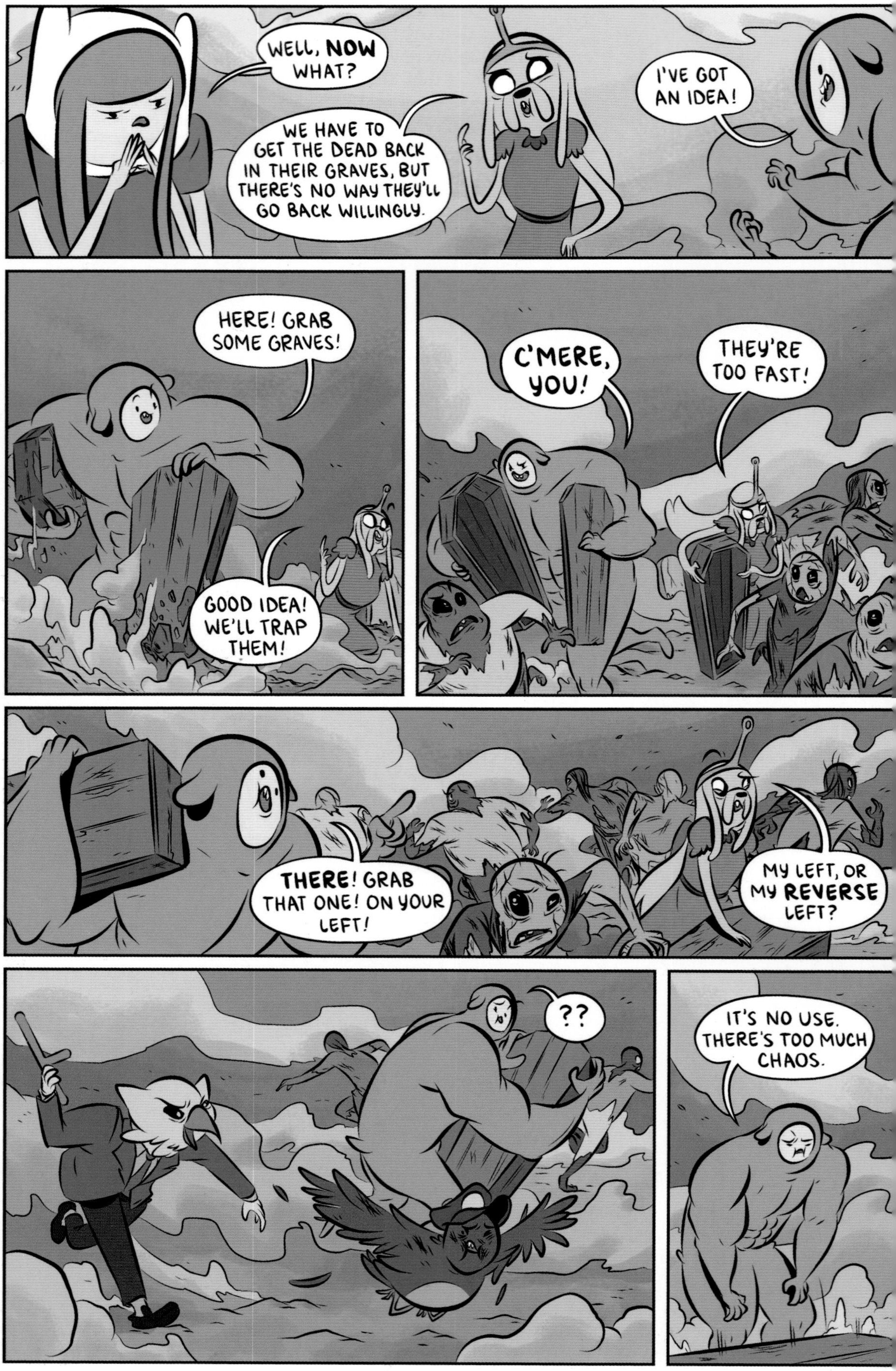
WELL, NOW WHAT?
WE HAVE TO GET THE DEAD BACK IN THEIR GRAVES, BUT THERE'S NO WAY THEY'LL GO BACK WILLINGLY.
I'VE GOT AN IDEA!
HERE! GRAB SOME GRAVES!
GOOD IDEA! WE'LL TRAP THEM!
C'MERE, YOU!
THEY'RE TOO FAST!
THERE! GRAB THAT ONE! ON YOUR LEFT!
MY LEFT, OR MY REVERSE LEFT?
??
IT'S NO USE. THERE'S TOO MUCH CHAOS.

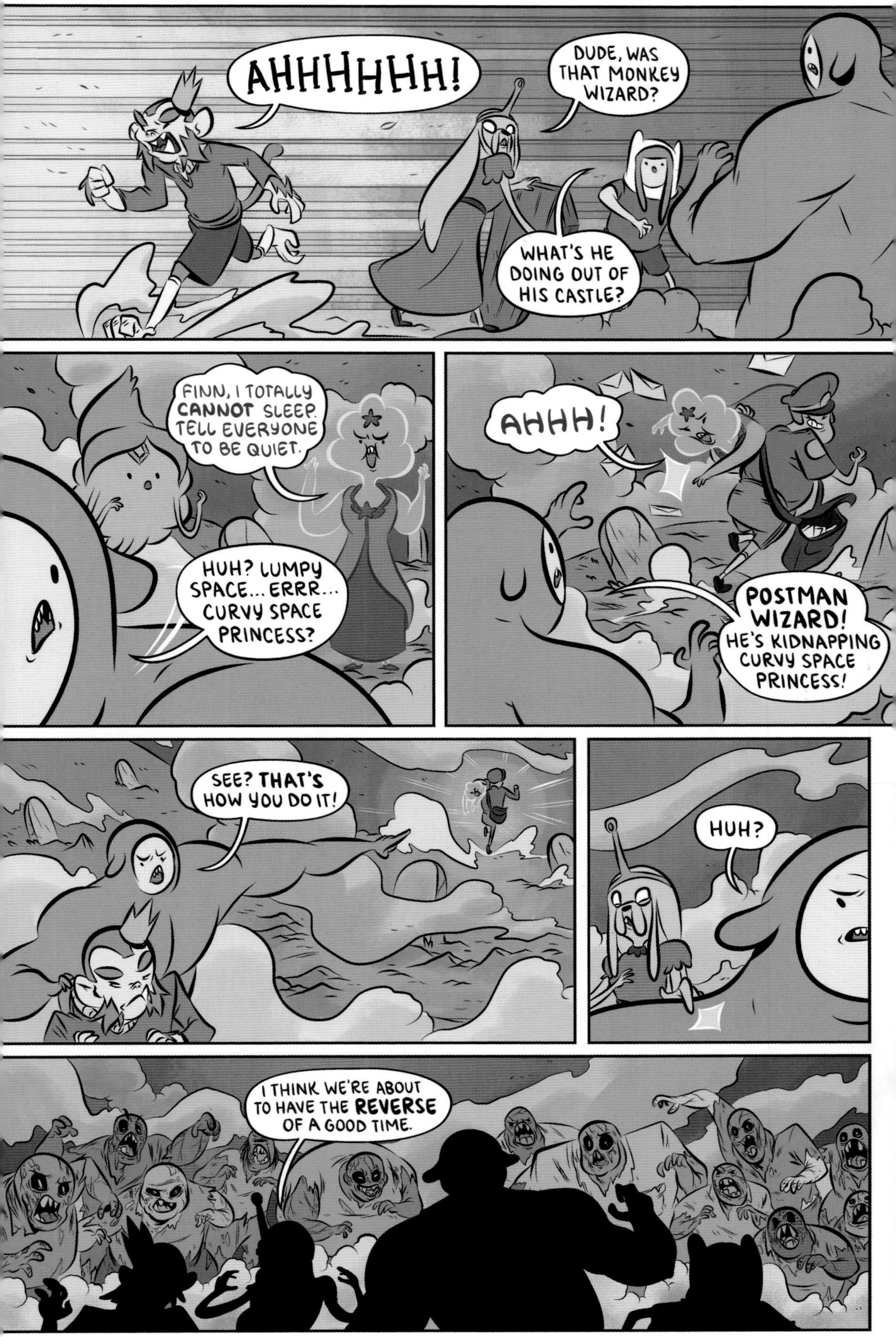
AHHHHHH!
DUDE, WAS THAT MONKEY WIZARD?
WHAT'S HE DOING OUT OF HIS CASTLE?
FINN, I TOTALLY CANNOT SLEEP. TELL EVERYONE TO BE QUIET.
HUH? LUMPY SPACE... ERRR... CURVY SPACE PRINCESS?
AHHH!
POSTMAN WIZARD! HE'S KIDNAPPING CURVY SPACE PRINCESS!
SEE? THAT'S HOW YOU DO IT!
HUH?
I THINK WE'RE ABOUT TO HAVE THE REVERSE OF A GOOD TIME.

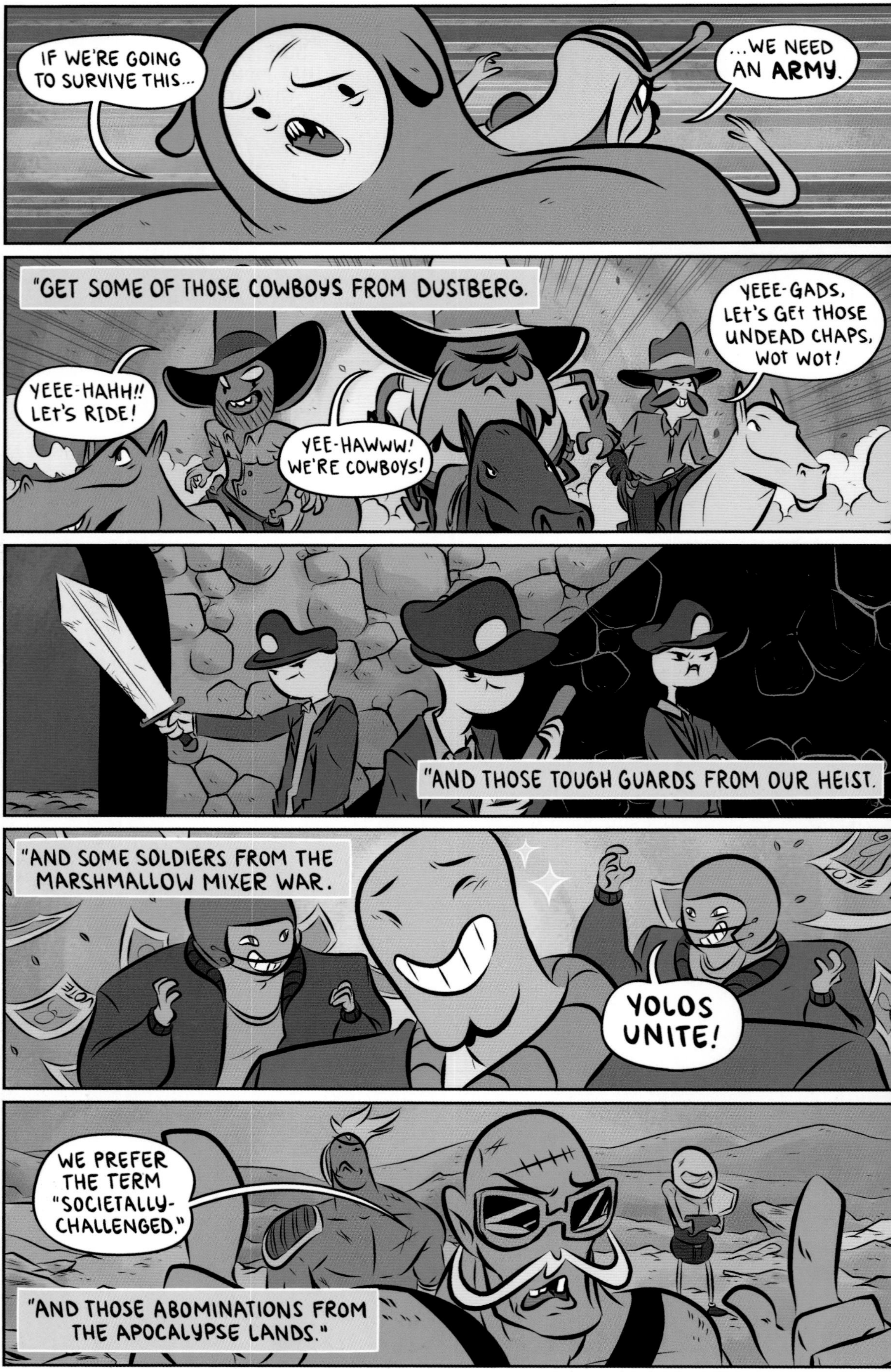
IF WE'RE GOING TO SURVIVE THIS...
...WE NEED AN **ARMY**.
"GET SOME OF THOSE COWBOYS FROM DUSTBERG.
YEEE-HAHH!! LET'S RIDE!
YEE-HAWWW! WE'RE COWBOYS!
YEEE-GADS, LET'S GET THOSE UNDEAD CHAPS, WOT WOT!
"AND THOSE TOUGH GUARDS FROM OUR HEIST.
"AND SOME SOLDIERS FROM THE MARSHMALLOW MIXER WAR.
YOLOS UNITE!
WE PREFER THE TERM "SOCIETALLY-CHALLENGED."
"AND THOSE ABOMINATIONS FROM THE APOCALYPSE LANDS."

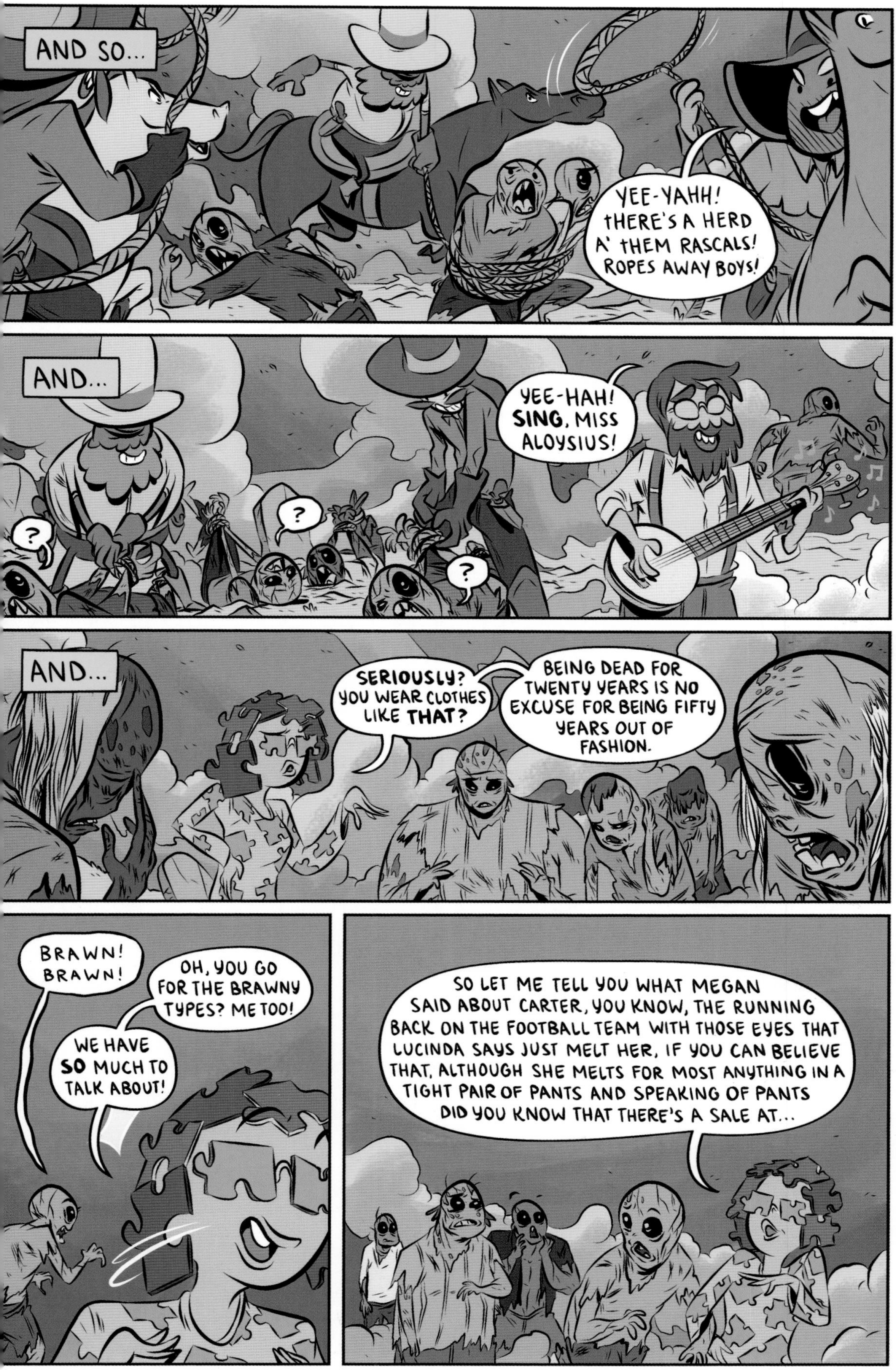

AND SO...
YEE-YAHH! THERE'S A HERD A' THEM RASCALS! ROPES AWAY BOYS!
AND...
YEE-HAH! **SING**, MISS ALOYSIUS!
?
?
?
AND...
SERIOUSLY? YOU WEAR CLOTHES LIKE **THAT?**
BEING DEAD FOR TWENTY YEARS IS NO EXCUSE FOR BEING FIFTY YEARS OUT OF FASHION.
BRAWN! BRAWN!
OH, YOU GO FOR THE BRAWNY TYPES? ME TOO!
WE HAVE **SO** MUCH TO TALK ABOUT!
SO LET ME TELL YOU WHAT MEGAN SAID ABOUT CARTER, YOU KNOW, THE RUNNING BACK ON THE FOOTBALL TEAM WITH THOSE EYES THAT LUCINDA SAYS JUST MELT HER, IF YOU CAN BELIEVE THAT, ALTHOUGH SHE MELTS FOR MOST ANYTHING IN A TIGHT PAIR OF PANTS AND SPEAKING OF PANTS DID YOU KNOW THAT THERE'S A SALE AT...

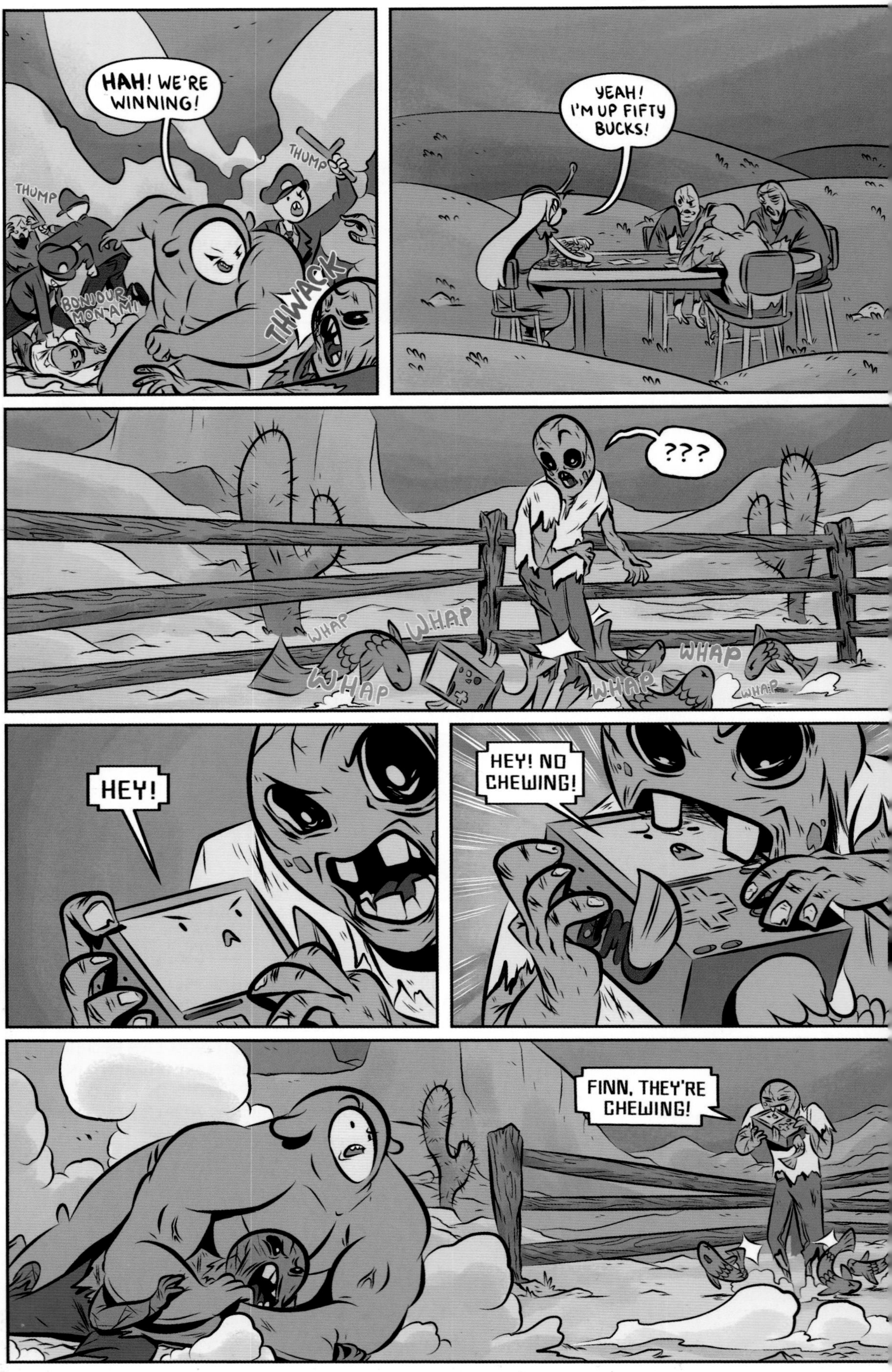
HAH! WE'RE WINNING!
THUMP
THUMP
BONJOUR MON AMI
THWACK
YEAH! I'M UP FIFTY BUCKS!
???
WHAP
WHAP
WHAP
WHAP
WHAP
WHAP
HEY!
HEY! NO CHEWING!
FINN, THEY'RE CHEWING!

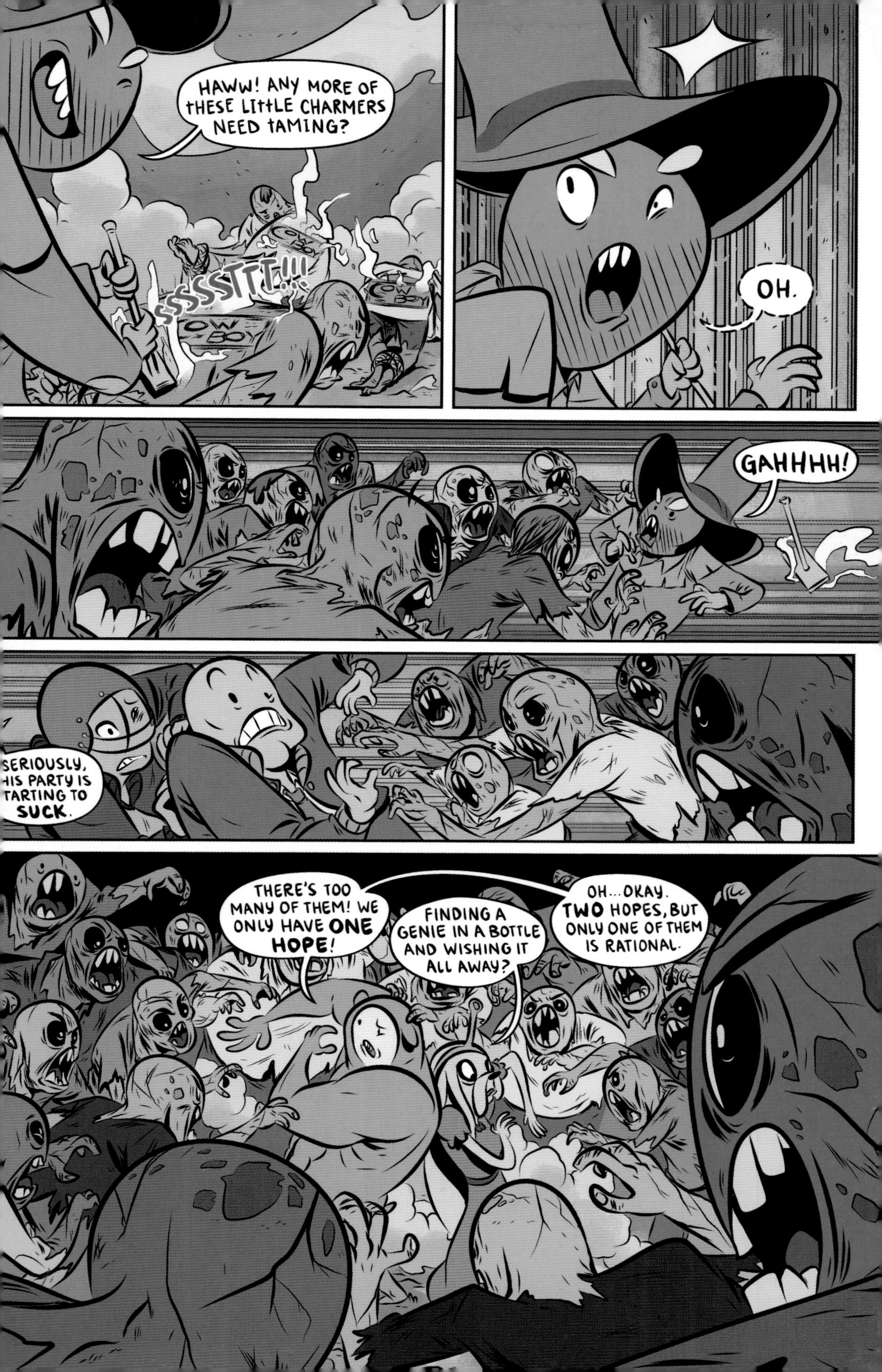
HAWW! ANY MORE OF THESE LITTLE CHARMERS NEED TAMING?
SSSSSTTT!!!
OH.
GAHHHH!
SERIOUSLY, HIS PARTY IS TARTING TO SUCK.
THERE'S TOO MANY OF THEM! WE ONLY HAVE ONE HOPE!
FINDING A GENIE IN A BOTTLE AND WISHING IT ALL AWAY?
OH... OKAY. TWO HOPES, BUT ONLY ONE OF THEM IS RATIONAL.

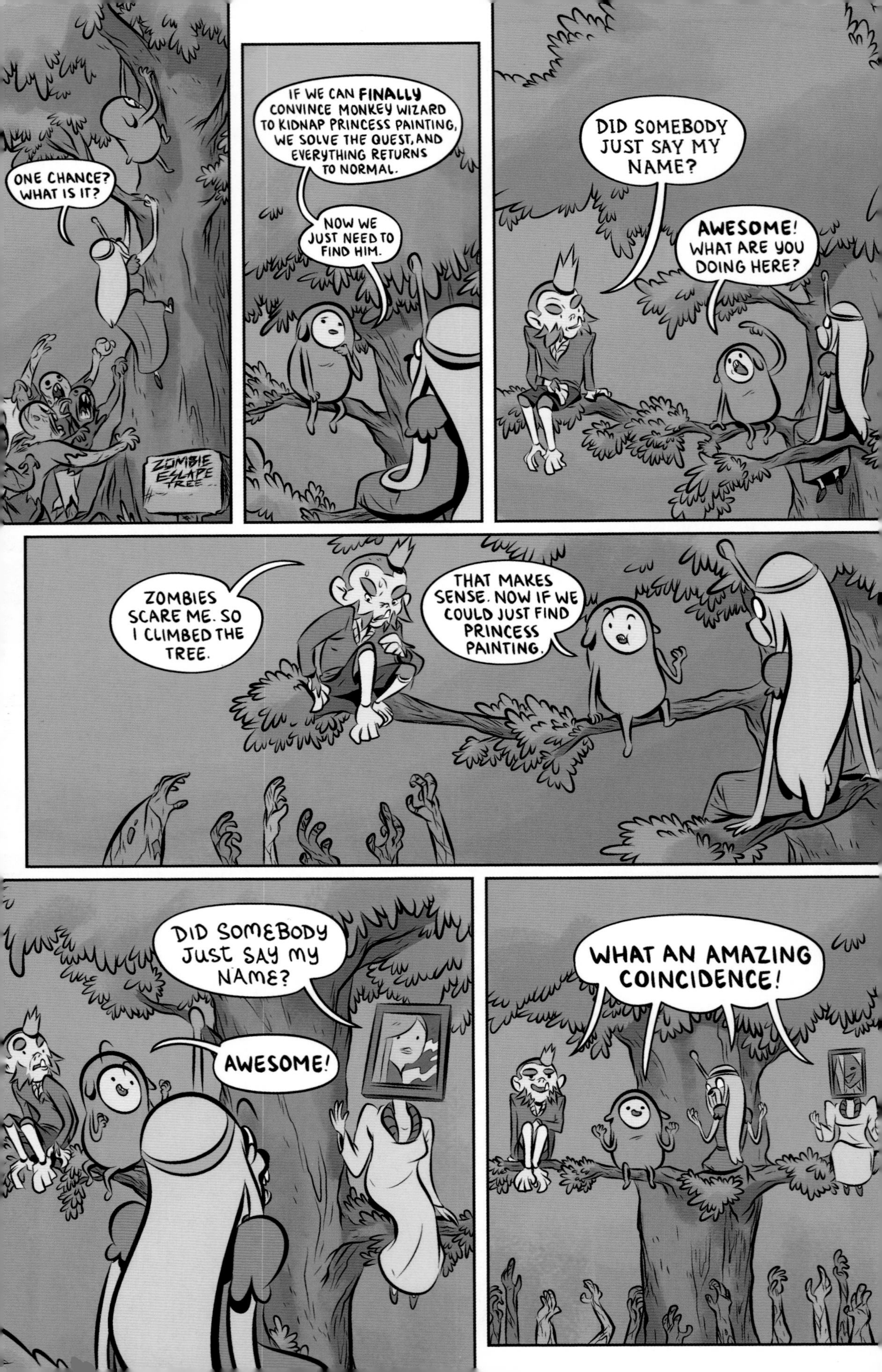
ONE CHANCE? WHAT IS IT?
ZOMBIE ESCAPE TREE
IF WE CAN FINALLY CONVINCE MONKEY WIZARD TO KIDNAP PRINCESS PAINTING, WE SOLVE THE QUEST, AND EVERYTHING RETURNS TO NORMAL.
NOW WE JUST NEED TO FIND HIM.
DID SOMEBODY JUST SAY MY NAME?
AWESOME! WHAT ARE YOU DOING HERE?
ZOMBIES SCARE ME. SO I CLIMBED THE TREE.
THAT MAKES SENSE. NOW IF WE COULD JUST FIND PRINCESS PAINTING.
DID SOMEBODY JUST SAY MY NAME?
AWESOME!
WHAT AN AMAZING COINCIDENCE!

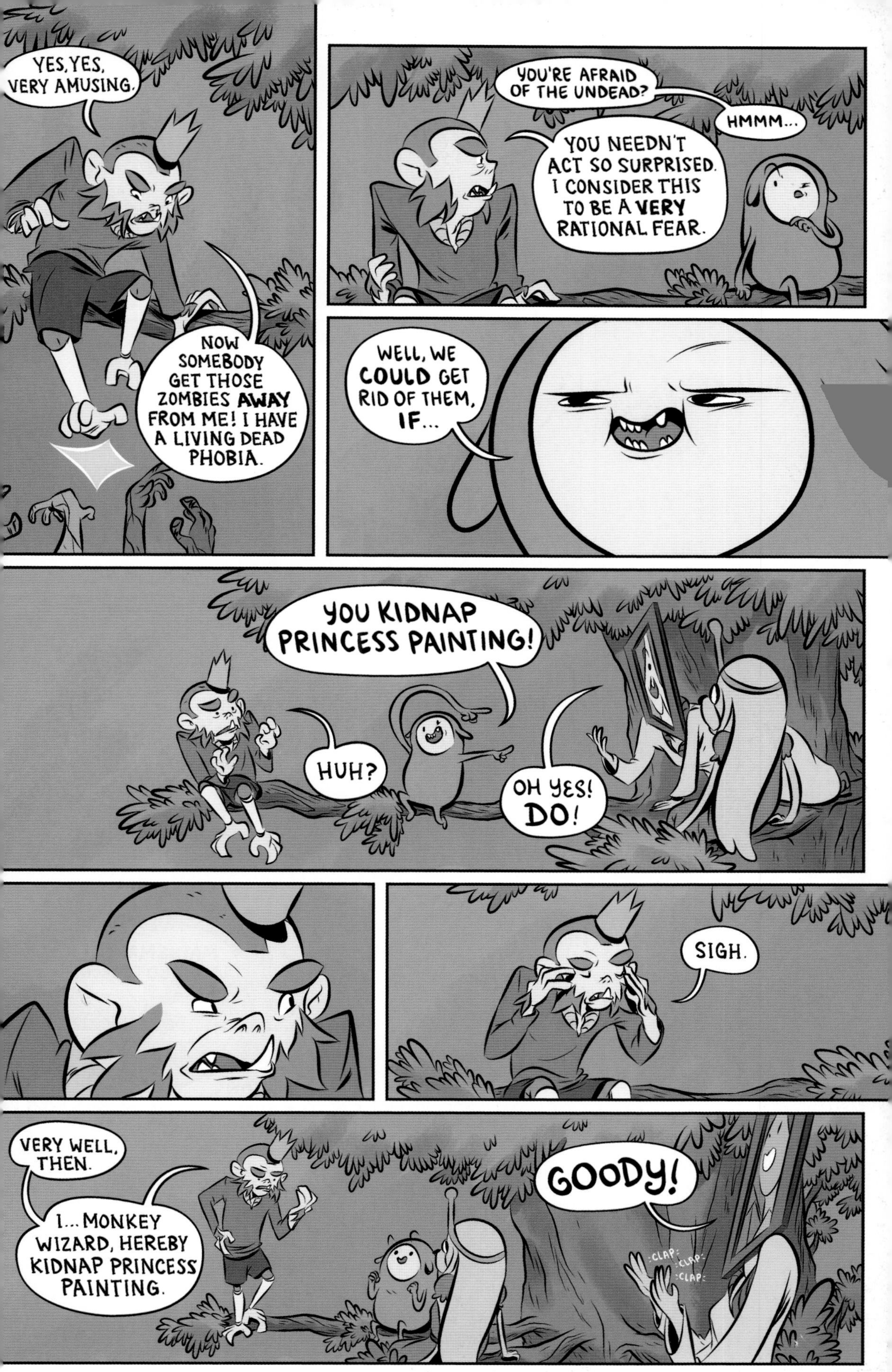
YES, YES, VERY AMUSING.
NOW SOMEBODY GET THOSE ZOMBIES AWAY FROM ME! I HAVE A LIVING DEAD PHOBIA.
YOU'RE AFRAID OF THE UNDEAD?
HMMM...
YOU NEEDN'T ACT SO SURPRISED. I CONSIDER THIS TO BE A VERY RATIONAL FEAR.
WELL, WE COULD GET RID OF THEM, IF...
YOU KIDNAP PRINCESS PAINTING!
HUH?
OH YES! DO!
SIGH.
VERY WELL, THEN.
I... MONKEY WIZARD, HEREBY KIDNAP PRINCESS PAINTING.
GOODY!
CLAP CLAP CLAP

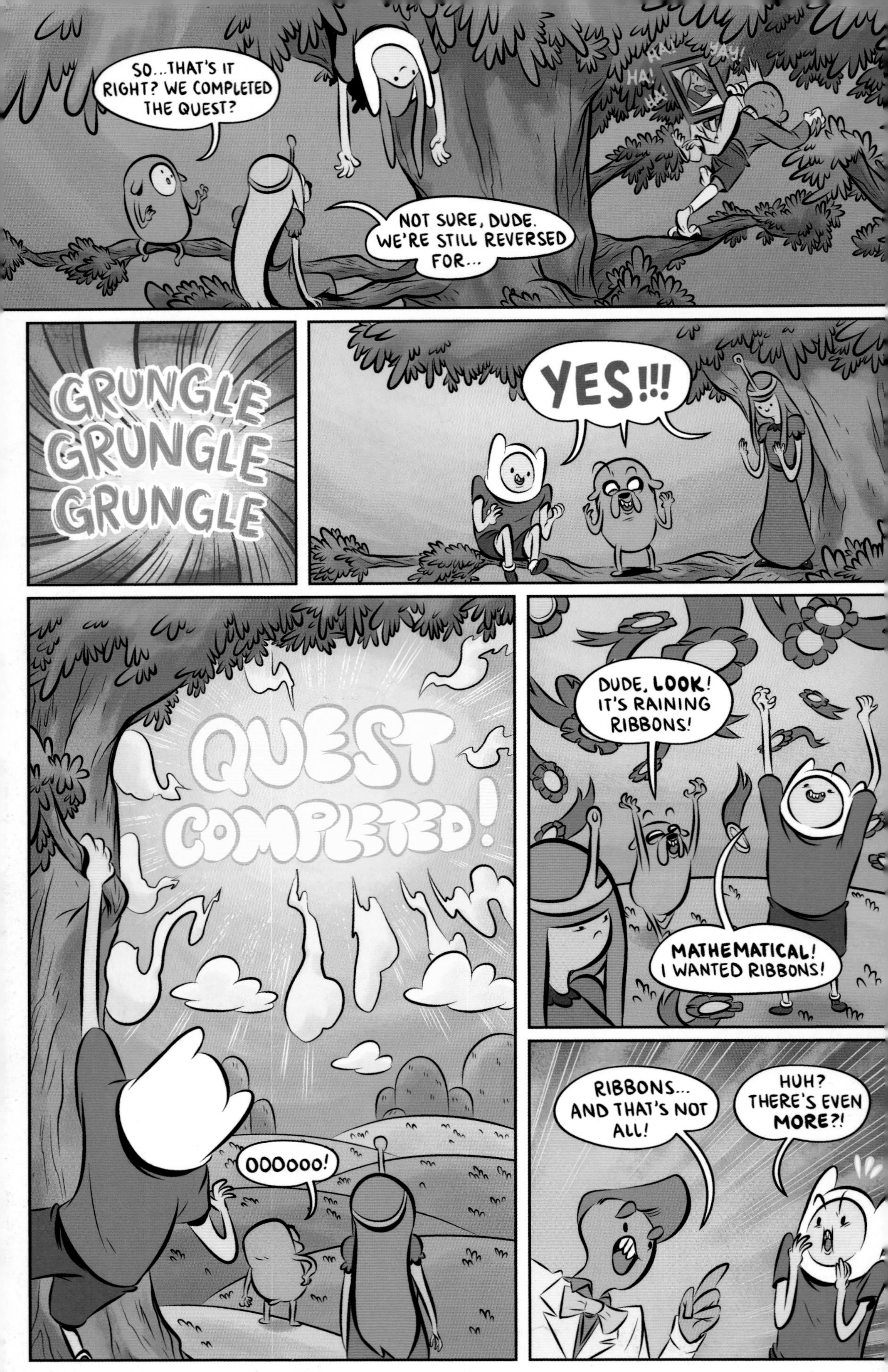
SO...THAT'S IT RIGHT? WE COMPLETED THE QUEST?
HA! HA! HA! HA!
YAY!
NOT SURE, DUDE. WE'RE STILL REVERSED FOR...
GRUNGLE GRUNGLE GRUNGLE
YES!!!
QUEST COMPLETED!
OOOOOO!
DUDE, **LOOK**! IT'S RAINING RIBBONS!
MATHEMATICAL! I WANTED RIBBONS!
RIBBONS... AND THAT'S NOT ALL!
HUH? THERE'S EVEN **MORE**?!

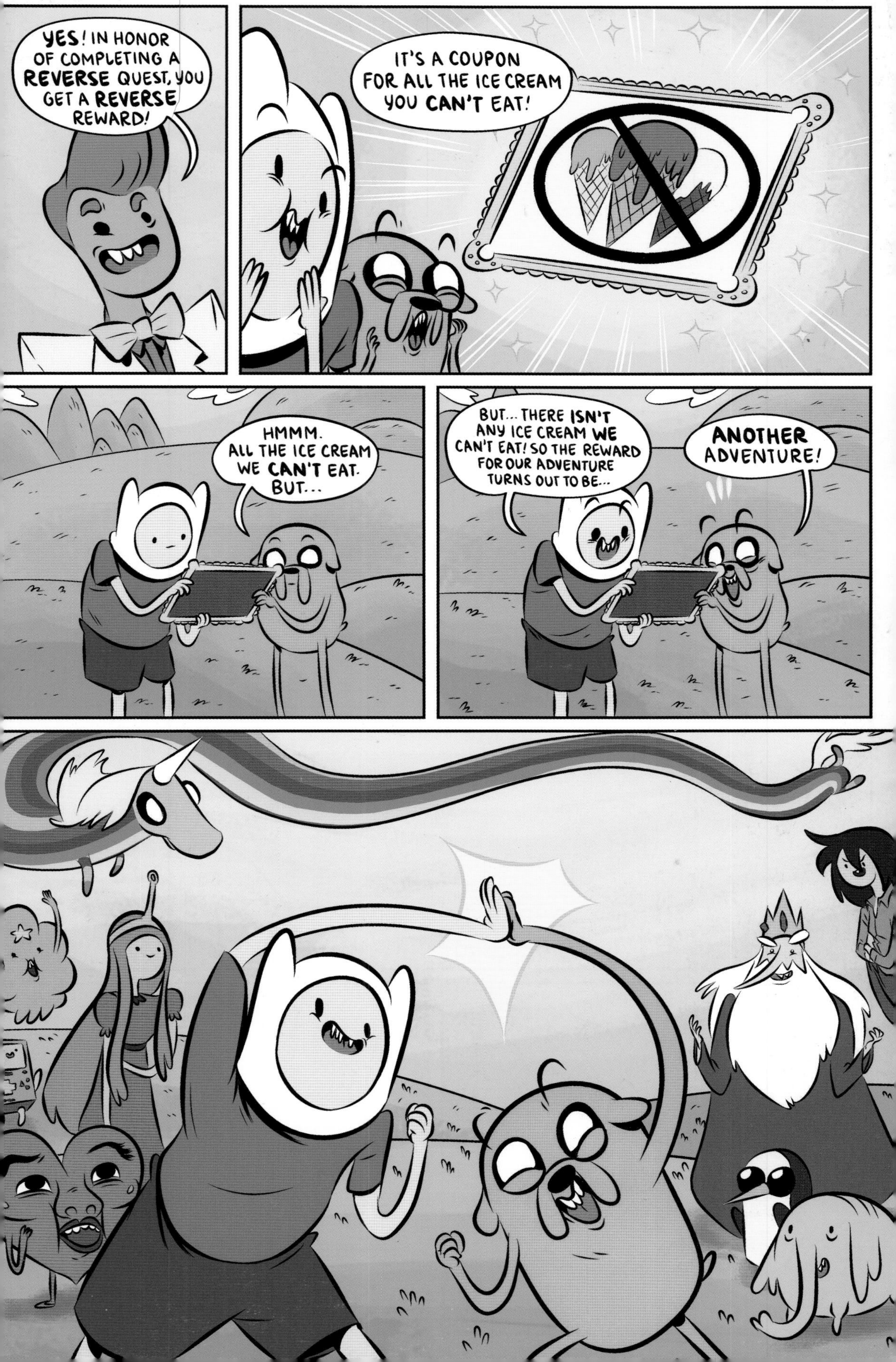
YES! IN HONOR OF COMPLETING A REVERSE QUEST, YOU GET A REVERSE REWARD!
IT'S A COUPON FOR ALL THE ICE CREAM YOU CAN'T EAT!
HMMM. ALL THE ICE CREAM WE CAN'T EAT. BUT...
BUT... THERE ISN'T ANY ICE CREAM WE CAN'T EAT! SO THE REWARD FOR OUR ADVENTURE TURNS OUT TO BE...
ANOTHER ADVENTURE!

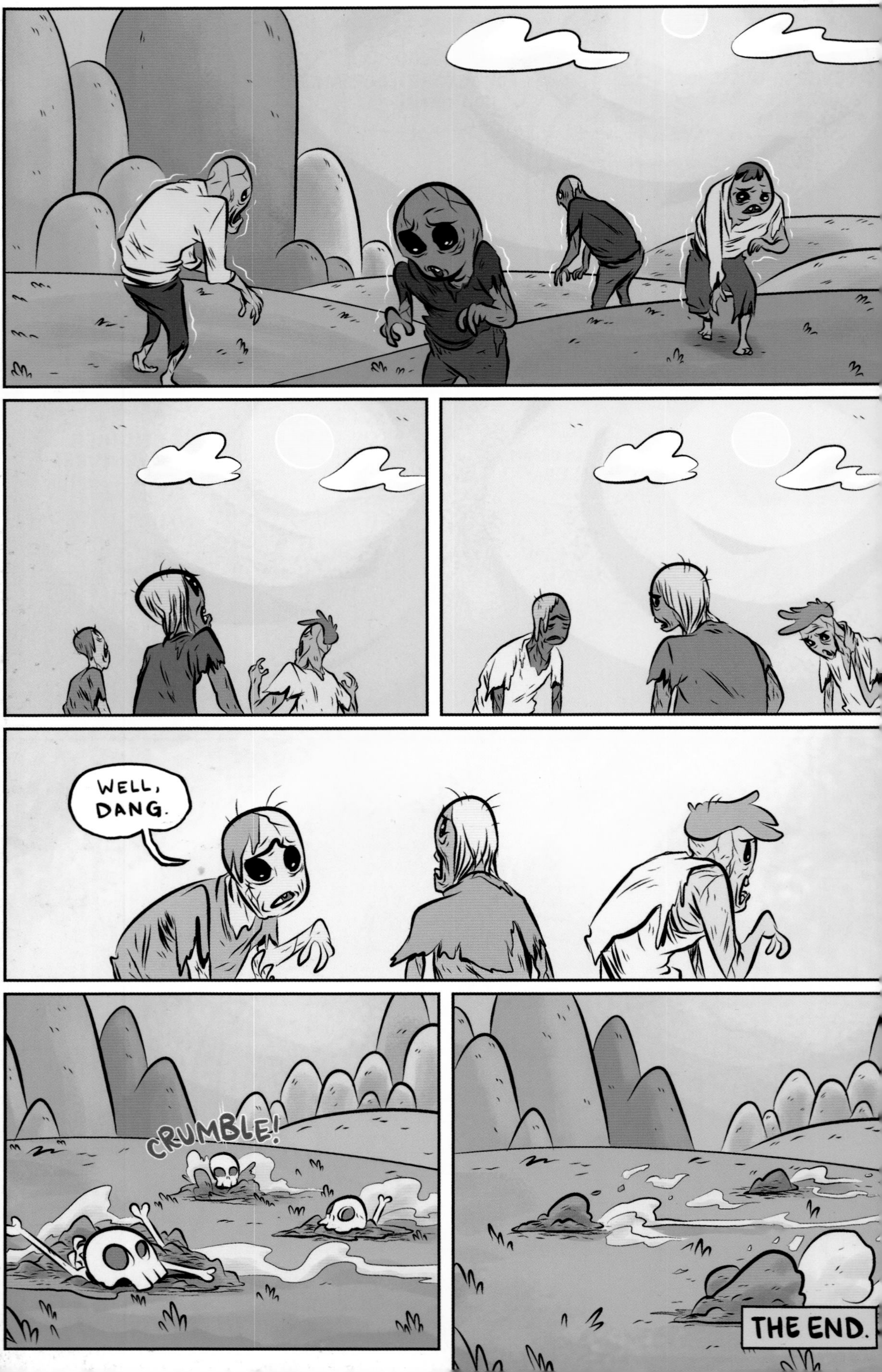
WELL, DANG.
CRUMBLE!
THE END.

COVER GALLERY

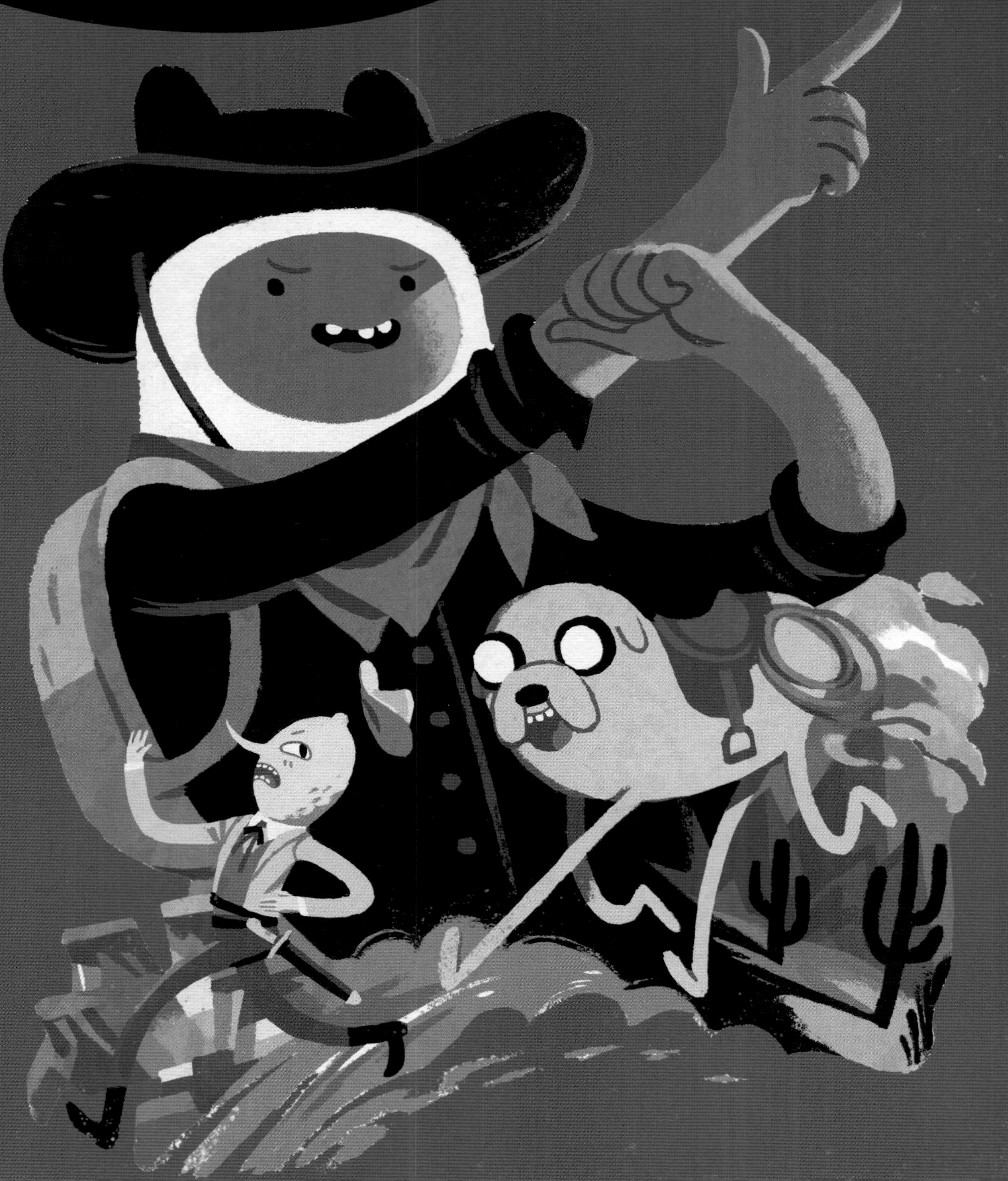

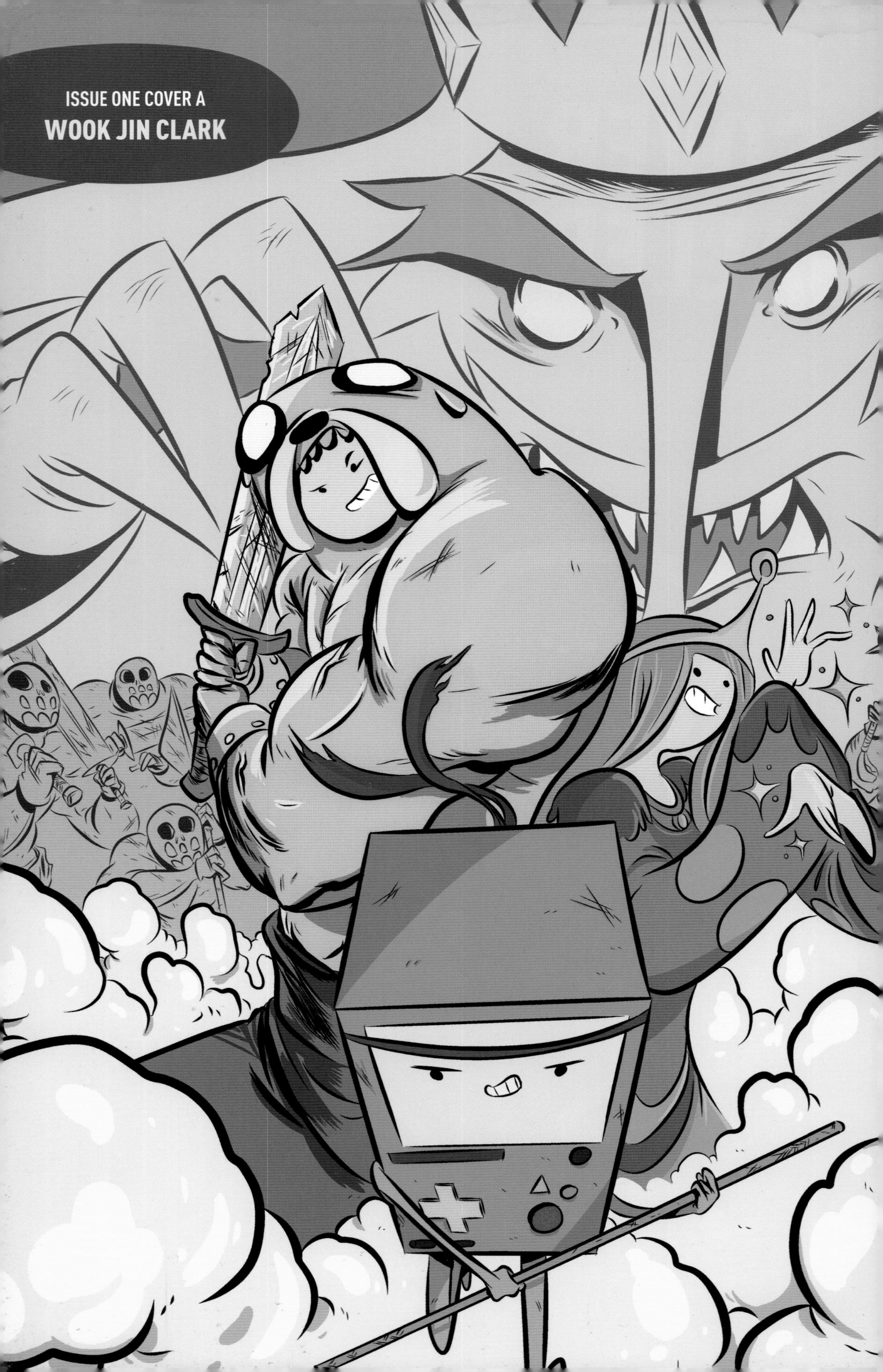
ISSUE ONE COVER A
WOOK JIN CLARK

ISSUE TWO COVER A

WOOK JIN CLARK

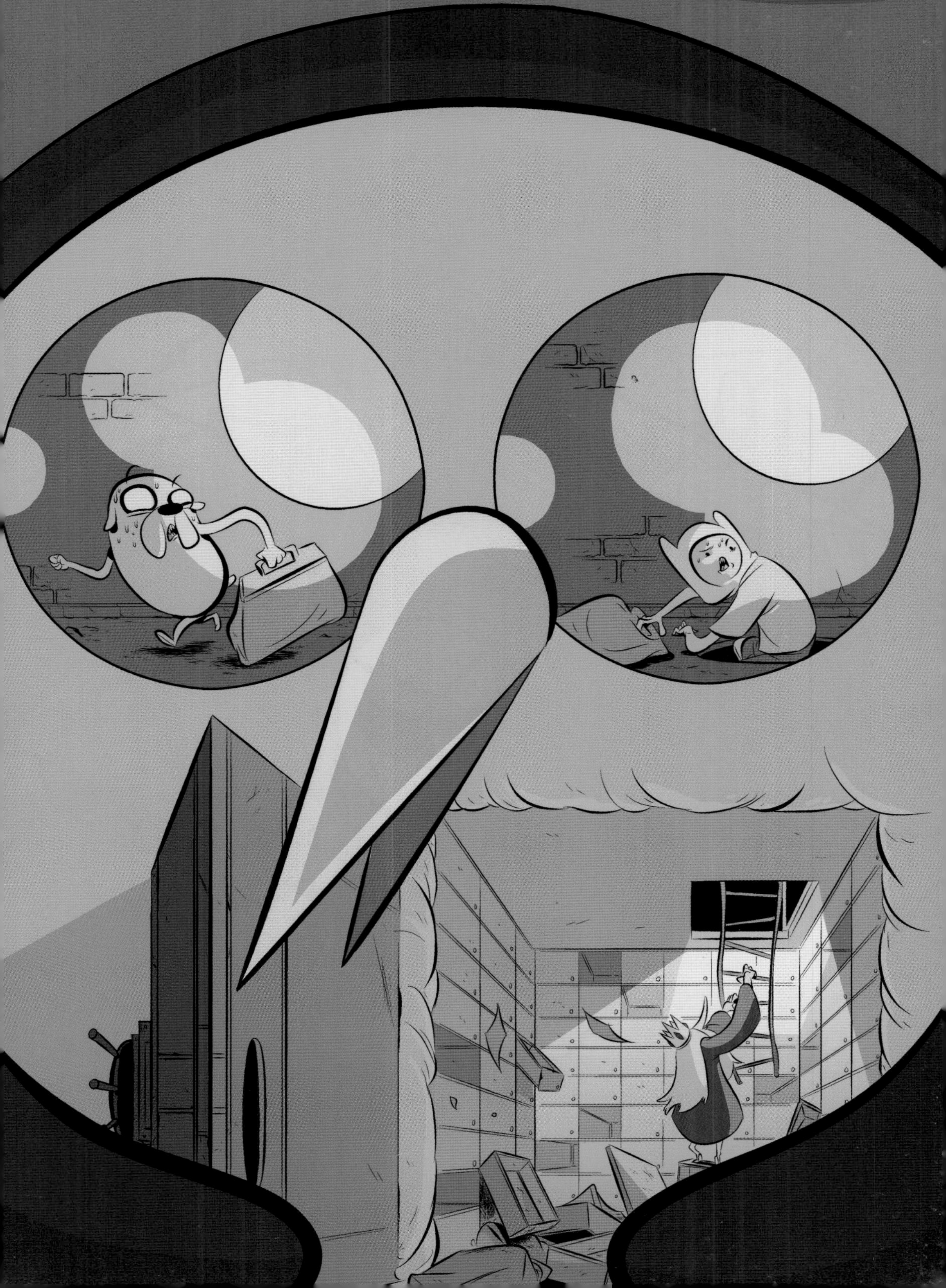

ISSUE THREE COVER A
WOOK JIN CLARK

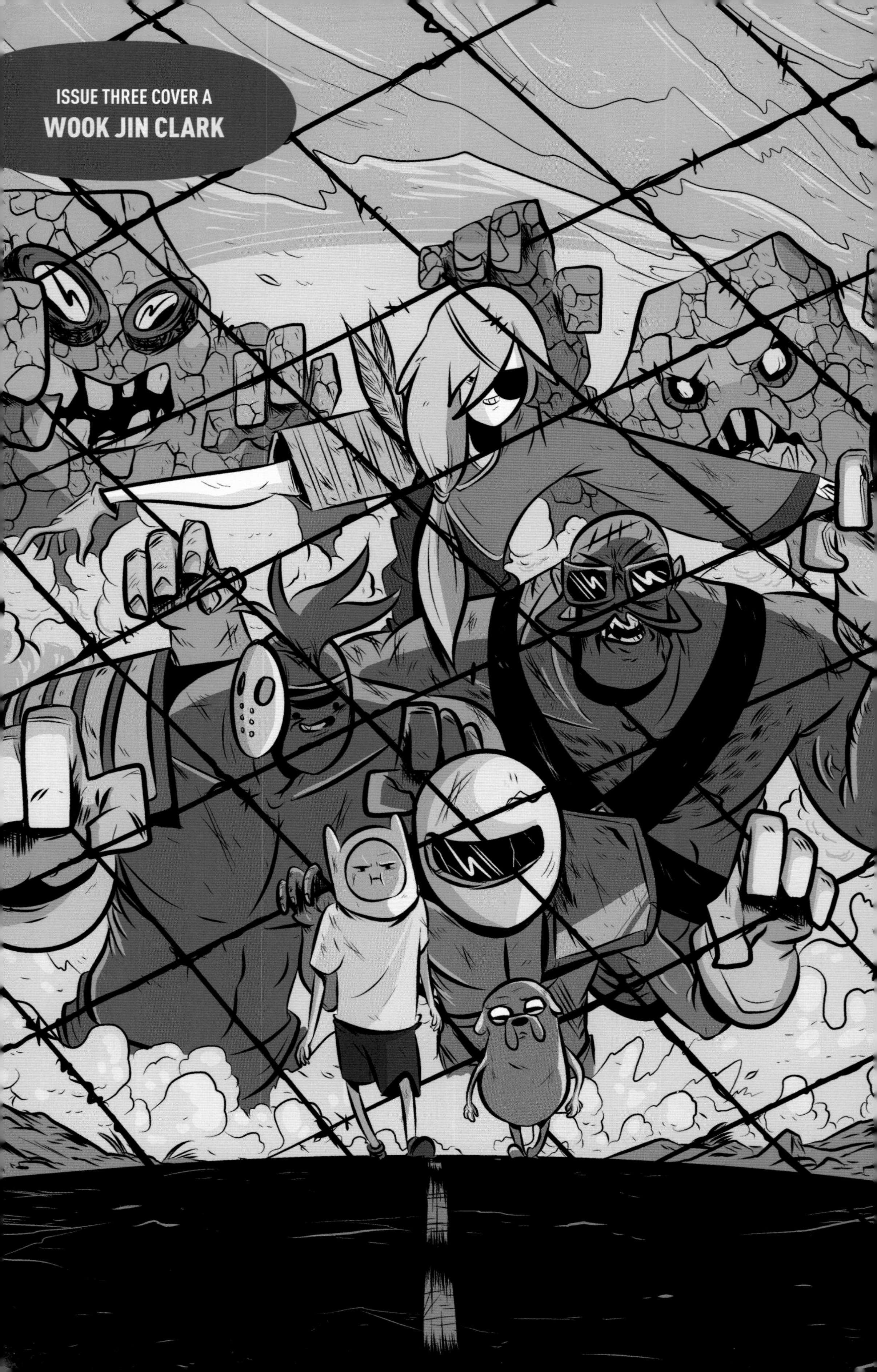

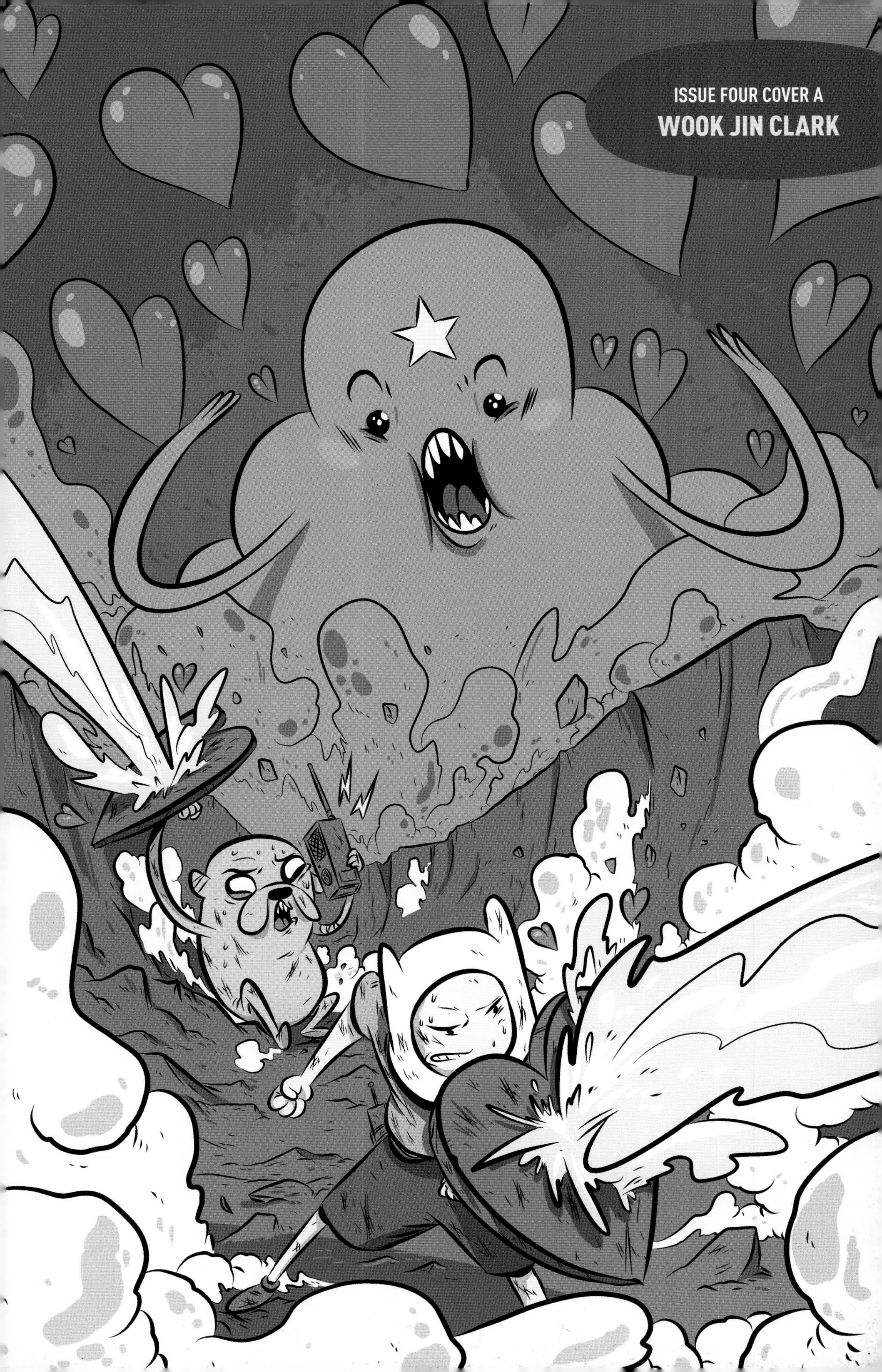
ISSUE FOUR COVER A
WOOK JIN CLARK

ISSUE FIVE COVER A
WOOK JIN CLARK

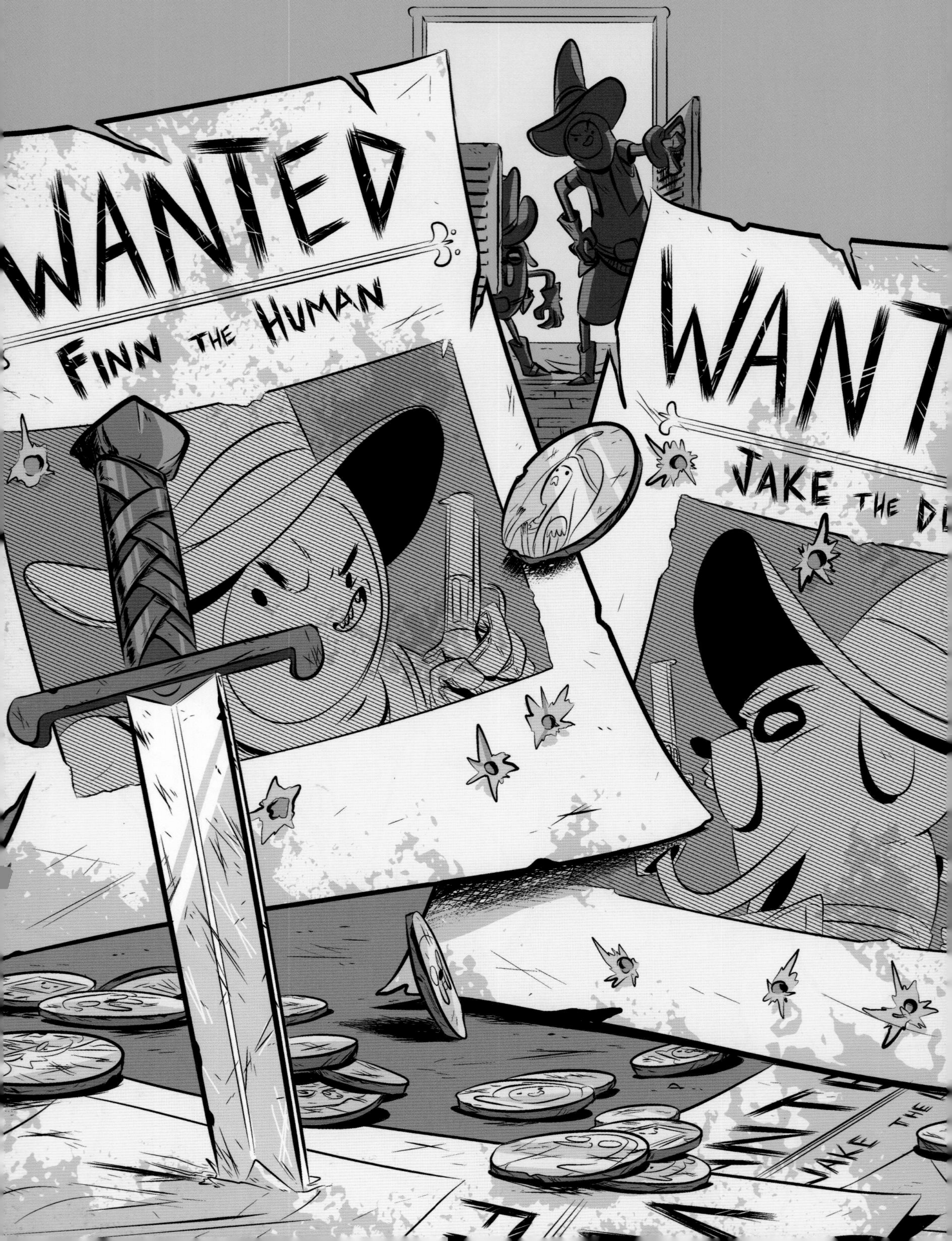

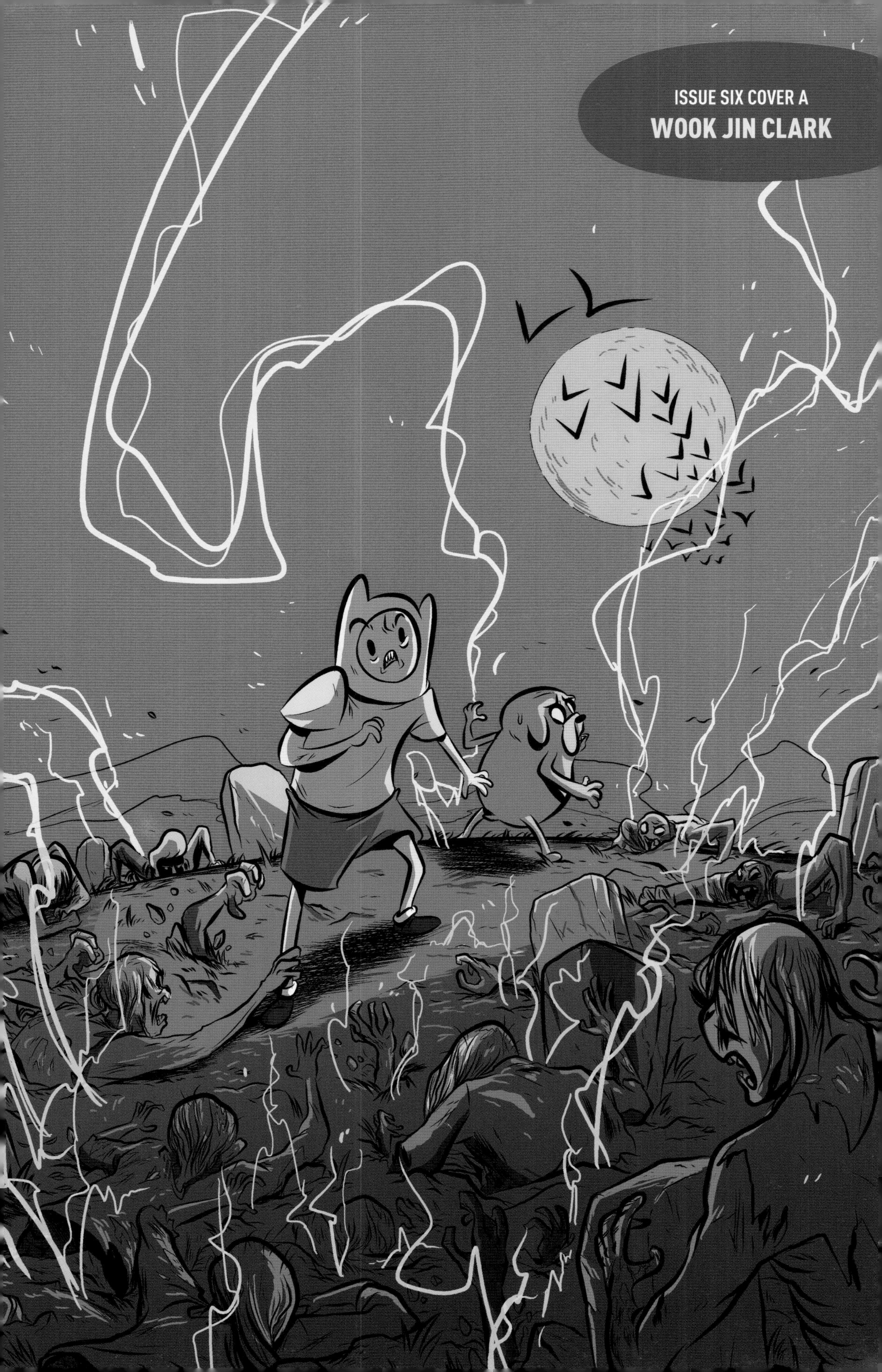

ISSUE SIX COVER A
WOOK JIN CLARK

ISSUE ONE COVER B
RU XU

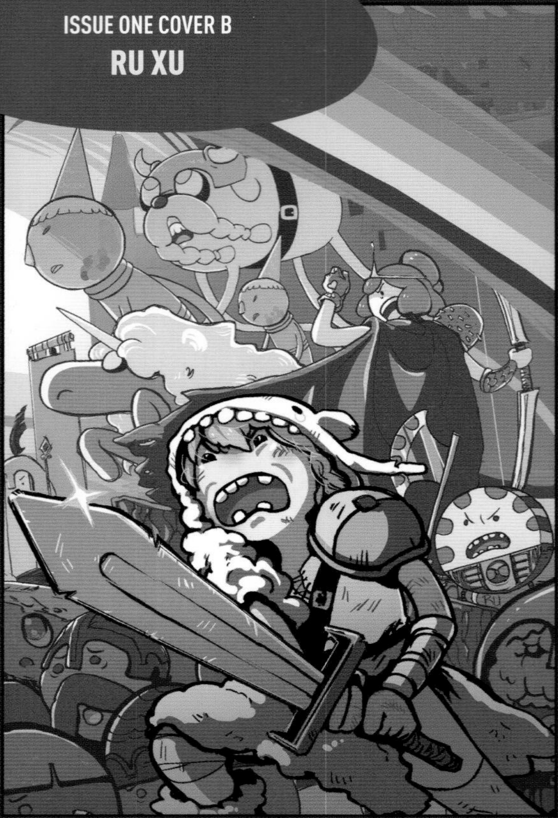

ISSUE ONE COVER C
ELLEN ALSOP

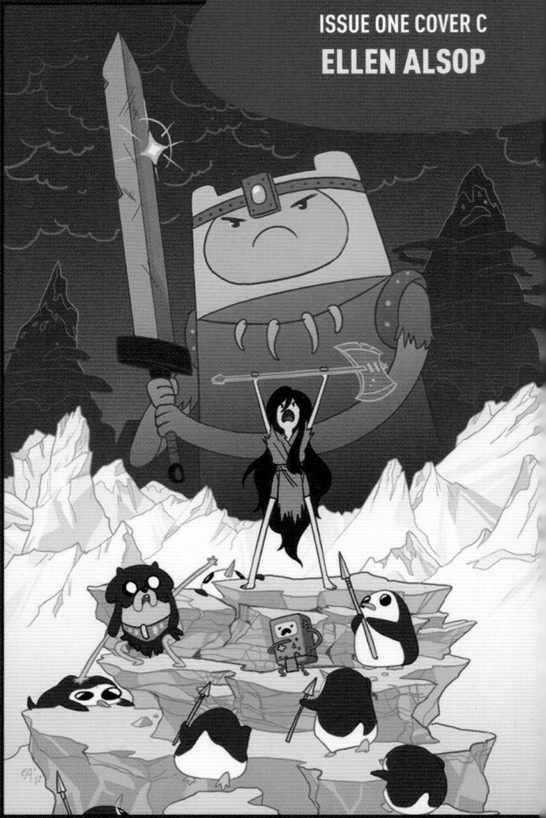

ISSUE ONE COVER D
BRITT WILSON

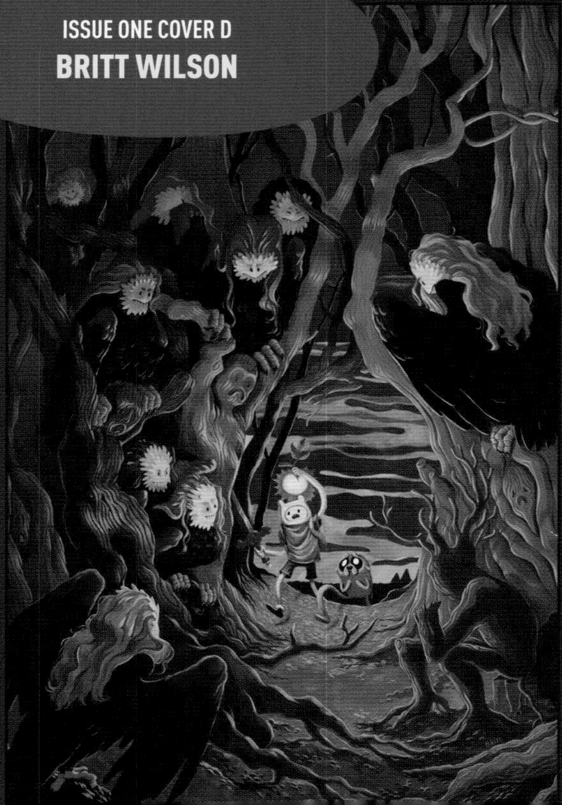

ISSUE ONE BOOM! STUDIOS
EXCLUSIVE COVER
COLLEEN COOVER

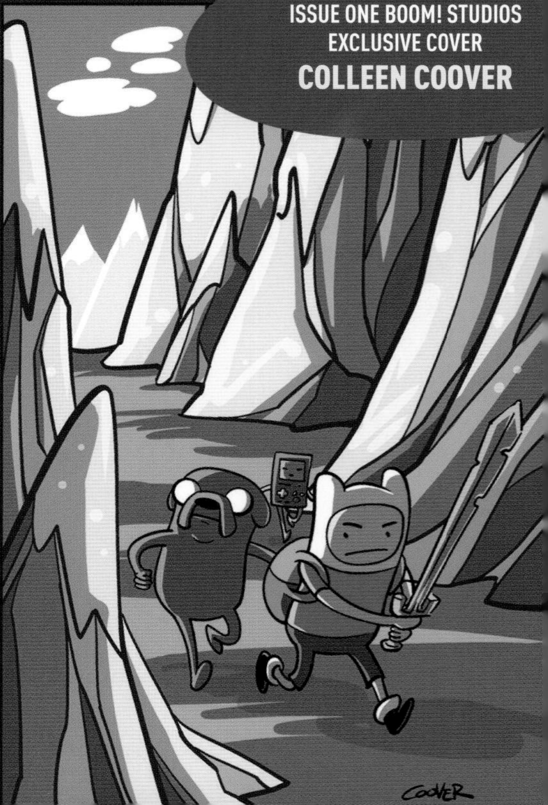
COOVER

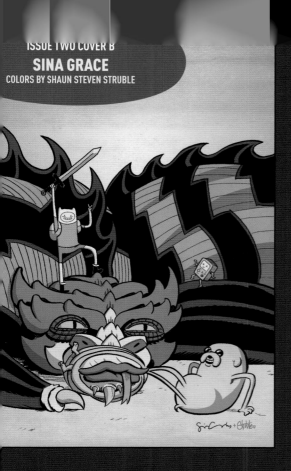

ISSUE TWO COVER B
SINA GRACE
COLORS BY SHAUN STEVEN STRUBLE

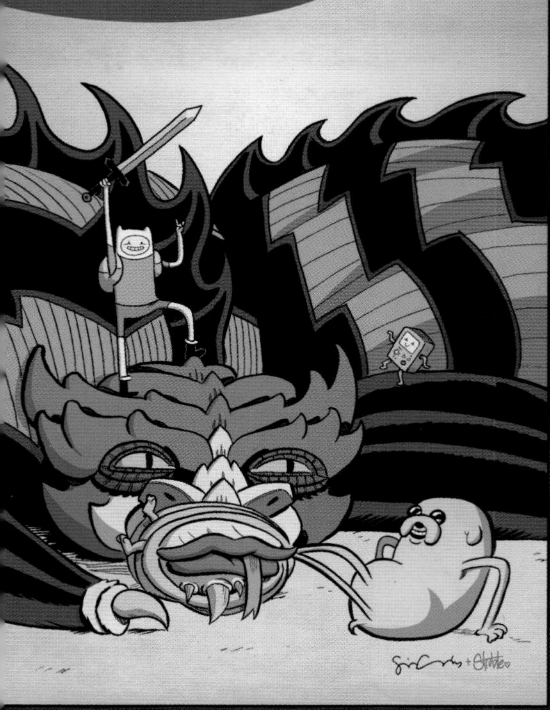

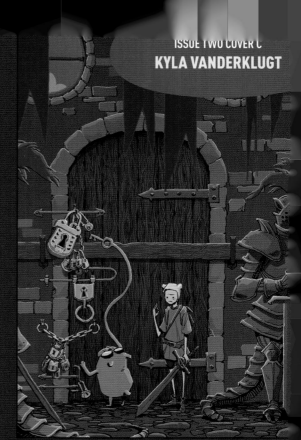

ISSUE TWO COVER C
KYLA VANDERKLUGT

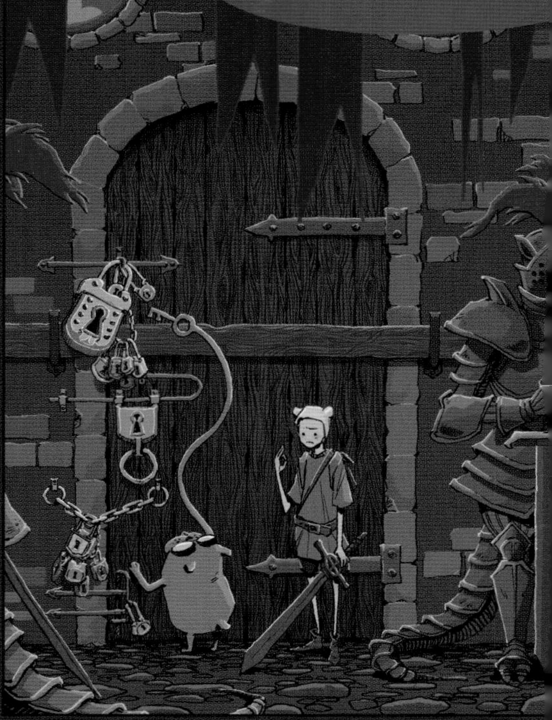

ISSUE TWO COVER D
NICK ILUZADA

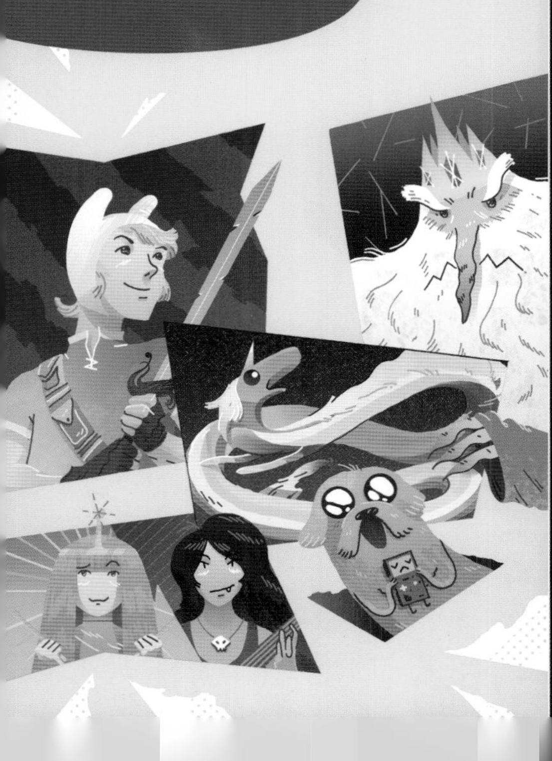

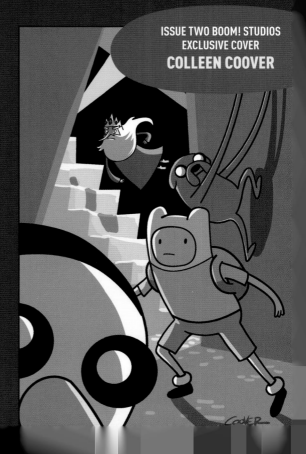

ISSUE TWO BOOM! STUDIOS EXCLUSIVE COVER
COLLEEN COOVER

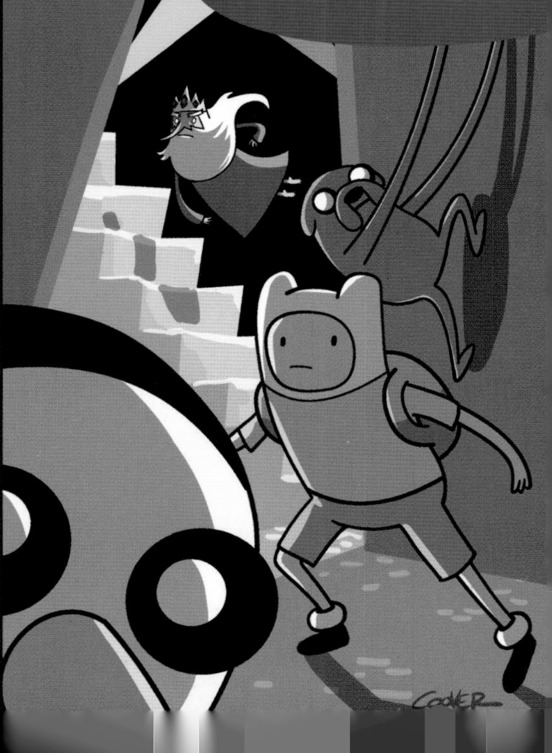

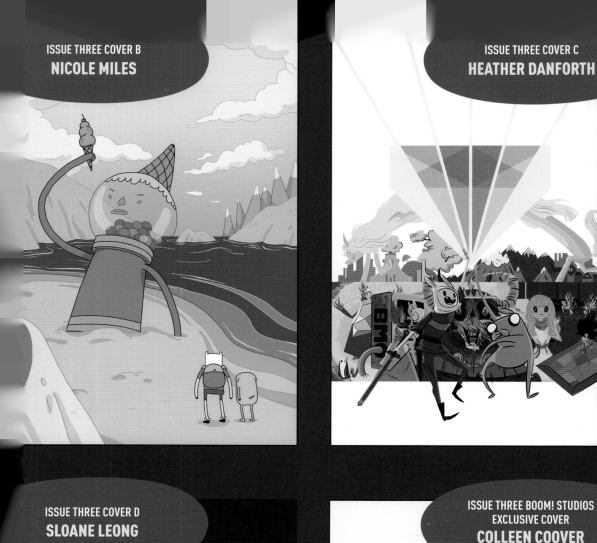

ISSUE THREE COVER B

NICOLE MILES

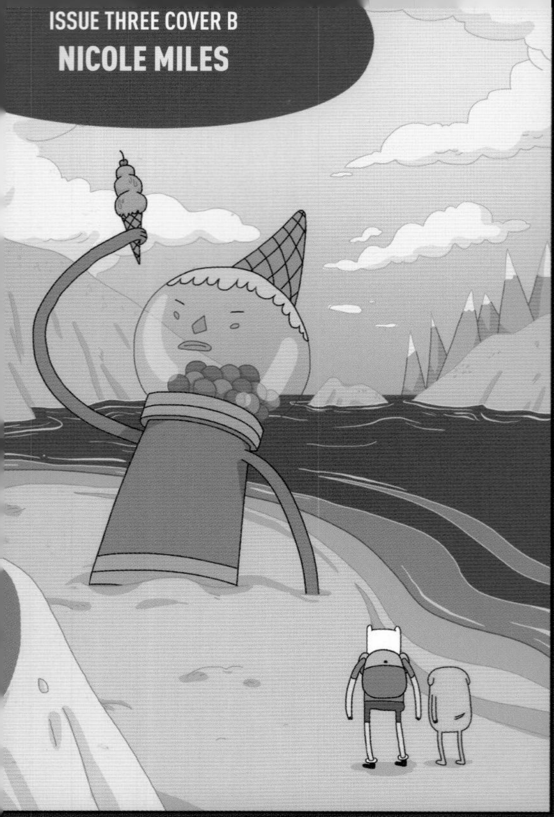

ISSUE THREE COVER C

HEATHER DANFORTH

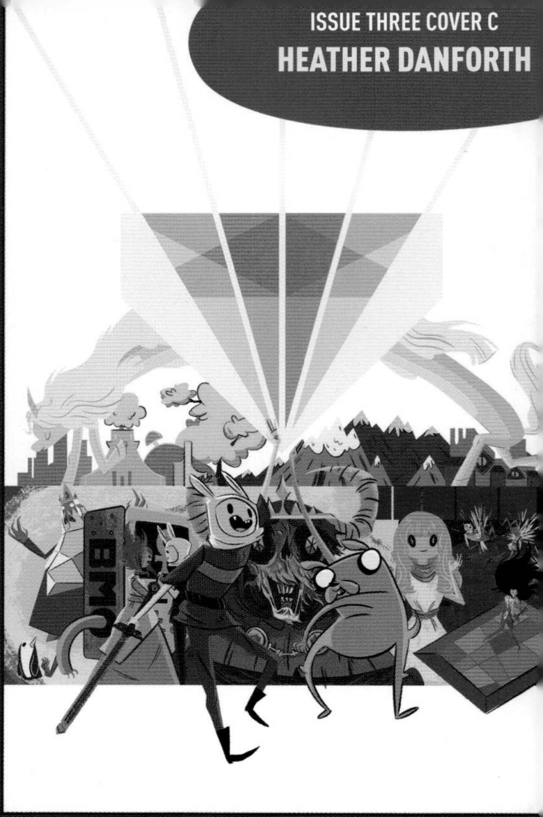
BMO

ISSUE THREE COVER D

SLOANE LEONG

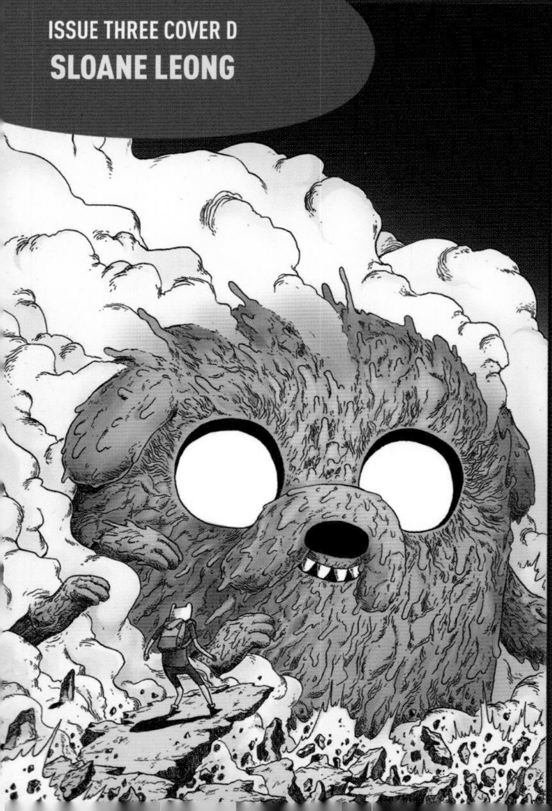

ISSUE THREE BOOM! STUDIOS EXCLUSIVE COVER

COLLEEN COOVER

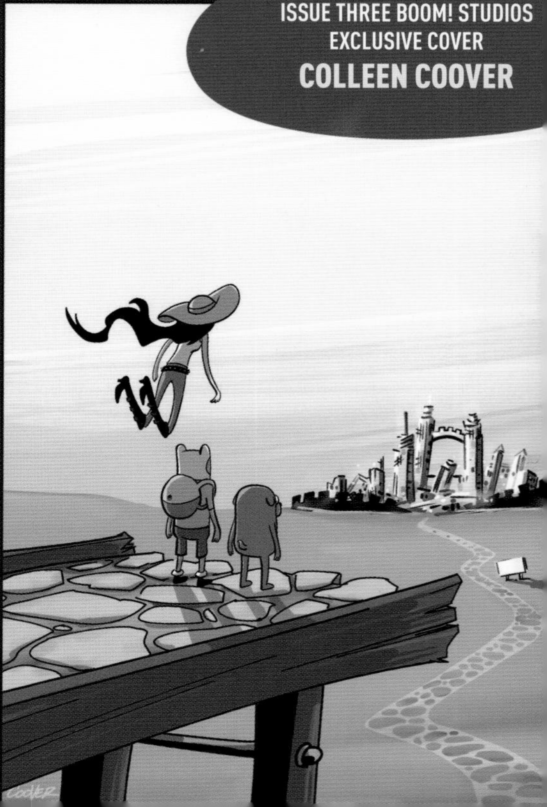

ISSUE FOUR COVER B
COURTNEY BERNARD

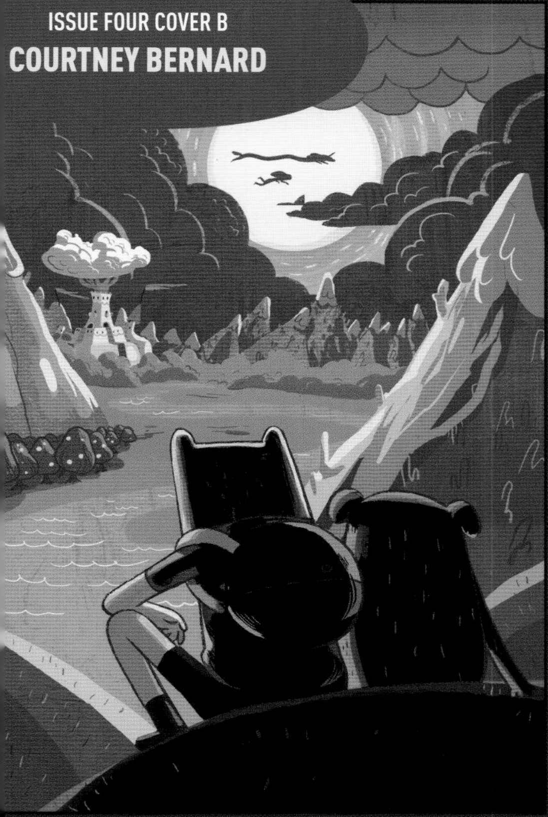

ISSUE FOUR COVER C
REBEKKAH DUNLAP

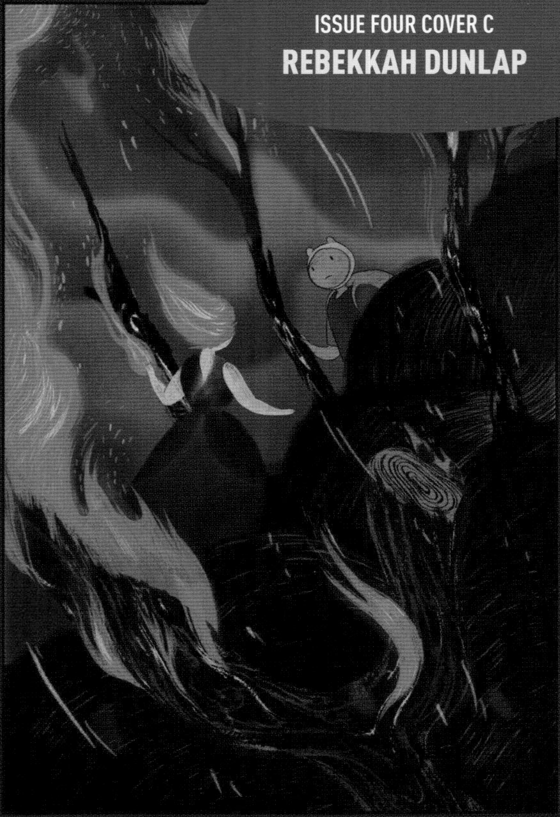

ISSUE FOUR COVER D
MARGUERITE SAUVAGE

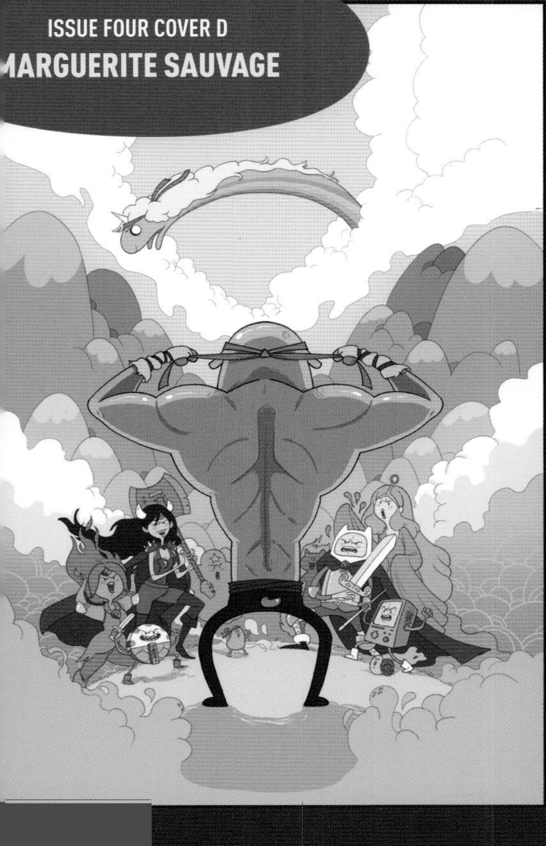

ISSUE FOUR BOOM! STUDIOS EXCLUSIVE COVER
COLLEEN COOVER

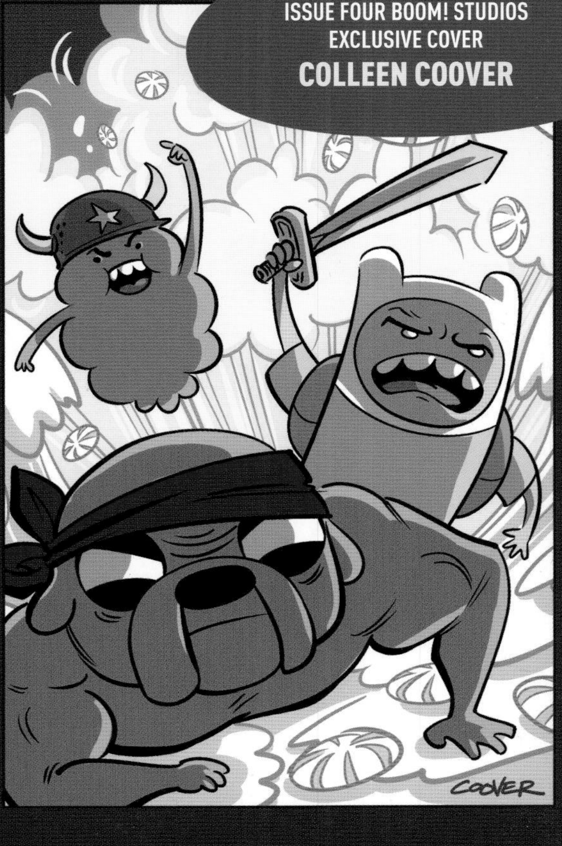
COOVER

ISSUE FIVE COVER B
MELISSA PAGLUICA

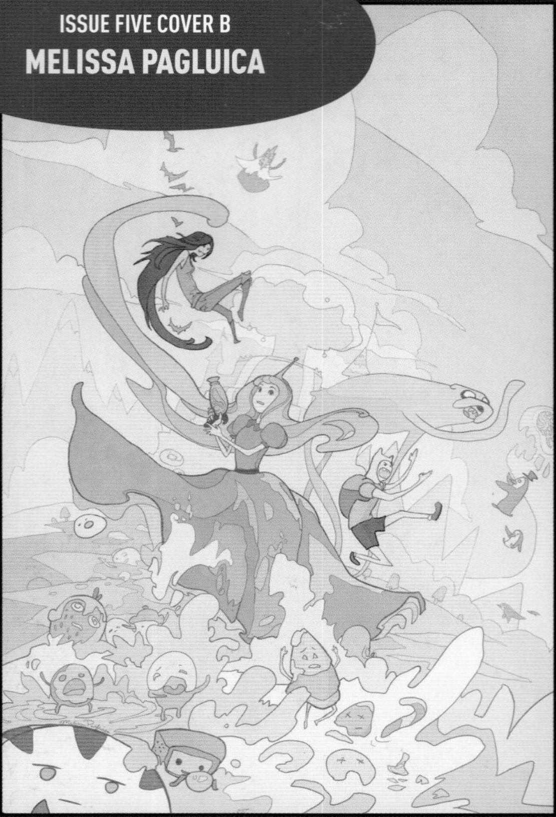

ISSUE FIVE COVER C
YALE STEWART

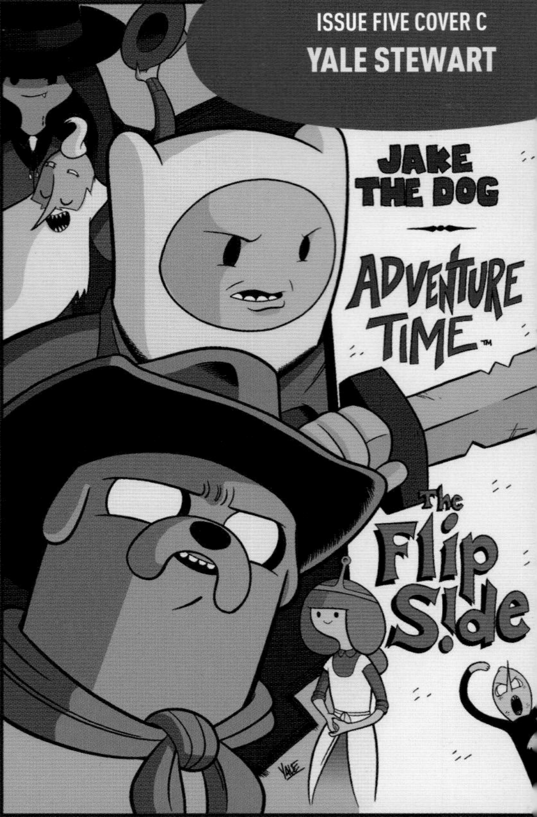
JAKE THE DOG
ADVENTURE TIME™
The Flip Side
YALE

ISSUE FIVE COVER D
KALI CIESEMIER

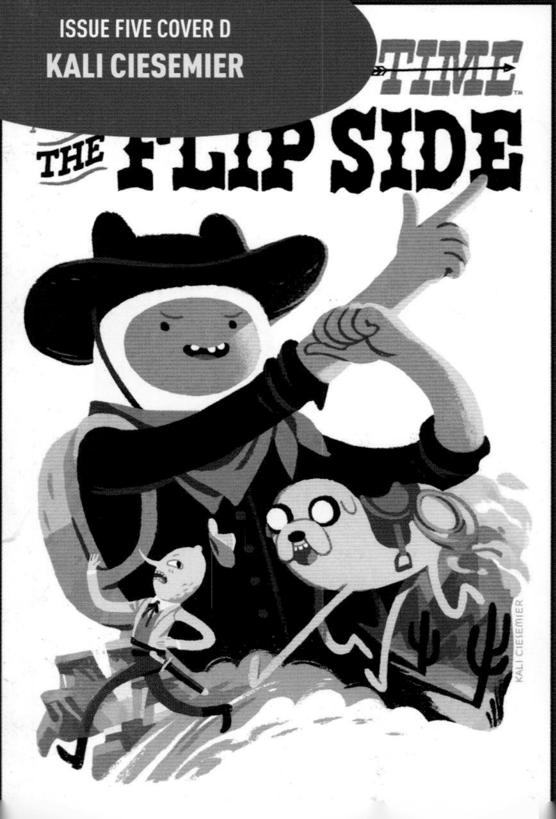
TIME
THE FLIP SIDE
KALI CIESEMIER

ISSUE FIVE BOOM! STUDIOS
EXCLUSIVE COVER
COLLEEN COOVER

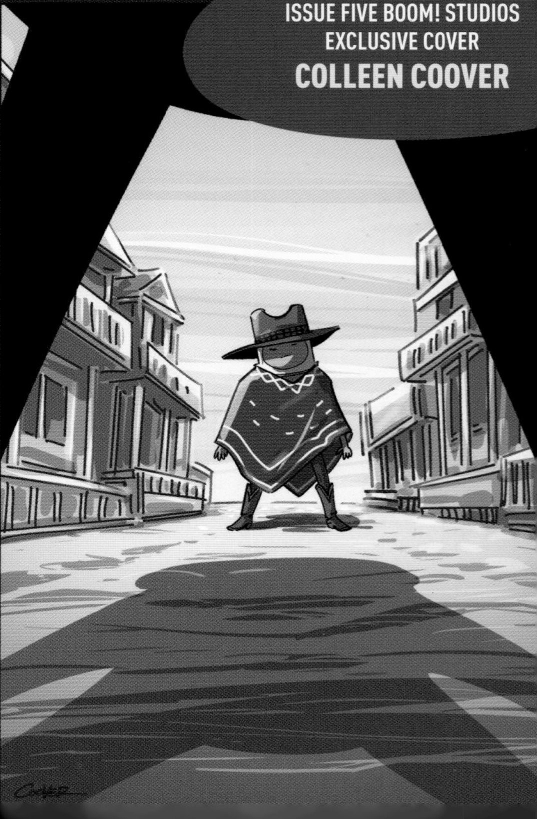

ISSUE SIX COVER B
DAVID CROSLAND

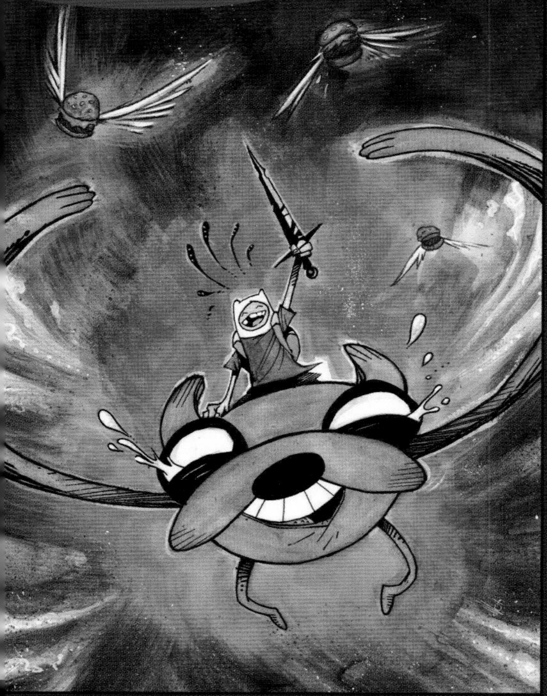

ISSUE SIX COVER C
KYLE HOTZ

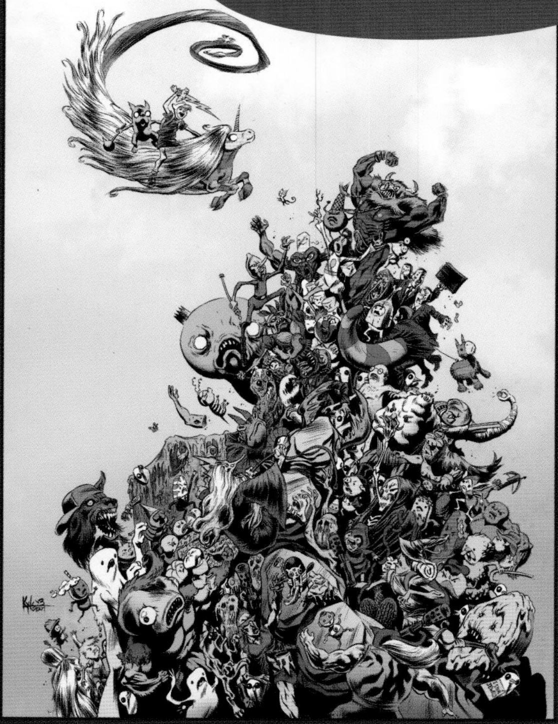

ISSUE SIX COVER D
SARAH STONE

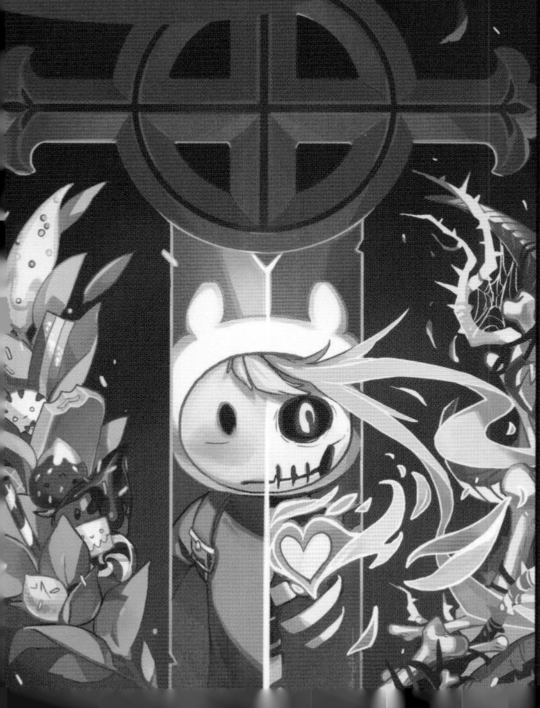

ISSUE SIX BOOM! STUDIOS EXCLUSIVE COVER
COLLEEN COOVER

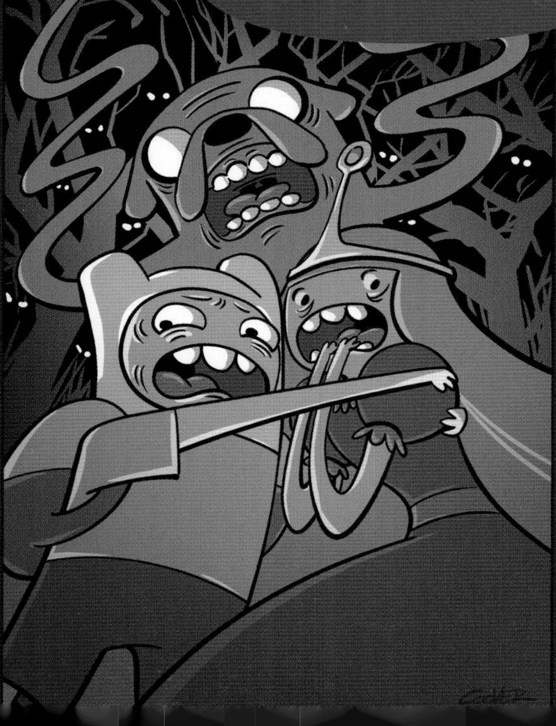